FANDANGO'S GOLD

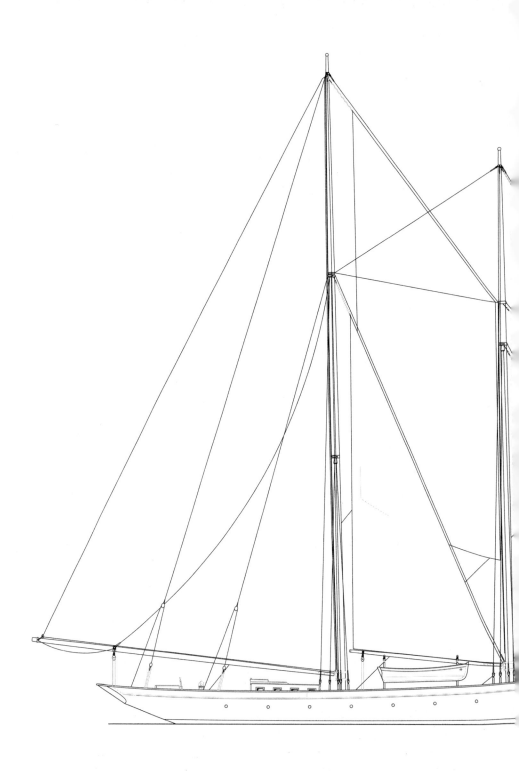

FANDANGO'S GOLD

Capt. Robert Louis Boudreau

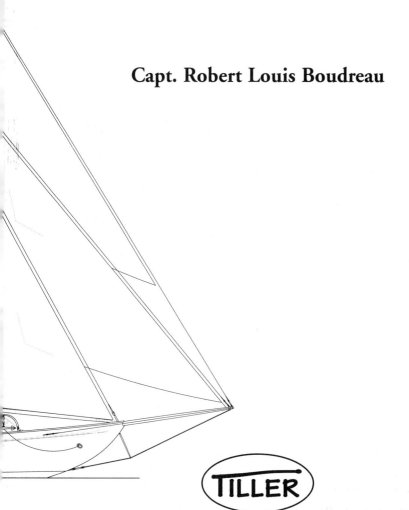

TILLER

ISBN-10 1-888671-19-X
ISBN-13 978-1-888671-19-3

Fandango's Gold is a work of fiction and any similarities between characters in the
book and real people are purely coincidental. Although not shown on many
charts and maps, Aves is real. It sits in a lonely spot some 300 miles to the west
of the Windward Islands in the Caribbean Sea. There are no boulders there. The
great boulders and baths at Virgin Gorda in the BVI are the model for Aves in
the book. All other geographical localities mentioned in the book are for the
most part accurate.

Cover art courtesy of Yarmouth Maritime Museum. It was my father's schooner
Doubloon.
Author photo © Christian Stalley

Graphic design and production by:
Scribe, Inc., 842 S. 2nd St., Philadelphia, PA 19147

Printed in the USA by:
Victor Graphics, 1211 Bernard Drive, Baltimore, MD 21223 USA

Questions regarding the content of this book should be addressed to:

TILLER Publishing
605 S. Talbot Street, Suite Two
St. Michaels, Maryland 21663
410-745-3750 • Fax: 410-745-9743
www.tillerbooks.com

AUTHOR'S NOTE

For S-J

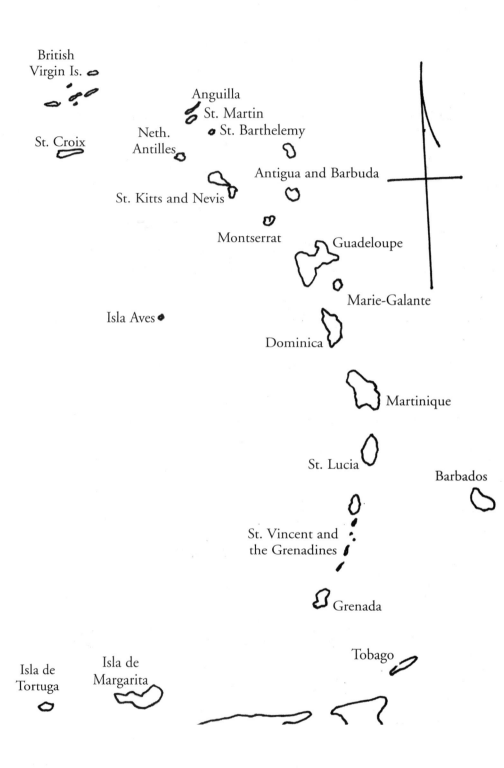

British
Virgin Is.

Anguilla
St. Martin
St. Barthelemy

Neth.
Antilles

St. Croix

Antigua and Barbuda

St. Kitts and Nevis

Montserrat

Guadeloupe

Marie-Galante

Isla Aves

Dominica

Martinique

St. Lucia

Barbados

St. Vincent and
the Grenadines

Grenada

Tobago

Isla de
Tortuga

Isla de
Margarita

PROLOGUE

1653, Cartagena

The stone citadel stood guard on the bluffs east of Cartagena harbour it's sun-bleached walls contrasting sharply with the lush green mountains in the background. The Spanish soldiers on guard duty sweated and swore under their thick blue tunics as they paced in the tropical heat.

Spain's major outpost in the New World, the small town comprised a collection of squalid buildings with the occasional stone house built by the Spaniards. A surrounding barricade of wooden posts opened to the sea and a recently constructed stone quay.

A big galleon lay anchored in the harbour. For over a year the gold, silver and other valuables had come across the mountains and the *San Idelfonso's* hold was almost loaded. Scores of wooden casks and chests filled with gold coins and bars lay in her fat belly. There were leather pouches filled with the exquisite pink pearls of the Pacific coast and a number of five libra powder kegs filled with emeralds. Hundreds of silver ingots each the weight of a good musket lay near the keel like so much lead ballast. Every piece of bullion carried the stamped letters DDV so that the queen would know who had so dutifully rendered her treasures.

His Excellency the Consul General Don Davilla supervised the wrapping and packing of a magnificent jewel-encrusted gold sacrificial knife himself. The hilt was capped with a large ruby and a spiral of polished emeralds ran down the handle of the thick golden blade. Although all treasures were personal property of the Queen, Don Davilla had a few small boxes in the privacy of his cabin where he secretly stowed a number of gold bars. He also filled a large brass tube with a selection of large uncut emeralds. He planned to retire rich with his young wife and daughter in the manner he was now accustomed.

The galleon's crew worked sluggishly in the fierce heat. Riggers overhauled cordage and tightened deadeyes. Sailors replaced worn ropes and re-stitched sails. They greased the pumps and coated her standing rigging with tallow and linseed oil.

Pedro Delgada had come to Cartagena as a seaman on the *San Idelfonso* but he was uncertain if he would ever see home again. Arnal, the Consul's pock-faced maggot of a cook servant had caught him stealing a little cheese and reported him. The soldiers came shortly afterwards and brought him bound to the Consul's offices.

Now he struggled to endure the torture of Davilla's wooden horse. Perched six feet off the ground the oversized four legged creation was the Consuls own cruel invention,

"To maintain discipline," he said.

The edge of the eight-foot long plank cut into Pedro's groin with unbearable agony. Rivulets of sweat ran down his naked body and flies tormented him, buzzing into his eyes, nose and mouth. The sun beat down mercilessly turning the stone ramparts of the castillo into an open oven. There was no wind, just the terrible heat and Pedro's pain.

Don Davilla glanced out the window of his apartment at the suffering sailor before turning. Captain Juan Dapena of the *San Idelfonso* had come with yet another unreasonable request.

"Your Excellency," he said, "I beg your pardon, but if you break any more of my seamen we will never see Spain. The swamp sickness has taken more than thirty now and I have a dozen more useless and crippled by this horse of yours."

Captain Dapena was not afraid of challenging the Consul, at least not on this side of the Atlantic Ocean. He was the only one who knew how to get the *San Idelfonso* back to Spain.

"You fail to see Capitan, that I must maintain discipline here, if I allow things to go unpunished, then there will be no order at all."

"Excellency, I implore you. We are very short-handed as it is and if you hope to sail the ship next week, then I must not lose any more men."

"So, you want me to pardon this dog who has stolen from me?" Don Davilla growled.

"Yes, Your Excellency, he is one of my most capable seaman and I need him. The Indians are useless on the ship; you are aware of their practice of throwing themselves into the sea?"

Don Davilla tried to look pensive for a moment, wiping the open sore on his neck with a silk handkerchief before replying.

"I will do as you ask, Capitan, but only because of your dire need. I will not have it known that I showed mercy or weakness to a thief. That would be most unwise. I shall deal with the wretch when we reach Spain."

The soldiers came to the horse and cut Pedro down but through the delirium of pain he could only imagine what was happening. As evening fell they carried him to the dock and released him to his shipmates who rowed him out to the *San Idelfonso* in the gig. The pain between his legs was agonizing and he would walk with a heavy limp for the rest of his life, but it slowly dawned on him that he was indeed alive.

Once aboard, the ship's physician gave him a strong potion and that night he fell into a deep sleep. He dreamed of a brightly painted new sardine boat and his family in Cadiz. He would have Alfonso, the shipwright, build the prettiest boat on his return and he would fish the tasty Biscay sardines for the rest of his life.

The *San Idelfonso* put to sea sixteen days later. It was the first of October 1653 and Captain Dapena was delighted to see the green mangrove-lined coast disappear astern of him.

"It is a godforsaken place," he said to no one in particular.

The wind was well south of east and the galleon was laying a far better course to the north than he had expected. It was usually a long hard beat to windward from the South American coast to Cuba, requiring many laborious tacks. Their present course was very good however, and would get them across the Caribbean all the faster. His only real complaint on this day was that he would have Don Davilla aboard as a passenger for the duration of the voyage. The man was a scab on the backside of humanity, Captain Dapena thought.

A group of wishful soldiers stood on the stone ramparts of the castillo watching the galleon's sails grow smaller as she sailed away to the Northeast. They were the last to see her. She never made it to Havana. The *San Idelfonso* and her precious cargo of gold and jewels disappeared off the face of the earth without a trace.

CHAPTER ONE

July 1967 – The Guadeloupe Passage

Jack Carlton watched the ominous smudge on the windward horizon carefully. A West Indian line squall was building fast and he knew how dangerous they could be. Twenty minutes later the dark rainstorm covered the final mile towards his schooner. It came quickly, whipping the surface of the blue Caribbean Sea into a white froth. The first outlying puffs arrived and he felt the cool, damp change of temperature on his face. It was time. Reaching into the cockpit seat locker for his old yellow sou'wester, he pulled it over his head and turned to his first mate.

"Stand by the main sheet, Cobb, going to run off for this one."

The heavy band of rain hit the seventy-five-foot staysail rigged *Fandango* hard and she heeled over sinking the lee rail below the sea. Jack had experienced his share of West Indian squalls, but this one was vicious. Water sloshed up the deck on her port side till it met the teak deckhouse coaming and as she went even further over it began to rush into the cockpit itself.

"Slack away," he called over his shoulder.

"Aye skip," Cobb replied.

The schooner's rail sunk deeper in to the sea and the muscular West Indian willed the line to run even more quickly over the brass deck fitting.

The Brookes and Gatehouse anemometer recessed into the cockpit bulkhead climbed to 40, then 45 knots. The schooner's Dacron sails and every sheet and halyard stretched to the limit. Over the whine of the wind he heard the sounds of pots and pans falling to the galley floor.

Jack hauled the helm to port as gust after gust hit, and the laboring schooner slewed erratically off to leeward. By running in the same direction for a few minutes, he would take the bite out of the squall and reduce the risk of blowing out a sail or worse.

Heavy raindrops, driven almost horizontally by the wind, stung his exposed face and legs.

As he struggled to steady her on the leeward course the schooner picked up speed. Suddenly a violent fifty-knot gust hit. Her varnished masts and booms trembled as if shaken by a giant hand and then with a report like a cannon shot the jib sheet parted and the sail trailed out to leeward, flogging like crazy. The whipping sail thundered and cracked and then, as the crew of the *Fandango* looked on, suddenly ripped along the mitre line.

"Get it down quick," Jack shouted.

Cobb quickly ran forward to the foremast pin rail, throwing off the halyard, but nothing happened. Under the strain the steel hanks were binding on the jib stay and the sail was jammed aloft. Small bits of Dacron flew away to leeward as it continued tearing itself to shreds.

"Got to get that sail off before it shakes the rig to pieces," Jack yelled, but the mate was already moving. The mate was strong and capable, but he would need help.

"Benny, come help me nuh," he yelled to his buddy.

The *Fandango's* deckhand got up from the cockpit where he was hanging on and followed the mate.

"Watch it, it's going to be rough out there," Jack shouted to them.

Bent at the waist the mate led Benny past the foremast to the varnished bowsprit. It stuck out some fourteen feet past the stem of the yacht, and they would have to go out along the wildly plunging spar to try and get the renegade sail down. Jack watched anxiously as they stepped out onto the footropes under the wooden spar and edged outwards. Halfway out to the jibstay they paused momentarily as the wind tried to pluck them off.

"Benny, keep a hold tight," Cobb shouted to his friend.

A moment later they reached the end of the bowsprit and Cobb placed his hand on the wire. It was taught as a guitar string. The heavy steel cable vibrated with the strain as if it would part at any moment. They wrestled with the tattered sail, but it took a good ten minutes to get it down to the bowsprit. The last few hanks remained jammed six feet above the turnbuckle.

"Got to climb up to cut de damned ting," Cobb yelled to Benny, brandishing his seaman's knife in his right hand. His left was locked to the jibstay with a vice-like grip.

"Hold me steady."

Grabbing the mate around the waist, Benny locked his legs around the bowsprit.

"Got you, do it quick man," Benny shouted to the mate.

Despite a small wiry stature, he was strong.

Cobb quickly put a foot up on the wire and climbed upward. As soon as he could reach he placed the sharp blade to the hank lashings. Two or three slices and the marlin parted. The tattered jib washed away to leeward a second later and quickly disappeared beneath the sea.

Jack continued to run her off as the fast moving squall passed over them, and then it was gone as quickly as it had come. In the lull behind the rain he put her back on course as Cobb and Benny cleaned up. Apart from the torn sail there was no other serious damage.

"You guys alright?" Jack asked as they returned to the cockpit.

"Sure ting, skipper Jack," Cobb replied wiping raindrops and salt spray from his face.

"You want us to bend on the spare jib?" the mate asked.

"Yes, you guys did a hell of a job out there," Jack told them.

Below decks the *Fandango*'s cook dove behind the saloon table with hands outstretched, but she missed. Megan Fairchild usually liked cats, but she hated this creature. On the next try she cornered it at the galley door.

A moment later her red head appeared briefly in the companionway. Her arms came up and she pushed the cat into the cockpit.

"This animal just threw up all over my wardroom," she snapped at Jack, and after glancing at the wet cockpit she gave him a dirty look before returning below.

Patch cowered near his feet. A mangy calico with an odd dark patch over his left eye, one of his front teeth stuck out crookedly to the side, giving him a roguish but comical look. He had been a little put out by the vessel's wild gyrations of a few moments before and seen fit to unload his ample breakfast in a number of hidden locations inside the yacht.

"In trouble again, Mr. Patch?" Jack said, smiling briefly at the cat.

If there was ever an instance where the pet and owner exhibited the same characteristics, then this was it. Both Patch and Jack drank, romanced women and got into fights. The difference between the two was that Patch scored more often.

Cobb and Benny carried the spare sail out onto the bowsprit and bent it on. The sky cleared and the indigo expanse of the Caribbean stretched as far as the eye could see. White crested waves sparkled in the tropical sunlight and puffy white clouds drifted across a powder blue sky. The speeding schooner seemed almost inconsequential on the empty sea. Her graceful spoon bow dipped and rose northwards and a surging quarter wave rose under her transom. Apart from the frothy, white wake astern, there was no record of her passage through the sea; it was as if she had never passed that way.

Jack sat in the cockpit at the helm, turning a spoke or two to keep her on her course. It was mid-afternoon and the tropical sun was halfway down the Tradewind sky.

"This is why I'm here," he smiled to himself.

A second later he opened the cockpit cooler and popped a cold Carib beer. It tasted good.

The former Navy test pilot had bought the sleek, white-hulled schooner in 1964 and put her into the West Indies charter trade. With his crew of three he operated out of English Harbour Antigua on charter cruises to the islands of the Eastern Caribbean. They had just finished a three-weeker in the Grenadines and were headed home for a break and some maintenance. Wealthy clients looking for sailing adventure booked her four double cabins, and the winter months were usually pretty busy.

There were old world ports and secluded out of the way anchorages. The passengers could go fishing and snorkeling on the coral reefs, or just plain beach combing while Jack and his crew took care of the cooking, maintenance and day-to-day operation of the schooner. His first mate Cobb and deckhand Benny had been with him since day one and were good men. They were originally from Bequia but had found their way to Antigua to work on the charter boats based there.

He'd hired Megan as cook for the trip. She'd come out to the islands to take a four-month, hands-on sailing voyage aboard a New Zealand sloop. Loving it, she decided to stay and put her culinary skills to work. Tall and slender, the thirty-year-old woman had long, flaming red hair and beautiful green eyes. Originally from a group of islands off the Cornish coast, she'd left a boring job at a London perfume house in search of adventure. She was an excellent cook but had a temper.

Although Antigua remained hidden to the north, the low island was there, just below the horizon. For a moment Jack mused that they were alone, but they were not. Flocks of sea birds accompanied them on their way; small dark petrels dove to disappear between the troughs of the waves, fluttering madly to keep up with the yacht. Brown boobies skimmed the wave tops, diving occasionally for a small fish that had dared to venture too close to the surface. Dark, scissor-tailed frigate birds wheeled above her masts, seemingly curious of the vessel below. The birds seemed happy, almost playful, and not in the least concerned about their isolated location.

Dolphins came and played under the schooner's stem, leaping and frolicking just under the bowsprit netting. Their silvery grey, streamlined bodies seemed to move effortlessly through the water, and when they breached for a quick breath there was the loud whoosh-pop as they exhaled and breathed in.

The Marconi rigged schooner was close-hauled on the wind and although there was a good twenty-five knots out of the northeast, Jack kept her under full sail.

"You pushing her hard, skip," Cobb remarked.

"Got a strong hankering for a drink and dinner at the Admirals Inn tonight," he replied, taking another swig of Carib.

They needed to make English Harbour before nightfall. A small slot between high rocky bluffs, the port's entrance allowed no room for error and if he made a mistake in the dark and the schooner went ashore on the adjacent reefs, it would be all over. A natural harbour comprised of three large lagoons, it was well protected by the surrounding hills and one of the best "hurricane holes" in the islands. Lord Nelson had based his fleet there and over the years built a comprehensive dockyard. The natural deepwater bays were just as attractive to present day seafarers, as they were to those of a hundred years past.

As evening came and went Jack, Cobb and Benny sat together in the schooner's cockpit, and the abruptness of nightfall in the tropics made the bad news obvious.

"Tough luck, guys," Jack said, "Doesn't look as though we're going to make it."

Antigua's low-lying landmass was visible on the horizon ahead, but the light was fading fast.

"You mean I got to sleep in my bed alone another night, skip?" Benny asked only half joking.

"Shut you mout', Benny, you want de skipper to wreck de vessel or what?" Cobb teased him.

Although Cobb was disappointed, the mate knew enough about sailing to understand the risks of entering English Harbour in the dark. Sharp rocky ledges lay along the coast and although there was deep water close to the entrance itself, a nasty coral reef extended into the small passage. Treacherous Cades Reef lay to the west of English Harbour and if the schooner made too much leeway, the jagged coral reef could prove deadly.

"All those women of yours are going to have to wait, my friend," Jack told him, smiling.

By seven o'clock it was pitch black and the island had completely disappeared, but Jack held his course. Reaching in the direction of his unseen first mate, he put his hand on Cobb's shoulder.

"Keep an eye open for Shirley Heights," he told him.

Jack had faith in his navigation and planned to take the schooner close to the island before making a final decision. If they managed to get a bearing on a recognizable bluff or a light inside English Harbour, then there might be chance of getting in.

He steered through the dark night and the dolphins came again. Streaking towards the yacht they left magnificent phosphorescent trails like torpedoes. Jack liked the nights at sea; they were kind of special. The eerie glow of the port and starboard lights threw ghostly colour into the salt spray as it rose from her bow. Like an endless kaleidoscope show, sudden flashes of red, then green, then darkness again.

Jack sat just forward of the wheel where the red tinted binnacle light gave his face a bizarre demon-like quality. A few feet away the glow of the Cobb's cigarette stood out like a tiny red beacon in the night. The schooner felt more alive than ever in the darkness. Perhaps because he could no longer see her, he more consciously felt her. Lifting her stem gently, she reaped the night wind and then heeling slightly took sustenance from it before rolling on. Under her lee bow a wave of white water rose up, higher even than the rail, but as the schooner surged forward, it curved away to fall on the dark ocean, rolling away to leeward with an angry hiss. White water raced along the lee rail in almost magical form before disappearing into nothingness. The zone of blackness ended as Jack glanced aloft. There, the tips of the Fandango's masts traced a meandering course through an endless sea of stars. It was almost hypnotic.

"Skip, look Shirley Heights," Cobb shouted suddenly and Jack was pulled from his reverie.

Standing, he held the wheel in his left hand as he peered intently into the night. He knew just where the bluffs should be, close ahead and to starboard. At first he saw nothing, but a moment later they emerged from the murk.

The high cliffs rising precipitously from the Caribbean were far closer that he had calculated. They were suddenly only a few hundred yards from English Harbour. The Antigua port authority had not seen fit to place a light on the entrance, and it remained unmarked and unlit.

"Lower away from forward," Jack called urgently and as he bent to the small console in the cockpit bulkhead, his fingers found the key and starter button for the main engine.

A moment later the big diesel roared into life. Spoking the wheel to starboard he pushed the Morse control forward and throttled up, bringing the schooner into the wind. He couldn't see the bow, but he recognized the sounds of metal on wire as the jib hanks made their way down the steel stay. It wasn't long before Cobb and Benny had the main and foresail down.

"What you tink, skip? Can make a try?" Benny asked him as they returned to the cockpit.

For a moment Jack remained silent.

"Maybe."

Although the high bluffs were barely discernable ahead, the entrance to English Harbour remained hidden. He needed to see something definite and recognizable before he'd risk an entry.

"Cobb, you take the port side, and, Benny, you take the starboard, we'll motor slowly in for a while. If we can see the entrance, I might give it a try. Otherwise it's rolling around out here till daylight," Jack replied.

His words were motivation enough. They ran quickly forward to the port and starboard shrouds, peering intently into the darkness.

The schooner moved slowly towards the land, rolling in the easterly swell. Jack peered into the dark void ahead, but there was still no sign of Fort Berkely's ramparts to port or the low, jutting stone spit to the starboard. The high promontory of Shirley Heights loomed, but of the small entrance there was no sign. Judging from the height of the bluffs he had only a few more seconds to go. And then there was a sound that made Jack shiver. The unmistakable hiss of waves crashing on the shore. Putting his left hand on the top spoke of the wheel he prepared to turn the schooner to starboard. They would hit the coral soon. Then they had a lucky break.

"Skip, look Plantain's lantern," Cobb shouted aft, unable to keep the tone of excitement from his voice.

The local Rasta angler was fishing in the outer bay and had his kerosene light hung on his short mast. Looking forward Jack spotted the faint light in the distance, and the low rocks of the point to starboard became barely discernable.

"I see him, got the starboard point now too," he said after a moment.

He throttled up slightly, giving the schooner a bit more steerage and they made for the tiny light. He couldn't completely see the small entrance to English Harbour, but Plantain's lantern got brighter by the second and he knew that the fisherman always chose the same spot in the bay. Suddenly the ramparts appeared as if by magic to port, just where they should have been. The schooner's decks ceased to roll and there was calm.

"We're in, guys," Jack called forward, "get that anchor ready."

The lights from Nelsons Dockyard came into view a moment later and the Admirals Inn loomed to the left. Jack smiled; he knew exactly where he was.

"Stand by the anchor," he called forward and imagined Cobb crouching with his hands on the winch brake.

Coasting into the center of the bay he reached down to the Morse controls, putting the diesel in neutral.

"Let her go, Cobb," he shouted and a second later he heard the sounds of the chain rattling out. They were home.

After securing the anchor they squared away the deck and launched the Boston Whaler. Cobb set the anchor light from the headstay and Benny closed the hatches in case of rain. At nine o'clock they were finally ready to go ashore. Megan appeared on deck with her shoulder bag and a moment later, the others followed.

"I'll need to get paid tomorrow, Jack," she told him. "I've got travelers cheques, so I'll be at the bank when it opens first thing in the morning," he told his crew.

He thought about asking Megan to join him at the Admirals Inn for dinner, but judging by her expression she wasn't in the mood. Benny and Cobb weren't any too happy about not getting paid, but at least they understood that the banks were closed.

Before leaving, he took Patch's bowl from the galley floor and put a generous measure of kittybits into it. He also took his milk saucer up to the cockpit and slopped the cat's usual dollop of Mount Gay rum into it. Patch came over, arched his back and started lapping it up.

"You goin kill de cat, you know, skip," Benny admonished, laughing.

"Naw, he loves it," Jack replied, smiling, "Helps him sleep after a rough trip."

"It helps him fall down," Cobb said, feigning disinterest.

He was used to the skipper's idiosyncrasies. Megan just rolled her eyes.

"I don't believe you sometimes," she said.

Jack carefully locked the companionway hatch and the four climbed into the Whaler. Cobb went to the stern and began pulling the starter cord on the 25 hp Johnson outboard. After about thirty pulls it reluctantly fired and started.

"Dis ting going kill me, skip," he complained as they made for the shore.

They heard the Admirals Inn before they arrived. It was Saturday night, and the tinny ping-pang of Fat Bubba's three-piece steel band echoed around the bay. What an awful racket, he thought, smiling, but he knew that after a couple of stiff rums they would sound great. The historic watering hole stood on the shores of the innermost cove in a grand old building that had once housed British Naval Officers. Across from the stone patio there was a small wooden dock where dinghies and launches from the anchored yachts tied up. Jack brought the Whaler in next to a large rubber Zodiac, and Cobb and Benny jumped out with the bowline and made it fast to the wooden piling. Megan stepped ashore, followed by Jack.

"OK, see you tomorrow," he told his crew.

Megan bid him a curt good night before walking off in the direction of the Inn while Cobb and Benny made for the bus stand. Jack watched them thoughtfully. Cobb, the big former fisherman and lobster diver, was black as coal and strong as an ox. A tough man with years of experience on the island trading schooners, he had been with Jack since he first arrived in the West Indies, and the two men had developed a respect for each other. They had a friendship as well, which stemmed from their mutual love of spear fishing. Whenever possible, they indulged their passion on the outlying reefs of the islands. Jack even trusted Cobb to move the boat in an emergency if he wasn't there. Cobb had an Antigan wife and four kids in St. Johns and that's where he'd be headed now.

Benny was a different story. Bow-legged Benny. Jack was the closest to family he had in Antigua and he knew exactly where he was headed right now. The cathouse up behind Frederick Street where his girlfriend worked, and Benny would stay there until she kicked him out.

Jack watched as they disappeared behind the Admirals Inn where the jitney buses left for St. Johns, and then he walked across the patio to the entrance. Red roofed with bright green window shutters, the stone building sported a large sign in gold italics over the front entrance. The legend Admirals Inn had an irreverent addendum wired beneath it on a pine board. Its crudely painted red letters read, "Seaman's Club, Women Welcome."

Entering the smoke filled room, Jack recognized a half a dozen or so of the English Harbour regulars standing at the long teak bar. It was the end of the charter season and apart from a couple of American tourists on the patio listening to the steel band, the place was almost empty. A small man wearing glasses along with a Latin looking fellow occupied a couple of stools at the center of the bar. Big Billy Ramsey stood leaning at the end under the painting of *HMS Boreas* orchestrating the proceedings as usual. The rawboned Ex-Royal Australian Air Force pilot had done a lot of things over the years, including running a pearl lugger in Northern Australia, before winding up in Antigua. His 'Digereedoo Air Charters' service was well known in the islands, and his beat up old PBY Catalina flying boat sported a big, red kangaroo logo on the fuselage. He flew out of English Harbour for anyone who would pay him. Rumour had it that he'd won the plane in a Florida poker game and forged the ownership documents, but nobody gave a dam and anyway you didn't pry into people's pasts in these parts. Billy was a hard drinking, red faced man who wasn't overly particular about what he carried, "Just as long as they paid."

"Hey, Jack," he shouted over, "Come and 'ave a brew."

Jack smiled; Billy was a good man and the kind of friend you could count on when things got rough. Crossing the cobblestone floor he joined the Australian at the end of the bar.

The Antigua charter community was made up of interesting folks. There were ex-Royal Navy officers, RAF pilots, some wastrels and a few men who didn't want anyone to know where they'd come from at all. Jack was no exception. His past held a few secrets and there were things he wouldn't tell anyone. The skippers and crews of the charter fleet congregated at the heavy teak bar where stalwart British Officers had propped their elbows so many years before. The strong rum was dispensed across its varnished surface just as liberally as it had been in the old days.

"What for you, skip?" Raphael the bartender asked.

"Cuba Libra, and throw in some extra lime."

"Pronto," Raphael said.

"Good trip then, mate?" Billy asked.

"No complaints, nice weather and I got paid," Jack replied.

"Get lucky with that saucy, redhead cook of yours?" the Aussie inquired.

"Not even close," Jack replied with an unmistakable trace of regret.

"No worries, mate, no worries, she'll come round."

Jack smiled and took a sip of his Cuba Libra. It was a nice thought.

Reaching inside his shirt neck Billy pulled out a huge tooth about three inches long. It had yellowed over the years and there was a hole in the big end where he had strung the leather thong.

"Now, I was just telling this rabble how I shot a big, salty rock in the territories one year and when me and me mates hauled him ashore he was twenty foot and had six inch teeth," Billy continued, gesticulating with his big hands.

"This one's only three inches," Jack pointed out.

"Well, I had to give the big one to me mates to show my appreciation for pulling that big bastard out of the water," Billy explained.

Everyone burst out laughing and by twelve thirty the regulars were getting a little drunk. Raphael's rum supply diminished and the tall tales got taller. An older, unassuming little fellow with round glasses sat next to them listening. He wasn't one of the regulars and didn't join in the conversation.

Jack looked at the floor for a moment and then held up his hand for silence.

"One day in my F84 over Inchon I shot down a Commie Mig 15 with only a two second burst of fire," he told his friends.

Billy looked puzzled; the story was probably true but Jack held up his hand and continued.

"There was another commie fighter right behind the first one and my bullets went right though it and flamed the second one at the same time."

Billy's mouth opened. For a brief moment he wasn't quite sure whether Jack was lying or not but then through the haze of rum he smiled and pointed a sausage-like finger at his friend.

"You're lying, sport," he said grinning, "No way you could 'ave done that."

Jack laughed as he reached across the bar for a handful of nuts.

"You're right, no chance in hell, but how about this," he said.

Pulling out his green Velcro wallet he took a large gold coin from one of the safety pouches. Holding it up he tilted it so that the piece glinted in the light.

"Oh beauty," Billy exclaimed, "Where'd you get that then?"

"On one of the islands," Jack offered, smiling.

Billy looked puzzled again.

"But there's hundreds of islands around here," he exclaimed.

"Then you know where to look," Jack replied, nodding.

"That's Spanish by the looks of it." An English voice interrupted.

Jack turned to his left. The little man with the round glasses leaned forward, looking intently at the coin. He held it out so the fellow could see it better and his swarthy companion looked on with interest.

"Yes, it's definitely a Spanish one all right," he said confidently.

'And how would you know that?" Jack asked him.

"I deal in antique coins," the man replied, leaning even closer, "See the faint cross stamped on it? Well that's a sure sign; the old Catholics you know."

Jack was intrigued.

"So where do you reckon it came from?"

"Probably South America," the Englishman said, sounding suddenly hesitant, "Where did you find it?"

"In the West Indies," Jack replied, smiling.

"Well, if you ever decide to sell it, please come and see me," he said suddenly nervous, "I'm Harold Bartram and I have a shop in town, on Market Street."

"I'll remember that," Jack said, returning the coin to his wallet, but he didn't. Billy was trying to promote a PBY flight to St. Barts the next day for some liquor, and Jack's brief conversation with the nondescript Englishman quickly faded.

As the subject changed Harry Bartram left. No one noticed, he was just an unremarkable kind of man. The swarthy character that had been sitting next to him left a few moments later. He'd seen the coin as Jack held it up to the light.

A little while later the manager of the Ad's Inn came down the stairs from her room. Blond and vivacious, the former London dancer was in her late fifties and still looked good. Mabeline and the big Australian had a thing going for a long time.

"Billy Ramsey, it's time for bed," she said in her lilting cockney accent.

Billy quickly took of his slouch hat and got serious.

"Yes luv, I'll be there in a little bit, just finish me brew," he said obediently.

"Now Billykins," she replied, putting her hands on her hips.

There were loud guffaws as the boys laughed.

"Don't keep the lady waiting," Jack chided, poking the Aussie in the ribs.

Finishing their round they toasted Admiral Nelson and Raphael closed the bar. It was two a.m. Jack drove the Whaler back to the anchored schooner and tying the boat alongside, climbed to the deck. The long day and Raphael's rums were taking effect. He was feeling pleasantly mellow and failed to notice the small rowboat tied on *Fandango's* opposite side.

Going below he made his way down the darkened hallway towards the teak door of his cabin. As he slid his hand inside to turn on the light he realized something was different. His door was open and he'd left it closed. Catching a slight movement from the corner of his eye, he instinctively turned to protect himself.

"What the hell?"

It was too late. He felt an explosion in the back of his head and as he collapsed to the teak and holly cabin sole, his mind went blank.

CHAPTER TWO

July 29th, English Harbour

Running his hand through the redhead's luxurious hair, he kissed her again. Jack's rapturous dream quickly faded when she spoke. There was no mistaking Patch's nasal snarl. The feline crawled a little higher up his chest and delivered a raspy lick on the lips. As the early morning sun shone through the skylight he groaned, raising his arm to shield his eyes.

"You're one ugly cat, you know that?" He said pushing an offended Patch away.

Rolling over to his pillow, he found it wasn't there. He wasn't in his bunk bed at all. He was still lying in the hallway floor outside his cabin. For a moment he thought the heavy throbbing in his head was due to Raphael's rum, but then he remembered. Squinting through blood-shot eyes, he sat up and ran his right hand over the bump on the back of his head. It hurt like hell. The open door, the sudden sense that someone had been near him in the hallway, he tried to picture his attacker, but nothing came. It had been too quick. The man had waited until he turned to enter his cabin, and hit him from behind.

Putting a hand on the teak doorframe, Jack rose unsteadily to his feet. Entering his cabin, he turned to the small adjoining bathroom on the right and opened the tap in the wall sink. Splashing cold water on his face, he shaved quickly before brushing his teeth. His clothes stank of rum and smoke, but he decided to wait until he had seen the police before changing. Turning to re-enter his cabin, he took in a deep breath. The six drawers below his bunk on the aft bulkhead were open and pieces of clothing were scattered over the floor.

"What the hell?" he exclaimed, as his anger rose.

Going quickly to the back of the top drawer, he breathed a sigh of relief. The brown envelope with his charter fee was still there. Although it had been opened, the thirty-five hundred in American Express was still intact. Odd, even an island thief would know that you could cash them on the Antigua black market. Even more strange was that the two fifty in petty cash was still there too. Placing the traveler's cheques aside he repacked the drawers and turned to the narrow mattress on his bunk. Lifting the forward end, he folded it back on itself exposing the outer bulkhead. Running his hand along the edge, he felt the slight give of the hidden latch and pulled away the teak panel exposing the secret compartment. It was so well built that even close scrutiny revealed nothing. If you didn't know about it, you would never find it. Putting his hand inside, he felt for the small chamois bag. At first he couldn't feel it and instead pulled out his long barreled Smith and Wesson .38, laying it on the plywood bunk sole. Sticking his hand back into the cubbyhole, he felt around and just as he began to panic he located it. The small heavy sack had shifted during the squall of the night before and was lying against the steel hull. Taking it out he carefully loosened the drawstring and poured five heavy gold coins into his hand. Patch rubbed his foot, telling him it was breakfast time

"Wish you could talk old friend," he said to the cat.

He'd found the coins by luck the previous summer. During the months of the hurricane season sea turtles congregated to lay their eggs on Aves island, a remote atoll in the middle of the Caribbean. Some two hundred and fifty miles to the west southwest of Antigua, few people had any reason to go there, other than for the turtles. Jack had first heard about the place from Neddy King, a cagey, West Indian schooner captain. While they shared a glass of rum on the stern one evening, the grizzled, white haired seafarer told strange tales about the far away islet. The last of the old time schooner captains, he was a real sailor's sailor. There were few men with the courage and skill to sail out to Aves during the hurricane season, but Neddy was one of them

"Jack man, let me tell you 'bout dat place," he had said. "Plenty men drown out dere, is a real bad luck piece of nowhere. Some people say dat you could even hear de dead sailors cryin' when de sea rough."

"How about you, Neddy, you ever hear them?" Jack had asked only half jokingly.

"When you go dere, mon, you listen, maybe you goin' hear dem, I don't know," and old Neddy had said no more.

Jack had sailed down there in late July of the previous year and caught nearly thirty big green turtles. They'd anchored the schooner in the tiny lagoon, and that night he, Cobb and Benny had walked around the atoll's sandy shore, waiting for the big female turtles to crawl up to lay their eggs. They would wait until they'd finished laying before capsizing them on the sand. The turtles weren't able to right themselves and so would lay there helpless until the morning when the crew of the *Fandango* returned to collect them in the Boston Whaler. They were hoisted aboard with the gantlines and stowed on deck. Every few hours Benny would take the salt-water hose and wet them down, keeping them alive.

Jack pulled it off, catching the turtles and sailing on back without getting mauled by bad weather. It was a good way to make money during the off-charter season, and he had no trouble selling the meat to the hotels and restaurants back in the Islands for top dollar.

A couple of the other charter skippers thought he was nuts going that far to leeward during the hurricane season. Nature protected the great sea turtles, and they came to lay their eggs during the height of the hurricane season. Maybe he was nuts, but the turtle meat paid for summer expenses and some paint and varnish.

The bird eggs were money too. Cobb had brought a cardboard box filled with them back to Antigua. He quickly sold them all to the local men.

"Does give you plenty iron," he'd explained to Jack.

Many of the locals in the islands strongly believed in their aphrodisiac qualities.

There had also been the nice bonus of the coins. He'd been walking around the north end of the atoll along the water's edge when something caught his eye. Bending to pick it up, he noticed another a few inches away. They were gold coins burnished bright by the sand at the water's edge. The markings were almost gone, but he could just make out a cross and a faint date, 1653. He'd picked up six within a few minutes, all in a ten square foot area, but after searching for another hour he'd found no more.

Jack's throbbing head pulled him back to the present. Slipping the coins safely back into the felt bag, he returned them to their hidden compartment and slid it shut.

"One of these days I'll have another look," he thought to himself.

He would go back to Aves again this coming turtle season and snoop around the island for any signs of an old wreck.

Suddenly he remembered his wallet. He'd kept one in it for good luck. He quickly checked his pocket, but it and the gold coin were gone. He vaguely remembered the odd little Englishman at the bar but couldn't recall his name. The little man certainly wasn't the burglar type, too timid and too old. But he'd certainly been interested in the coin. Popping the

.38 open, he made sure that it was loaded and then after putting the gun on safety, placed it under his pillow.

"Going to have to go see the Major," he said quietly to Patch.

The fact that somebody had broken into his boat was not that unusual. Theft was part of the scenery in the islands, but something about this particular incident bothered him.

His crew would be back for their pay soon, so he pocketed the traveler's cheques and took the Whaler ashore.

Major Ewan Balfont was the police chief in Antigua. A living anachronism, he was a true product of the British Empire. Pompous, and only slightly corrupt, the dapper army major was on permanent loan from the British government to Antigua.

"To train up the lads," as he liked to put it.

He made the most of his billing as chief of the Royal Antigua Police Force, enjoying all the little perks that turned up from time to time. Although the main station was in St Johns, Balfont liked to conduct business from English Harbour where he could take his twenty-foot sloop out for afternoon "patrols". Jack came through the door to the little English Harbour station as the khaki clad man was playing with some papers on his desk. He knew him from the odd social function and occasionally brought him a case of Gilbeys Gin from St Barts in return for which he provided Jack with the odd small "favour."

It was eight when Jack knocked on the door. Balfont was in his office with a couple of the local constables, going over some papers.

"So old chap, you say that you were burgled last night do you?" He asked, raising one of his bushy eyebrows.

"Yes, went back aboard late. Caught me from behind."

"Did he take anything?"

"My wallet and lucky gold piece. Jumped me in the hallway and then took off," Jack replied.

"Any ideas who?" The Major asked.

"No, really odd though, didn't take my cash and traveler's cheques and they were right there," Jack told him.

"Ah, lad, that's island life. Give me a full written report in duplicate and I'll start an investigation."

"Write it up today," Jack told him.

He wouldn't though. It would be a waste of time. Officially the Major would start an investigation, but nothing would really happen. So after bidding the mustachioed officer adios he left.

Walking towards the tiny English Harbour bank a mile up the road in Falmouth, he pondered Balfont's attitude. In the islands incidents like this were rarely solved. It was par for the course.

Depositing the traveler's cheques, he withdrew enough to cover his debts, which was just about the same amount, and left. He got back aboard the anchored schooner by ten and made some coffee before grabbing a quick shower. Standing momentarily in front of the vertical door mirror on the tiny bathroom, Jack glanced at himself. At forty-five, his tanned, well-muscled body was still lean and hard. The sandy blond hair was still there, albeit a trifle thinner, and the creases at the corners of his brown eyes wrinkled cheerfully when he smiled. The almost unnoticeable kink in his nose was due to a recent altercation in the Dominican Republic, that he'd rather forget, but it added a roguish dimension to his still boyish good looks. There were the visible scars of a lifetime of hard usage including a shark attack. Running his hand over what was left of his rear end, he recalled the unnerving event. While spear fishing in the Dry Tortugas he'd shot a forty-pound Nassau grouper under a coral head when a ten-foot bull shark came up behind him and tried to take out his left buttock. He lost the grouper and his stainless steel spear but managed to save most of his butt. Jack realized the shark almost certainly had mistaken his rear end for the grouper, but that had done little to assuage his pain.

Closing the door to the shower stall, he turned the water on cold. It was invigorating, and he had to admit he felt better afterwards.

A few minutes later he heard the sound of oars and a rowboat coming along side. One of the local fishermen had brought his crew back aboard.

"Skip, you awake?" Benny called down the hatch.

"Yes," he called back, running the towel across his back, "I'll be right up."

Stepping into a pair of clean tennis shorts and old polo shirt, he walked through to the wardroom where his crew was waiting and eased himself into the padded chair in front of the small mahogany writing desk on the port side.

"Morning guys, and ladies," he added, glancing at Megan.

Cobb and Benny sat on the settee near the galley door. Looking a little impatient, Megan remained standing in the center of the room. Watch out, he thought to himself. Jack had been impressed with her though. Despite the restrictions of working in a small space, which tilted to thirty-five degrees at times, she'd produced an excellent selection of gourmet meals. Megan had a temper though. One night she caught Jack romancing the leftover roast in the fridge.

"Hey! Get you paws off of that. It's for cold cuts for the passengers tomorrow," she had scolded.

The galley was her domain and not even the captain was allowed in there.

Megan could be pretty funny at times, but there seemed to be a wall there and whenever Jack thought he was getting closer to her, the invisible wall would come up. She quickly noticed his delicate condition.

"What happened to you? You look like something that alcoholic cat of yours dragged in," she laughed, her mood turning lighter.

He winced slightly as Megan looked a little closer at him. Benny and Cobb noticed too.

"Skip, but you looking real rough, you know," Benny observed.

"I don't feel much better than I look. Got robbed last night," he explained.

"What?" Cobb exclaimed.

"Caught me in the hallway and took my wallet," he said, rubbing the large bump on the back of his head.

His three crew dutifully examined the egg.

"Yeah Skip, for true somebody plant a good one on you," Cobb said solemnly.

Benny nodded in agreement. They were more impressed with the actual size of the protrusion than the incident itself, but Megan was skeptical.

"Don't tell me. You and Billy were drinking last night and you fell down the companionway?"

Realizing that he would get no sympathy there, he changed the subject.

"So, how much did you make on your tip?" he asked.

"One fifty, but I should have got a lot more the way I worked my backside off for those people," she remarked, flicking a tress of red hair back from her forehead.

"Sounds decent to me," Jack replied.

She gave him the smile, the one that meant he really was a heel.

"I suppose you would think that, after all, you spent the whole charter sitting on your bum at the steering wheel telling stories to the passengers," she pointed out.

His head started to feel better and his normal good humor returned. Pulling open the drawer, he took out her pay.

"Here's your money, now be a sweetheart and go beat up on somebody else," he teased, handing her the white envelope.

"Thanks, Jack. If you need me again, you know how to get hold of me," she said, giving him a quick pat on the cheek before disappearing up the companionway.

He watched her flaming red hair disappear as Benny ran her ashore in the Boston Whaler. He and Cobb would stay a while to clean up the yacht before taking off.

He smiled to himself; he really liked Megan and would probably hire her again, even if she did have a mouth that wouldn't quit. He felt a brief twinge of loneliness as he thought about his first and only marriage.

The admiral's daughter had been a good catch but a wrong match.

It was getting on past eleven and he'd better run the guys ashore, if they'd finished cleaning up. He found Benny and Cobb waiting on deck.

"You guys done squaring away the boat?" he asked them, smiling.

It was amazing how quickly the two men worked when they were due a few days off.

"Yeah skip, but you forget someting," Cobb smiled at him.

"Oh yeah, you're right," Jack laughed a little self-consciously, and he went back to the wardroom desk to get their pay. He handed them each an envelope and they jumped into the Boston Whaler laying alongside. The decrepit 25 hp Johnson outboard rattled into life after two dozen pulls, and they cruised slowly towards the shore.

"Is time you get another motor, skip," Benny told him, "Dat damn ting sound jus' like a cement mixer."

He was probably right, and it would bite the dust soon, choosing the worst time. The small U.S. dollar bank balance he'd managed to save from the charter season would see him through the schooner's annual haul-out, but there would definitely be no extra.

The gold coins came to mind again; they would be worth something, Jack thought to himself. Maybe he could sell them; Spanish or whatever, they might buy him a new outboard. He'd check it out later on in the day.

"When you need us back?" Cobb asked, shaking Jack from his reverie.

"I'll check the charter office, but I don't think there'll be anything more, so you guys should take a week off," he told them.

A moment later Jack brought the Whaler alongside the dock.

"We go check wid you after a week den," Benny said as he jumped ashore.

They were good guys, Benny and Cobb. Jack knew he was lucky to have them and as they stood there on the dock, he handed them each ten extra Bee Wee dollars from his pocket.

"Have a couple of beers on me," he said.

Tying the Whaler to one of the old cannons embedded in the stone quay, he strolled across the dry grass towards the charter office. Plantain, the dreadlocked Rasta man, was sitting on the low stone wall surrounding the hibiscus flowerbed making his straw hats, and they had their customary friendly exchange.

"How 'bout a straw hat for you today, skipper Jack?" he asked, smiling.

"Not today, Plantain," he replied.

"Got some good Jamaican splif, skip," Plantain tried.

"And cut into my rum drinking money?" Jack grinned.

He got a kick out of the rasta's persistence. Plantain always made a joke of offering him marijuana, even though he knew Jack didn't use the weed.

Approaching the peeling green painted wooden door of the charter office, he thought briefly about going to the bar for a Carib beer to ease the pain a bit but then thought better of it.

He stepped into the room. There were pictures of sailing yachts from around the world pasted on the white painted walls. Jenny Craig, the young girl from England, stood behind the long, Formica topped desk. Big Billy Ramsey sat on the bench across the room smoking his usual cigar and talking to her. Jack wondered if he owned a change of clothing, he always had on what seemed to be the same pair of voluminous khaki shorts and white cotton shirt. The inevitable slouch hat covered his curly red hair and shielded his bulbous nose from the sun.

"Morning mate, what's up?" the big rawboned Australian drawled in his broad accent.

"Someone broke into the boat last night, hit me from behind," Jack replied, rubbing his head.

"Oh no," Jenny exclaimed, putting her hand to her mouth.

"You clobber him then?" Billy asked, frowning.

"As soon as I find him," Jack replied, turning to Jenny.

"And how's my favorite English gal?"

"Better than you, you look terrible," she observed.

"You're the second person who's told me that today, and it's not even noon yet," he grinned, "Any mail or charter inquiries?"

"Nope, nothing today, but if anything comes in, I'll get a message to you," Jenny replied helpfully.

"By the way there was an English guy in the bar last night a Harold something or other. Said he was a Jeweler. You know him?" Jack asked.

Her eyes brightened.

"Oh wow Jack, what's the skinny? You're not looking for one of those sparkling stones, set in a gold ring are you, you know, the ones you stick on the left hand of a lady?" she teased.

"No," Jack replied with just a noticeable touch of regret.

"Oh, I just thought after a two week cruise with Meg, tropical seas and moonlit nights, well you know."

"I'm not the fish she's angling for," Jack replied slowly.

"Our Jacko spliced?" Billy chortled, "When roos fly I reckon."

"Oh well, we just wondered." Jenny said, turning back to her desk.

"We?" Jack asked suspiciously.

"We, the ladies who run this charter office to keep you guys in beer money," Jenny said, glancing at him out of the corner of her eye.

"So what about the jeweler guy?" Jack asked again.

"There's a Harry Bartram of Chandlers Jewelers down on Market Street, you know it?" she asked.

"I can find it, you have the number?" Jack inquired.

"Hang on a mo," Jenny said as she went to get the phone directory.

"Well, got to tend to a sticky stabilizer on my Cat, later sport," Billy said, walking through the door.

Running her finger down the page, Jenny had the small phone book on the counter.

"Here it is. Now I suppose you would like to use the phone," she said, writing down the number on a note pad.

"'A' for efficiency, Jen," Jack said ,winking at her.

She placed the office phone on the counter and Jack dialed the number. After a few rings Harry Bartram answered.

"Yes?"

"You the man who was in the Admirals Inn last night?" Jack asked.

"Yes, who's this please?"

"Jack Carlton. I had a coin and you said that if I ever wanted to sell to call you."

"Ah yes, I'm interested," he said, "When can you bring it in?" Bartram asked.

"How about around noon?" Jack suggested.

"Okay, I'll see you then," Bartram replied.

He hung up the phone and turned to Jenny. She looked at him quizzically.

"You found some treasure, Jack?"

"My, what big ears you have. No, nothing that exciting. Anyway, gotta fly and see a man about a.... ring was it?" Jack winked at her before leaving the office.

Wandering down to the dock, he untied the Whaler from the old cannon barrel and sped back to the *Fandango*. Going below to his cabin, he took the coins from their hiding place and put them in his pocket. He made a quick check to make sure the anchor was secure and then turned off the power, locked her up and sped the Whaler back to the shore.

Walking briskly to the bus stand behind the Admiral's Inn, he caught Speedy's brightly painted jitney just as it was leaving for St. Johns. The bus was full, and the long ride into town was a real pain in the ass, literally. As usual, Speedy went way too fast, hitting every rut and pothole in the uneven road. Whenever the crowded bus hit a bump, it jumped momentarily into the air before crashing down again. The passengers clapped and cheered the driver on as he careened around sharp corners on two wheels.

"Yeah man, plenty speed, plenty speed, de man could really drive, you know," one guy kept on saying.

Jack was of a different opinion along with an old lady who kept crossing herself, until she couldn't stand it any longer.

"Ay man, you tryin' to kill all we? Slow dung de ve-hickle ah tell you. You is an ass or what? Ah tell you slow dung de ve-hickle," she shouted desperately trying to hold her pink-feathered hat on her head.

Dreadlocked Speedy ignored her completely and continued on with the radio blasting out calypso music.

"I envy de Congo man..."

"He bettah dan me ah feel to shake he hand..."

"He wid he stomach upset..."

"And me, I never eat a white meat yet..."

Jack quit worrying about Speedy and after getting a firm grip on the door handle, settled down to try and keep himself in his seat.

At the first intersection outside St. Johns, the jitney bus passed crazy Mama De La Rose standing at her regular location on the right hand side of the road, under the red and yellow Milo chocolate milk sign. She was a wizened, bowlegged old crone with a pipe, who wore her colorful full-length island style dress and Madras headpiece to direct all traffic passing through the intersection. She believed this was her solemn duty and took it very seriously, energetically waving every single car past with a sharp tweet on her silver whistle. Jack wondered why the police force didn't just hire her. She had a great work ethic and if they could train her to pass out speeding tickets, well...

Pulling into St. Johns, Speedy screeched to a halt in the center of town. Everyone disembarked quickly, glad to have made it alive.

"I'll never take this damned thing again," Jack muttered to himself, but then he'd said that before.

He stood for a moment trying to recall how to get to Market Street. The old British capital of Antigua hadn't changed much since the colonial days of empire. Open gutters flanked cobblestone roads and sidewalks that spread outwards from the town center where the occasional paved street took over. Brightly painted, two-storied wood buildings stood side by side with interesting signs over dark shop entrances. "Braithwaites Dry Goods" spanned a whole block while "Ripplestones Sundry Grocery" was much smaller. A flight of rickety steps on the side of one building boasted a larger sign with "Bebbington & Faquart, Barristers at Law" in large white letters. A smaller reminder beneath the names said that the above were "English Educated". Louvered red and green doors on handmade black wrought iron hinges hung from the beams while windows and ancient brass padlocks hung on foot long hasps. A few stevedores pushed huge wooden handcarts fitted with old car tires from the waterfront to various town destinations while a local captain of commerce strutted about wearing a dark suit and tie trying to convey personal importance despite the sweltering heat.

The hot noonday sun shimmered off the tin roofs, and Jack's deck shoes soon began absorbing the heat as he strolled in the direction of Market Street. The old, British-style wooden buildings with their brightly painted shutters lent a carnival-like atmosphere to the town.

There was a big cruise ship at the main dock and tourists in white knee socks and red baseball caps braved the heat to explore the old town. Near the waterfront local women in brightly colored Madras dresses and head-bands enticed tourists to buy their wares. Beads, straw hats and baskets of a dozen types, painted conch shells and the inevitable tee shirts with "Yeh Mon Antigua" emblazoned across the front were all for sale. The heat was a lot more oppressive here in town than in English Harbour, and he hoped he wouldn't have to stay too long.

Strolling down Newgate Street, he turned left into Market Street. When he passed the market stalls the smells of fresh local produce and spices filled the air. In the fish section some local fishermen had hauled up a twenty-foot black pilot whale that they had harpooned and were chopping it up with machetes and selling the dark red meat to an eager crowd.

The jeweler's shop was located towards the end of the street, and Jack almost missed the small sign. It read "Chandlers" and underneath, "Harold F. Bartram, dealer in fine gems and precious metals". Wiping the sweat from his forehead, he walked up to the door and turned the knob. It was locked. He muttered under his breath and was just about to start banging when he noticed a small sign saying, "Please ring bell." So he did.

CHAPTER THREE

St. Johns, Antigua

The door opened halfway, and as Jack peered in he recognized the man from the bar the night before.

"Bartram?" Jack asked.

"Yes?" he answered suspiciously.

"Jack Carlton, we spoke at the Admiral's Inn," Jack said, pushing the door slightly.

"Oh yes, come in," Bartram replied, motioning for him to enter.

The Englishman's handshake was damp and weak. Inside, the shop was large. Rows of glass cases stood against the walls filled with a surprisingly large selection of jewelry. Each case was secured with a solid looking padlock.

"I brought the coins I told you about," Jack said, taking the small felt bag from his pocket.

"Jolly good," Bartram said, watching, "Actually, I think it would be better if we go into the back room where I keep my equipment. This way please."

He motioned politely towards the curtain at the back of the shop. There was a long bench against the back wall with the various tools of the jewelers' trade. Bartram pulled up a chair for Jack. He took the small stool next to the workbench.

"Now, let's have a closer look, captain, shall we?" Bartram said expectantly.

The British were always so formal, Jack thought to himself. He opened the felt bag, and after pouring the coins into his hand, offered them to the jeweler.

"I don't have the one I showed you last night," Jack told him, watching to see if there was a reaction. "These are different," he pointed out.

He didn't even blink.

"That's because they weren't molded," Bartram said, laying the gold pieces out on the workbench, "These coins were just poured from a weight measure and stamped on each side when the metal was still soft. How many do you actually have?"

"I found six of them. But the one I showed you got stolen last night."

"Oh, unfortunate. Happens in the islands you know. Good job you still have these."

Bartram's eyes didn't flicker. He knew nothing about the incident.

Using his jeweler's loupe, he examined the coins one by one, tilting his head and pursing out his lower lip.

"What do you think?" Jack asked.

"Good, pure gold, and Spanish in origin."

"In the bar last night you said they were minted in 1653 right?" Jack asked curious.

"Well yes," Bartram replied, shrugging his shoulders, "although you can't see it clearly on all of them, the date is stamped on each of the coins,"

Jack reached for the loupe to take a look. The jeweler's tool made the faint numerals easier to see. Squinting through the small magnifier, he followed the indentations of the Spanish cross in a circle with the year below. The centuries had taken their toll and each coin bore signs of erosion. On three of them the first digits of the date and parts of the cross were gone while the other two had the last digits erased. There was one though, that had the date almost intact: 1653.

"There's some other marks on this one here, below the date, like little DDvs," Jack pointed out, handing back the loupe.

The Englishman had seen them as well and although he had never come across that particular code before, they were definitely identification numbers of some sort. The Spaniards of that era were meticulous in their records, and their gold minting in particular usually carried some sort of identifier in addition to the date. He didn't see any harm in letting that out; there was no possible way the charter skipper could ever know the true significance of the small letters, but he quickly changed the subject.

"They're the minter's identification marks," Bartram said, swiveling around. "You want to sell them?

"That's why I'm here," Jack replied.

"Where did you say you found them?" Bartram asked suddenly.

"I didn't," Jack replied.

"It would be nice to know where you got them, for my records you know," Bartram pressed.

"In the Caribbean," Jack replied in a way that left no more room for argument.

"Right oh then, give me just a moment and I'll give you a price," the Englishman said, sounding slightly disappointed, "I'll just weigh them and take a photo for my book."

Jack had no objection. He left him with the coins and walked to the side of the workshop where there was another glass case filled with what looked like antique jewelry.

Harry Bartram worked quickly. Taking his camera from the shelf, he carefully photographed each coin. Then he put them on his mini scale, making sure to subtract a decimal off the reading. He always made sure that he got a fraction more than he paid for when buying gold.

Jack was getting a little impatient when Bartram finished fifteen minutes later. He wondered how much the old bandit was going to offer him.

"Well captain," he smiled ingratiatingly. "I'll buy all five."

"How much?" he asked, getting straight to the point.

Bartram hesitated for a moment before replying.

"Seventy five each, I think that's a fair price."

"Uncle Sam's best?" Jack queried.

"Who? I've never heard of..."

"US, American Dollars."

"Oh my, yes of course," Bartram replied, sounding affronted.

Jack considered it for a moment. The Englishman obviously wanted them and he had a feeling he could go higher.

"Make it a hundred a piece and you've got a deal," Jack offered.

It took him only a split second to decide.

"Done," the Englishman replied moving to his desk.

Unlocking the drawer he pulled out a wad of cash. Carefully counting the bills one by one, he handed them over.

"Thanks," Jack said and they shook hands.

Walking out of the jeweler's shop five hundred dollars richer, Jack headed straight for the Johnson outboard dealer two blocks away. He bought the new 25-hp outboard sitting in the shop window.

"You want it delivered, skip?" the dealer asked

"Can you get it to English Harbour this afternoon?" he asked.

"Yeah man, no problem, gonna send it wid Speedy. He de bes' driver in town, fast an' reliable."

Jack just shook his head. Smiling, he counted the cash left in his pocket; he still had some left.

The little jeweler waited until Jack disappeared down the street before going to the bookcase on the opposite wall. With a little difficulty he pulled a heavy volume from one of the shelves. Returning to his stool, he placed the encyclopaedia of gold coinage on his workbench and quickly began leafing through the pages.

There were a half dozen pages dedicated to the lost Cartagena bullion, and the minter's identification of that horde was DDV. A heavily laden Spanish galleon disappeared without trace after leaving Cartagena in 1653. Bartram's hands began to shake. If they could find out where Carlton found the coins, perhaps there might be more, even the wreck of the ship. After reading the pertinent paragraphs again he snapped it shut and reached for the phone. As he dialed Bartram felt excited. The coins he had bought could just be from the famed lost Cartagena bullion and no trace of that treasure had ever been found.

He had a wealthy client who had purchased coins from him in the past. The amateur treasure hunter was always on the lookout for interesting pieces. Ed Henderson had been around the Eastern Caribbean for a number of years, searching for some mysterious Spanish wreck. He rented a beautiful home on the north coast near Hodges Bay, and he had recruited Bartram to be on the lookout for coins of the vintage that had just come to light. They had a sort of standing agreement that whenever he came across anything special, Henderson got first refusal. He liked doing business with the American. He always paid whatever he asked without question, especially for old gold coins of Spanish origin.

The phone rang four, then five times and just when Bartram thought he'd have to call back, someone answered.

"Yes?"

"Hello, Mr. Henderson?"

"Speaking," the voice was confident and deep.

"Yes, Harry Bartram here in St. Johns."

"Got something interesting for me?"

"Possibly. I've just purchased some new coins," he said cryptically.

"What have you got, Harry?" Henderson asked his tone changing.

"Well, this chap came in with five gold pieces. They're unusual, but more important they're marked, Cartagena 1653, and the book says most of the bullion in that batch was lost."

"That's great, Harry, did you take them?" Henderson inquired.

"Oh yes, I've got them right here but there's more," the jeweler added, making the most of his new possessions.

"What?" pressed Henderson?

"One of the coins has an identification mark that I recognize."

"What's it look like?" Henderson asked impatiently.

"Odd really, just two capital D's and a smaller v," Bartram explained.

At the other end of the phone Henderson sat up and took a deep breath.

"You've got the five coins in your possession now?" he asked cautiously.

"Yes, I just this minute bought them from a charter captain out of English Harbour called Jack Carlton, and paid through the nose I might add. I do hope that you'll take them off my hands."

"Don't worry about that, I'll definitely take them," Henderson assured him, "You're sure it was Carlton you bought them from?"

"Oh yes."

"Where'd he get them?" Henderson asked casually.

"Well, I'm not sure really. When I asked him, all he said was that he found them somewhere in the islands. He wouldn't tell me exactly where."

"But he was the one who found them?" Henderson pressed.

"Oh definitely. I heard him say so in the bar last night. Said he found them last July. Would you like me to hold them for you?" Harry Bartram was going to make sure his investment was covered.

"Yes, I'll definitely buy them," Henderson assured him.

"I need one fifty a piece," Bartram said nervously.

"Fine, Harry, fine. Have you told anyone about this yet?" Henderson inquired casually.

"No, just you, Mr. Henderson. You know I keep my business relationships private," Bartram said, sounding slightly hurt.

"And I appreciate that a lot, you and I will do a lot of business together, Harry," Henderson told him.

"There is one more thing," Bartram said slowly.

"What's that, Harry?"

"Well supposing there was a bit more to this than meets the eye, I would of course expect..."

"Harry, I understand perfectly and I intend to take good care of you."

"A small finder's fee perhaps, for my assistance."

"Absolutely you have my word. Just keep this quiet for now, between you and me, OK?"

"You can trust me, sir, and when do you think you'll be along to collect them?" Bartram inquired.

"I'm going to send Garcia right now with the cash. Just make sure you hold those coins for me," Henderson told him.

"Right oh then, I'll be waiting," Bartram said.

Henderson hung up the phone. The Englishman knew too much already, but it sounded like he had really hit the jackpot this time. If he was right, this was the *San Idelfonso* horde.

Walking to the front porch of the beach house, Henderson waved to the man standing at the end dock with a Casting rod. He kept Garcia Perez employed full time and although he sometimes wondered about the Puerto Rican's intelligence level, he was at least motivated by something they both understood, money. He paid him to be loyal, and given Garcia's personality it was a sound arrangement. A small time crook with big time aspirations, he'd paid him to smuggle some artifacts from Puerto Rico into the United States three years ago and kept him on salary ever since. A few minutes later Garcia walked into the house.

"Si Eduardo, what is it you want?" he asked dully.

Henderson explained exactly what it was he wanted him to do. He nodded slowly but showed no emotion whatsoever.

That night around eleven Garcia returned.

"You get the coins?" he asked.

"Yes, Eduardo, here," he said, handing over a small velvet bag.

Henderson poured the coins on the glass topped dining room table. His hand shook as he picked up the magnifying glass. Sure enough on each coin there appeared the telltale minters marks, DDv.

"And the Englishman?" Henderson asked, his back to Garcia.

"He will not talk Eduardo," the Puerto Rican answered.

Henderson shivered slightly. The man had no personality; he was cold as ice.

With the coins in his possession Henderson was able to confirm that they were from the *San Idelfonso* horde. Later he placed a call to Bimini in the Bahamas.

"Hello?" A woman with an American accent answered sleepily.

"Is this Laura?" Henderson asked.

"Who's this? It's two o'clock in the morning," she replied angrily.

"It's Ed Henderson, I need you now for a few weeks. Have you still got your equipment available?"

"Yeah, I've got all the stuff you need, but it's going to cost," she replied, yawning.

"Not a problem, so long as you hold to your quote," he replied.

"What do you want me to do?" she asked.

"Come to Antigua. You can use some of the mobilization fee I gave you, and we'll settle up later," he told her.

"How soon do you want me there?" she asked, sounding more alert.

"Take the first flight you can tomorrow and I'll meet up with you at the Admirals Inn, in English Harbour. There'll be a room booked for you," he told her.

Laura Feldman was a freelance marine archeologist Henderson had met diving in Bimini four months ago. They'd met at the local bar one night, and over a few drinks he'd made an arrangement with her.

Henderson's last call was to the Admirals Inn. Speaking quickly to Mabeline, he booked a room. Afterwards, he sat back in his chair, smiling for a moment. After a long chase things were finally coming together. He had been on the trail of the lost Cartagena bullion for years and the DDv identification marks were on the old documents he'd received from the translators in Spain. They meant that the coins had been minted and packed by Don Davila in 1653 in Cartagena, Colombia. All he had to do now was get the Carlton guy to show him where he'd found them.

Meanwhile, Jack was happy. Towards evening he motored slowly around English Harbour with the new outboard. The dealer had said to break it in at slow speed over a full tank of gas. The needle of the tank gauge showed about half, but Jack didn't mind. The new outboard was sounding sweet after the rattle of the old one, and anyway, he still had a couple of cold Carib beers in the icebox. He had the light, twelve pound Mitchell casting rig with the yellow jig on the seat, and if the bonito showed up at the mouth of the harbour, as they usually did at sundown, he'd give them a try. As the sun went down, he let the engine idle just in time to see the fabled green flash on the horizon. It was a good one. The bonito never showed, but he hooked a nice four pound yellow-tail snapper, just the right size for dinner.

CHAPTER FOUR

The Anchorage

A day later the *Fandango* lay gently at her anchor in English Harbour. The wind died down towards noon, and Jack rigged the sun awning over the cockpit. Sitting on the port side he tinkered with a 4/0 Penn fishing reel, fitting new washers in the drag. The peaceful afternoon suddenly ended as Moses's water taxi came roaring out from the shore with two people aboard. Watching in disbelief, Jack saw the green, wooden hulled skiff slew alongside the schooner way too fast, slamming into his glossy white hull with a nasty thump.

"What the…" he shouted angrily jumping up.

Leaning over the rail, Jack saw an eighteen-inch long scratch in the paint.

"Look at what you did to my topsides," he said angrily.

The Antigan launch driver held his boat alongside, not looking in the least bit apologetic.

"Ah bring someone out to see you, skip," he said.

"When are you going learn to drive that thing?" Jack growled.

"Sorry, skip, but dis gentleman did want to see you urgent like," Moses explained, flashing a huge, white-toothed smile.

The well-heeled looking man in bow of the water taxi wore an expensive polo shirt with new topsider deck shoes. About six-foot with dark slicked back hair and big square hands, he wore a fancy, gold watch on his left wrist.

"I'm looking for Capt. Jack Carlton," the man said.

"You just ran into him," Jack replied testily, looking at the gouge in his hull.

"Sorry about the damage to your boat, I'll pay you for it," he said in a self-assured manner, holding out his hand, "I told him to hurry, I didn't want you sailing away."

"Ed Henderson," he said, leaning over and stretching out his hand.

"I'm interested in chartering a yacht for a couple of weeks and Moses here said that you're the only one with a dive compressor aboard."

"That's right," Jack said, his annoyance disappearing fast, "I've got a new Mako compressor and dive gear for six people."

"Can we talk?"

"Sure, come aboard for a beer and I'll run you back, then Moses here can be on his way," Jack suggested, scowling at the Antigan.

At the mention of a possible charter, Jack felt his anger over the scratched topsides slowly evaporating.

"Fine," Henderson said, turning to the Antigan, "How much do I owe you, Moses?"

Jack smiled. He'd seen it a hundred times, the old island shake down. He was curious to see how this man would handle it.

"Well sir, I go give you a special price. Mostly I charges ten dullah U.S. to come across de bay, but for you, well jus' make it a low five US dullah," Moses told him.

Henderson hesitated for only a second. There was just the slightest hint of anger at first, but then he smiled quickly and whipped out a wad of bills from his pocket, peeled off a five and handed it to the Antigan.

"Righteous, yeah man, you need to go anywhere, you jus' call Moses."

The actual charge was in fact one dollar Bee Wee and given the exchange rate of two and a half to one, Moses had just made out like a bandit. After seeing his passenger aboard the *Fandango*, he sped off, grinning from ear to ear.

Henderson easily climbed the boarding ladder and made his way to the cockpit. He'd obviously been on boats before. Jack offered him a cushion, and they sat down on the port side just ahead of the brass binnacle.

"Carib or Heineken?" Jack asked.

"Ah, Carib," Ed replied.

Reaching into the small Igloo cooler, he chose two cold ones and popped the caps. He passed the local island brew to Ed.

"So where are you from?" Jack asked.

"New York, but I'm renting here for a couple of months," Henderson replied.

"Where abouts?" Jack was curious.

He hadn't seen the man around Antigua before.

"Hodges Bay on the north coast," Henderson replied.

Jack knew the house. There was only one in Hodges and he had seen it from the water. It was large modern place with pool and dock in front.

"So what do you have in mind?" Jack inquired.

"Diving," Henderson said taking a sip from the Carib bottle, "two weeks would be good."

He looked like he had the money, Jack thought, noticing the designer logo on his shirt and the sleek gold watch.

"I know some good dive sites around the islands we could sail to," Jack offered. "What are you looking for though? There's a couple of good wrecks off Anguilla, or if you want to spear some big grouper, we can probably find a few out around Barbuda."

Jack was a perceptive man, and he saw a slight flicker in Henderson's eyes when he mentioned the word wreck.

"What I really had in mind, Jack, was something exciting, like exploration diving, or some treasure hunting," Henderson countered.

"Most of the wreck sites around here are already pretty well picked over, but they still make good dive sites and you might even find a cannon ball or two," Jack told him. He wasn't about to say he'd found coins the previous year. They were probably just a fluke anyway, a one time deal.

What Henderson said next surprised him.

"What I'd really like to do is go out to Aves."

Jack digested that for just a second to make sure he had heard right. "Aves?"

"I understand there's a couple of unexplored wrecks there."

"There could be, but I never saw one. Any wooden ship that piled up on Aves probably disintegrated and went deep years ago," Jack said, "There's little shoal ground there to hold anything."

He suddenly felt exasperated. It was the same old story; whenever things looked too good to be true they usually were. Up until a few seconds ago it had been shaping up nice. Some good sailing, and a few days of good shallow water diving out in Barbuda and maybe another two or three in Anguilla. Coral reefs, nice beaches, feed them lots of lobster and bring them home fat, tanned and happy. An easy buck on a milk-run charter, but no, he had to get a guy that wanted to go to Aves Island. All of a sudden the prospective easy charter had turned into one where he would have to work his butt off. And in a dangerous place too. He'd made one dive at Aves last year and it had scared the hell out of him. There wasn't even a decent anchorage out there, and the days when you could actually dive outside the reef were limited. It was usually just too rough. The water inside the small lagoon was shallow, and outside, well that just dropped down into the abyss all around with no shelving or ledges at all. It was like swimming in the ocean. No, it was swimming in the ocean, and with a whole lot of big goddamn fish there, the kind that ate people.

"Let me tell you, Ed, I was out there last July for some turtles and it's a dangerous place. The water's real deep and there are some bad currents. We're just starting the hurricane season here now too, and it's not a good time to go."

He waited a moment to see if that had discouraged Henderson but the New Yorker didn't seem impressed.

"I wouldn't recommend Aves for recreational diving. In fact I wouldn't recommend it for any kind of diving," Jack continued.

"Sorry to hear that, I kind of had my heart set on going out there," Ed sounded disappointed.

"How'd you hear about Aves anyway?" Jack asked curiously. "Nobody much knows about it and it's hard to find, like a damn needle in a haystack. It's not even marked on a lot of charts," he added.

Henderson shifted in his seat and hesitated for a few seconds before answering.

"A bird watcher friend of mine, he read about an expedition out there a couple of years ago. They saw some rare migratory birds that stopped on their way from the Arctic to the marshes of Venezuela."

"That's why they call it Aves, Bird Island, there are a lot of birds there," Jack replied, "probably thousands."

Henderson was deep in thought. He shrugged slightly and after taking another sip of beer turned to give Jack a serious look.

"What's your regular rate, skipper?"

"Three thousand U.S. dollars a week, all inclusive, except your booze."

"I tell you what, skipper. I'll pay you double that for two weeks and if I need to stay longer, I'll pay the same pro-rated on a daily basis."

Jack did a double take. What did this guy want out at Aves this time of year? He was either nuts, or maybe I am even listening to him. He really had to think this one through carefully. Like most of the people in the charter business, Jack Carlton carried no insurance. Men like him relied on their skill and smarts to stay out of trouble, and it worked just fine as long as you were careful.

"When would you want to leave?" Jack asked.

"As soon as possible."

They talked for another twenty minutes and Ed asked the usual questions. He was particularly interested in the schooner's radio equipment, what its range was and which channels were available. He asked specific questions about the crew and wanted to know how many would be aboard for the trip. He also wanted to know about the machinery, electrical voltage, speed, range under power and so on.

"Have you got a twelve volt battery charger on board?" he inquired.

"Yes, we can rig you up one if you need it," Jack replied.

Henderson was beginning to look a touch impatient.

"So how about it, skipper, is it a deal?"

Jack thought for a moment. He'd have to be careful, real careful, and at the first hint of bad weather he'd get out of there fast.

The atoll was some two hundred and fifty miles to leeward and west of the islands of the Eastern Caribbean and the cyclonic storms of the Atlantic formed far to the east, off the African coast. The big weather systems fed on the warm waters of the Atlantic, occasionally forming into the huge spinning storms known as hurricanes. They always moved westwards, sometimes as fast as twenty knots, so if you were caught to leeward of safe harbour with a hurricane bearing down on you, well you could get into a whole heap of trouble. Jack had talked to Captain Neddy King the previous summer. The old West Indian skipper had been going down to Aves for a lot of years on his venerable schooner, *Ruby C,* and he made no bones about the dangers.

"Listen to de radio, man, every day, even three times a day. Get de weather reports and if you hear of a tropical storm anywhere to de east of de islands, well get out of dere right away," he'd said dramatically. "And don't you never tink about staying ashore at Aves in a storm you know. Big storm waves could just wash Aves away. Ah went dere one year after a storm and even though ah could see some rock, most of de sand was gone. A month later de sea wash de sand back up and Ah could land dere for my turtles again. Let me tell you my friend, don't play with Aves, she'll kill you."

It was strong advice. But as Jack sat there in the *Fandango's* cockpit, he couldn't help thinking of the money. Two weeks charter at six thousand, plus any extra time at eight-fifty a day. Jack mentally deducted the amounts for his crew's salary and other expenses and he was still left with a real tidy sum. He'd hire Megan again and although he'd have to put up with her mouthing off in the galley, for that amount of money, I can put up with a lot. He'd have to make some special arrangements for his crew though, maybe give them a little extra something for 'hazardous duty'.

The *Fandango* was pretty much ready to go. All he needed to do was make the oil and filter changes, grease the bearings, fuel up and do a few small maintenance jobs that had come up during the last trip. If he could get a hold of Megan in time, she'd be able to get the provisions aboard tomorrow morning and they'd be ready to go. He already knew that he would do it. He just couldn't pass up that kind of cash. Even though it was the beginning of the hurricane season and not the best time to sail down to Aves, it could be done.

After moment, a slight grin crossed his face.

"Well, skipper?" Henderson asked expectantly.

"Why not," Jack told him evenly, "but only on certain conditions."

"What conditions?"

"For starters all decisions regarding the safety of the vessel are mine and if we have to head home because of bad weather, that's my call. Secondly, if you lose time, there's no refund."

Henderson hesitated only slightly before replying.

"Fair enough, you're the boss."

"Also, you pay up front."

"Not a problem," Henderson replied agreeably, "I can pay right now if that helps."

"Great, how many are there going to be in your party?"

"There'll be just the three of us. Myself, Laura and Garcia."

"You'll have lots of space then."

"That's good. Laura's a photographer and she'll be bringing along some underwater equipment," Henderson told him.

"You're all certified divers? " Jack queried. He didn't want any learners out at Aves. If somebody got injured or lost out there and the authorities found out he was diving uncertified clients, there would be hell to pay.

"Yes, we're all certified."

Henderson reached into his pocket and came up with the two cards and handed them to Jack. They were PADI (professional association of diving instructors) licensed Jack noted, but while Henderson's card was dated four years prior, the card for Garcia Perez had been stamped in Puerto Rico only four months previously.

"What about the other person, Laura?" Jack asked.

"She won't be diving. She's just along to handle the camera equipment."

"All right, you've got a deal," Jack told him.

Henderson seemed happy and they shook hands to consummate their arrangement.

"We can do the money thing right now if you want," he offered.

"Works for me. Let's go below," Jack replied.

The generator was purring away, and he turned on a couple of lights in the red carpeted wardroom and opened the overhead skylight using the polished brass screw handles. They sat down in the padded chairs at the varnished mahogany dining table.

"Cash alright, skipper?"

"Cash is fine," Jack replied, smiling.

Charter fees were often paid by traveler's cheques into the charter office but cash was all right; in fact it was very all right.

Henderson pulled a thick billfold from his jacket pocket and, opening it began to count crisp new hundred dollar bills onto the table. Jack watched as the thousands piled up. He was sure carrying a wad.

Ed Henderson placed the last of the one hundred twenty hundred dollar bills on the polished surface of the mahogany table and slid them across towards Jack. They totaled twelve thousand of Uncle Sam's best kind.

"Go ahead and count it, skipper."

Jack counted out the bills.

"It's all here," he confirmed and after squaring the bills in his hand he stood up from the table.

The twelve thousand felt nice and heavy and he was happy with the arrangement. He had a good schooner, a good crew and 195 good horses in a big diesel to get him home if the going got rough.

"Just give me a minute while I put this away," he said, putting the cash into a brown envelope.

Leaving Ed in the wardroom, he went to his cabin. He took a thousand out before hiding the rest in the secret compartment. Tucking the sheet in again around the mattress, he returned to the wardroom.

"When can get under way, skipper?" Henderson asked him.

Jack detected a suddenly more authoritative tone and thought for a moment before replying. It was something you learned quickly in the yacht charter business. When clients paid the kind of money that Ed Henderson was paying, they all wanted to be in control. The trick was to let them think that and still keep a hold of the reins.

"If I can get everything ready, we might be able to get away tomorrow, how about that?" he offered.

"That'll be fine. When can we bring our stuff aboard?"

Jack checked his watch. "I'll tell you what, let me have tomorrow morning to get my crew together, provision and fuel up, then we'll be ready for you say, around three o'clock in the afternoon."

"Alright, we'll be on the dock at three."

"Great," Jack said, smiling, "get your taxi to bring you to the fuel dock across from the charter office. That's where we'll be."

Jack took his new charter client ashore in the Whaler, and they shook hands at the dock in front of the charter office.

"See you at three tomorrow then."

"Thanks for the ride," Henderson said before turning to walk away towards the Admirals Inn. Jack threw a clove hitch around the barrel of the big cannon planted in the ground and ducked into the charter office. Jen was there, working behind the desk.

"Hello Jack, you're looking brighter today," she said with a smile.

"I'm feeling better today. The egg on the back of my head has gone down a little," he said.

She frowned disapprovingly.

"Trouble just seems to follow some people around."

Jack smiled. It was more accurate a statement than she could ever know.

"I got a diving two-weeker to Aves," he said, changing the subject.

"Lucky you, that means you'll be able to pay us the commission for the last charter we gave you," she said pointedly.

"Do I still owe you for that? Jack tried sounding contrite, but it didn't work. Jen just glared at him.

"It must be the guy who came in here late yesterday," she said.

"Henderson?" Jack queried, putting an elbow on the chest high counter.

"He didn't give me his name, but he was asking a lot of questions about you and the subject of Aves came up during the conversation."

"Really, how's that?"

"Hang on, let me think," Jenny said, her forehead creasing in thought, "Yes, first of all he came in asking about you specifically, saying someone around here had recommended you for a dive charter. Then he asked me what places you'd been to at this time of year. I remembered you had gone out to Aves last July for turtles, so I told him and he sounded particularly interested in that."

"Anything else?" Jack asked.

"No, that was pretty much it. He asked how he could get hold of you and I told him that I could get a message to you out in the harbour, but he said not to bother and then he left."

"He must have come out to me right after he left you then. It's a cash up front deal and no agent," Jack pointed out, smiling. He wouldn't have to pay any commission on this one.

"I just hope you know what you're doing going down there again this time of year," she warned him.

"Hey, don't worry about me, Jen, 'Lucky come back Jack' they used to call me. Oh by the way, can you get a hold of Megan for me? We'll need to leave tomorrow."

"She's probably at the Ad's terrace; I'll ring there right now and leave a message if you want?" Jen offered.

Jack thanked her and walked out past the back of Admirals Inn to the taxi stand. He scanned the terrace as he passed by, but Megan was not in sight. Maybe she had already left. The taxi stand was empty except for two cars. He was looking for the driver who did all his charter transports and spotted him sleeping in his Ford station wagon.

"Hey Sando, I need you to go and get Cobb and Benny for me. I need them tomorrow morning, we've got a two week charter leaving in the afternoon."

Sando knew where the two crewmen would be found.

"Yeah skip, you pay me when I get back?" Sando asked.

"As always, just make sure that you bring those guys back in time tomorrow."

He couldn't understand why Sando always had to ask about money. He always paid him. He watched the taxi scream away in a cloud of dust before walking back towards the charter office. Inside, Megan and Jen stood in the corner near the wall phone, chatting away and drinking iced tea. Jen was dying to hear how Meg had got on with Jack during their last charter. He was a bit of an unknown quantity with the girls around English Harbour, a real mystery, which was a shame as they all thought he was gorgeous. The mystery surrounding him inevitably made him even more fascinating in their eyes.

"Come on, Meg, tell all. What's he really like?"

"He's a bit of a dark horse," Meg answered, not looking at Jen.

"Oh come on, you're blushing Meggie! Did something happen between you two on the trip?" she asked slyly.

"No, of course not."

"I don't believe you."

"Nothing happened, Jen," Megan repeated a little more defensively.

"Well that's a shame, because you two look great together," Jen glanced at her good friend, whose face had taken on a wistful look.

"Maybe you'll have something more exciting to tell me when you come back from this charter. Actually, I'll be pretty annoyed with you if you don't."

Meg laughed at her friend and picking up her bag, she gave Jen's nose a quick squeeze.

"This is getting far too inquisitive," she said. As she walked towards the door she was just about to open it when Jack beat her to it.

"I was just looking for you," he said, stepping back to let her out the door.

She wore a light green one-piece swimsuit with a matching sarong tied around her waist, emphasizing her athletic figure.

"Hi Jack, Jen tells me you need me?" she asked in her lilting English accent.

"Yes, we've got a charter for two weeks, maybe more. Can you do it?"

"What's it about, Jen mentioned something about diving out at Aves?"

"Well I've got this guy who wants to do a little diving out there."

She thought for a second.

"You'll have to pay me a bundle of money this time, Jack, to get me to go all the way out there," Megan told him half seriously, "especially this time of year."

Jack smiled.

"Have you ever known me not to look after the best interests of my crew?" he teased, "How about I double your salary, that okay with you?"

Her eyebrows lifted in surprise.

"Double? Skinflint Jack, forgive me, thrifty Jack is offering double? What are you up to?" she asked, putting her hands on her hips.

Megan was naturally the suspicious type.

"They're paying me double, so I'm paying the crew double, it's the only way to keep the best."

"Alright, I'll come." It took her only a split second to decide. She respected his abilities and thought no more about it.

"Great," Jack said, smiling; he was glad she was coming along again.

"And not because of the flattery, when do we leave?" she asked.

"I'm going to try for tomorrow afternoon, so you'll need to provision right away."

"You don't leave a girl much time, do you? How many guests?" She always shopped by the head.

"Only three, plus Benny and Cobb and the two of us, so it'll be an easy one for you."

He pulled a wad of hundreds from his pocket and peeled off four crisp new bills.

"Here's four hundred. Get some nice stuff to get us through a month if we need it and treat yourself to a quick lunch in town," he said expansively.

Megan broke into wide grin as she took the money.

"Oh wow, aren't you the big spender today," she laughed, blinking her eyes and acting impressed.

"I think you should just get a good selection of..." he stopped as he caught the expression on her face, "You know what to get, Meg."

"Yes, I think I can manage."

She bent down and stuffed the bills into her purse. Then she pulled out a cheesecloth shirt from her tote bag and put it on. Jack knew that she was a good shopper and that he'd get his money's worth. He was surprised how relieved he felt that she could come. He'd been a bit worried that she might have some other plans already. It would have been a bummer not to be able to do this charter because he couldn't find a chef. Mind you, he thought, for twelve large ones he would have cooked himself.

Back on the *Fandango*, Jack relaxed in the cockpit for a half-hour to watch the sunset. Everything was looking good. Fine weather, cash up front, his crew would be there tomorrow. Life was sweet.

CHAPTER FIVE

The Charter

The following morning Jack woke with a clear head. He felt good, in fact better than he'd felt for days. Lying quietly for a moment in his cabin he looked through the skylight at the edge of a puffy white cloud drifting across the sky. There would be a sailing breeze later on.

His thoughts returned to Ed Henderson and his charter. The just-after-you-wake-up, relaxed feeling disappeared and Jack felt his body tense. Running down to Aves atoll was risky this time of year, but he understood West Indian weather patterns. Modern day weather reporting facilities and the work of the National Hurricane Center in Miami, Florida, made tropical storms and hurricanes far less dangerous. Nonetheless the fickle storms remained both a fact of life in the islands and potentially deadly.

"What the hell, I had no problems last year," he said to himself, rolling from his bunk.

Slipping into his worn Tahitian swim trunks, he closed the door to his cabin. The morning quiet hung fleetingly over the bay as he came up through the main companionway and the sun peeked over the red sandstone bluffs of Shirley Heights. The stirrings of other early risers on their boats echoed around the bay. Walking to the rail, he looked down; the crystal clear water looked inviting. The usual small red snappers hung around just above the turtle grass eighteen feet below, and a school of silvery little Jacks drifted back and forth under the schooner's hull. Perching his feet on the teak rail, he took a deep breath before plunging into the warm water.

He made two circuits of the anchored schooner before climbing back aboard. Using the freshwater deck hose, he rinsed off before going to his cabin to change. Slipping a braided leather belt through the loops of his shorts, he made sure the lanyard of his clasp knife was clipped comfortably on his right side, and the old, blue polo shirt with the words

"*Fandango Crew*" embroidered on the front was stained but clean. Making a quick cup of coffee and a couple of pieces of toast, he ate while standing. It was going to be a busy day. Patch whined around his ankles, indicating that he was hungry so Jack opened a can of tuna fish.

"Spoiled cat," he said, placing it on the galley floor.

Jack began his maintenance routine in the engine room. Opening the small door at the aft end of the salon he entered feet first. The six cylinder 195 hp GM main engine lay gleaming on the centerline. On the port side the 12 kW generator provided electricity to charge the ample battery banks as well as for the ship's main systems. Changing the oil in the GM and the generator he replaced the oil filters and the three in-line fuel filters. Bleeding the lines, he fired up both engines for a moment to check for leaks. There were none, so he shut down and gave the alpine green engines a careful wipe down.

When he was all done he glanced at his old Rolex. It was ten o'clock. The watch had been with him since Korea. There was a diagonal scratch across the crystal where a tiny piece of shrapnel had hit it. The little red-hot bandit had zinged though the cockpit of his F4U Corsair, hitting the Rolex. The watch had survived, but his wrist had been fractured.

Washing his hands in the galley sink with some gunk, he closed the engine room door and went up on deck. Spotting his two sailors on the dock near the charter office, he jumped into the Whaler and sped in to get them. He would check the weather report while he was ashore as well.

Cobb looked fine, but Benny looked like he had just crawled out of a rum barrel, and that was probably the truth.

"Sorry about dragging you back so soon, guys, but I'll double your money for this trip," Jack told them.

They seemed happy.

"New engine, skip," Cobb said, looking at the new outboard on the stern of the Whaler.

"It was time."

"It was past time," Benny said.

"Ready to go aboard?" Cobb asked.

"Just give me five, I'll check Jen at the office. See if there's any messages."

"We wait for you here," Cobb told him.

Leaving them to tend the Whaler, Jack walked briskly towards the green door of the charter office.

Jen was already there behind the desk sorting out the morning's mail, putting the letters into the rack of named letterboxes on the wall.

"Morning," he said cheerfully, "got the latest weather report yet?"

"Yes," she said, smiling, "It's on the board already."

Going to the cork message board on the opposite wall, he read the brief synopsis.

"There are no tropical weather systems affecting the North Atlantic at this time. Weather remains normal for the month of July. Winds NE at 15-20 knots. Seas moderate 3-5 feet. Swells northerly at 6 feet, occasional brief squalls."

Every morning Jen called the met office at the airport and they dictated the report to her. She then typed it up before pinning it on the board.

"Looks fine, Jen," he said, turning to leave, "especially the 'no tropical weather systems.'"

"Have a good one then," she said, looking up from the desk, "and look after Meg for me."

"I'll do that," he replied, and leaving a busy Jen to her sorting, walked out the door.

Cobb and Benny cast off the Whaler and they ran back to the anchored schooner. Stashing their sea bags on their bunks in the fo'c'sle, they quickly coiled the dock lines and ranged the fenders along her topsides in preparation for the fuel dock. Jack and Benny managed to put some fast drying epoxy filler in the scratch on the topsides. He didn't want to go to sea with any bare metal on the hull. It would weep red rust very quickly.

"Let's get under way then," Jack said when everything was ready.

He fired up the main engine and Cobb started the anchor windlass, washing the chain with the deck hose as it came up through the hawse-pipe. Benny lay on the floor in the crew's quarters, packing it carefully as it came down into the locker. Soon the chain came up vertically and the windlass tone changed as it picked up the additional weight of the anchor.

"Off the bottom," Cobb called aft, and Jack gave the engine a good shot of ahead while swinging the wheel to port, bringing the bow around towards the fuel dock.

He maneuvered his schooner with skill and prided himself in being able to dock her without a lot of screaming and shouting. He was a professional. Bringing the *Fandango* up to the fuel dock until she was a foot and a half off, he gave her a touch of astern, bringing her to a gentle stop. Cobb and Benny got the lines ashore fast and soon the schooner was secured with bow, stern and two spring lines.

Buster, the dockmaster, came over to find out how much diesel they would take.

"Morning, skipper Jack, what you need today?" He was his customary cheerful self.

Jack made some quick mental calculations. This time of year the wind could just die out, leaving the Caribbean Sea calm as a millpond.

"Buster, we'll fill her right up, don't want to be stuck out to the west with no wind and short on fuel. Could buy me a whole heap of trouble this time of year."

"You got dat one right, skip," Buster said smiling.

He went to the dock shack and after setting the meter to zero slowly spooled off the heavy fuel hose. He liked Captain Jack; in fact most folks around the islands did. He was just a good kind of guy. And of course Buster knew that he could expect a little tip for taking care of him.

Cobb unscrewed the brass deck water intake, and Benny put the water hose in. The water tanks held a thousand gallons, but there would be no more once they left for Aves.

Jack thought momentarily about the fuel. The *Fandango* carried fifteen hundred gallons of diesel and the dipstick read three hundred left on board. It would take all of an hour to take the twelve hundred gallons needed to fill her up.

"Fill all of the five-gallon gasoline jerrycans and put aboard a couple of extra five-gallon drums of lube oil, Benny, and don't forget the outboard oil this time," he warned him.

"Yeah skip" Benny replied, smiling.

A few months ago they had found themselves in the Tobago Cays with eight passengers ready to go snorkeling, with plenty of gasoline but no outboard oil. They'd done a lot of paddling that trip.

By two thirty the fuel tanks were full, and Buster took the diesel hose ashore. Benny and Cobb got the water hose to scrub the deck where they had spilt some diesel. Jack stepped ashore to the fuel shed and paid Buster in cash, making sure he added a tip. Megan chose that moment to arrive at the dock with Sando's taxi overflowing with groceries. Jack and Benny went over to help her, and Buster carried some of the groceries aboard too.

Fifteen minutes later, the Henderson party arrived in their taxi. He got out, followed by another tall dark man and a blond woman. Jack and Cobb strode over to help them with their luggage, and Henderson introduced his friends.

"This is Garcia Perez and Laura Feldman," he said.

Jack did a double take; Laura was an extremely attractive woman. He shook hands with them both.

"Good to meet you," he said, "Cobb and I'll help you with your luggage."

Jack found his eyes drawn to the blond woman, and he got caught each time. Laura smiled right back at him. About five foot eleven with cropped, white-blond hair and piercing blue eyes, she had the kind of figure he'd thought only existed within the pages of Playboy magazine.

"Good to meet you too, captain," Laura replied smiling.

Garcia was typically Latin looking, tall with long, black curly hair and a moustache. He had dark beady little eyes that reminded Jack of a ferret. He didn't smile, but then in this business you met all kinds.

"Haven't I seen you before? Jack asked.

"No, Capitan, ees not possible, I 'ave not been 'ere long," Garcia replied with a smile.

"Funny I always remember a face," Jack said.

"Not mine I think," Garcia assured him.

"Well let's get you aboard," Jack said.

Funny, he thought to himself, the guy did look familiar. Probably saw him around English Harbour somewhere.

Garcia and Henderson carefully unloaded their photographic equipment from the van. There were two large aluminum cases the size of flat steamer trunks, weighing at least thirty pounds apiece, and a number of heavy duffel bags.

"Fragile stuff, so let's be careful with it," Henderson warned.

Jack and Cobb helped carry the cases and luggage aboard, bringing it below and stowing it in one of the spare cabins. Magically, Megan had managed to slip into her blue *Fandango* uniform polo shirt and khaki shorts and was already standing by the rail waiting to greet the new passengers.

"Hi, I'm Megan," she said, shaking hands, "I'll take you below and show you your cabins."

They acquainted themselves with the boat, and she showed them how to use the heads.

"Don't put anything down there you haven't eaten first," she told them. Like all marine boat heads, they clogged easily.

"You've got four cabins to choose from, so I'll just let you take your pick, Megan explained.

"Thanks," Laura said to her.

Cobb and Benny took the sail covers off and made the schooner ready for sea. Stowing the deck gear they checked the sheets and running rigging. The final chore was to lift the Boston Whaler. Megan helped them sling it aboard using gantlines from the masts. It sat on teak chocks on the port side amidships.

Three forty-five saw the *Fandango* motoring past Fort Berkeley into the open. Taking advantage of the lee under Shirley Heights bluffs, Jack held the schooner's bow into the wind as Cobb and Benny hoisted sail. They set the main first, then the main staysail, jumbo and finally the big Yankee jib. Shutting down the engine, Jack feathered the propeller and let her fall off on the starboard tack. Her sails filling, the *Fandango* took off like a scalded cat.

An hour later, with a freshening northerly trade wind breeze off the quarter, she sank her shoulder into the deep blue Caribbean. After clearing the land, a long low swell came up but the schooner remained steady under her press of sail and rolled only slightly. Real schooner conditions, Jack thought to himself. He knew what his ship responded to and he could tell she was at her best. Making a good ten knots without any fuss at all, she rose to the crests and took the wind full, on and the knot-log rose another two points before dropping to ten again. Jack smiled; it was going to be a good sail.

"Better rig preventers on the main and two staysails," he told Cobb.

He didn't want any of the schooner's three booms to jibe if she went off course.

The two crew rigged tackles from the ends of the booms to points farther forward. Cobb left the jib full and free and Jack set the schooner's course just far enough to the north to keep it from being blanketed by the main. Towards five the sun began falling towards the western horizon, and the *Fandango* sailed swiftly on.

It was Jack's favorite time of day. Sitting next to the teak wheel box in the cockpit, he handed a spoke or two from time to time, keeping his schooner on her course. With his passengers below in their cabins he savored the quiet time. Megan busied herself in the galley while the two deck hands sat resting in the lee of the deck cabin. He didn't have to speak to anyone.

They were making just to the south of due west and the *Fandango* was tracking well, her long keel keeping her from wandering too much. He planned to pass between the mountainous island of Montserrat and the rock of Redonda, and as the sun touched the horizon he could see the two landmasses rising abruptly from the sea in the distance.

He thought about the atoll. He didn't relish the idea of diving out at Aves, but he was experienced and what the hell, chances of getting hit by a shark twice in your life had to be slim. From a strictly practical stand-point his passengers were another matter.

Jack was a good, careful diver and had been at it since he was a kid.

He was twelve when he first tended the diesel air pump on his father's sponge boat in the Florida Keys. He handled the winch as his father picked sponges off the bottom, seventy-five feet below. When he was fourteen, his father sent him on his first dive and he loved it. Although the old hel-meted suit was bulky and restrictive, he found the sensation of working underwater soothing. He was a natural.

There were a lot of big fish around the Keys in those days, and Jack took to spear fishing as a sport. The surrounding reefs and channels were home to large jewfish and groupers, while the open areas held snapper and other species. He dove for stone crab and lobster and caught sea trout with the old cast net. These were slim times in the Florida Keys and Jack's family benefited from the sea's bounty. He became an excellent spear fish-erman and made a few extra bucks selling grouper fillets in Key West.

A dollop of spray came over the rail, hitting Jack on the face. He made a slight change of course as his schooner ran down the deep channel between Montserrat and Redonda just before nightfall. The low hills of Antigua disappeared over the horizon astern, and as the sun went down Henderson and Garcia came up on deck and sat in the cockpit.

"We're making great time. How are you feeling?" Jack asked.

He needn't have asked; they were both suffering the effects of mal de mer.

"Lousy," Henderson replied.

Garcia made no response, but the greenish tinge on his cheeks left no question as to how he felt.

Laura had been lying on a towel behind the main hatch, but as it got darker she joined the others. The schooner's motion didn't seem to bother her, and she felt fine.

The cockpit was comfortable. Cushions on each side ran fore and aft from the helm position forward to the main hatchway. The coamings to port and starboard served as seat backs and the teak folding table sat cen-terline. It was the focal area where crew sat to steer the yacht and while in port Jack usually rigged an awning for rain or sun. Cobb lifted the flaps on the teak table running forward from the compass binnacle, and Benny laid the knives and forks. More often than not passengers chose to eat there instead of the salon below.

The *Fandango* rolled gently, but the plates stayed easily inside their wooden guards. Megan offered drinks and although Henderson and

Garcia declined, Laura accepted a Carib beer. Jack refused his regular rum and coke and went about rigging a light over the table.

Megan served a delicious veal casserole. Jack finished quickly so that he could steer and let Cobb eat. Laura seated herself next to him, and Megan didn't miss her obvious flirtations. She fawned over him, touching him on the arm whenever she had the opportunity and leaned closer whenever he spoke. Some women are so obvious, thought Megan

"You must tell us about your adventures, Jack," Laura said to him.

"I've had some funny experiences over the years," Jack offered, and he began to tell the story of the shark attack in the Tortugas. At the end Laura whispered to Jack that she'd just love to see the scar sometime.

After dinner Megan brought up coffee, while Jack was regaling Laura and the other two with his story of the Corsair crash on the aircraft carrier in Korea. Henderson and Garcia seemed bored; they hadn't eaten much but Laura was lapping up every minute of it.

"Oh wow, you crashed the plane on the carrier deck?" she exclaimed.

"Had to, no landing gear."

He was swallowing the attention like a dumb codfish, Megan thought, and if Laura flutters her eyelashes at him once more, they're going to fly off into her coffee. I bet they're false anyway. Jack noticed Megan glaring at him, and feeling slightly guilty, ended his story. By the time coffee was over, it was getting on towards eight and the passengers went below.

As it always did in the tropics the wind dropped a little for the night, but there was still enough to keep the *Fandango* going at six or seven knots. The night was clear and soon the sky filled with an impossibly brilliant myriad of stars. It was magical. A glowing phosphorescent wake trailed astern, and the red and green running lights probed eerily into the emptiness of the night. The only sounds were those of the schooner making her way through the sea and the music coming from an old guitar. The bow wave made a merry gurgling sound and there was the occasional hiss of spray as it came over the rail. Benny sat in the lee of the companionway for while playing and singing the only song he knew.

"Brown skin gal go home an' mind baby..."

"Brown skin gal go home an' mind baby..."

"I'm going away, on a sailing ship, 'an if I doan come back..."

"Go home an' mind baby."

The guitar was old and slightly out of tune, but Benny sang with a lot of passion and he sounded good.

The waves rose and fell around the schooner as she sailed swiftly on, and the tiny bulb of the compass light shone weakly upwards casting a dim reddish glow on the helmsman's face. The night was clear. There weren't any squalls and she was far from land. Jack divided his crew into two watches. Cobb and Benny would take the first until midnight, and he would take the second with Megan. He trusted Cobb with the schooner and both he and Benny were good wheelsmen. Jack had traditional rules about standing watch, and he insisted that the two crewmen stick to them religiously. There was a complete inspection of the vessel every hour, including a look in the bilges and engine room. The rig and sails were also inspected and there was a standing rule that if a squall or another ship approached, they would call Jack right away.

"Keep her heading southwest," he told Cobb and before turning to go below, he made a final check of the rig and deck. Everything seemed fine.

He passed Megan in the main salon. She'd just finished putting away the last of the dinner dishes and had her feet up on the lee side settee. Jack joined her.

"You did a great job today," he told her.

"I'm surprised you noticed," she replied tiredly.

"Of course I did, why would you say that?" Jack queried innocently.

Megan ignored the question.

"I never knew you used to be a pilot."

"That was a long time ago."

"Air Force?"

"Navy."

"You're not that old, Jack."

"Got out of Annapolis and went straight into flight training in Pensacola. Almost got kicked out for punching one of the instructors."

"Must have deserved it."

"He did. Made some cracks about my poor white trash ancestry. Said I had no right to be there."

"And you clobbered him as Billy Ramsey likes to say."

"Broke his jaw, and went straight to the brig for the night, but I managed to graduate and become a naval aviator."

"You've led a dangerous life."

"Very, married an Admiral daughter, Marjorie was her name."

"What happened?" she asked intrigued.

"Stalled after less than a year, we didn't want the same things out of life. She wanted domestic bliss, a home with five kids and security. I still hadn't grown up."

"And?"

"And we split. Father-in-law got real hot collared. Told me I'd get a promotion when pigs flew jets or when hell froze over, whichever came along first."

"Ever thought of getting hitched again?" Megan asked him.

"I'm getting kind of rough around the edges. Think I'll just keep on sailing. It's a good life."

Megan looked at him quizzically, but he turned away.

"You try and get some sleep, I'll be calling you at midnight," he said to her, and he got up and went to his cabin.

With the vessel sailing safely in clear water and Cobb at the helm, he turned in for a couple of hours sleep.

Back in English Harbour the nautical chiming clock in the charter office rang in eight bells as Billy Ramsey and Jen finished an invoice for Digeree Air Charters. Billy couldn't type or write very well, so Jen did all his invoicing for him. Suddenly Major Balfont came through the door.

"Evening, Major, should have let us know you were coming we'd have got some ice for your gin," Billy chided, but the police chief appeared serious.

"Sorry, old chap, not a social visit I'm afraid," Balfont replied gravely.

"Oh what's up?"

"You know that Harold Bartram fellow?" he asked twirling the ends of his moustache.

"The jeweler, in St. Johns, why?" Jen asked.

"Raphael the bartender at Admirals Inn says you were having drinks together a couple of nights ago," Balfont said, addressing Billy.

"I don't organize seating at the Admirals Inn, sport, people come and go as they please," the big Aussie replied.

"Sorry, old chap, but I'm going to have to ask you a few questions," Balfont told him.

"What the hell for?" Billy asked indignantly.

"Bartram was murdered last night."

"What happened?" Jen asked, her face turning white.

"Rather nasty really, poor chap had his throat slit ear to ear."

Jen turned white, putting her hand to her mouth.

"Steady on there," Billy said, putting his big arm around her.

"Where's your friend, Jack? I'd like to have a chat with him as well," Balfont said.

"He's long gone mate, won't be back for weeks."

"Ah, pity."

"Hold on sport, you don't think that we did it?"

"Course not, my good man, but I want to know exactly what time you all last saw him. We fully intend to find the perpetrator."

Balfont was persistent if anything. As for Jack leaving on a cruise, well the Major wasn't worried, he knew Jack had a lot at stake in English Harbour and would be back at the end of the trip.

"And do you know where our Jack is headed then?" Balfont asked.

"Well yes, to Aves atoll with some American treasure hunter," Jen replied.

"Indeed?" Balfont said, raising his eyebrows, "Very interesting indeed."

CHAPTER SIX

Twenty Fathoms Deep

Jack and Megan had been on watch since midnight. Sitting together in the cockpit they talked quietly, each steering for an hour at a time. She could only see his shadowy outline in the dark, but as she listened to his voice she found herself warming to it. It was their first real quiet time together. During the previous trip they had sailed mostly during the day, and each had been busy with their chores.

"How did you end up in the Navy?" Megan asked.

"I was eighteen. My father rescued some yachtsmen in trouble off Key West. One of them was an Admiral, out on his fishing boat. The gas engines blew up. They jumped for it and Dad was nearby in the sponge boat. Got a free pass into the Academy."

"I guess you flew those fancy American jets," she told him.

"Mostly prop Corsairs off of carriers in the Korean War, then I was a civilian test pilot for a few years."

"Must have been thrilling," Megan said.

"When we weren't getting killed. We were considered pretty much expendable."

"Sounds like a tough business," Megan said.

"Some designs were just never meant to fly."

She found that she was interested in the things that he had done.

"I quit while I could still walk, away but I knew, a lot of guys who didn't. There were a lot of beat up pilots around then, and good work was hard to find. The big airlines wouldn't train any of us older guys to fly the new jets; they wanted the young kids that would spend the next twenty years working for them."

"I heard you say something about the CIA last night," Megan said, referring to the dinner table conversation.

"I flew for Air America for while. We dropped leaflets and propaganda in the Far East. One mission we pushed sized fifty-waist men's cotton underwear out the hatch. They were supposed to convince enemy soldiers that U.S. troops were giants. It didn't work; they just though that U.S. soldiers were fat and lazy."

"It's hard to believe what people think sometimes," Megan said, amazed.

"You're right there. The pay was good, and I stayed with Air America for a couple of years, but the Piper aircraft we used were susceptible to small arms fire, so I got out of that too. Mine got hit twenty-seven times. I figured that I survived the Korean War and testing, there was no way I was going to let myself get shot down by an AK 47."

"And here you are," she said, smiling.

"Here I am, and alive too," he grinned.

"How about you? What's your life story?" Jack asked her.

"Men are allowed to tell. Ladies never do," she replied coyly.

"You're down here in the islands, makes you different."

He let her nap on the cushions under a blanket while he steered and although a little tired, he was used to the odd hours. He'd catch some sleep after they arrived. She was delighted when he brought her a coffee and roll after one of his hourly checks.

"You're just full of surprises, Jack Carlton," she told him, and he felt good about the way she said it.

Dawn broke in a blaze of red glory. Even though he wasn't superstitious, Jack remembered the old sailor's adage.

"Red sky in the morning sailors take warning, red sky at night sailors' delight," he said.

"What?" Megan asked.

"Nothing. Just some old sailor's drivel."

The wind, which had dropped a little through the hours of darkness, picked up a few knots again, and the *Fandango* took notice, forging westwards with a renewed sense of purpose. Reaching down he switched off the navigation lights on the console. He'd have to fire up the diesel generator to charge the batteries later on.

The blue Caribbean sparkled in the morning sun, and flying fish skittered away from the schooner in schools of twenty or more, like little silver missiles. They often flew for a hundred yards or so before disappearing into the face of a wave. Occasionally, there would be a larger splash as a dorado or some other predator fish broke surface after the flying fish. Overhead, clouds sailed briskly across the azure sky. It was sure going to be a spectacular day, Jack thought to himself. These were the times he loved best. For him it was a dream come true. He took great pride in sailing his schooner well and encouraged his crew to do the same. The *Fandango* was known as a happy ship in the charter fleet.

As the sun rose and the wind picked up slightly. Jack couldn't help but notice Megan's long, tanned legs as she sat next to him in the cockpit. She caught him looking and smiled to herself. Her long red hair blew across her face, and she whipped an elastic band out of her shorts and put her hair into a ponytail.

"Better," she said while looking out at sea, "How about some scrambled eggs?"

"Now, that's the best offer I've had today."

"Well, it's still early Jack. I'm sure it won't be the only one you'll get," she said before moving away. She returned fifteen minutes later with coffee, a plate of eggs and toast.

"You know, Meg, she's not my type," he told her.

"Sure could have fooled me. I'll take over while you eat," she said, handing him the plate.

"Thanks."

She was a good helmsman, and Jack gave her the wheel as he ate. The eggs were warm and tasty.

"Any sign of our guests yet?" he asked.

"Nope, they're all still asleep. Want me to wake them?"

"No, let them sleep. I'm kind of enjoying the peace and the company," he replied. She noticed the whimsical smile on his face.

After eating he made a round of the decks, checking the set of the sails and making sure that everything was still lashed down properly. At eight o'clock Benny came up and hoisted the Stars and Stripes on the flagpole on the stern, and it billowed out to leeward. The wind was picking up slightly and as it did the waves became slightly more boisterous.

"I'll go below and check the weather report," Jack said, leaving Megan on the helm. She was doing a great job.

In the chart room he turned on the am to the weather channel in Barbados and took note of the important part.

"There are no tropical weather systems affecting our area at this time."

"Excellent," he said to himself.

Turning to the big communications set on the bulkhead he tuned in on 2638 English Harbour. There was a lot of interference and static, a fairly common occurrence at certain times of the day.

"English Harbour radio, English Harbour radio, schooner Fandango, do you read, over."

The static crackled and buzzed but there was no reply.

"English Harbour, this is Fandango, over."

"Fandango this...is...glish arbour...we...over."

He barely recognized Jen's voice through the static.

"Go ahead, English Harbor, over."

"Fandan...essages...Balfont...over."

"English Harbour, you are unreadable over."

"Fandango, Fand...English Harb...over."

It was no use. The ether was full of static, and it probably wasn't important anyway. He'd try again later.

After breakfast Cobb sat near the stern, rigging one of the heavy deep-sea trolling lines with the new yellow patent feather bait he'd bought the day before at the marina store. He carefully measured out twelve feet of heavy stainless steel leader wire, twisting it around the big hook before threading it into the lead head of the feather lure. At the top end he twisted on a big swivel and knotted it to the three hundred-pound test fishing line. Setting the line out over the stern he gave it about two hundred feet before making it fast to the backstay.

"What you going to catch today, Cobb?" Jack asked him.

"Anyting dat comes along," Cobb replied with a grin. "You know me, skip; I ain' fussy when it comes to fish."

Jack really liked Cobb; he was a good man, and the kind you could depend on when the cards were down.

Around nine o'clock, Henderson came up on deck looking a little green around the gills. He sat down in the lee side of the cockpit and tried to make himself comfortable. Laura and Garcia made an appearance a moment later and sat near him. Garcia looked a bit queasy but not as visibly ill as Henderson, while Laura on the other hand seemed to be more at home on the boat.

"How long till we get to Aves anyway?" Henderson asked.

Jack was slightly irritated by his tone. Aves was a special place to him. Few human beings had ever seen the atoll and he felt that he was sharing something with his passengers that they should be grateful for. Aves was a primeval kind of place, remote and unspoiled by man. It was dangerous but clean and without humans who seemed to ruin everything they touched. Putting aside his annoyance he answered Henderson.

"I've planned it so we should make landfall at about three this afternoon," he explained. "That way the sun will be falling to the west, and we should be able to spot the surf on the reef. It's a tiny little spit of land and hard as hell to see. A lot of vessels have run up on the reef trying to find the place."

There was a momentary flicker of interest in Henderson's eyes and then as the "mal de mer" returned his eyelids drooped again.

"Is it going to stay rough like this for the whole trip?" he asked his voice shaky.

It wasn't rough at all. The conditions were just perfect for the *Fandango,* and she was rolling along as happy as could be. It was clear that Henderson and Garcia had done little or no sailing. He hoped they were better at diving. Aves was no place to open a Jack Carlton deep-sea scuba school. He told a little white lie in answer to Ed's question.

"It should smooth out a little after a while."

It wouldn't though; the *Fandango* would sail on just as she was, and Jack would be happy for it.

As the morning wore on the wind picked up until it was blowing a good thirty knots. It was a classic Trade wind day, with all the trimmings. Although some heavy looking cloud had appeared on the distant horizon, the bright sun shone down out of a powder blue sky and puffy clouds scudded along over the schooner. The surface of the Caribbean Sea took on more aggressive mien and the waves broke in sparkling white caps. As the schooner surged ahead her bow wave rolled away to leeward while astern she left a straight and true wake. A huge flock of seabirds appeared about a mile off the port bow, and Cobb took notice.

"Got some action ahead, skip," he said.

"Want me to alter course?" Jack asked.

"No, we goin' pass close anyway," the burly mate replied.

Below the yacht a school of fifty big wahoo traveled north. Oceanic members of the mackerel family, each fish weighed just over one hundred pounds and measured six or seven feet. Swimming at more than twenty knots their long streamlined shapes were well suited to the predatory life. Pointed heads held rows of razor sharp teeth in the top and bottom jaws, and they were notorious for striking with a speed unrivalled in the fishy world. Long powerful flank muscles ended in a highly effective scimitar shaped tail that propelled them almost effortlessly through the sea. The iridescent blue of their backs contrasted silvery sides with vertical stripes.

The Caribbean was a vast expanse of water, and these predators had to move fast in their endless search for food. Inevitably, they would locate a school of smaller fish such as jacks, herring or mackerel of a pound or two in size, and they would stay with the school for days, feeding voraciously.

Often there were symbiotic feeding frenzies. The wahoo weren't the only predators that followed the tons of small fish. There were tuna, dorado, shark and billfish of two or three different types. As the wahoo carried out their lateral attacks the tuna would lurk below, preventing the smaller fish from diving to escape the carnage.

The dark hull of the schooner rolled along above and ahead of the school. The leader, a huge bull, spotted Cobb's tiny yellow feather bait speeding a few inches below the surface pounds and in its tiny brain there was a signal. It was the signal that had kept the species alive over the aeons of their evolution. It meant attack and feed.

Streaking towards the surface, the fish switched to attack mode. The blue and silver torpedo turned almost impossibly brilliant, and the iridescent azure stripes on its side became more highly defined. Hitting the bait with a fury designed to kill instantly, the fish broke surface and came six feet out of the water before diving.

"Fish on de line, fish on de line," Cobb shouted.

From the cockpit Jack looked two hundred feet astern where the long streamlined fish whipped up a froth of white. The shouting alerted the *Fandango's* passengers.

"What's going on? Are we in trouble?" Henderson asked.

"No, it's nothing, Cobb's just got a big fish," Jack reassured him.

Henderson watched the proceedings from the cockpit, along with Laura and Garcia. Jack took the helm from Megan while Cobb stood on the stern slowly pulling in the big fish hand over hand.

"You want the gloves?" Jack asked offering a canvas pair from the beneath cockpit seat.

"Gloves is for de tourists, skip, not fishermen," he replied disdainfully.

Cobb wrapped the three hundred-pound test mono around his big callused bare hands, working the fish. Running forward to fetch the long gaff, Benny stood near the windward rail, ready to sink the big hook into the fish when Cobb got it alongside.

"Can you see what it is?" Jack shouted.

"No, she gone deep. Can't see nutting yet, but she's heavy," Cobb replied breathlessly.

Tiring, the big wahoo stopped thrashing and swam from one side of the schooner's wake to the other, shaking its head in an effort to dislodge the sharp hook embedded in its jawbone.

The big fish slowly tired, and Jack brought the schooner around to starboard luffing the mainsail and slowing her down. Suddenly the long silvery shape emerged from the depths.

"Yeah skip, is a big, big wahoo. Slow dung de vessel a little bit moe for me please," he instructed Jack.

Jack didn't want to bring the schooner too far in to the wind because the sails would start to crash around and flap, but he came a few more degrees, slowing her down a bit more. Cobb finally brought the big fish to the surface alongside the schooner, and Benny sunk the gaff into its silvery side.

It was a magnificent fish, resplendent in its fighting colors and as they lifted it aboard Jack was surprised at the size.

"Got to be one hundred twenty-five pound, skip," shouted Cobb, laughing.

As soon as the wahoo hit the deck, Cobb pulled the big main sheet winch handle from its holder and delivered the coup de grace, a few well-aimed blows to the head. Megan winced.

"Does he have to do that?" she asked, grimacing.

"Yes, he does," Jack said to her. "You wouldn't want it flipping around and nipping somebody, would you?"

"Actually, I could think of someone," Megan said, glancing sideways at him.

After a few seconds the big fish lay still. Cobb ran his Dexter fish knife over the stone a few times and quickly filleted out half of the fish and steaked the other half. He and Benny carried the pieces down to the galley in a pair of buckets, where Megan divided them up into plastic bags and packed them away in the freezer. She kept out a good portion for lunch.

At eleven, Megan went below, and just after noon she served some fresh baked wahoo in the cockpit. Laura helped herself to a piece, but Ed and Garcia weren't in the least bit interested and tried to rest in the lee side of the cockpit, covering themselves with blankets to stay out of the wind.

Cobb and Benny had no problems with food; they just seemed to get hungrier at sea. The two men sat in the lee of the companionway hatch after they'd eaten, content to have a snooze during their off-watch.

At two o'clock Jack came up on deck with his old Plath sextant and took a series of sights. Megan took the times from him on the stopwatch, and afterwards he calculated their position.

Garcia noticed and turned to Benny.

"We are lost?"

"No, we ain' lost."

"Then whey he must use this instrument?"

"He does use dat to make sure we don't get lost," Benny pointed out, sounding a little exasperated.

"I think we are lost," Garcia said.

"No way. Captain Jack de bes skipper in de fleet. One time he done sail dis schooner trough a storm all by he self to rescue a frien' and get back safe an' soun'."

Jack plotted the LOP, and they were right on course. A few minutes later he started the generator to charge up the ship's batteries.

Henderson gagged as the exhaust fumes blew back over the stern into his face. He leaned out over the rail again and again.

"Can't you do something about that?" he asked weakly.

"I can change course, but that'll just put us back time-wise," Jack replied.

"Don't bother," Henderson replied quickly.

He wanted to get to Aves as soon as possible. He continued sitting in the cockpit with a towel over his face.

The afternoon wore on and the weather held. The schooner sailed on under big Yankee jib, main and main staysail. Everything seemed just peachy, Jack thought to himself, but there was a tiny nagging in the back of his mind. Perhaps it was the reality that for him, whenever everything seemed to be just fine, things usually started to go wrong.

Pushing those thoughts from his mind he focused on the business at hand. Still unseen over the horizon, Aves atoll crept ever closer. Three o'clock rolled by and Jack began to feel anxious. The *Fandango* had run her distance from Antigua to Aves and as the minutes rolled by so the extra miles added up. They needed to see the atoll soon, he thought to himself; it was so flat and low that a ship could run ashore on the reefs before seeing the land. Many had.

He decided that if they hadn't spotted land in another half-hour, they would tack and start running a ten mile grid to the north. Aves was there, Jack knew that. It was just a pain in the butt to find in all of this empty water. Old Neddy King had shared with him an old West Indian secret about the approaches to Aves, and as Jack scanned the western horizon the old sea captain's words came to mind.

"If you ever find yourself close to Aves but can't see it, just go to de bow and listen. Aves is an island of birds, man, and you'll hear de birds before you sight de land."

Cobb and Benny were stealing a nap in the lee of the coach roof, so he asked Megan to steer for while.

"Take the helm for a bit?" he asked her, getting up.

"Course?"

"Due west," he replied, smiling.

Leaving her on the helm he walked forward to the bow and stood facing west. At first he heard nothing but the sounds of the sea and wind in the sails. He was about to return to the cockpit when he thought he heard them. Cocking his head to the side he made sure. There was no mistaking the faint cries of sea birds that made their homes on Aves. Suddenly a group of perhaps forty brown Boobies passed them headed west. Returning from their feeding grounds they were undoubtedly headed for Aves, and he took careful note of their course. He returned to the cockpit and turned to Megan.

"You better call the guys, Megan," Jack told her, "We're coming up on Aves now."

Jumping up she put her hand up to forehead, scanning the horizon.

"Where? I don't see anything," she said, a little perplexed.

The horizon was clear all around and there was no indication that there was any land near the fast moving schooner.

"Straight ahead see it?" he teased.

"No, there's nothing there," she replied, squinting.

"Trust me, Meg," Jack said, smiling, "it's just over there. Look, can't you see it?" He added pointing across the empty sea.

There was of course nothing there to see yet; the low-lying atoll was still below the horizon, but Jack was intent on having a little fun with Megan. She looked at him doubtfully but went to wake the two men.

At ten to four they sighted Aves ahead on the starboard bow about two miles distant. They couldn't actually see the land itself, just the white surf breaking on the surrounding reef.

"How did you know it was so close?" Megan asked. "It just kind of appeared suddenly, didn't it?" She was genuinely impressed.

"Just put it down to intuition, Meg," Jack said chuckling.

"Only we females are blessed with that, Jack. I'd say you were just lucky," she replied, teasing him.

Cobb was coiling the main sheet a few feet away.

"You don't know de skipper, he could smell land twenty miles off you know," he told her, laughing.

They came to within a mile of the atoll before they saw it, a thin white line on the horizon. Jack pulled the wheel to starboard rounding up into the wind as the crew took sail off the vessel. He fired up the GM while Cobb and Benny dropped the jib and then the jumbo, main staysail and finally the main. They made up the sails and tidied up around the deck as Jack guided the schooner towards the paltry lee of the atoll where he hoped to find a little shelter from the wind and swell.

Aves was a strange, remote place, and Jack was once again struck by the feeling of absolute isolation. Approaching slowly, the tiny spit of sand and coral grew in size on the starboard bow until they could see the dark of the surrounding reef and the green scrub grass on the atoll itself.

"You can anchor here?" asked Megan.

"Small kind of coral lagoon on the leeward side, it faces the southwest," Jack explained. "It's the only place where there's any lee."

Closing the atoll the sea color suddenly changed.

"On soundings, skip, can se de bottom," Cobb shouted.

The sea floor suddenly came into view. Sandy patches contrasted small clumps of coral, and sea fans waved gently in the amazingly clear water seventy feet below. Peering over the side Megan spotted a big, blue parrot fish swimming slowly along.

"Stand by with the lead Benny," Jack called forward.

The *Fandango*'s depth sounder had given up the ghost a year ago, and anyway Jack preferred this more traditional method of determining the depth.

The sandy beach at the head of the small bay came into view, and Jack turned the schooner into the wind. He maneuvered carefully. The vessel needed to be in the center of the lagoon to afford the best of the limited shelter from the sea.

The bottom turned completely sandy, and Cobb went forward to get the anchor ready. Benny swung the lead line, calling out the soundings in fathoms.

"By de deep six."

"By de deep six."

"By de mark five."

"And a half four."

"By de mark three."

Eighteen feet. Jack threw the engine into reverse. They were close enough.

"Let go!" he shouted forward.

Cobb released the brake holding the Danforth, and the chain rattled out. Going to the bow Jack peered over the rail. The anchor was clearly visible sitting on the sandy bottom. Returning to the cockpit, he backed the schooner a bit more as the mate paid out chain.

"Lock her up at about one twenty-five, Cobb," he called forward and when the mate had slacked out the required amount, he tightened the winch brake.

In the last of the day's light the schooner settled and slowly swung to her anchor facing the northeasterly breeze.

Jack shut down the engine. They had arrived at Aves, and a thousand sea birds circled overhead screeching their displeasure at this invasion of their timeless refuge.

CHAPTER SEVEN

The Lagoon

Jack woke before dawn to sounds of the *Fandango* tugging on her anchor chain as she rolled gently. He lay in his bunk for a little while listening. She would be safe as long as the good weather held.

A hundred yards east of the schooner Aves formed a stage for the rising sun. The half-mile long sandy cay lay in the shape of a comma northwest to southeast with a maximum elevation of less than twenty feet. The narrow sand and coral beach stretched away towards the round boulders to the north.

The atoll was mostly made up of tons of sand although sparse bits of vegetation and dry scrub clung precariously to life between clumps of sun-bleached coral and shell. The detritus of a thousand years of relentless pounding by the Caribbean Sea, it was a brilliant white hue. The coral colonies grew and thrived only to be broken by the storm waves that ravaged the reef annually. It was life's eternal cycle, destruction and rebirth.

Marginally shielded from the wind and the sea by the coral reef the open lagoon was relatively calm, and with only a minimal surge on the shore it wouldn't be a problem to land the Whaler.

Jack was satisfied. The strong wind they'd enjoyed on the passage from Antigua was lighter and only a gentle breeze blew across the lagoon.

On the northeast tip of the atoll the lone outcroppings of rock stood, stained white with bird droppings. They were the only permanent part of the coral fortress. Having withstood the ravages of time, these guardians remained as silent sentinels protecting whatever secrets Aves held.

Over the centuries the sea had rounded the protruding tops of the hard stone and they appeared as a group of giant, uneven boulders and odd shaped slabs sitting half buried in the sand. At the base of one large rock face there was a dark triangular cleft three feet high by two feet wide, the entrance to an unusual grotto.

Jack had discovered it quite by accident the previous year and explored it briefly. He'd been poking around the rock formations after finding the coins and seeing the passageway, decided to see where it led. Crawling into the entrance on his hands and knees on the white sand, he had shuffled around cracked and weathered rock for more than eighty feet, before entering a forty-foot long chamber. Sunlight filtered in through a crack in the rock twenty feet over his head. Two huge slabs of rock rose from the sandy floor on each side of the chamber to meet unevenly at the top. Where bird droppings had never touched the stone, it was a light steely gray in color.

The ten-foot wide sandy floor of the chamber led into the sea at the far end, forming an underwater grotto. It was breathtaking. He'd heard of the famous blue grotto in Capri but had never been to see it. He could only imagine that this is what it must be like.

The grotto of Aves opened to the sea. The combination of unique geographic formation and sunlight made for an unusual and truly stunning natural phenomenon.

Brilliant rays of tropical sunlight shining into the shallows inside the reef penetrated the grotto, reflecting off the white sandy bottom upward onto the stone walls. Jack had stayed for some minutes, mesmerized as the reflected sunlight played in light blue waves on the stone walls.

Cobb's distant voice had shaken him out of his trance, calling him to help with the loading of the turtles, and he'd left the chamber. He'd never told anyone about his discovery, choosing instead to keep it his own secret.

The bulwark of coral reef circled the sandy shore opening into the sandy-bottomed lagoon. Jack had anchored the *Fandango* as far in as he had dared, leaving enough swinging room so if the wind died out she wouldn't go aground.

Jack rolled out of bed, pulled on his swim shorts and came on deck. When he looked over the side the shallow water was so clear the yacht seemed as though she was suspended in air. The turquoise water looked inviting, but below the serene surface lurked dangers not the least of which were the big sharks he knew were around. It was generally accepted that swimmers were far more susceptible to attack than scuba divers and he decided to forgo his customary dip.

As the sun peaked over the atoll the birds came alive. True to its name, Aves was permanent home to a half dozen species of sea bird and temporary home to a dozen more and before long there were hundreds of birds in the air above the schooner. Boobies wheeled and screeched overhead and above them dozens of frigates and albatrosses rode the wind on their broad wings. Seagulls and terns hovered low over the lagoon swooping periodically to snatch sardines from the surface.

The birds seemed to take particular pleasure in bombing the *Fandango*'s teak decks which were already liberally splattered with droppings. Cobb and Benny would have to keep that situation under control. He would have them wash down twice a day with the saltwater hose.

Before long the delicious smells of bacon and sausage wafted through the hatch, and all of a sudden Jack realized how hungry he was. Following his nose, he wandered into the galley. Stirring some eggs, Megan stood in front of the stove in her Madras colored West Indian apron. Patch, transparent as ever, clung to her legs begging for a handout. Jack reckoned he would give it a try too.

"Any chance the chef will give the captain a special breakfast, just because he's the captain?" he asked playfully.

"All depends on how good the captain is to the chef," she replied, looking at him out of the corner of her eye. Suddenly her face changed to a more serious expression.

"You going to dive today, Jack?" she asked him.

"Yes, I'm going to take Henderson out to the reef later."

"I want to tell you something," she said, looking over her shoulder to make sure no one was listening.

"What's on your mind?"

"I don't know exactly, but I've got a weird feeling, that's all," she said, almost not wanting to continue.

"About what?" Jack asked, daring to pinch a piece of bacon.

She didn't seem to notice and for once didn't scold him.

"Our charter party, there's something not quite right about them."

Jack shook his head.

"They're just eccentric, wealthy people looking for something out of the ordinary, that's all," he told her, grinning.

"Just be careful," she persisted.

"OK, I'm not sure what you want me to be careful about, but I will be. Now let's talk about more important business, like I'm starved. What are you going to do about that then, Meggie," he said lightly, trying to assuage her concerns.

"First, don't call me Meggie, and second, you can help yourself. Here," she said, giving him a plate.

Men can be so annoying, she thought furiously. She didn't know what it was about the Henderson party that bothered her, but her sixth sense was warning her something was amiss.

Jack took his breakfast up to the cockpit and began to eat. Cobb and Benny were gassing up the Whaler alongside. Ed Henderson came up a few minutes later looking pretty groggy, but after a coffee he began strutting around the deck impatiently.

"I'd like to make our first dive as soon as possible," he declared.

Although the sky was clear and bright, beneath the surface of the Caribbean it would still be gloomy. The sun needed to be higher in the sky for its rays to penetrate the sea. Jack wanted to wait until ten or so, but he was getting paid big bucks for this jaunt, so he'd dive.

"Let's have some breakfast and when the sun gets a little higher in the sky and, say, at nine o'clock we'll go dive, what do you say?"

"Alright," Ed replied reluctantly, "but can we take a look at the chart for a minute?"

"Sure," Jack replied, putting his empty plate on the table, "let's go below."

Following him down the companionway to the *Fandango's* tiny navigation station, Henderson looked over the chart. It was an Admiralty issue and while these were often the most comprehensive in the world, this one showed little of Aves. Perhaps it was because there just wasn't much to it. The chart depicted the atoll and the small, sandy-bottomed lagoon on the southwest side where the schooner was anchored. The surrounding reef showed at less then one fathom, but the outside soundings quickly dropped off to more than a thousand. One moment there was the thirty-foot depth just outside the reef and then it was a couple thousand feet.

"See here?" Jack said, running a line around Aves' southwest side. "We can dive anywhere in the lee here as long as the weather stays smooth."

"How about the edges of the reef around about here and here?" Henderson asked, indicating the southwestern arms of the coral lagoon to the north and south of the anchored schooner.

"I dove right there last year," Jack replied, pinpointing a location on the edge of the northern arm. "There's a good wall and it's probably as good a place as any to start."

"What about further to the northwest?"

"No way, couldn't even get the Whaler out there on the windward side. We'd swamp in a minute," Jack told him, "This side of the atoll is the only calm water we're going to get."

Henderson nodded his agreement, seemingly deep in thought.

They returned to the deck, joining Laura and Garcia. They had come up and were eating at the cockpit table. Jack went to the starboard side where Cobb and Benny were getting the Whaler ready.

"Got all four sets of gear loaded?" he asked.

"Yeah skip, and I put your lil friend in de boat too," Cobb grinned, pointing to Jack's big Arbalette speargun." "Just in case you see someting nice," he said with a big smile, showing off his incredibly white teeth.

A heavy-duty four-rubber job with a reel of two hundred-pound test tether line fired a six-foot stainless steel spear. It was big enough to nail any grouper that he might come across. Being a fisherman, Cobb was impressed at how skillfully his skipper handled the gun. Whenever Jack went down with that big Arbalette in his hand, there was a good chance that he would surface with a fish on the spear. After hearing the shark story and seeing Jack's butt, he was religiously respectful of his skipper's peculiar injury.

"Don't forget the long anchor line and float," Jack reminded them.

There was a scuba rig each for Henderson and Garcia, one for the skipper and one spare.

At about nine fifteen Henderson appeared in his flowered swim trunks.

"About ready, skipper?" he asked impatiently.

"All that's left is to get you aboard, let's go," Jack said and the three men climbed down the boarding ladder into the Whaler.

Garcia seemed less than enthusiastic and Laura stayed on the anchored schooner with Megan and Benny.

The new Johnson outboard fired on the first pull and a happy Cobb steered away. Leaning towards him, Jack pointed towards the north.

"You remember where we were last year?"

"Yeah skip."

"Let's try the same spot first."

"Right."

Cobb drove slowly towards an area to the port and ahead of the *Fandango*. One good thing about diving around here, Jack thought to himself, you never have to go too far from the schooner. They moved three hundred yards around the northern edge of the horseshoe reef surrounding the lagoon to a spot that looked vaguely familiar.

"It was right about here that I went down last year," Jack stated.

Cobb put the outboard in neutral, stopping the Whaler over a clear patch on the outside of the reef. To the left the water was deep blue while on their right the tops of the reef could be seen just below the surface. The bottom lay thirty feet below. Pitching the little Danforth anchor over the bow, Jack watched it sink to the bottom. Slacking out scope, he yanked it a number of times until it caught. He made it fast to the small bow bit and then they began to put on their dive gear. Cobb always stayed in the boat when they were diving in out of the way places. He and Jack had an understanding that if he ever came up shouting, he was to cut the anchor line and come and get him, but fast.

Jack and Henderson checked their regulators and wiggled into the backpack harnesses before cinching the heavy buckles secure. As Jack reached for his weight belt he glanced at Garcia. He sat unmoving, looking at the Arbalette spear gun in the bottom of the boat.

"Is to protect from the sharks, no?" he asked nervously.

"No man, lots of game fish in dese waters, if you a fish you don't want to let skipper Jack see you," Cobb explained, chuckling.

The swarthy Puerto Rican balked.

"I think I stay in the boat this time, Eduardo. It looks too deep for me," he said.

Eduardo didn't seem too happy at this turn of events.

"This is why we arranged for your lessons, so you could help me under the water," Henderson replied frustrated.

"I will drown here, it eez too deep."

"The captain and I will be close to you," Henderson told him. "You will be safe." But no amount of talking was going to convince him.

"I feel unwell today also, I have blocked ear and I cannot go down," he said, making another excuse.

Jack looked at Henderson, but he made no move to pursue the matter further.

"All right, just the two of us then," Jack said thoughtfully.

If the Puerto Rican was afraid well then that meant one less person to worry about down below. Just he and Ed would dive.

"We'll make this a familiarization dive," Jack instructed, "Then once we feel comfortable, we can shift locations."

Henderson grunted affirmatively.

Before rolling over the side, Jack went over a few safety procedures.

"Stay close to me and if I give the thumbs up sign, we head for the surface. We'll swim up current, so that if anything happens we can drift back to the Whaler, okay?"

"Yes," Henderson replied a little hesitantly.

"Skip, you watch yourself, you hear?" Cobb said as he watched the two men make some last minute adjustments to their backpacks.

The two men rolled over the side of the Whaler backwards. Cobb handed Jack the big Arbalette and the two divers disappeared below the surface. Cobb dutifully watched their air bubbles, keeping track of their movements in case something went wrong.

Ten feet below Jack glanced upwards. The surface shimmered like a translucent mirror. Below the view was awesome. Jack wondered just how many human beings, if any, had ever witnessed the vista that lay before them. The white Dacron anchor line led down into a blue world that must have looked just the same a thousand years ago. The little Danforth was stuck solidly into the bottom near the base of a large sponge. Sloping upwards on their right, the multi-hued coral wall teemed with life. The bottom quickly disappeared into the empty blueness on their left. It was like flying, he thought.

The visibility was excellent. They could see almost one hundred feet and the sunlight flickered down in shimmering rays, playing on the reds and bright yellows of the sea fans waving gently in the current. Schools of brightly colored wrasses and juvenile parrotfish drifted above tall tube sponges ready to dart into their circular openings at the first sign of danger. Jack paused for a moment to string the spear gun with all four rubbers, and then after putting it on lock, he slipped the eight-foot safety line over his wrist.

Motioning Henderson to follow, he sank to a depth of fifty feet and began swimming along the edge of the reef. A seemingly endless variety of brilliantly colored corals stretched from the surface above them to the blue abyss below. Near the top, antlerhorn and staghorn coral grew in wild profusion, sheltering the tiny metallic sheened copper sweepers that hung in shimmering schools under the flat, orange hued branches.

A few feet deeper, other types of coral thrived, each species different in shape, size and color. This was the protective bulwark that had saved Aves from total destruction over and over again, a living defense comprising billions of tiny, industrious coral polyps.

Occasionally, there was a coral ledge or small flat outcropping, but for the most part it was just sheer drop-off. The two men swam away from the boat slowly. There was a strong current and it required a lot of legwork to make headway.

The wall was alive with fish and marine life. Huge, electric blue parrotfish chomped audibly on underwater growths while schools of small jewel-like tropicals darted in and out of cracks and crevices, feeding on the tiny plankton travelling along with the current. The water was exceptionally clear. A group of six big amberjack appeared, looming out of the blue, lured by the schools of ballyhoo swimming near the surface. Deeper, a big school of twenty pound mirror-sided horseye-jacks of the same family roamed the drop off looking for prey. The fish seemed unconcerned by the two bubble-blowing newcomers, passing within a foot or so in complete indifference.

A lone cubrera snapper of at least a hundred pounds made a brief appearance below them. Ambling slowly up from the deep, it came to within ten feet and Jack could see its big dog like teeth. Its dull reddish hue reflected the sunlight off its broad, heavy back. After having a brief look at the two divers it turned and slowly returned to the deep.

In the distance ahead, Jack saw the unmistakable form of a large grouper. His hand automatically turned the barbed tip of his speargun towards the fish, but he'd decided to keep this first dive on a safe basis and reluctantly took his eyes away from the deep swimming fish. Maybe later, he told himself.

It didn't take long for the first barracuda to show up. Jack had a habit of looking over his shoulder every few moments, a holdover from his fighter pilot days. Making one of his usual over-the-shoulder scans, he saw it hovering just above and twenty feet behind them. The ancient seven-footer would probably tip the scales at a hundred pounds or more. Jack took a double suck on the mouthpiece of his regulator; he'd seen plenty of big barracudas over the years, but this one was huge. The fish was doing what barracudas always do, just kind of hovering there behind them, keeping pace exactly. Its silvery sides were blotched with dark spots, and there were scars on the gill covers where it had been in some recent fight.

It was the head that was intriguing. The long pointed snout held rows of surgical two-inch daggers, designed to slice clean. There had been many occasions when he had caught fish on the trolling lines, only to have them ripped in half by a barracuda. This one had the equipment to cut either man in half if it wanted to. Jack knew that barracudas didn't normally attack humans. But looking at the specimen behind them, he wasn't too sure. He left the barbed tip of his big Arbalette speargun pointed towards the bottom. He had no absolutely no intention of trying to spear the fish; that would just piss it off.

Suddenly Henderson, who'd been looking ahead, turned and spotted the cuda. Panicking, he ripped his mouthpiece out releasing a rush of air bubbles. Jack dropped the Arbalette on its safety cord and swam over to try and calm the terrified man. He tried to grab him around the waist, but the sonovfabitch was strong as an ox. After a few seconds, Henderson stopped struggling, and Jack managed to put the regulator back in his mouth. It was a good thing it was a barracuda, he thought. An underwater struggle like that could have provoked a spontaneous attack from a shark, but the big cuda was gone. They just weren't on the menu today.

Hauling up the safety line, Jack retrieved his spear gun and they continued swimming slowly along the edge of the drop off, at a depth of fifty feet. He was just starting to feel at ease again when the current took them. An invisible wave, more powerful than either man could possibly swim against, quickly swept them backwards and away from the coral wall. Signaling for Henderson to follow him in towards the reef, Jack struggled to make headway, but the current was just too powerful. They were swept inexorably backwards along the coral wall towards the end of the reef. Jack realized they'd have to do something quickly to avoid being swept out into the open sea. Currents often rode specific levels and he wondered if a change in depth would make a difference. Signaling Henderson, they swam as hard as they could towards the bottom near the end of the reef wall. A momentary swirl of current suddenly took them. As if in a giant washing machine they were spun even deeper. At a hundred and ten feet it grew dimmer and colder.

They quickly neared the end of the reef and the beginning of the blue abyss. Desperately swimming towards the wall, Jack suddenly realized they weren't going to make it. Signaling Henderson to grab hold of his backpack, Jack raised the Arbalette and fired it at the last of the coral wall. The spear hit solidly and the barbed tip held fast. Dangling horizontally in the current, Jack struggled to hold the gun's handle. The invisible current pulled their air bubbles across the blue void. Floating towards the surface above, they glittered like huge silver mushrooms before bursting in the air. Wave after wave of current swept over them, trying to suck them away, and Jack barely hung on. Glancing at Henderson over his shoulder, he saw the fear in his eyes. He was having trouble holding on as well. If either one of them lost their precarious grip, they'd be swept out into the blue and lost forever.

"Sods law," Jack thought, only twenty minutes into the first dive and already we're in big trouble.

Suddenly the barbed tip started to come loose and then the tether went limp on Jack's wrist.

"No," he muttered into his mouthpiece, but the current began to fluctuate and then as quickly as it had appeared the turbulence was gone.

The schools of fish that had taken refuge within the reef, nonchalantly reappeared, seemingly accustomed to the occurrence. Jack decided it was a good time to head back. They'd been down for only twenty minutes, but he'd had enough. Signaling Ed, they made a slow ascent towards the surface.

Drifting the last hundred feet down current to the waiting Whaler, Jack shook his head.

"What the hell am I doing out here?" he wondered.

At the side of the Whaler Cobb took the scuba rigs from the divers one by one, pulling them over the rail. Climbing aboard, Jack and Henderson sat on the thwarts absorbing the warmth of the sun. Garcia watched them, his face expressionless.

"What happen down dere, skip?" Cobb asked.

"It was overpowering. That current was an ace away from taking us into the big blue." Jack said emphatically as he wiped his face dry with a towel

Cobb understood. The big blue was a place nobody needed to go.

Henderson had gone very quiet.

"You okay, Ed?"

"I'm fine," he replied, looking a little dazed, "it wasn't quite what I imagined."

"We just picked a poor time. We'll do better next dive," Jack said, draping the towel around his shoulders.

Cobb hauled up anchor and Jack drove the Whaler back to the schooner. Benny helped take the gear aboard, while Garcia got out of the boat and walked away saying nothing as usual.

"What's wid him?" Cobb asked.

"Don't know but he doesn't like diving. I know that," Jack replied.

"Maybe his mother beat him a lot, dey say dat if your mother beat you plenty you don't talk much," Benny offered.

"But Benny your mother did beat you an, you still talk plenty, ain't it?" Cobb teased.

Benny had no response. As usual in their little verbal matches Cobb always got the last word.

They fired up the Mako compressor right away, putting the empty bottles on charge.

Megan noticed that Jack looked uneasy following the dive, but she knew he was a capable diver and wouldn't take any unnecessary chances. But there was something different about this trip. After straightening out the galley she went aft to begin cleaning the guest cabins. Walking down the hallway towards the stateroom occupied by Ed Henderson, Laura suddenly opened the door.

"Where are you going?" Laura asked her.

"I'm just about to clean the cabins," Meg explained in a friendly tone, "I do that as well as cook aboard here."

"You don't have to do that," Laura said, shutting the door behind her.

"Oh it's not a problem, all part of the service." Megan offered amicably.

"I don't care. I'll handle it," Laura continued.

"Look, I'm perfectly honest if that's what you're worried about," Megan said a little miffed. "I've worked for Jack for...."

"What's your problem?" Laura cut in, "Don't you understand English? We want you to stay out of our cabins."

Her voice was raised and she looked like a cat ready to pounce. It was obvious that the woman didn't like her and quite honestly Megan suddenly felt the same way about her.

"Alright," Megan said defensively, "suit yourself."

Laura made no response; she just stood in front of the door waiting for her to leave.

Megan was worried. She'd done many charters on a number of different yachts, but this was the first time anyone had acted with such hostility and distrust towards her. She was also puzzled. Why on earth wouldn't they want their cabins cleaned and made up? They were paying a lot of money for this charter. As Megan walked towards the galley, her intuitive mind clicked into gear. I don't care what Jack thinks, she thought, something is definitely wrong here and I'm going to find out what it is.

There was no more diving that day. Henderson had lost his earlier enthusiasm and was content fiddling with some expensive looking dive equipment in the cockpit. At three in the afternoon he, Laura and Garcia met near the bow. They spoke earnestly for a minute and then afterwards he approached Jack.

"I think we'll go ashore to stretch our legs a bit and explore the atoll," Henderson told him.

"No problem, I'll get one of the guys to run you in and you can just wave when you want to get picked up," Jack replied.

Benny drove them to the small sandy beach at the head of the lagoon, agreeing to pick them up later.

Peering from the companionway hatch, Megan watched the Whaler speed away from the anchored schooner. Jack lay in the cockpit, taking a nap. After waiting until the guests were safely on the beach, she turned and went down to Henderson's cabin, opening the heavy teak paneled door. She planned to tell Jack about her little encounter with Laura a little later, but for now she was going to have a quick peek. They were ashore now and this was her chance.

Bright rays of sunlight shone through the portholes into the cabin. It seemed neat and tidy. In fact, it was unusually tidy. Most charter guests unpacked at least some clothing, but not this one. Henderson's two pieces of luggage lay unopened on the bed: a large, aluminum-colored case and a smaller duffel bag. Taking a deep breath, Megan paused for a moment before closing the door. Moving to the large case, she checked to see if it was locked. It wasn't. For a moment she hesitated. This was strictly against the rules, but she had an uneasy feeling about these people, and felt she should find out what it was.

The two clasps flew open with such a loud clack that she was sure they heard it on the shore. After waiting a second she raised the top of the case. There were some shirts and a toilet kit, and at first glance everything seemed innocent enough. Lifting a few shirts and a bathrobe, she felt around the edges. Nothing. But then her hand touched something hard and cold in the top left-hand corner. Pulling back the yellow polo shirt, she felt her heart skip a beat. She was looking down at the blue, steel barrel of a gun.

"Oh oh, this is trouble," she whispered to herself.

She didn't know much about guns other than they could kill people, but she could see this was a powerful one. Megan picked it up. It felt alien and heavy in her hand. The name of the manufacturer and the caliber were inscribed on the metal block, Colt .45.

Suddenly there were footsteps in the hallway and she almost died of fright. She stood there frozen until she heard a familiar voice.

"Megan, you there?" It was Jack. She quickly slipped the gun back into the corner of the case and closing, it she opened the door. Jack came towards her.

"Hi," he said. "I just wanted to ask you..."

"Oh, thank God it's you Jack," she interrupted in a breathless voice. "You better come and see this."

"What, you got a blocked toilet again?"

"Why is it anytime I have a problem in the cabins, it has to be a blocked head?" she said in an exasperated voice, "It's a gun! Henderson's got a gun in his suitcase."

"Show me," he said, his voice quickly changing from the usual light tone Megan knew to a cold dangerous one that she had never heard before. It scared her.

"See, look," she said, opening the case again.

Megan peeled back the shirts, exposing the gun.

Jack picked it up. It was obvious by the way he handled it that he knew about guns.

"See," she whispered in an I-told-you-so kind of voice, "and that Laura woman had a fit this morning when I went to clean the cabins, told me to stay out."

"So that's why you're in here digging through their stuff?" Jack tried to look disapproving, but Megan just smiled and gave him a quick punch on the arm.

He carefully searched through the rest of the case while Meg rifled through the duffel bag. They found a box of shells for the .45 and an extra loaded clip but nothing much else. He expertly popped the loaded magazine from the heel of gun and held it in his left hand. Then he worked the slide back, ejecting the shell in the chamber. Henderson had wanted it loaded.

"Make sure that everything else is the same as you found it."

She made a quick run through the case with her hands making sure everything was just as it had been.

"Same as it was," she said, turning to Jack, "What are you going to do now?"

"I'm going to have a little chat with our passenger as soon as he gets back aboard," he replied.

"What if he gets angry?" she asked sounding unsure.

"Him angry?" Jack told her sternly, "Believe me, I'm the one who's going to get really pissed off if he can't give me a damned good explanation."

From his expression she didn't doubt him.

Jack knew enough about life to realize that it took all kinds to spin the world, and that meant bad ones as well as good. He knew that people didn't carry guns unless they had a good reason, and he needed to know what Henderson's was. As they left the cabin together, Megan turned to Jack.

"By the way, what was it you wanted to ask me?" she asked, "You know, when you came down to the cabin."

Jack stopped and thought for a second.

"Funny, I honestly don't remember. See the effect you have on me?" he chuckled, shaking his head slightly.

She smiled.

Walking back into the galley, she started preparing dinner while Jack went back on deck. Standing at the rail, he hefted the box of .45 ammo in his right hand before heaving it out into the deeper water behind the schooner. A second later the two clips followed. Taking a seat in the cockpit, Jack placed the empty Colt under a coil of main sheet. Popping a Carib from the cooler, he pulled one of the cockpit cushions behind his back. Henderson and his party were still on the atoll.

As the sun began to set, Benny came walking aft.

"Skip, de guests ready to come back. Look, dey waving on de beach," he said.

"Go and pick them up, Benny," Jack told him.

A moment later he watched the Whaler leave the schooner on its way to the shore. Getting up, he walked to the bow and shut down the dive compressor and then going below, he fired up the generator to charge the batteries.

Returning to the deck, he took the gun from beneath the cushion, holding it behind his back. As the Whaler came along side, Henderson climbed aboard followed by the other two. Jack was waiting for him as he walked aft along the deck and he stepped in front of him, blocking his way.

"Yours?" Jack confronted him holding the gun out.

Henderson was obviously taken aback. He glanced angrily at Garcia, but the Puerto Rican remained silent.

"Yes," he replied, "but..."

"What the hell do you think you're doing bringing a gun aboard my ship?" Jack asked angrily.

"Nothing, I didn't think you'd object," Henderson said lamely.

"Try again," Jack said.

"I've heard about drug pirates in the islands and all my friends told me to bring a gun, it's just to protect myself that's all," he explained, spreading his hands.

"And this is the only one, no more surprises?"

"No."

"Because if there are, then this trip is over and we head back to Antigua pronto. No refund."

"I'm sorry I should have told you, but it was an innocent mistake," Henderson said, sounding genuinely sorry.

"You get this mistake when we get back to Antigua, right?"

"Of course," Henderson agreed.

Jack decided to leave it at that. The evening was quiet without much conversation and after dinner the crew faded fast. Jack locked the Colt in the secret compartment behind his bunk. As he curled up under the sheet he thought that it had been one hell of a day. Later he fell into a fitful sleep.

CHAPTER EIGHT

The Deep Reef

The wind dropped during the night and the schooner drifted over her anchor chain. It rasped and vibrated across the bobstay and the sound transmitted into her steel hull, making odd sounds. At dawn the sun peeked up over the horizon bringing a gentle breeze. The *Fandango* slowly swung to face the northeast. The morning of their second day at the atoll dawned clear and calm.

At six o'clock Jack came up on deck and sat in the cockpit. Watching the sunrise to the east, he thought about the gun they'd found in Henderson's luggage. The guy was certainly an oddball eccentric, but he had to admit that there had been problems over the years with drug smugglers hijacking yachts. Jack was well aware of the situation, but it was mostly in the more remote areas of the Bahamas.

Shaking his head, he stood up and stretched his back. For now, he'd quit worrying. A lot of people in the islands carried guns anyway. His own long barreled Smith and Wesson .38 was locked away in his cabin.

The great sea birds were already rising in their hundreds from the atoll. Circling overhead, they seemed at first to be confused, screeching and weaving as if without motive. Then, at a moment precipitated by something known only to them, they swooped down to sea level to take up formation before heading out to some unknown location in the empty expanses of the western Caribbean.

After a while he heard Megan rattling pots and frying pans in the galley, and he wandered down to see if there was any coffee going.

"Morning, Meg," he said, "sleep well?"

"No, matter of fact, I was awake thinking a lot," she grumbled, rubbing her eyes.

"About our guests?"

"Yes, want a coffee?" she asked, still sounding sleepy.

"Great."

"What about the gun business, you going to head back to Antigua?" she asked him.

"No, I don't think we need to do that, but I'll be keeping an eye on Henderson. Where's that delicious brew of yours?"

Megan didn't pursue the matter and passed him a cup.

Thanking her, Jack took his mug of coffee back up to the cockpit, where he sat watching pelicans dive bombing a school of sardines in the shallows. After a while Henderson came and sat opposite him in the cockpit. Jack eyed him carefully.

"Have a good night?" he asked.

"Oh pretty good, but the boat was making some strange noises for a while," Henderson replied nonchalantly.

He showed no sign of animosity or unease about the gun incident.

"That was the anchor chain rubbing on the bobstay. She does that when the wind dies. So, what do you want to do today?" Jack asked him.

"When Laura and Garcia get up, I thought we'd unpack the equipment, maybe test it out," he replied.

"I'll have the guys help bring it up," Jack offered.

"Think the current will be down? Yesterday wasn't too good, was it?" Henderson questioned cautiously.

"It was bad, but I think it'll probably just kind of come and go. We'll just have to play it by ear and if it gets too strong, then we'll just quit for a while," Jack told him.

"We may just play with the camera today. I'll talk to Laura when she gets up."

She and Garcia came up shortly afterwards and Megan served breakfast on the cockpit table. Cobb and Benny washed down the schooner's decks with the saltwater hose and gassed up the Whaler. Going to the engine room, Jack made his daily maintenance checks and then fired up the generator to charge the batteries.

After breakfast, Henderson and Garcia went below to the spare cabin with Cobb and brought up the three aluminum cases, laying them on the deck near the boarding ladder. There were two large ones, bigger than Jack remembered, and a smaller one. Laura took charge at that point. Taking some keys from her short's pocket, she undid the locks and flipped the tops open. Each case held a three-foot aluminum torpedo cushioned in gray molded sponge. Designed to travel through the water, they were streamlined, with smooth, round noses and swept back stabilizing fins at the aft end. Each one had a stout towing eyelet at the top.

"What are these things exactly?" Jack asked.

It was pretty fancy underwater equipment, he thought to himself, as they huddled around the cases, curious to see the gear.

"I'll let her explain," Henderson replied, turning to Laura.

"Here Jack, let me show you," she said, lifting the front of the first torpedo, "This one's the underwater video camera."

He and Megan leaned over to get a closer look. The front ended in a transparent Perspex dome while inside, the large black eye of a camera lens peered out.

"And this is the screen that goes with it," Laura explained, turning to the smaller case.

Opening it, she displayed the foot square television screen and a small control console with a selection of knobs and switches.

It got hotter as the sun rose and the heat began reflecting upwards off the schooner's teak decks. Laura stood up, pulled her tee shirt off and after giving Jack a quick glance to make sure he was watching she wiggled out of her shorts. Underneath she wore a tiny white bikini that barely covered her. She had an extremely seductive figure and Jack couldn't help looking. Laura noticed and smiled sweetly as she explained how the camera worked.

"We'll tow the camera behind your Boston Whaler. Whatever picture the camera picks up gets transmitted to this screen," she said, tapping the monitor.

"We just need to hook it up to the battery here and it's all set."

"Pretty high tech stuff," Jack said, looking at the second case.

It held an exact replica of the first silver torpedo.

"What's this unit?"

"This one's a magnetometer," Laura told him, "We tow it about twenty feet above the bottom and if it passes over any ferrous metal it beeps. We'll pull it behind the Whaler the same way as the camera."

Megan noticed the small silver labels on the sides of the boxes.

"The cases say Nassau Oceanic Laboratories," Megan queried, curious as always.

"I used to work for them," Laura answered without looking at her.

When Laura spoke to her, she spit venom but when she talked to Jack, it was all sweetness, touching him or leaning against him at every opportunity. It was really starting to bug Megan.

Her thoughts were interrupted by Jack's voice.

"You guys are really into this treasure business, you looking for something specific?" he asked, turning to the dark haired man.

"No, but hey," Henderson laughed a little self consciously, "you never know."

"Yes, you never know," Laura said lightly, "maybe we'll find a shipwreck or something."

Henderson glared at her and even Garcia looked a little uneasy for a minute.

"I've been lucky over the years," Henderson continued, "Found a few coins here and there, cannon balls, bronze buttons. We even got a small brass swivel gun off of Anegada last year. Laura's a marine archeologist and all of this equipment is hers."

Jack had heard it all before. People came to the islands with treasure on the brain. From Chicago and New York and a hundred other places they came to the West Indies and South America searching for things that had little basis in reality. Atlantis, El Dorado or the fabled Janganati, the legends were a dime a dozen. Only a few people had ever struck it rich in the islands and they had paid heavy prices for their lucre. If there ever was anything substantial at Aves, it had been washed away by the sea long ago. He'd let them have their fun. If they did find a few coins or a cannonball, well, all the better.

"Hey skip, de Whaler ready now," Cobb shouted from below the rail.

Henderson and Laura decided to try the camera first. It was equipped with a spool of quarter-inch rubberized towing cable that would be attached to the stern of the Whaler. Climbing down the boarding ladder to the boat bobbing gently alongside, Laura took the roll of duct tape and strapped the small console case to the forward seat. Benny passed the twelve-volt battery down to Cobb and Laura started plugging in the coaxial cables connecting the screen and the console to the rubber towing cable. Lastly, she snapped the two rubber coated pole caps over the battery terminals and plugged the lead into the back of the console.

"All set," she said after five minutes or so. "We can give it a try whenever you're ready."

Henderson and Jack climbed down the teak boarding ladder to the Whaler, and Jack gave the new outboard a pull. It started right away.

"I'll drive while you guys play with your stuff," Jack suggested.

Henderson nodded and Cobb cast off the bowline from the deck of the schooner. Garcia would stay aboard with Megan and the two crew members this time.

The sun was well up in the sky as they pulled away from the *Fandango*. The day was brilliant and Jack thought that the underwater camera would see all the better for it. Damn I'm getting excited about this myself, he thought.

He drove the boat slowly off to the left and ahead of the schooner. They would start towing near the spot where he and Henderson had gone down the day before. As they crossed the lagoon, a pair of spotted leopard rays glided under the Whaler's bow, their wide wings skimming the bottom as they searched for morsels in the sand. They swam gracefully and in unison, their seemingly gentle movements belying the six-inch poisonous barbs hidden in their tails.

The Whaler soon crossed the divide between the shallows and the drop off. The light blue of the lagoon suddenly changed to the dark blue of the Caribbean. Jack slowed the boat to a crawl.

"You're going to have to watch you don't hook it on the bottom," Laura said to Jack. "I'll let out about fifty feet, of cable to start with and if you can stay in water deeper than fifty feet, we'll be just fine."

It was obvious she'd done this before and knew her stuff.

"There's not going to be any trouble there," Jack replied, "Your problem is going to be seeing anything. The water's really deep here."

"Oh yes, we will. The camera has a wide angle lens and it looks sideways as well as down, so as you drive along the edge of the wall the camera should capture the coral reef."

The camera housing was actually pretty light and as soon as Laura had connected the cable to the silver torpedo, she and Henderson lifted it over the side, letting it sink below the surface.

"Just keep us going slow, below three knots should be good," Laura told him, "The 'fish' swims best at that speed."

Henderson slacked out the cable, as Jack motored the Whaler slowly forward. When the colored markers on the cable indicated there was fifty feet out he stopped, making the wire fast to the stern cleat with the special non-crimping clamp Laura had provided.

The little foot square screen came to life and Laura bent over in front of it adjusting the knobs. She had rigged a cardboard canopy around it with duct tape to shield it from the sun's glare, and Jack could look into it as well from where he sat at the steering wheel.

The sea was fairly smooth as he brought the Whaler onto a course parallel to the edge of the reef and drove along it about thirty feet off. The day was clear and bright and the dark of the coral was clearly visible on his right while on the left the water was blue.

The face of the screen steadied as Laura focused the camera from the console. Jack was impressed at the quality of the picture. Although black and white it was really distinctive, with excellent contrast. The sunlight penetrated to a good depth in the crystal clear water.

"Look, there's the coral wall where we had our little problem," Jack said.

The undersea vista looked calm and inviting in the small screen.

Driving the boat slowly along he veered to the left anytime the 'fish' seemed to be getting too close to the reef. The sea floor to the right of the reef wall was generally clear, and the screen showed every detail. This was the northwest edge of the reef and the bottom geography seemed to be pretty uniform.

"Head a little more to the east for a while," Henderson said. "Maybe we'll see something there."

The same schools of small fish that had been there the day before drifted in and out of view and occasionally a few larger ones.

"There's turtles down there," Laura said as a large specimen swam in front of the camera.

It stayed for a good thirty seconds, looking back over its carapace at the odd little silver fish as it wobbled along. They'd seen them on the surface earlier and occasionally one would swim across the small monitor. They swam using just their powerful front flippers, steering with their smaller hind ones.

"Females coming to lay their eggs," Jack said, "They come in runs and looks like there's one building now."

Some of the females weighed more than three hundred pounds and if he had time, Jack thought, maybe he'd go ashore and take one during the night. He liked turtle steak.

"That's interesting. Maybe we can dive with them later," Henderson said, glancing at Jack.

"You may not want to. A good run of turtles brings those big ocean-roaming sharks in here like clockwork."

Somehow the large carnivorous predators knew exactly when the turtles congregated here, and they uncannily showed up at Aves for the annual runs. Turtles, however, weren't the easiest ideal food for them and even the biggest teeth had trouble crunching through the hard carapace or shell. The big sharks had a cruel feeding tactic that worked fairly well. Zeroing in on a prospective victim, they would grab one of their flippers as high up as possible where the skin was softer and chomp it clean off. The thought made him shudder, and unconsciously he put his hand into the back of his swim trunks and rubbed the rough scars on his left buttock.

They continued to pull the 'fish' along that section of the reef until Henderson was satisfied there was nothing of interest to be seen there, and towards noon Laura announced the battery was getting low.

Returning to the schooner, they passed the gear up on deck. Jack and Cobb put the depleted battery on charge, replacing it with a hot one. Megan had prepared a lunch and the ravenous crew dug into the meal. Sitting around the cockpit table, they discussed plans for the afternoon. Henderson wanted to try out the magnetometer.

"Why don't we tow it around the edge of the reef around this end of the island and if there is anything, it'll tell us, right Laura?" he asked her.

"Yes, it's really sensitive. If there's so much as a nail down there, it'll detect it right away, even at depths of seventy or eighty feet."

When she'd finished eating, Laura pulled out a bottle of sun tan oil from her bag.

"Jack, rub this on for me please," she said, handing him the bottle.

"Where do you want it?" he asked feeling a little unsure.

Laura looked straight at him.

"All over, but you can start with my back."

Turning her back to him, she flicked off the strap of her bikini top, so he could apply the oil unhindered. She leaned forward then, and a little self consciously, Jack rubbed the oil on her back. Megan looked furious as she noisily clattered the dirty plates together.

After lunch, Laura unpacked the other 'fish'. It was a duplicate of the first housing; just the guts were different. The machine held a very sensitive magnetic field detector according to Laura, who seemed very knowledgeable on the subject. Apparently, every piece of metal had a magnetic field and her magnetometer was sensitive enough to detect even the faintest trace. She finished fiddling with the set and was ready to put it in the Whaler.

"Jack, can you get Cobb or Benny to help put this in the boat?" she asked him. "This one is a little heavier than the camera."

"Sure," he said, turning to the foredeck where the crewmen were sitting. "Cobb, give us a hand here, will you?" he called through cupped hands.

The burly mate came over and the three of them lifted the magnetometer from its case and carried it to the rail. The bloody thing was certainly a lot heavier, Jack thought to himself. They lowered it into the

Whaler, laying it on an old vinyl cockpit cushion. After a few more minutes of chatting, Jack, Ed and Laura took off again.

They began towing near the spot where they'd made the first dive. As soon as the unit was at the desired depth Laura tested the alarm.

"This is what it'll sound like if it finds any metal down there," she said, turning the squelch knob all the way up. The little receiver made a loud beeping sound.

"It's working," she said happily.

Henderson nodded affirmatively.

They towed the new equipment from the far northwestern limit of the reef to the lagoon where the schooner lay anchored.

"You better pull in a bit on the cable," Laura remarked as they crossed the sandy bottom.

Henderson hauled in about twenty feet as Jack slowed the Whaler to a crawl. After a few minutes they passed the *Fandango*'s stern and the depth began increasing again. The bottom sloped downwards into the deep and the little silver fish went down once more. They towed it to southeastern edge of the reef. There wasn't a sound from the speaker.

"Looks like there's nothing down there," Jack said. Neither Laura or Henderson replied and they continued on.

Towards late afternoon when the sun was getting near the western horizon, Jack looked at the gas tank; the gauge was nearing the empty mark.

"Time to head back, we're getting low on gas," he told them.

Henderson looked frustrated.

"Can we just go over there for a moment?" he asked, pointing to the south. There seemed to be an area of darker water where the reef was cut by a deep underwater ravine.

"Alright, five more minutes," Jack replied, checking the fuel gauge again.

Unconsciously he glanced under his seat at the oars he'd asked Cobb to take from the lapstrake skiff. Steering the Whaler towards the dark looking area, they turned north. Moving up the up the deep channel for fifty or sixty feet, Jack peered over the side. There was a massive rift in the reef running seawards towards the land. The depth seemed to carry quite far in towards the shore.

"Looks like there's nothing here either and we're almost out of gas so we'll have to..."

The machine went crazy. All of a sudden it was beeping and howling like a banshee.

Laura smiled. "There's a whole lot of some kind of metal down below us."

Jack was surprised at the sudden turn of events and intrigued. Henderson leaned over the side to have a look, but there was nothing visible. The bottom sixty feet below was dark, with clumps of coral and rock.

"Can we mark this spot?" Henderson asked excitedly, "Then we can come back and dive here tomorrow."

"We can use the anchor and pick it up again tomorrow. Let me just get to the bow a minute," he told him.

Opening the bow hatch, he took out the coil of quarter inch Dacron anchor line and tied the bitter end to one of the little white boat fenders he kept under the seat. It was white and would float well.

"Here we go," he said, tossing the little Danforth over. He slacked the line after it and when the anchor took hold he threw the fender in.

"Thats not going anywhere," Jack said, turning to Henderson.

There was a feeling of excitement aboard the Whaler as they approached the *Fandango*. Climbing aboard, Jack tied up the bowline to the foremast cap rail turnbuckles before joining his guests in the cockpit. Popping himself a cold Carib, he listened as Henderson talked animatedly to Garcia.

"The machine just went crazy, beeping like mad," he told him.

"It means treasure?" Garcia asked dully.

"It means ferrous metal, lots of it," Henderson explained.

Jack turned to Laura.

"So, what does your machine tell you is there?" he asked her.

"Something magnetic probably, I'd say quite a lot judging by the reaction we had today," she replied.

"We'll get out there again first thing tomorrow," Henderson said his eyes bright with elation.

Jack considered the latest developments. If his charter party found a few odds and ends around the reef, it wouldn't be a problem, but what if they found something more? It was remotely possible that there might be something of value out on this piece of sand and coral, but what if? Gold, even small amounts of it, bred trouble like rabbits. There was usually either too much or not enough. Either way it was trouble.

But there was no law against accidentally finding a few artifacts or even a coin or two, Jack thought to himself, especially if you kept your mouth shut. After all he'd only just sold the gold coins he'd found the year before for a nice piece of change. He glanced momentarily over the rail at his new outboard and smiled slightly.

There was also a good chance that whatever had set off the machine was a piece of metal from one of the many turtle schooners that had come to grief on the atoll over the years.

Over dinner the conversation seemed stilted and Henderson quickly steered any talk of the afternoon's find off to another subject. After dinner they dispersed to their cabins for an early night.

Sitting in the small chair at the navigation station, Jack listened to the weather report from Barbados. There was nothing to worry about in the forecast, but the wind had come up a little over the past few hours and the schooner was pulling on her chain. Switching off the set, he made a last round of the deck with Cobb. The two men walked the bow and Jack placed his bare foot on the anchor chain. Any movement would indicate that the anchor was shifting in the sand. The night was dark with only a few stars visible. It meant that there were clouds aloft and there was always the possibility of a squall during the night.

"We better give her some more chain, Cobb," Jack told his mate, "Don't want her dragging tonight."

The burly West Indian eased the winch brake, slacking out another twenty-five feet of the three-quarter inch chain.

"Dat should hold her, skip," he said.

"Yeah, but keep an ear open tonight just in case."

"Always do, skip," Cobb replied, putting the chain dog on.

After double checking the brake the two men turned in. The crew slept in the fo'c'sle of the schooner and would be the first to know if she started to drag. The noise of the chain dragging over the bottom would make an easily recognizable sound as it was transmitted into the schooner's steel hull.

Sometime in the middle of the night, Jack came half-awake. In the dim light shining through the porthole he imagined someone slowly closing his teak paneled door. A female form moved towards his bunk while pulling her tee shirt up over her head.

Jack lay on his back in the warm cabin. He usually slept naked during the balmy nights and as he tried to sit up, warm hands suddenly touched him and began caressing his chest, pushing him back down on the mattress. Suddenly he realized he wasn't dreaming.

"Megmmm?" he whispered unbelievingly.

"Shhhh," a female voice answered huskily.

She climbed over the edge of the bunk and lay down on top of him. Her skin felt warm and silky under his hands. Completely naked, she pressed herself against him seductively.

"Meg," Jack whispered still in a dreamy state of mind.

"It's me, Laura."

Jack came fully awake now, but before he could say anything further, Laura pushed him back on the narrow mattress with surprising strength and, straddling his waist, began kissing him feverishly.

"You need a real woman," she whispered between kisses.

Laura had been flirting with him, but he hadn't expected this. He should have been enjoying it, but he felt guilty. He knew it was Laura there on top of him, but it was Megan's face that kept drifting into his mind.

Suddenly, there was a loud knocking. He half expected an angry Henderson or Garcia to explode through the door. With a great sense of relief he heard Cobb's familiar voice ringing through loud and clear.

"Skip, Skip, you best come quick, she dragging de anchor," he called.

Pushing an unhappy Laura to the inside of the bunk, he grabbed his old swim trunks that he always hung on the sink. He couldn't think of anything to say to her on the spur of the moment, so he left her there in the darkened cabin as he ran out the door and up on deck.

Megan had heard the commotion and came running from her bunk to see if they needed her help. She arrived just in time to see Laura standing in the doorway of Jack's cabin, draped revealingly in his towel. She smiled wickedly at her before retreating into his cabin.

Megan stopped in her tracks, unable to believe her eyes.

Surely Jack couldn't be taken in by someone like that. Didn't he realize what she was? There must be less to him than I reckoned and none of it good, she thought to herself.

She turned and went back to her bunk, not wanting to go up and speak to him.

Meanwhile, Jack was tending to the schooner. As soon as he'd hit the deck, it was obvious she was dragging anchor. It was still very dark, but a pitch-black smudge loomed close on the horizon to windward of the vessel which was drifting broadside to the gusting wind. Already he could feel the motion of the sea outside the protection of the lagoon, but at least she was dragging away from the atoll's reefs and away from danger. The first strong gusts of the squall hit at about thirty-five knots, he thought. Cobb and Benny stood by on deck, ready to act.

"She dragging bad, skip, an' de wind picking up too," Cobb said.

"I'm going to fire up. Go ahead and heave up the anchor as soon as you hear the generator going," he told them.

Jack fired up the generator and main engine from the cockpit switches and when they were both running, he flicked on the compass lights and sidelights. Spinning the teak wheel to port, he gunned the main engine, trying to get the schooner's head to the wind. The clink clank of the anchor winch faded as the full strength of the rainsquall hit. Jack pulled his yellow slicker on as the *Fandango*'s bow slowly came into the eye of the wind. The anchor finally broke surface and Jack took his schooner cautiously away to the southwest, away from the lagoon.

The situation was dangerous. Close to a treacherous reef in pitch darkness, they were unable to see a thing. There was nothing for it, Jack thought, they'd have to stand off and motor around in the lee of Aves until daylight. It was still only three in the morning, so he would have a long wait.

The squall passed, leaving a damp stillness. Cobb and Benny secured the Whaler astern on a double towline and hoisted the anchor into the hawsepipe. It was wet and chilly on deck after the squall and Jack wished someone would bring him a coffee, but only Henderson came up.

"What's happening? We're not leaving are we?" He was in a panic.

"No, just a squall and we dragged anchor a little, but we'll have to wait until daylight before we can get back into the lagoon. I can't see a thing and it's too dangerous to poke around in the dark."

Henderson looked relieved and went back to his cabin. Cobb finally made a coffee for Jack and a little while later Jack sent his two crew back down below. There was nothing more for them to do and they might as well get some sleep.

He would stay on deck and keep the engine running, making sure that the schooner didn't get near the atoll. He'd let the *Fandango* drift dead to leeward until dawn. Hopefully then he'd be able to motor straight onto the wind again to Aves. It was only two hours more till daylight, and he hoped they wouldn't drift too far from the atoll.

Sitting alone in the cockpit of his schooner, Jack experienced an odd sensation. Closing his eyes for a moment, he wondered if he'd been dreaming. The warm naked body that had crawled into bed with him had been real enough, he was sure of that. The surprising revelation was that he found himself wishing it had been Megan instead of Laura. He was convinced though that Megan would probably laugh at the idea. But neither woman came on deck, and Jack was left alone with his thoughts as he motored around under an overcast sky.

CHAPTER NINE

The Wreck of the San Idelfonso

Jack's rear end itched where he'd been sitting on the wet cockpit seat and he felt cold. Dawn broke and the horizon to the east turned the sky an angry red but he remained alone on the schooner's deck.

The Caribbean Sea seemed empty and there was no sign of the atoll, but as the sun rose above the horizon the first of the great sea birds left Aves for their day's fishing. Taking note of their direction for the second time in a week, Jack revved up the main engine bringing the *Fandango* onto a course opposite to that of the sea birds.

"My friends, you never let me down," Jack said to himself.

Unless the current had taken them too far to the east or west, it should take them back to the atoll.

With the throttle at 1850 rpm, the big diesel pushed the schooner easily through the water. She gradually built momentum until the speedometer read a solid nine knots. Hearing the change of tone in the engine, Cobb and Benny appeared on deck and began tidying up. Benny got his lead line ready again in case it was needed and Cobb prepared the anchor.

Jack's assessment was correct and after an hour Aves came into view again. During the night the schooner had drifted only a few miles to the southwest. There was a low swell rolling in from the north this time though, and the sea was a little rougher than it had been the day before. He made a mental note to get the weather report from Barbados at eight a.m.

Megan came up looking venomous.

"Sleep alright?" Jack asked.

"I slept fine, but you didn't get much did you."

"No, I didn't, was up here freezing my butt off half the night."

Megan spun round, fastening her emerald green eyes on him.

"That's not what I meant."

He was stung by the animosity, but before he could respond she went below again, leaving him alone in the cockpit.

Twenty minutes later Cobb dropped *Fandango*'s anchor in the lagoon where she'd been before. Jack shut down the main engine and went below in search of a badly needed cup of coffee. Strolling into the galley, he prepared himself for an onslaught from Megan, but she wasn't there. He quickly made himself a mug of strong black and taking it to his cabin, he placed it on the dresser top while he stripped. The soft towel felt good on his skin and he put on some clean dry clothing. When he returned to the cockpit he sat down, pulling a dry cushion between his back and the teak wheel box. The coffee was hot and tasted good.

The clatter of the anchor chain going down woke his charter party. They appeared one by one up the companionway hatch.

"Bad squall last night?" Henderson asked.

Jack nodded.

"We dragged anchor, had to drift around till daylight to get back in here."

"Think the weather will be OK today?" Henderson asked, glancing aloft.

Although the breeze had risen only slightly there were a few gray smudges lurking on the distant horizon, and the usual Trade Wind clouds overhead were thicker and heavier looking.

"We'll have to watch it," Jack replied, "Probably be some rain by the looks of it."

"When do you think we can dive?" Henderson asked impatiently.

It wasn't even eight o'clock.

"We'll go around nine thirty. It's cloudier today and the sun needs to get a little higher in the sky," Jack replied, rubbing his eyes.

He left no room for argument.

Henderson nodded and a few moments later he and Garcia left Jack in the cockpit. They stood around on the foredeck waiting for Megan to appear with the morning coffee. Henderson pointed towards Aves once or twice. Laura stood near the hatch quietly looking toward the shore. Jack thought it was probably a good time to clear up any misunderstandings about her nocturnal visit to his cabin.

"Last night," he began, but she cut him off.

"Forget it, it didn't happen," she replied coldly.

"Fine by me," Jack said.

I can do without that kind of bitchiness today, he thought to himself.

Megan served breakfast in the cockpit. Silently placing the tray on the cockpit table, she returned below. Jack managed to secure himself a plate of overcooked scrambled eggs and a scowl. Henderson and Garcia came aft then, and joined him at the table, helping themselves to some juice, toast and eggs.

Henderson seemed agitated and in big hurry to get diving, but after the last few hours, Jack wasn't going to move anywhere without getting a bite to eat and an hour's rest. There seemed a lot to think about today all of a sudden, and though he should be concerned with his guests and their activities, his mind kept wandering back to Megan.

After breakfast he instructed Cobb and Benny to start getting the Whaler gassed up and the scuba gear ready. Leaving his passengers in the cockpit Jack went below to the *Fandango's* small chart room and tuned in the AM radio. After a few moments the marine weather report from Barbados came over the ether.

Leaning on the chart table, he took another sip of coffee and frowned as the announcer droned on.

"There is a weak tropical wave or depression east of the Lesser Antilles. The depression is moving west at about eighteen knots and remains at latitude fourteen degrees. Heavy squall activity and gusty winds accompany the system."

"That's all I need now," he said to himself.

"There are no signs of cyclonic development at this time," the announcer concluded.

There were no guarantees in the hurricane lottery. There was another report in the afternoon and Jack would decide then about whether to cut and run, or stay at Aves another night. Under normal conditions they could reach secure harbor in twenty-four hours. Discovery Lagoon in Marigot Bay, St. Lucia offered superb storm shelter.

By nine thirty they were approaching the rift in the reef.

"There it is," Cobb said, pointing.

The squall hadn't shifted the white fender; it was still there marking the dark channel where the magnetometer had gone crazy.

Cobb steered the Whaler right up to it and Jack leaned over the side, picked up the line, making it fast to the bow. The water was dark and uninviting. He had a sense of uneasiness as they prepared to make their dive.

Laura and Garcia had insisted on coming along, even though it crowded the Whaler. They sat in the bow as Jack and Henderson checked their gear. Cobb would stay in the boat as usual while they were down.

"Skipper, you watch it dung dere today," he told him. "Dis water ain't lookin' nice at all."

"And you keep one eye on the clouds and another on the bubbles. If there's even a hint of a squall ahead, just start the outboard and we'll come up right away," Jack replied and after nodding quickly, he slid the back-pack over his shoulders.

Good old Cobb, everyone else on the schooner was treating him as if he had a social disease. Laura hadn't said another word to him and was distant and cold. Big change from last night, he thought. Megan hadn't said anything more to him either and was avoiding him like the plague.

Rolling over the rail, Jack took a breath and adjusted his facemask. The compressed air coming through the regulator tasted cold, dry and rub-bery. As the bubbles cleared he looked down. This area of the reef was unusual and the bottom terrain different from the north reef. Fifty feet below, a long underwater ravine ran from the open sea to the shallow reef near the shore. The coral walls prevented sunlight from penetrating to the bottom, lending a shadowy aura to the location. Only when the sun was high in the sky would any light filter through.

Jack motioned for Henderson to follow and they descended to thirty feet, swimming slowly towards the shore. As they sank deeper, the walls on either side rose menacingly. Where the coral had grown into bizarre tortured arches, deep crevices and caves loomed. Dark openings gaped wide as if beckoning the unsuspecting towards some unknown end. Huge sea fans waved slowly in the murky shadows and Jack gave an involuntary shiver as the water turned cooler.

Patches of turtle grass and clumps of low coral and sponge made an eerie field along the bottom. The usual brilliant colors were gone and the surrounding reef looked obscure and gloomy. There was little current in the ravine though, and the swimming was easy.

Suddenly, a pair of big green turtles appeared above them headed for the deep sea. Jack watched motionless, as their powerful front flippers pulled them effortlessly through the water. He noticed the smaller of the two had one of its hind flippers shredded and there were white scrapes in the heavy carapace from a shark attack. Jack shivered again.

The creatures never ventured onto the land during daylight. They would hang around on the edge of the reef, waiting for nightfall before dragging themselves ashore to lay their eggs. Using their hind flippers, the great turtles dug deep holes in the soft sand where they deposited as many as three hundred soft-shelled, golf ball sized eggs. It was an interesting process and when the females had finished they returned exhausted to the sea, where the smaller males waited. The males never went onto the land, spending their entire lives at sea. It was during this time when the females came to lay their eggs that the two sexes met.

Suddenly a shadow appeared below him on a patch of sand. Figuring it was Henderson, he turned but his heart skipped a beat. There was no mistaking the long sinuous shape of the big tiger shark passing close above them. It swam purposefully down the channel after the turtles. Jack's chest tightened and he found it difficult to take air from the regulator. The shark was nasty looking with the usual broad square snout and angled teeth. Its belly seemed starkly white against the surface of the water and the sunlight flickered menacingly along its flanks, highlighting the trademark vertical stripes. At least fourteen feet long it had a pointed dorsal and large wing-like pectoral fins. A pair of ugly looking black and white remoras had attached themselves to the underbody. Using the suction cups on their heads, they hung like three-foot parasites. They would stay with their chosen host for as long as they lived, letting go only to feed on the scraps of their master's dinners.

The shark's head turned slowly and there was no doubt that the beady black eyes were scanning the two divers. Suddenly it seemed as if there was some sort of recognition. It was not an intelligent creature; in fact it was little changed from its ancestors of a million years ago. The huge predator's senses were finely tuned as a deep-sea eating machine and Jack and his diving partner had perked its interest. Banking like an aircraft, it turned along its powerful length, swimming almost casually back towards them. Sinking down to their own depth, it circled them, staying about twenty feet off.

Jack's blood ran cold and turning to Henderson, he held his hands up in a stop-don't-move position, but he had already done just that and was hanging motionless in the water.

"That's it, man, don't make any sudden moves, just stay like that for a minute," Jack thought to himself.

If Henderson threw a fit right now that shark would have him in a second.

"Just play dead, stay still, good, good."

No bubbles were coming from Henderson's regulator; he was holding his breath.

Jack turned slowly in the water facing the shark. Eye to eye he winced at the two-inch teeth in the slightly opened jaw. Shaped like huge bent commas and roughly serrated on the edges, they were one of the distinguishing features of this species Jack had seen pictures of men who'd been mauled by tigers and they weren't pretty. He held his breath as the huge fish evaluated them. If an attack were going to come, it would come within the next few seconds. Without knowing it he rubbed the old wound on his rear end.

Suddenly, the big tiger shark turned and banked in towards him. Feeling his bowels clench, he instinctively raised his legs. His hands were empty; he didn't even have the Arbalette to ram down its gullet. The big square snout leveled and the jaws opened slightly, but when it was only three feet away some primitive reason prevailed and it turned. The left pectoral fin lightly brushed Jack's arm as it swam by. The shark's minuscule brain had already punched in the code for turtle, and Jack and Henderson just didn't register as food. The big tiger made one more quick circuit of the divers and swam off in chase of the turtles.

The two men started breathing again, and a rush of bubbles rose from their regulators. They quickly swam away from the deeper water until the depth gauge on Jack's wrist read twenty feet. He was ready to call it quits. This kind of stuff was far beyond the call of duty. Spotting Henderson moving towards the shallow end of the ravine some fifty feet ahead, he took off after his charge. It was time to call a halt before someone got hurt. They would surface closer to shore and signal for Cobb to come and get them.

The shallow reef was alive with schools of small multihued fish and sea life. Jack noted the abundance of lobster feelers sticking out of holes in the coral and under different circumstances he might have had a little more interest, but right now he had other things on his mind. Swimming closer in towards the wall on his left-hand side, he caught a slight movement from the corner of his eye. Out of curiosity he swam a foot or so closer but then quickly pulled back. The eye of the huge green moray eel was the size of a small apple. Hanging half out of a crevice in the coral, the eel moved its mouth rhythmically, opening and closing slowly over razor sharp teeth. Jack knew this was the creature's natural breathing action and was probably benign. He was glad Henderson hadn't spotted it. Another scare might just finish him off.

He caught up with Henderson pausing for a moment to catch his breath. Floating at a depth of ten feet, Jack thought the bottom of the ravine looked about five or six feet below his fins. Near the surface an abundance of staghorn and antlerhorn coral grew. Beneath the branches hundreds of small copper sweepers and a few bigger, glassy eyed snapper hovered.

Just ahead a massive flat slab of coral stretched out from the south wall, almost spanning the ravine. It was only a few feet under the surface and it opened below in a shadowy cathedral. He was about to signal Henderson to the surface when he noticed something on a sandy patch of bottom within the coral cathedral. Moving closer, he peered down. After a moment he made out the unmistakable form of a cannon.

Motioning for Henderson to follow, he descended towards it and as they got closer, its size became fully evident. It was at least ten feet long and heavily encrusted with coral, but there was no mistaking the shape. A half dozen more lay scattered just twenty feet further in. The first of the cannons lay in water less than fifteen feet deep, and the next two in only ten or so. They weren't in any order, just spread out helter skelter as if thrown there by some giant hand.

Jack looked at his pressure gauge; it was time to go up. Pulling a reluctant Henderson, he surfaced and waved to Cobb who was waiting patiently in the anchored Whaler with Laura and Garcia. Treading water, they watched as he pulled in the anchor and motored carefully towards them.

"You can anchor it right here," Jack shouted and the big Bequia sailor threw the little Danforth back into the water where it quickly sank to the bottom, catching hold under one of the cannons.

Swimming the last few feet on the surface to the side of the Whaler, they held on to the gunwale while Cobb and Garcia lifted the near empty scuba bottles from their backs into the boat. Then Jack and Ed Henderson climbed aboard.

"Probably a dozen or more big cannons right below us," Henderson said excitedly. "There must have been a wreck."

Jack dried himself with the towel and nodded in agreement.

"Looks like it must have been there for a long time, there's nothing left of the ship itself."

"You're right," Henderson was suddenly serious, "I think we've got ourselves a very old wreck. I'd like to go down again for another look. Did we bring spare tanks along?"

"Yeah," Cobb said, "I put a refill set in de bow."

"Let's change them," Jack said.

Undoing the stainless steel cir-clips, they slid the empty bottles from the backpacks and replaced them.

"Watch it with the o-rings," Jack said, attaching the double hose US divers' regulator to his J valve. "If they're not seated right you'll leak air like crazy."

Henderson carefully reattached his regulator and Cobb slid the empty bottles under the aft seat, and then Henderson seemed to hesitate for a second.

"What about the shark?"

"He's gone after the turtles. I don't think we're on the menu today," Jack replied.

The water was a lot shallower at the head of the underwater ravine and they were unlikely to run into another big shark.

Back on the schooner, Megan and Benny sat in the cockpit having a soda. They finished their chores just before ten thirty and were taking a quick break. Megan pressed her eyes to a pair of binoculars to check out the scene at the dive site. After a moment she passed them to Benny.

"Can you see what's going on over there?"

Taking the glasses from her, he looked through them for a second.

"It look like dey change de dive tanks. Yeah, Skip and de Yankee man going down again."

Megan decided to go for it.

"Listen, Benny," she said. "I'm going below for a little while to check on something. Stay here and keep a lookout for me and if you see them getting ready to come back, call me right away."

"Sure ting, Meg," Benny replied.

She left him looking through the binoculars and went below to Henderson's cabin. Opening the door, she crept in and closed it behind her. Megan was even more nervous this time and kept on listening out for the sound of Benny's voice. Henderson had unpacked since the last time she and Jack had been in the room, and there was stuff all over the place. There were clothes piled on the upper bunk and in the drawers and on the small side dresser there was a large cream file folder with a sheaf of papers inside. Without expecting anything much she took them out and began reading the first page.

After the first few lines she took in a sharp breath and her hands began trembling. Her instincts had been right all along. These people weren't just here for a diving holiday and as she continued to read on, her fear for their safety grew with every line.

CHAPTER TEN

1692, Father Sebastiano

Perching on the edge of the bed, Megan read the documents. They were typed in English, and the first pages spoke of a translation by a company in Barcelona. By the date shown, they'd been commissioned more than a year ago, at the request of a Senor Eduardo Hernandez.

Alameda Translation Services,
El Puerto Viejo 152,
Barcelona, Spain.
10th July 1967

Snr. Eduardo Hernandez,
88 Sutton Place,
New York, N.Y. 10666

Dear Sir,
Following your instructions, we have finally completed the last translations of the documents from the Royal Spanish Archives.
Since you first contacted us a year ago, we have worked to try and piece together the fragments of photocopied paper and this is the result. It has been most difficult, as the fragments were in no order. However, we have managed to place them in correct chronology.
We have carried out the actual translations as carefully as possible, taking into account the differences of the 17th Century Spanish language. We have also followed your instructions with regard to making the English text as close to the old Spanish as possible.
It appears this is the testimony of an illiterate Spanish seaman, who was the sole survivor of a shipwreck in 1653. The account was recorded in 1692 by one Father Sebastiano, a monk serving at the Lady of Mercy Mission in Cartagena in that year. It seems as though the story was recounted to the monk

over a period of three days when the seaman was on his deathbed. According to the text, he died within a few moments of uttering his final words.

Please note the attached invoice, listing the hours at the agreed rate of five hundred pesetas per hour. I would appreciate your settlement of this final invoice as soon as possible.

Sincerely yours,
Jose Rodriguez (Head Translator)

The next document was even more fascinating. Megan quickly read on.

Mission of Our Lady of Mercy,
Her Holy Majesty's Port of Cartegena, 1692

Today began a very strange incident. At the evening hour, a wretched look-ing soul appeared at the doors of our Mission asking for the Bishop. We have no Bishop here, but being the master I was summoned. At first, I took the man to be an Indian so dark was his skin, but upon closer examination it was revealed the swarthy complexion of a man of my own race, albeit very old. His grey hair was braided in the style of the Indians of this coast and his face greatly lined, as if from many years in the tropical sun.

He stood, bent with age on our steps, but he smiled weakly at me as if sat-isfied of some great accomplishment. I inquired of his needs and in the Spanish of old Cadiz he replied to me.

"Padre, I have held a great secret in my breast for all these years and now before I die I wish to lift that burden from my soul. I have walked these five days to find you and I beg that you take me in and that I may give you my last testimony."

Being good Christian servants of his most Holy Majesty and curious of this strange old man, we decided to take him in and so doing took him to the ser-vant's kitchen, where we gave him some porridge. He walked with a crab-like gait as if suffering from some old wound and when I made inquiry of this he smiled slightly saying that it was related to an old horse-riding injury.

He ate slowly and sparingly of the porridge and when he was finished I asked him to tell us of his reason for coming to our mission.

"Padre," he sighed, "I have a heavy secret that I have need to divulge of before I die. It is like a great weight and I must rid myself of it, lest my soul not rest in peace."

I inquired of him as to the nature of this great mystery and he replied thus;

"My name is Pedro Delgada, but what I have to say will take much time and I am very weak and tired. Will you not give me a pallet upon which to sleep and we will begin on the morrow?"

My curiosity was most aroused and I decided to let him stay the night. We gave him one of the small penitent's cubicles and having seen him lay himself on the wooden cot, I bade him good night and left him.

I returned at daylight to his chamber followed by my Indian servant carrying some bread. He was awake but made no effort to raise himself from the cot save to prop himself against the headrest. He seemed very frail and although he ate little of the bread, he was very appreciative.

"Good morning, Padre," he said, "Are you ready to hear my tale?"

I replied that I was most anxious to hear what it was that he thought so important.

"Padre," he began, "you are a good man and I will tell you my secret, but pray give me a little wine as none has passed my lips all these years."

I ordered my Indian servant to bring a cup of wine and after partaking of a few sips he began speaking in a slow, steady voice. I have recorded the account on paper and this is what he told me.

"I hold the key to a great mystery. The treasures of which I will speak have been mine alone for there is no other who has knowledge of this. My secret has lain hidden from the eyes of men on a far off coral reef for many years, but wait, I go ahead of myself."

"I was a poor sardine fisherman out of Cadiz and for the sake of my wife, Elena, and my baby daughter, I came to the galleon San Idelfonso to try and improve my position in life. I wished to save sufficient money to buy a sardine boat for ourselves. I came to Cartagena in 1653 in that ship under the command of Captain Dapena. He was a good man, but gone now like all the rest."

The old man paused for a moment and took another very small sip of wine. I could see that he was very weak and even talking seemed to tire him much, but he continued.

"We spent many months anchored in the port of Cartegena, waiting for the gold as it was slowly carried over the mountains. The Consul General Don Davila was in command of the garrison and all that took place. He was a cruel and evil man. It was he who tried to break me upon his wooden horse. You have seen the way I walk, Padre. It was Davila's horse which caused me this agony."

The old man described to me the instrument of torture used to render him and many others crippled. I cringed at the thought of such cruelty.

"*Padre, you look unwell. Have you not yourself stretched the life from hundreds of the poor inhabitants of this coast upon your rack in your quest to Christianize them?*"

I explained to the old man that he misconstrued, as that was God's work, and that which he described was of course not.

"*It is the same, Padre, but in any case let me continue before I tire, for I have much to say. We loaded the ship with the treasures from over the mountains for many months. Don Davila made us smelt the metal in the castillo, casting it into coins and ingots before taking it to the ship. Only the most beautiful pieces were saved. The Don himself supervised the packing of a number of beaten gold masks and intricately woven chains.*"

I inquired as to the fate of the man Don Davila. After another small sip of wine the old man smiled slightly and replied.

"*Padre, you are like a young boy with your impatience. Worry not, I will make known to you the whole of my story before I go. The man Don Davila came aboard the night before we sailed, with his wife and his young daughter. With them came their servants including some six Indians, two young females and four men. The Don and his family installed themselves in his quarters towards the after part of the ship. He professed his fidelity to wife, but the man spent many hours in the company of the two young Indian women he brought along for his pleasures.*"

I asked how he knew this, not of any desire for base or lustful information, but to understand how one of her Holy Majesty's good Christian servants could lay with not one, but two heretic women at once.

"*I know this, Padre, because I am a man, or I was once. Don Davila came every night to the small cabin of the Indian women, which was close to the place where I slept. I heard the cries of the women in the night as they performed his duties and I saw the marks and scars upon their skins where he had caused them to suffer. He was an evil man.*"

I crossed myself again. Such blasphemy comes from the mouth of this old man, but I bade him to continue and I dipped my quill into the inkpot again.

"*Yes, Padre, the fat belly of the San Idelfonso was finally filled with the gold and treasures from beyond the mountains and we made to leave the port of Cartagena. We sailed for 5 days to the northeast. How do I know this? I am not versed in the arts of navigation, but the compass I know, after all was I not a sardine fisherman of the Biscay? We sailed for 5 days and at which time the disaster took us.*"

"*A storm arose upon the sea and the wind and waves became most violent. Great seas broke over the San Idelfonso and our Captain bade us to reef down*" *the sails. Even though I still suffered greatly from my injuries upon the horse, I carried out my duties with the other men. The galleon was a stout and fine ship and we feared not for our lives. Through the night the tempest raged and Captain Dapena stayed on the deck, looking to the needs of his ship. In the final hour of darkness the ship struck hard, as if hitting a wall of solid stone.*

"The course of events following came to pass thus. Our ship leaned to one side and her masts broke off, falling into the sea. Many of us were washed into the turbulent waters then and drowned. As the storm raged I clung to the windward bulwarks under the cap rail. If I was to drown, then it would come to pass, but I would not invite this experience before its time.

"I felt the ship shudder and shake as she was pounded mercilessly upon the reef, for indeed it was a reef. Her bottom was ripped asunder and water flooded the hull quickly. Captain Dapena conducted himself with great honor, trying to lead the men in unlashing some spars that we might float upon them, but he and a number of others were killed instantly when a heavy cannon came loose from the windward side and fell upon their bodies, crushing them.

"As the dawn broke, the hopelessness of our situation became most apparent. It was clear the San Idelfonso was hard upon a coral reef, some of the jagged teeth visible through the surf. I searched for the shore but saw none. It seemed that we were upon the open sea with no land in sight. Then, from the corner of my eye I saw it, a pitifully small spit of sand with a rocky outcrop at the end. This land was almost awash in the huge seas. and I doubted that it was to be our salvation.

"Some of the men who still lived became mad and made to enter the hold where the Queen's treasures lay. Don Davila, however, was determined that this would not come to pass and he stood at the remnants of the hatch and with his blade ran through a number of those who tried in vain to pass. I felt sorry for his wife and daughter. Of them there was no sign. It was a certainty that they perished within the first few moments of the flooding of the hull as their accommodation was deep within the bowels of the San Idelfonso."

Megan paused for moment, hardly believing what she was reading.

"A small spit of land with a rocky outcrop at the end," she said to herself.

He's talking about Aves, she suddenly thought. So, that's why Henderson was out here, he was looking for the *San Idelfonso*. They were after the treasure, she thought in a panic, she'd have to warn Jack as soon as he got back.

121

Leaving the cabin for a moment, she popped her head up through the companionway hatch. The Boston Whaler was still anchored far over near the reef edge and Benny was still looking through the binoculars.

"Don't forget to call me if they start heading back," she reminded him before darting back into the cabin.

"Don't worry," Benny smiled, but he had stopped looking at the Whaler and had focused the binoculars at some birds ashore on the atoll.

Picking up the papers again, she read on.

The old man gave a great cough then and his spittle was flecked with blood. He lay back and closed his eyes momentarily. He had been speaking for a great time now and was near to collapse.

"Padre, I am greatly weakened, let me sleep again and when I have rested for a little while we will continue."

I thought for a moment about the old man's name and his tale. If this were indeed true, then this Pedro Delgada was a Christian man and one of his most Holy Majesty's subjects. I inquired of him that if he was a Christian man, then let me administer the Extreme Unction, lest he die unholy in his sleep and be forever damned. I asked him to confirm to me then that he had enjoyed the Holy Baptism that I might minister to him. He replied in the greatest of blasphemy.

"Padre, I have long since left the ways of your God. I have stood with my adopted people to worship their many gods and they have served me well. I will not change now on the eve of my departure from this earth."

Clearly I was in the presence of a true heretic, a servant of Satan. I crossed myself a number of times and said a special prayer to ward off the evil auras which must surely be emanating from the dark heart of this man.

"You must not speak thus in my presence." I told him, "I am bound not to witness heresy or pagan testament."

"Padre, fear not, I am no more evil than the Indian servant who prepares your food, but I am weak now and beg of you, leave me to sleep."

I left him then to rest again in the small penitent's room. For me, there was little rest that night. I proceeded to the offices of the monastery where documents from the beginning of our time in Cartagena were kept. I searched for the records of the San Idelfonso. I was not long at this task, for indeed the incident was at the time cause for much concern and was well recorded.

There were a number of pages concerning the ship. We Spaniards are meticulous in our records and soon the story of the San Idelfonso's time in the New World lay before me. I carefully examined the pages before coming to the ones of interest. There were work lists concerning the careening of the ship. Caulking, orders, tarring, etc. There were quartermaster's lists and pursers requisitions. There were orders of punishment and lists of the dead, which the foul fevers had claimed. Lists of supplies landed and supplied to the castillo and lists of arms and armaments.

But the one document that was of the most interest was the ship's manifest, prepared by none other than His Excellency Don Davila. It read as follows:

In Her Most Holy Majesty's Port of Cartagena
The Year of Our Merciful Lord, 1653.

May it please your most Holy Majesty,
Please look upon the manifest below as an accurate and complete list of your own Majesty's treasure loaded and secured on the galleon "San Idelfonso". May it also please Your Majesty that your humble servant Don Davila has seen personally to the loading and care of your goods that they will arrive at your Courts intact.

Item	Weight
148 oaken casks of silver Santa Maria coin.	12193 libras.
142 teak chests gold coinage	13149 libras
118 oaken casks gold ingot	6559 libras
4 brass tins large uncut emeralds	20 libras
2 brass tins medium uncut emeralds	8 libras
1 oaken powder keg small uncut stones	130 libras
1 large brass tin semi-precious stones	6 libras
1 oaken cask woven gold chains	75 libras
2 teak chests Gold Indian artifacts	112 libras
2 teak chests misc. gold pieces	157 libras
1 brass tube of large uncut emeralds	9 libras

Your most Holy Majesty's humble and obedient servant,
Don Davila

Megan's breath came hard and fast. She didn't know how much a libra was, but even if it was a small measure it meant there had been a huge quantity of gold and other valuable jewels on that old ship. Hardly believing, she read on.

There had indeed been a great treasure in the hold of the San Idelfonso. I resolved to try upon the morrow to get from the old man the location of this wreck.

At dawn, I went to the penitent's room and the rays of the morning sun shone through the barred window upon the face of the old man. He was clearly near to death, unable even to raise himself from the cot. He did not partake of the bread and cheese my servant had brought, but he opened his eyes and seemed eager to finish his tale. I firstly inquired of him the fate of the man Don Davila.

"Padre, let me go back. As the sun rose on that day, the winds and seas reduced as quickly as they had come up, but many of us had already perished. Even in the earliest hour of the day, I could hear the screams of my shipmates as they were cut up by the great fish. Yes, Padre, as they floated upon the sea the sharks came up from the deep and dismembered them. I was fortunate in that I had secured a large piece of bulwark upon which I was able to drift towards the shore. It was big enough to keep all of me out of the sea. Many of the others were not so lucky.

"You asked of Don Davila? Fear not, for I will tell you what fate befell him. As I floated upon my wooden raft, I saw him near to me. He was paddling in my direction. It was clear to me his intent and as he came to within a few feet he began to rave.

"I am the Consul General and I claim this raft as my own, you must leave go as I have the Queen's interest."

He began to push me from my raft then and struck me with a long heavy brass tube the length of my arm.

"Move, you dog." he screamed at me, "Leave go as I have need of this wood."

"He had the strength of one gone mad and he threw me from my raft, hitting me about the head with the heavy tube. I had been grievously injured on his horse, but I was a seaman and a strong one. We were not far from the shore then and so I was able to swim to the sand.

"His Excellency drifted in later and as the tempest receded those of us who were still alive came together on the barren shore. There were not twenty of us left of the whole complement, and from where we stood that terrible morning we looked out onto the reef to what remained of the great ship. The seas had broken her so there remained little of her form. There were however the last of her bilges held to the shallow coral by the weight of her guns.

"Don Davila bade us to walk out onto the sharp corals and to bring the Queens treasures onto the land, as much of it was for the most part intact. We could walk to this part of the wreck in the sea only in depths to our thighs, so

the great fish could not devour our flesh. There were others though, and as the sharp reef cut our feet, voracious eel-like creatures took hold of some of us by the legs and mauled the flesh terribly. It was madness.

"We had no water and not a crust of bread to eat and we could not eat gold, but when one of our numbers made to protest this useless work, Don Davila drew his blade and ran the poor man through.

"At the end of the first day on our small purgatory, we began to suffer greatly from the sun and four more of our number perished. The night was worse and none could sleep, for our thirst was terrible. On the morning of our second day, the mad man forced us to carry the casks and boxes of the Queen's belongings to a strange cleft in the rocks to the north end of this devil's isle. It was an odd place and found quite by accident. One of the men fell through the loose sand as he made to relieve himself behind a rock. He forced us to secure the portion of the ships' cargo we had rescued inside a stone cavern, where it at least would be safe. It was a useless maneuver, for who would ever come upon this God forsaken place?

"In the night that came, two of the men became crazed and entered the sea, whereupon they disappeared. I decided to leave that place. I was a fisherman and if I was to die then I would die upon the sea and not on this spit of land. And so I went to the edge of the shore in the darkness and prepared a raft. I found the same piece that Don Davila had stolen from me after the wreck and with bits of cordage I lashed other timbers together. Before daylight I had fashioned a serviceable craft. But first there was something I had to do."

The old man paused for a moment, for he had been long speaking but he was anxious to get this tale out and he made to continue.

"Padre, you asked of the fate of Don Davila? Listen now to what I tell you. At dawn I went to him as he lay exhausted on the sand and I took him by the hair, dragging him to the edge of the shore, which was not far. He seemed weakened, as we all were, and did not struggle. I pressed my face close to his then. Do you not remember me then, Your Excellency? It is I, Pedro Delgada, the poor seaman that you made to ride upon your horse. I think there was vague recognition, but it made no difference. I slammed his head upon the coral a few times and then I held his head below the surface of the water. I felt him struggle and as the life left him I released him for the huge eels which had come into the shallows to scavenge the remains of our dead. I took from his breast coat the brass tube with which he had struck me. Will it surprise you, Padre, to know that I took much pleasure in killing him?"

I crossed myself again as the old man paused for a moment. He had killed a nobleman and servant of her Holy Majesty. Could I in honor continue to allow myself to hear this? I decided that as it were I must hear all. I inquired of him then the location of the ship.

"Ah yes, Padre, this is the most important part for you, is it not? But wait, I have more to say, do you not wish to hear of my rescue and my life as it followed?"

I was not in truth interested in this part of his tale, wishing rather to secure the important details, but he continued his rambling.

"Padre, I pushed my raft into the sea and drifted for days, until I thought that I would surely perish. The hot sun peeled the skin from my back and my tongue swelled, becoming like a huge dried slug within my mouth. My eyes grew opaque and near the end I could see no more.

"The great sharks circled my raft endlessly, waiting for me to assuage their hunger, but I denied them this. I fell asleep on the last night knowing I would not wake to see the next day, but I was wrong. My raft was washed ashore on one of the coastal islands to the west of here and I was saved by the Indians who lived and fished there."

I implored the old man again to shorten this aspect of his tale. He was very weak and I wanted him to say the name of the place where the San Idelfonso lay before he died.

"Padre, you are most anxious to hear of the treasure? Fear not, you will know of its location soon enough. But first, let me finish. It is my wish that you hear all of my story."

I resigned myself to the fact that I would listen to his ramblings and I dipped the pen again.

"The Indians adopted me, Padre. They took me as one of their own. Their women nursed me back to health and after some months I was able to stand and walk again. They called me Mang, the Indian name for crab, because of the way I walked. I lived with these, my new people for the next thirty-nine years, Padre, and life was good.

"In the passage of time, the memory of my wife and family faded, for I knew in truth I would never return there. The Indians taught me to catch the fish of these waters and I took four good wives from amongst them. Can you believe, Padre, that I am a grandfather many times over?"

What heathen filth had this old scoundrel committed? Four wives indeed. However, I implored him to continue.

"When it became evident that I would die soon, they took me to the cliffs above the village and left me facing the sun, as is their custom. But I did not die, Padre, I have walked five days along the coast to reach you."

I interrupted then, inquiring as to the location of these Indian peoples, as they would surely be in need of Christian instruction, but the old man would not divulge this to me.

"*Padre, I will not tell you this for it would sadden me greatly to have them corrupted by you. They are a simple, good folk and that they remain so is important to me. Now Padre, you have been most patient. The treasure of the San Idelfonso lies some five days sailing to the northeast of Cartagena, upon a coral atoll no bigger than this town.*"

I asked the old man if he could be more specific and he gave me this reply.

"*Padre, that is all I can or will tell you and it is enough, but do you truly understand why I have walked five days through the jungle of this coast to tell you this story?*"

I bade him to tell me.

"*Because, Padre, I know that you will tell my words to your masters in Spain and they will swallow them like a fish takes the bait. My words will be like worms in their guts causing them to kill and connive to find the treasure of the San Idelfonso. You see, Padre, I leave you with a bad joke.*"

At this time, the old man's face broke into a wide deathly rictus revealing his rotting teeth. I told him that revenge was God's alone and that he should not seek to punish for the injustice he had suffered at the hands of Don Davila. I told him that in any case none would believe his tale, a crazy old man with a crazy story. Then he died. As the life left his emaciated body he laughed at me, a loud, rasping death rattle.

In the final seconds he grimaced and opened his tattered robe. A long brass tube fell from his gnarled hand to the stone floor where the top became undone, allowing a flood of huge uncut green emeralds to roll out. The old man's eyes closed then, the life having indeed left him. I picked up the brass tube, replacing the emeralds.

In closing this I must say that I brought the emeralds and this tale to the present Commander of Cartagena, His Excellency General Don Alfonso Ramierez. He gratefully agreed to take custody of this evidence and he bade me speak to none about this lest men search for it wrongly. Save for this record which I have kept, I have told no one. The General plans to immediately dispatch a ship to search for the wreck of the San Idelfonso.

Our Lady of Mercy Mission,
Cartagena,
This Year of our Lord, 1692

Megan felt as weak as a kitten. This was a crazy story, but it had to be true. There was one last page and she quickly finished it.

Father Sebastiano.
Our Lady of Mercy Mission,
Cartagena,
This Year of our Lord, 1694

As I prepare to leave this unholy land and return to Spain, I wish to record that although the General's ships and others have searched the Caribbean sea for months, no trace of the San Idelfonso has been found. The General's soldiers have searched also for the Indians of whom the old man spoke. Of them, there is also no trace. I adhere to his wishes, however, and I will disclose to none the contents of this record.

Father Sebastiano

Drained, Megan sat on the edge of the bed with the file in her hand. She was shocked by what she'd just read, but one message seemed to ring through loud and clear. There was going to be trouble over this, a whole lot of trouble.

Back at the reef Jack and Henderson had donned their full scuba bottles and rolled backwards over the Whaler's low gunwale into the water above the cannons. They quickly descended twenty feet to the bottom.

CHAPTER ELEVEN

Fandango's Gold

The visibility was much better as they descended to the head of the underwater ravine. Bright flickering rays of sunlight played over the coral arch into the small amphitheater where the coral incrusted guns lay. The shallow depth made diving easy and there was no current. Pulling his dive knife from the plastic sheath on his calf, Jack poked around the muzzle of a large cannon. Small fish crowded around his hands as he stirred up the sand. Little wrasses and juvenile snappers rushed in, grabbing tiny crabs that suddenly found themselves floating a foot above the bottom. After twenty minutes he still hadn't found anything. He ran his hands through the soft sand around the breach of the big cannon, but that's all he found, sand. The entire ship seemed to have vanished leaving only the iron guns.

Suddenly, the tip of his knife hit something solid. Brushing away the sand, he slowly uncovered a thick curved object, but after chipping away at it with the blade it turned out to be a piece of whitened dead coral. About twenty feet to his left Henderson dug around another of the guns with his hands. His lack of diving experience was evident by the massive rush of bubbles escaping from his regulator; he was using a lot of air.

Then his eye caught something. An unusual looking circular clump half-buried beside a sea fan. Swimming over, he cleared the sand with sweeping motions of his hand. Gradually he uncovered a coral incrusted object the size of a trash can cover. Henderson, noticing that he'd just found something, swam over hovering at his elbow. With difficulty Jack picked it up.

"Heavy," he mumbled into his mouthpiece.

He was surprised at the weight; it pulled him down to the sand immediately. Henderson swam over and knelt on the sand next to him. He reached out and took the object for moment, examining it closely. He seemed excited;

it was definitely manmade. Jack signaled to surface. The Whaler floated less than fifteen feet above them and they could more easily check out what they had found aboard the boat. Adding air to their inflatable safety vests, they ascended slowly. Henderson reached the rail of the boat first and Jack surfaced a second later. Raising his left hand, he took a hold of the gunwale.

"Grab this thing," he said, spitting out his mouthpiece while raising the disk with Henderson.

"Heavy, skip," said Cobb his big hands grabbing the disk on both sides.

Passing it to Garcia, he turned to help the divers out of the water.

Surrendering their backpacks, they pulled themselves over the low gunwale into the boat.

"Is a rock?" Garcia asked, holding the flat clump of coral on his knees while running his fingers over it. About eighteen inches across, it was about six inches thick.

"Don't think so, but let's find out," Jack replied and taking a large heavy steel-backed dive knife from below the seat, he gave the mass a few good whacks.

It split open laterally exposing a stack of four blackened plates. They were ornate with engraved rims. Using the edge of his towel, Jack wiped the top one with a circular motion. The black oxidation of the centuries disappeared and bright metal appeared, sparkling in the Caribbean sun. Even after all those years the silver was as brilliant as it had been when it was first minted.

"Alright!" Laura yelled, clapping her hands.

Crowding around Garcia, they ran their fingers over the plates. talking excitedly and then Jack noticed something.

"Look at this," he said rubbing the boarder rim. The words *San Idelfonso* appeared as if by magic. "Must be off of a very old ship," he said, taking a closer look.

Henderson stopped talking and Laura and Garcia turned to look at him.

"You recognize the name?" Henderson asked guardedly.

"No, but it's Spanish. Lots of Spanish cargo vessels in the West Indies back in those days. This one ran into a piece of bad luck called Aves," Jack replied.

There were a few seconds of silence as Henderson glanced at Laura, but they said nothing.

"You want to dive again while we're here?" Jack asked, pointing into the water, "There could be more artifacts right below us. It's very shallow and I'm betting we won't see any more sharks this far in."

Henderson shook his head.

"We'll pass on anymore diving today, skipper. I don't like being shark bait." Henderson replied, "I'm going to spend the afternoon doing something relaxing."

"We are agreeing completely and totally," said Garcia.

"You're the one paying," Jack said, climbing towards the stern and the outboard, "but you need to know that there's a change in the weather coming and if the afternoon report says anything about storm development, we may have to leave tonight."

Jack's prognosis on the weather didn't seem to register. Henderson's mind was somewhere else.

"Want to walk around the island?" Henderson asked, turning to Garcia.

"With pleasure. I will collect some eggs to eat as well."

Well, he was from Puerto Rico, Jack thought, and bird's eggs were a delicacy there too.

"That's it then. Garcia and I will go ashore for while. It's too early to go back to the boat for lunch."

Back on the schooner Benny took another quick look through the binoculars at the Whaler. The divers were back aboard, but it was still anchored. He had a pressing need to go to the bathroom. Megan was still below, but he wouldn't be too long, he thought, heading forward towards the fo'c'sle hatch.

A moment later Jack started the outboard and sat down behind the steering wheel. Cobb hauled the anchor line in and after yanking it a couple of times, he felt the Danforth jump free from its position under the cannon. Jack checked his watch. It was ten past eleven. He didn't really care if the diving was over. He was already planning a return trip to Aves. If there was anything more below them, he would be back for it.

Steering out the channel and around the edge of the reef, he had a thought.

"We'll just swing by the boat, and drop off the dive gear and I'll tell Megan we'll be back for lunch at about one thirty," Jack said.

"Drop me off too, I'm not up for any hikes today," Laura replied, glancing at Henderson, "and I'll tell Megan about lunch."

"Good," Jack said as they crossed the lagoon.

A few minutes later the Whaler slid easily alongside the *Fandango*.

"Back around one thirty," he said to Laura as she got up from the varnished seat.

"Sure," she mumbled, climbing the boarding ladder.

When she was on deck, Cobb stood up in the bow and called for his shipmate.

"Benny, you lazy buggah, where you is nuh? Come help me," he said, but his friend was nowhere to be seen.

Cobb lifted the dive gear up over the rail piece by piece laying it on the deck near the rail.

"Dat buggah always in de toilet," Cobb muttered to himself, "Must have worms."

"Laura, pass us the Pentax, and the big lens, will you?" Henderson asked.

Nodding, she disappeared into the cockpit and returned a second later with a small black camera bag and handed it to Garcia.

"In case we see one of those tourist panoramas," Henderson said, smiling.

"Lots of willing subjects ashore if you like birds," Jack replied.

They sped off quickly after that, heading towards the north end of the beach.

Down in the cabin, Megan was shaken out of her numb reverie by the sound of footsteps approaching. She jumped up nervously, spilling some of the loose papers onto the floor.

"Benny, is that you?" she called out urgently, but there was no reply.

As she dropped to her knees to try and pick up the papers, the door burst open. Laura appeared with a dangerous look on her face. In one swift glance, she took in the scene, Megan on the floor with the translation papers in disarray.

"Thought I'd find you in here," Laura said caustically, standing in front of her.

After her initial shock, Megan realized she wasn't afraid. Instead, she felt a resentment stir deep within her.

"I knew there was more to you three than met the eye. Now I know exactly what it is," she said angrily.

Picking up the rest of the papers, she stood up.

Laura moved slowly over to the teak dresser as she spoke.

"And what is that?"

"I'm sure you know all about these documents. I'm going to show them to Jack," she finished defiantly, waving them at Laura, and with a flick of her hair she moved towards the door.

Before she had taken a step Laura blocked her exit. Megan suddenly found herself staring at the business end of a snub-nosed .38 pistol.

"Don't think so, sweetie," Laura said in an almost bored voice.

Megan looked at her with contempt. She thought for one crazy moment about tackling Laura. She was taller than the blond was, but the gun canceled that idea.

"Up on deck," Laura ordered her.

She motioned with the gun for Megan to leave the cabin.

Benny came up the forward hatch just in time to see the two women appear in the cockpit. Megan watched helplessly as he walked aft along the deck towards them.

"Benny, you were supposed to warn me," she said frustrated.

"But I was in de toilet," he replied a little confused.

Megan just shook her head, and then Benny noticed the gun in Laura's hand.

"Come back here to the cockpit where I can keep an eye on the both of you," Laura told him sternly while motioning with the .38.

"What kind of joke all you playing, Megan? How she have a gun in she hand like dat?" he asked totally bewildered.

"They're after treasure out there," Megan told him.

"Treasure? Ain't no treasure out dere. Too many people look already."

"There's treasure," Megan replied.

"There's treasure alright, and I'll use this if I have to," Laura assured him as she waved him closer with the gun.

"It's no joke, just do what she says," Megan warned him.

Laura had Megan take one of the Dacron sail ties from the deck box and tie Benny's hands securely behind his back. Laura watched closely so there was no chance of her making a loose job of it. When Megan was finished she stood up and turned to Laura.

"You'll never get away with this. No one does," she warned her.

Laura smiled and then hit her in the face with the pistol. The snub barrel caught her on the right side of her lip. When Megan put her hand to her mouth, it came away wet with blood.

"No one cares what you have to say," she snapped.

Lightheaded, Megan half fell on the cockpit cushion next to Benny. I hope Jack comes back soon, she thought to herself. But then the thought crossed her mind that Jack and Cobb might be in the same trouble. Where were they anyway?

Cobb and Jack sat quietly on the bow of the Whaler as Henderson and Garcia walked away to the north along the sand. The hint of a low northerly swell had gradually appeared on the reef to the north over the last two hours and the sky was beginning to look a little suspicious. They knew enough about West Indian weather to realize that something was up.

"Skip, de weather changing you know," Cobb said, looking at the sky.

"I know, my friend, I know. I'll get the report this evening and then we'll decide. By tonight we may be running east as fast as the *Fandango* can get us there."

"We goin wait for dem?" Cobb asked, indicating the receding figures.

Jack looked towards the lagoon for a brief second.

"No. How 'bout some good old Bahamian conch chowder tonight?"

"Count me in, skip," Cobb replied, smiling.

"There's all kind of big ones here in the shallows," Jack replied. "We'll just walk along and see how we do."

Launching the Whaler, they pushed it in front of them as they waded the shallows at the head of the lagoon. Never venturing deeper than their waists, they began picking up really big conchs and putting them in the boat.

Walking over the warm sand towards the north end of the atoll, Henderson and Garcia left the lagoon. The sky was gradually turning overcast and low-lying clouds scudded overhead. Twenty minutes later they reached the rocky outcroppings at Aves' north end. The gargantuan boulders and monolithic slabs looked like a giant's rock pile, as if planted there for a reason.

"The rocks all look the same," Garcia said.

"Yes, but the cave is here somewhere. The *San Idelfonso* cave is here. I know it."

"If you say so, Eduardo."

"See those rocks?" Henderson said, pointing to some high slabs amidst the jumble of thirty-foot high boulders, "The entrance to the cave has got to be somewhere in there."

It was the only place they hadn't searched. Leading Garcia into the rock maze, he tried to imagine where the entrance could be. They had found nothing the previous day but the plate with the name *San Idelfonso* confirmed everything.

"This is definitely the atoll in the documents," Henderson said. "There is a cave here somewhere. We just have to look harder."

Like ants navigating paths of white sand amongst islands of stone, the two men walked around the boulders. They looked for some recognizable feature that would lead them to the entrance. One huge boulder looked much the same as another and the stone ramparts rose above their heads hiding any reference points he might have remembered. After twenty minutes Henderson was frustrated. They had wandered more than three hundred feet through the rock formation to the water's edge. He gazed for moment out over the Caribbean. The swell was beginning to break on the barrier reef and the air was damp with the sea. This was the windward end of the atoll and the wind had clear access to the shore. The strong, northeast trade wind lifted little sandstorms, blowing grit into their faces.

"Where is this cave?" Henderson asked impatiently.

Suddenly, there it was, a triangular entrance at the base of a high stone slab. Walking over to the four-foot high tunnel mouth, he dropped to his knees.

"This must be it," he said over his shoulder, "I'll go first and you follow."

Crawling into the small opening single file on their hands and knees, they dug a little trough in the white sand.

"It ees dark in here," Garcia said.

"Just stay behind me. The cave must be ahead," Henderson replied.

The winding trail took them around giant slabs of rock and pieces of boulder, until suddenly they entered a high roofed grotto.

"This is it, the cave of lights," Henderson said, "Just like the old papers say."

He was thrilled by the strange and eerie phenomena. It was the same play of lights that Pedro Delgada had seen all those years ago.

They stood there for a few minutes watching the light reflecting on the stone walls. It was beautiful, but Henderson seemed disappointed.

"It's open to the ocean."

"What do you mean?" Garcia asked, puzzled.

"Well, after three hundred years whatever was in here has probably gone into the sea along that deep wall we were diving yesterday."

Recalling the dive, he knew that if anything had been washed out of the grotto, it was irretrievable. It would have gone deep, real deep.

"There must be more," Henderson said, trying to stem his feelings of disappointment.

Garcia began wandering around the edges of the chamber. He made his way to the far end where the sunlight from outside hit the sandy bottom and reflected up onto the cathedral ceiling and walls. The crystal clear water lapped gently on the sandy edge of the grotto where the underwater tunnel to the outside began. As his feet touched the water Garcia let out an exclamation.

"Look, Eduardo, there is another place."

"What, another cave?" Henderson asked.

"Possible, come and look."

Garcia moved aside so that he could look. Peering into the cleft, he saw a narrow crack in the stone. It was visible only from the seaward end of the cavern. From where they had been standing it was just a narrow seam in the wall.

"There's another chamber about twenty feet further in," Henderson said. turning.

It was actually a rift in one of the giant boulders, where some titanic force had cracked it millennia ago.

"Big enough to go through?" Garcia asked him.

"It's straight. May be enough for us edge along sideways. I'm going to try it out," he said, edging his shoulder into the cleft.

Henderson took the lead and Garcia followed. The sand became noticeably drier as the path took on a slight rise. Just enough light filtered in from cracks in the formation above for them to see.

Twenty feet further along they exited the cleft. Immediately there was another tiny sand corridor with yet another tiny opening directly ahead at the base of two massive boulders. Similar to the one on the outside, the small triangular opening formed where the two colossal stones met the sand.

"Hope nobody's got claustrophobia," Henderson said.

"No, Eduardo, I 'ave been in many tight places," Garcia said, attempting humor.

There was barely space for one person and they crawled in on their stomachs, slithering along the tunnel for fifteen feet. Suddenly it opened into another much larger stone cavern. Although similar to the first, this one however was higher above sea level and inside the air was still and dry. The only light seemed to come from a small opening in the ceiling, giving the place an eerie atmosphere.

Their eyes slowly adjusted to the gloom and Henderson took in the layout of the cavern. It was longer and bigger than the first and the grey steely colored stone rose in two huge slabs at the top, one overlapping the other. At one end was the entrance they had just come through while the other was blocked by a twenty-foot boulder.

He was the first to look down. The stone floor was uneven with deep parallel rifts. From about two feet across to a few inches the channels ran lengthwise in the chamber. As his eyes adjusted to the dimmer light, Ed Henderson suddenly became aware of what lay at their feet.

"Garcia, look at this!" he shouted, falling to his knees.

His quavering voice echoed strangely off the stone walls. Garcia stooped down to get a better look at what Henderson had found. There, littered in the crevices, lay the lost treasure of the *San Idelfonso*. Human eyes had not seen what lay before them in more than three hundred years.

Over the centuries the wooden chests and casks had disintegrated. Part of the long lost treasure had itself been washed out of the caves by violent storms and hurricanes, explaining Jack Carlton's coins of the year before. But most of the heavy gold, silver and other artifacts remained where they had originally been stowed, settling into the natural rifts of the stone floor. Henderson greedily ran his fingers through the glittering horde. He laughed and shouted like a man intoxicated. The men seemed crazed by the gold, tossing coins into the air by the handful.

"Can you believe it?" Henderson exclaimed again joyfully.

Garcia dropped to his knees, and began lifting gold bars and coins. Even he was animated for once. Picking up a beautiful ceremonial mask of beaten gold, he placed it against his face, laughing like a deranged fool.

"El Dorado, it is the treasure of the El Dorado. You have done it, Eduardo. It is just as you said and we have found it," he said almost religiously.

There were scores of gold ingots visible, ranging in size from a bar of chocolate to a book and everywhere there were hundreds of coins. The bottom of each crevice was littered with whatever had fallen there. Each was a shimmering melange of treasure mixed with sand and dried seaweed.

A second later Henderson spotted an unbelievably large emerald lying on a pile of gold coin. He tried to pick it up but it seemed a little stuck, so he gave it a good yank and it came loose, all twelve inches of it. The ceremonial dagger had an eight-inch gold blade and the huge emerald crowned the top of the hilt. Looking at the dagger, he suddenly realized the magnitude of the fortune they had stumbled on, and he fell silent, deep in thought.

There was almost an equal amount of silver. Where the gold had proven impervious to the salt air the silver had been darkened over the passage of time. The ingots looked almost black and many of the coins had been fused together into lumps. Underneath though, was the gleam of clean, bright metal waiting for someone to restore its luster. Garcia scratched one of the black bars against the edge of the stone and the shine of silver immediately shone through.

Henderson looked at his watch. They had been in the caves for over half an hour, although it only seemed like a few minutes.

"Alright, stop playing with that stuff," he snapped at Garcia, "You'll have plenty of time later, right now we need to go back to the yacht for a couple of duffel bags and the aluminum cases. We'll use them to carry this stuff."

Henderson put a few choice pieces in the black Pentax bag to show Laura.

Walking along the shore towards the spot where Jack had dropped them off, Henderson and Garcia talked.

"We'll have to deal with Carlton now," Henderson said, outlining what they would do when they reached the Boston Whaler.

"I understand, Eduardo."

As they came in sight of the beached skiff, Cobb stood up. He had been sitting on the bow as Jack knelt in the sand, cleaning conchs with his dive knife.

"Skip, they coming back now."

"OK, I'll leave these conchs here. I'll come back and clean the rest later," he said dropping his dive knife to the sand.

Suddenly Jack's blood ran cold. As he looked at the two approaching men his instincts told him something was wrong and a second later they were confirmed. From a distance he saw Garcia reach into the black Pentax bag and pull something out. He quickly placed it beneath his flowered shirt.

"Cobb my man, we've got trouble," Jack said urgently.

"What, skip?" his friend asked.

"Our Puerto Rican tourist just pulled a gun from that black camera case of his."

"Dat's trouble alright, Skip," Cobb replied.

"Get the boat in the water now," he said in a low voice, motioning for him to launch the skiff.

Cobb had seen the gun too and needed no encouragement. They pushed the boat into the water, but just as she began to float Garcia suddenly took off and sprinted the last seventy feet.

"Jump in," Jack shouted, climbing over the bow.

Garcia realized what they were up to, and quick as a cat pulled a big colt .45 from the small black camera bag.

"Quick, push off," Jack shouted, but it was too late.

Garcia reached Cobb before he could get in. Grabbing him around the neck, he pushed the gun to his temple.

"What the hell do you think you're doing?" Jack shouted angrily.

"Sorry, this is as far as you go," Henderson replied calmly, catching up a few seconds later. He pulled a heavy gold chain from the bag. It had a six-inch cross at the end.

"Captain, I present the newly discovered treasure of the *San Idelfonso*," Henderson smiled.

"Where? There's nothing in that cave but wet sand," Jack said.

"Correct, not in your cave, the second one. Had you looked a little harder last year you might have found it and saved yourself all this trouble."

Jack felt the world brake, and time seemed to pass in slow motion. He waited for Garcia to pull the trigger of the big pistol and blow Cobb's brains out, but he didn't. He kept it pressed against the seaman's head and Jack felt a tiny ray of hope. He slowly eased over the rail into the knee-deep water.

"Get into the boat," Garcia ordered Cobb.

He and Henderson climbed in afterwards, leaving Jack standing there.

Suddenly a pattern formed. It was as though someone had just handed him the final piece of a puzzle, and it all fell into place. The theft of the coin in English Harbour, selling the others to Harry Bartram, Henderson's sudden arrival and request to come out to Aves. They hadn't just stumbled upon the treasure.

A find like this was reason enough for men to kill, Jack thought to himself. In fact he'd come up against a few who'd kill for a whole lot less, but he wasn't exactly sure how far Henderson was prepared to take it. His gut instinct told him that he and his crew were in trouble. He was convinced now that Henderson had purposely come here to find this treasure. It all seemed to fit now, like a glove. He had to keep calm and think quickly.

"You knew about this horde, didn't you?" Jack asked.

Henderson leaned over the rail towards Jack a little, so that he'd be able to hear him clearly.

"Oh I knew about it alright, but you and that Bartram character led me to it."

"Bartram, the English jeweler?" Jack asked, thinking aloud.

"Yes, but he has no throat now, not possible to talk," Garcia told him with a half smile on his lips.

"You killed him?"

It was more of a statement than a question.

"He was a liability," Henderson told him.

"What about everybody else that knows we're out here?" Jack asked angrily.

"Come on, Carlton, who else knows? As far as the rest of the world is concerned you're off on charter for another week at least. I plan to be long gone by then."

Henderson was probably right. They weren't due back for a week and he hadn't been in radio contact since they left.

"Just tell your crewman to cooperate, otherwise my friend here will put another opening in his head," Henderson instructed.

As Jack glanced towards Cobb, the full realization of what had happened hit home and a hard look came over his face.

"The penny finally drops?" Henderson said sarcastically, "I have to thank you, of course, for helping me find it. Unfortunately I have no further use for you now, only your boat and your crew."

Jack believed him.

"Just do like they say, Cobb. Don't try anything that'll get you into trouble."

Even as he said it he knew it was a little late to be offering that kind of advice.

"Okay Skip," Cobb said, looking pretty unhappy.

A moment later the Whaler sped away from the beach and Jack waded from the warm water and sat down on the sand. He was suddenly worried about Meg. If they laid one hand on her, there would be hell to pay. He'd make sure of that. But how?

CHAPTER TWELVE

Marooned

Cobb brought the Whaler alongside the *Fandango*'s boarding ladder and Garcia smiled for the first time since the trip began. Laura stood on deck holding the .38 police special in her hand. They climbed aboard and Henderson glanced over at the two sitting in the cockpit.

"What happened to her?" he asked.

Megan had crusted blood on her chin and her bottom lip was swollen.

"Caught her reading the documents in your cabin."

Henderson didn't seem worried.

"Doesn't matter now. It's all over, we've found it."

"How much?" Laura asked excitedly.

"Tons of it, just lying around inside the cave," he replied, laughing loudly.

Henderson handed her the ornate gold cross and cross-studded with emeralds that he had brought aboard. She noticed that Jack wasn't with them.

"Fantastic," she said, "Where's Carlton?" she asked, glancing towards the shore.

"On the beach for now."

She wasn't sure what the "for now" meant but didn't pursue the question.

Cobb finished tying the Whaler's bowline to the forward turnbuckles and went to sit with Benny. Henderson walked over and stood above them.

"You two have got an important choice to make, so listen up. You with me so far?" Henderson asked him coldly.

"Ah listenin'," Cobb said, scowling.

He'd seen the gold pieces that they had brought back and put together most of what was going on but was still finding it hard to believe. Benny just seemed dazed.

"You help us to sail back to the islands and I'll turn you loose when we get there or I'll have Laura run you over to the island to join your skipper. What'll it be?"

Cobb didn't doubt that he would carry out the threat. It wasn't much of a choice, but at least if they stayed with the boat, there was a chance that maybe later he could somehow get back to rescue his friend. Cobb replied for them both.

"Okay, man, we'll do what you say, but what about skipper Jack, you ain't goin leave him dere?"

"Just worry about your own hide, not Carlton's. Now, we're just going to tie you up for a little while and you can explain the choices to your quiet shipmate."

Henderson nodded to Garcia and they ushered the two West Indian seamen down to the master stateroom and after trussing up their hands and ankles, locked the heavy teak cabin door shut, so there was no chance of escape.

Afterwards Henderson went to his cabin. Emptying two large army duffel bags onto the bed, he tossed the clothes aside. Stripping the false bottoms, he removed the three firearms hidden underneath. Folding the bags under his arm, he carried them and the guns back up on deck.

Placing the Uzi machine gun and two Colt .45 pistols on the white canvas cockpit cushions, he opened a small black Adidas bag with extra ammo. Checking the clips carefully, he made sure they were loaded and ready to fire. Garcia picked up the Uzi and slung it over his shoulder.

"We need to empty her camera trunks," Henderson said to him, pointing to the aluminum containers containing the equipment, "We'll use them to stow the gold."

"I will do it now," Garcia said.

Laura looked hesitant.

"Those cost me a lot of money."

"Don't worry. I'll get you new ones," he told her.

Garcia dragged the two trunks forward until they were near the rail and removed the camera and then the magnetometer. Stripping out the form-fitted Styrofoam packing, he pitched it over the side.

"They are ready, Eduardo," he told Henderson.

"Alright, let's go. Got a lot of work to do," he replied enthusiastically.

"What do you want to do with her?" Laura asked him, motioning towards Megan with her gun.

"Take her to the beach when we go in. She can keep Carlton company."

Garcia climbed down the boarding ladder to the Whaler, and Henderson passed the light trunks and duffel bags over the schooner's caprail to the Puerto Rican, who placed them in the bow.

Henderson turned to Laura.

"You said you knew how to drive one of these things?" he questioned, pointing to the Whaler.

"No problem," she replied, "Driven small boats all my life."

"Let's go then," Henderson said.

Laura turned to Megan, sneering at her.

"Alright you, get your scrawny butt in the boat. We're going to give you your chance to be alone with Jack. That's what you've always wanted."

Megan said nothing. She picked up her little pouch purse from the cockpit, climbed down the ladder and into the launch.

Laura drove the Whaler to the beach with obvious skill. As the bow hit the sand Jack stood up, walking towards them, but Henderson waved him off with his pistol. Laura was carrying now as well and the Puerto Rican had a goddamned Uzi on his shoulder.

"I have no problem using this if I have to," Henderson warned him.

"Meg, are you alright?" Jack asked concerned.

Noticing her cut lip, his anger began to mount.

"No, I'm not alright," she snapped angrily, "I should never have come out here with you in the first place."

Garcia waited until she stood to get out of the Whaler and then smiling he thumped her hard in the small of the back, catapulting her headfirst into the shallow water. Jack quickly waded over to help her.

The two men got out of the boat and Garcia picked up the sail ties he had brought along. Motioning for Jack and Megan to move up the beach, he followed with the Uzi. Using the sail ties, he tied their hands behind their backs.

"You greasy dago, when I get loose I'm going teach you a lesson you'll never forget," Jack told him.

The Puerto Rican pushed him to his knees on the sand.

"Si, and how you are going to do that, gringo, grow some wings?" Garcia said laughing and then walloped him on the back of his head with the Uzi's barrel.

Jack saw stars as blood oozed from a nasty inch-long gash, but he flinched as Garcia bound Megan's hands behind her back. She was still standing and he was enjoying it, smiling as he twisted her arms, hurting her. She gave a little whimper, head down.

"Eh, gringo, your red haired woman is hot, yes? Perhaps she needs something to remember me," he said, turning to Jack.

Sneering, he ran his hand up the front of her tee shirt. Laura studied Jack's face with a contemptuous little smile. She was curious to see how he would react. Garcia moved behind Megan and held her roughly around the waist with his left hand as with his right he pulled her t-shirt up and ripped the bikini top down, exposing her round white breasts. He began running his hand over them.

"Leave her alone," Jack shouted, struggling with his bonds.

Henderson stopped the sick charade before it could go any further.

"Leave that. We have things to do," he shouted.

The grinning Puerto Rican stopped immediately, pushing Megan down on her knees in the sand. Henderson really had some kind of a hold over the guy. Jack felt an icy anger and he knew he would kill Garcia the first chance he got.

"Later, little one, later," Garcia promised her and as a parting shot he planted a well-aimed kick in Jack's stomach. Retching, Jack rolled over in the sand.

Leaving the larger aluminum cases in the Whaler, Henderson and Garcia turned towards the caves with the duffel bags.

"If they even so much as twitch, shoot them both," Henderson instructed Laura as they walked away.

When the two men left, she turned to them.

"Just keep your butts right there and no one will get hurt."

She backed off twenty feet to perch on the Whaler's bow. Jack and Megan lay on their sides in the sand. His hands were already beginning to swell from lack of circulation and his stomach hurt like hell, but he rolled onto his side facing Laura.

"You've never heard of anyone getting away with something like this. They'll find you in the end," he told her.

"That just it, Carlton. If you get away with it, no one ever hears about it," she replied.

"How'd you get mixed up in this anyway?"

"Money, but you were quite a bonus too," she added as an afterthought.

Jack said nothing and she turned to Megan.

"Your honey of a skipper and I had a real hot little adventure in his cabin last night. We just steamed up the portholes," Laura goaded.

"Don't listen to her. Nothing happened," Jack began, but she cut him off.

"Oh? Did he ever show you his shark bite?" Laura asked contemptuously.

"I saw her standing in your doorway naked. What? Was she reading you a bedtime story?" Megan snapped back at him.

Jack could see there was no use trying to explain how he really felt. He'd tell her later, but right now he needed to think of a way to get them both out of the mess they were in.

Laura bent over the boat and got a floppy sun hat out from under the varnished seat. Realizing her two prisoners couldn't possibly go anywhere, she wandered off a ways and began poking around for shells near the water's edge with her foot. Momentarily she turned back to check on her captives.

After a while the pain in Jack's head receded until it was just a dull aching throb. He sat up in the sand and turned to Megan. He decided to take a moment to try and put her in the picture.

"We're in trouble. There's enough gold up in those rocks over there to finance a revolution."

"I know all about it; it was a galleon called the *San Idelfonso*," she replied, sounding pissed off.

"How do you know that?" he asked, surprised.

"While you were out diving, I slipped down into Henderson's cabin again and found some documents. They were a translation of some old papers from the Spanish archives. It's the whole story of how this ship got wrecked here in 1653, loaded with bullion."

Taking it in, he put all the pieces together.

At the north end of the island Henderson and Garcia dragged the two duffel bags into the treasure chamber. The Puerto Rican laid them out on the floor, unzipping the tops.

"Don't worry about the silver," Henderson directed, "Just pick out the gold and jewels."

"Si, Eduardo. I will pick only them."

They spent the next hour loading the two heavy canvas bags with the treasures of the *San Idelfonso*. Beaten gold masks and chains appeared out of the crevices. They shook the sand from them before packing them in the cases. The beautiful artifacts that had been so laboriously handcrafted by the Inca people three hundred years ago were being readied yet again for another sea voyage. The gold ceremonial dagger and the assorted gold ingots that Don Davila had ordered melted and cast in the castillo of Cartagena all those years ago went in to the cases. They threw in gold coins by the handful, along with large gems of two or three different kinds. Huge green emeralds, both cut and uncut and beautiful pearls of impossibly large size and luster passed through their hands. Gold brooches and pins adorned with precious gems, along with a dozen other forms of jewelry, all went into the bags.

They worked for the most part silently, their minds totally absorbed by the task at hand. Finally, they were satisfied they had taken all that they could carry in one trip. They would come back for a second load later.

"Let's get this out to the schooner and then we'll come back for more," Henderson said already out of breath.

"Si Eduardo, they are very heavy now," Garcia replied, hefting the handling strap of the duffel bag closest to him.

It was true, they were incredibly heavy and the two men could hardly lift them. They only just managed to drag them through the series of small openings, and they had to make two trips along the rift holding a bag at a time between them. They ended up dragging them one by one over the sand and through the openings to the outside. At one point one bag got jammed in the rift and it was doubtful for a few minutes they were going anywhere with their treasure. But Garcia kicked it loose and after a struggle they managed to drag it out.

By the time they approached the Whaler the two men were sweating heavily. Laura took a small piece of line from the boat and helped to pull Henderson's bag last few hundred feet.

There was still no chance for Jack or Megan to do anything.

"Let's get this into the trunks," Henderson ordered breathlessly and after thinking for a moment he turned to Jack and Megan, motioning for them to get up.

"Get over here and help."

Garcia untied them. Jack was about to refuse when he caught the look on his face. The guy was just waiting for an opportunity to use that Uzi, he thought.

They helped load the bags into the Whaler, sliding them over the rubrail onto the seats. Jack winced as they made deep scratches in the impeccably varnished mahogany, but he realized the scratches were the least of his problems right now.

"Empty the bags into the cases," Henderson said.

A moment later they strained to push the Whaler down the sand until it was just afloat.

Laura climbed in after her two companions and with a quick pull the outboard roared to life. Jack couldn't help but wonder at the irony of it all. It was the gold coins that had paid for the new outboard that Laura had started so easily. She would never have been able to get the old one going.

Megan made a move to get into the Whaler, but Laura waved her off.

"No, you don't, you get to stay here and play castaways. How romantic for you both," she said, breaking into laughter.

Sitting down behind the steering wheel, she put the outboard in reverse, backing the boat away from the shore.

Jack and Megan waded out of the water and sat on the beach. Megan looked terrible. The cut on her mouth wasn't threatening in any way, but her lower lip had swollen into a lopsided pout. Her eyes told the real story though. Megan's were very special and they could light up bright as emeralds whenever her mouth even hinted at a smile. But now they just looked terribly dull and hurt, and Jack felt his stomach knot up.

"They're not really going to leave us here, are they?" Meg asked quietly.

"Reckon so. Wherever they're going, they aren't going to want us with them."

Jack saw the hopelessness in her eyes.

"Hey, did Jen ever tell you what they called me in the navy?" he asked.

"What?" she asked, looking sideways at him.

"Come back Jack," he told her, "No matter how bad my plane was shot up, I always made it back."

She buried her head between her hands.

"Is there any chance at all of us getting off of here or are you just trying to make me feel better?"

"I'm going to get my boat back. There's always a chance," he replied.

Lifting her head, she looked up at his face and she almost believed him. Sitting on the sand, they watched as the Whaler reached the anchored schooner.

Garcia climbed aboard and quickly went below, returning a moment later with Benny and Cobb at gunpoint.

"Rig your rope and lift the cargo from the boat to the deck," he told them.

They were reluctant but even from a distance of one hundred yards, Jack could see Garcia coaxing them on with his weapon. They rigged gantlines from the masts and got ready to lift the heavy cases aboard.

Meanwhile, Ed and Laura seated themselves in the cockpit.

"What's next?" she asked.

"We keep on loading, get as much aboard as possible," he replied.

"I need to know exactly where we're headed," she told him.

"Beef Island in the Virgins, safe harbor, air strip and no cops or customs for miles," he replied confidently.

"What about Jack and the woman?" she asked.

"They aren't going anywhere," he told her.

"You didn't say anything about killing, Ed."

"We're just going to leave them here that's all."

"And them?" she asked, glancing forward at the two seamen rigging lines to the big main halyard winch and knotting a strap for the heavy aluminum cases.

"We need them for now. You said you can navigate, but we'll need them to do the bull work."

"What happens when we get to the Virgin Islands?"

"Don't worry, I tell you. I've got it all planned. We'll discuss it when we get there. I'm getting hungry, you want to whip something up?"

"No, I think I better go down and check the charts."

Henderson turned to Garcia.

"It's time we ate, why don't you go down and fix us something?"

"Eduardo, that is woman's work," he complained.

"Can you do navigation? Make some food. I'll keep an eye on these two."

Garcia grudgingly went below and hunted around for something to eat. Megan hadn't prepared anything, but he found bread and mayo in the fridge and some canned tuna fish in the cupboard. Patch tried to charm him into a handout, but all he got for his efforts was a swift kick. He scampered away to the skipper's cabin where he hid under the pillow.

Laura went down to the navigation station to look at the charts. There was one of the West Indies already on the table and Jack's tools were laid out on the little shelf above. There was a set of parallel rules and dividers and a selection of plastic triangles and compasses.

The AM weather radio was mounted just above her head and she turned it on. It was tuned in to Barbados and the time was three fifty five. Sparrow was singing the popular calypso tune about "three white women travelling through Africa". There would be a weather report on the hour, but she had no reason to expect anything unusual.

Opening the drawer, she leafed through the various charts. Jack had a good selection and after a few moments she pulled out one of the Virgin Islands.

"Let's see. Beef Island, that's where he wants to go," she said to herself.

She'd been there before, on a dive boat cataloguing wrecks in the area a year ago, but this time would be different. She had to navigate the boat safely there herself. She remembered that there was a good anchorage.

Then the weather announcer came on and Laura stopped reading the chart. Standing in the small navigation room, she listened as a lilting Barbadian voice came over the radio.

"Here is the latest weather bulletin from the meteorological office in Bridgetown, Barbados. There is a tropical storm warning in effect for the islands of the eastern Caribbean from St. Vincent to Antigua. The tropical depression east of the Lesser Antilles has been upgraded to a tropical storm. This is the second storm of the season and has been named Beatrice. Tropical storm Beatrice is located some fifty miles to the east of Barbados and is moving in a westerly direction at a speed of twenty knots. Highest sustained winds near the center of the storm are fifty knots gusting to sixty and gale force winds extend from the center some hundred miles to the north and west. Conditions are favorable at this time for further strengthening. All marine interests in the eastern Caribbean should now take the necessary precautions and seek shelter where possible."

Laura suddenly felt faint. She'd heard Jack talk about the hurricane danger before they left Antigua. Even with her limited experience it was clear that they were in a bad position. The forecast was repeated. Throwing the dividers on the chart table, she ran up on deck to find Henderson.

As he supervised, the two crewmen lowered the treasure-laden cases to the deck.

"Slowly, slowly, good," he said.

The cases were heavy and he planned to stow the bullion in the wardroom. Garcia came up at that moment with a huge wicker basket filled with tuna sandwiches.

"Think you made enough?" Henderson asked.

"Come from big family."

Laura met them on the foredeck.

"We got big trouble, Ed," she said urgently.

"What? What kind of trouble?"

"I was checking the charts and I turned the radio on. The weather report from Barbados, it looks as though there's a bad storm on the way. We've got to get out of here fast."

Henderson thought for a moment.

"We're not going anywhere yet. We have to go back ashore to the island, there's a ton of stuff still there."

"We don't have time to mess around this place. We've got to leave right away. If we keep the engine on, we can be in the Virgin Islands the day after tomorrow."

"So what's the rush all of a sudden? The weather looks fine to me," he argued. Laura was frustrated.

"You see those clouds? They're coming towards us. There's a storm on its way and this boat is our only ticket out of here. If it sinks, we're all going down and the gold too," she added a second later.

That seemed to decide the issue quickly.

"Jack said the schooner was full of fuel. He said it's got a range of fifteen hundred miles under power. That enough?" he asked, suddenly sounding worried.

"That would take us all the way to Miami. The distance to the Virgin Islands is around three hundred miles or so. It'll be more than enough," she said, trying to sound confident.

Henderson made his decision.

"Let's get going then."

He called Benny and Cobb over. They'd just finished lowering the second heavy aluminum case to the schooner's deck.

"We're leaving. Just do exactly as you're told, understand?"

"What happenin'?" Benny asked, "Where we goin' and what 'bout Skip and Meg. You're ain't goin' just leave dem dere?"

"Enough questions. All you have to do is help Laura get this boat going and I'll let you go when we get to the Virgin Islands."

Benny swallowed the promise, but Cobb didn't buy it. He realized that they would kill them when the time was right, but for the moment he had no choice. He would bide his time.

"Get the Whaler aboard and when it's on deck get this boat ready to leave."

The two seamen went about it halfheartedly. They'd never put to sea without their skipper. Benny was stunned and confused but Cobb was torn and in a silent rage about leaving him and Megan.

"What we gonna do, Cobby?" Benny asked, laying out a jib sheet.

"Just quiet an' do de work. If a chance come up, den I know what to do. Sometimes when de sea rough people does just fall overboard," he told his shipmate.

Laura opened the Plexiglas panel in the cockpit and pressed the start buttons marked Main Engine and Gen. Set. There was a satisfying rumble as both engines started up.

On the beach Jack heard the familiar growl of his GM diesel and realized the worst.

"They're lifting the Whaler."

Cobb and Benny hooked the gantlines to the bow and stern and hoisted her aboard. With Garcia's gun wielding encouragement, they lifted the Boston Whaler aboard and secured it on the deck. Henderson was going to abandon them there on Aves. Megan noticed the activity too.

"Cobb's lifting the anchor, they're leaving us, aren't they Jack?" she asked him, her voice rising in fear.

Jack couldn't think of anything to say. Suddenly, all the pent up frustrations of the trip came to a head. She stood up in front of Jack, legs spread with hands on hips and exploded.

"Stubborn mule."

"Not his fault, he's got a gun to his head."

"I mean you. I told you these people were trouble, but you didn't listen, you had the hots for that silly blond and now we're here," her voice raising to screaming pitch.

Jack stood there letting her vent her fury. Suddenly Megan lost it and, taking him completely by surprise, punched him squarely on the jaw, twisting his head sideways. Rubbing his chin, he turned back to her.

"That hurt," he said quietly, rubbing his face.

Her emotions running amok, she collapsed onto the sand and began crying. "What are we going to do?"

He knelt beside her, put his arms around her, trying to reassure her.

"Please tell me what we're going to do," she sobbed.

As they huddled together on the lonely atoll Jack felt an incredible sense of frustration, but he could do nothing. The sound of the anchor winch carried loudly to the shore as the chain came up clanking over the wildcat. Cobb stood on the foredeck glancing shoreward from time to time, and Jack pictured Benny laying on his stomach below at the chain locker packing the chain as it came aboard, his bow legs sticking up in the air. He felt no animosity towards either of his men. He knew they had no choice.

The anchor came off the bottom and Jack made out the people standing near the stern and in the cockpit of the schooner. Laura handled the helm while Henderson stood to one side. They shared the task of maneuvering the schooner out of the lagoon. It was easy enough because as soon as the anchor was off the bottom, the *Fandango*'s bow automatically fell off to leeward, and it was only a matter of turning the helm to port and advancing the Morse engine control to the ahead position and steering. The schooner turned slowly, making her way out the lagoon.

Jack and Megan stood on the sand watching their only hope of survival grow smaller and smaller. It was a surreal experience watching his beloved *Fandango* sail away without him, but she rounded the western point of the reef surrounding the lagoon and turned to starboard, leaving the atoll.

There was more activity on the deck then as the crew set the main staysail and fore staysail. The last sound Jack heard was the sound of the main engine as it revved up then the schooner quickly moved away on a northerly course.

All too soon, Jack and Megan were alone on the barren sands of Aves, with only the birds to keep them company. They watched until the *Fandango* was only a speck on the horizon and as she disappeared, Megan turned and put her head on Jack's shoulder. Despite the fact that it was still mid afternoon she was shivering. He put his arm around her.

"Please tell me what we do now," Megan asked with a sinking heart.

Looking at him, she realized he wasn't really paying attention. His eyes were focused on the line of dark storm clouds forming on the horizon far to the east.

"First thing is to get some shelter. I think there's a storm coming," he told her.

The *Fandango* rounded Aves's north reef and immediately started bucking into a steep sea.

"It's really rough," Laura shouted, but no one was close enough to hear her.

The long, ominous Caribbean swell rolled in from the east-northeast and the schooner's bow rose and fell in sickening dips.

Struggling with the teak steering wheel, Laura began wondering what she had let herself in for. When Henderson first contacted her about going on a treasure hunting expedition in the Caribbean, he'd asked her about her boating skills.

"Can you handle a boat?" he had asked.

"I sure can," she'd replied, eager to secure the job.

Like most families who grew up on Florida's East Coast, Laura's had owned boats and she'd learned to operate them competently enough, making a number of trips to the Bahamas and the Keys. But this was a different story. Her family's thirty-eight foot O-Day sloop was a far cry from the *Fandango*. This was a big ocean sailing yacht. She wasn't happy about it, especially now this storm was coming.

"No way am I going to do all this for what he's giving me," she said to herself angrily.

She resolved to hit Henderson up for a bigger payoff.

Aves quickly sank below the horizon astern of them and Henderson turned to Cobb and Benny.

"Trim the sails like you would normally do for this kind of voyage," he ordered them.

Reluctantly they sheeted the main staysail and fore staysail for the course they were steering. The schooner's motion improved a bit. As the strong wind filled her sails, she stopped rolling. She continued to pitch heavily though, and occasionally took a good-sized sea over her bow. Under Garcia's ever-watchful eye, Cobb stuck some rags into the two hawseholes where the anchor chain went through the deck to the fo'c'sle to stop any water from going below.

Towards four p.m. what was left of the daylight faded. The sky clouded over and sudden gusts of wind seemed to come from nowhere, bursting across the schooner's deck. The great Caribbean Sea that had so recently shone with its customary rich, blue sparkle took on an unfriendly leaden mien.

Henderson worried about handling the big sailing yacht on the open sea. It was one thing talking in the safety of harbour, but this was different. He'd been uneasy enough when Carlton was in charge, let alone now. It was a good thing they'd kept the two West Indian seamen aboard. At least Cobb knew how things worked, and he wouldn't do anything to jeopardize his own skin. He'd coerce them into doing whatever was necessary.

Laura sat in the cockpit spinning the helm, struggling to keep the schooner on course. The woman had been helpful with her technical instruments, but now she didn't seem too sure about herself. He'd asked her specifically about her boat handling abilities when they'd first spoken.

"Hope she can get us to the Virgin Islands alive with this bad weather business," he mumbled to himself.

Laura kept the radio tuned in and she listened to the hourly weather reports. The radio was piped through to the companionway speaker, and by ducking inside for a moment she could listen to the brief bulletins as they came over the ether. It didn't sound good. Henderson and Garcia sat near her in the cockpit, looking out to the east where the black line of squalls was slowly bearing down on them.

"Maybe this wasn't such a good idea," she said bluntly.

"I thought you were tough enough to see this through," Henderson challenged her.

"Shut up. When you asked me about boats you never mentioned a seventy-five foot schooner, Henderson," she snapped.

He noted it was Henderson now, not Ed anymore.

"I hired you because you said you knew about boats, so stop whining and get this thing to the Virgin Islands," he ordered.

Laura hated to be bossed around by anybody. Abused as a child, she had quickly developed an attitude problem, which progressed into a life-long judgment flaw. This had gotten her in plenty of trouble throughout her young life and now she was about to get herself into more. She turned to face him.

"You're a real jerk. I should never have got mixed up with you," she yelled angrily over the noise of the wind.

Henderson watched as she sat there gripping the schooner's helm. Peculiar, he thought. The woman was like a chameleon. One moment she looked like a sultry angel, blue eyes and short blond cut blowing in the wind. The next minute she could change into a snarling vixen.

"Just do your job," Henderson warned her, his voice taking on a more ominous tone.

He'd already paid her five thousand up front and there was another five for her when they parted company. Now the gold was aboard and he had run his hands over the precious yellow metal, his feelings were more mercenary. There would have to be another trip back to Aves as soon as possible and in the meantime the fewer people that knew about the *San Idelfonso* the better. If Laura gave him any trouble, well Garcia was totally without emotion of any kind. He'd do exactly what he was told to do. He'd let Garcia take care of her. Laura spoke up again and what she said next sealed her fate.

"I want a cut of the gold," she said as loudly as she could, running her hand through her hair.

He looked at her in disbelief, but she glared right back.

"Ten grand won't do it, man; there's millions in those cases and I want a share."

Henderson remained silent for moment, his face expressionless, but inside there was an icy rage brewing. He turned to her smiling.

"Fair enough," he said, leaning towards her." I'll cut you in for a share, just get us safely to the Virgins."

She didn't believe for a second that he would keep his word. For the moment she held the upper hand and things were just beyond his control. As long as they were aboard the *Fandango* she had some control. She would play on and when the time came she would make her move.

"I'm going to keep the engine going," she told him, feigning acceptance. "Hold the wheel, while I go below to look at the chart. If you can manage," she added sarcastically.

Reluctantly, he took the helm as she went below. The schooner's bow immediately began wandering from the course.

In the small navigation room, Laura laid the chart on the table. She took the rules from the shelf, laying a rudimentary course just to the right of due north on the chart. The pencil line took them to the west of St. Croix, over the Great Saba Bank and across the Anegada Passage to the Virgin Islands. It was an easy piece of navigation and she was satisfied it would be impossible to miss the island chain. They would run aground first.

Coming back on deck, she checked the main engine revs, 1250 RPM. The knotlog in the cockpit showed their speed at five and a half knots with the two sails and the engine. It was slow, she thought, but even with her limited experience she realized it would be dangerous to push the yacht any faster. She recalled her father's advice so many years ago when he was teaching her how to sail the sloop.

"When it gets rough, just keep it slow."

Under an ever-darkening sky, the schooner pitched and rolled her way north. Laura flipped on the overhead light in the companionway where the console was. She hit the little rubber-capped switches marked Nav. Lgts. and Compass Lgts., and then she poked her head up through the sliding hatch to check they were on. She left the overhead on in the companionway hatch and it shone out onto the deck and the figures crouching in the cockpit.

Henderson tried to steer for a little while, but his lack of experience was obvious. The schooner's bow roamed all over the place in an arc of more than forty degrees.

"Cobb," he shouted towards where he and Benny were sitting in the lee of the companionway hatch.

They'd donned their yellow foul weather gear but offered none to the others. He motioned for him to come to the helm.

"Jack told me you were good on the wheel, so let's see what you can do," he told him, pointing to the steering wheel.

Cobb took over and after a moment the schooner steadied on her course, and he and Benny took turns steering from then on, two hours on and two hours off.

Total darkness fell and the swell came around to the east. They had built to a good twenty-five feet. The *Fandango* was thoroughly wet. Stinging raindrops pelted across the deck and the salt spray blew from the crests of the waves over the swiftly running schooner. She was taking it well though, and was in no danger. Cobb took great satisfaction in noting that both Henderson and Garcia were scared witless. They crouched desperately in the cockpit holding onto the coaming each time she rolled. Laura looked a little better. After an hour he called for her to come over to the helm.

"We need to make de checks every hour, so tell de Spanish man not to shoot, OK?" Cobb told her.

"What checks?" she inquired suspiciously.

"Jack always check de engine and de bilges every hour to make sure everyting alright."

"Alright, but don't do anything without asking me first, got it?"

"Ah got it clear as could be."

Laura went over and filled Henderson in on the crew's activities. Cobb checked the hatches and deck skylights again, but there were only a few drips getting into the accommodation areas.

At nine that evening, Henderson went to the navigation room to make a call on the ship's radio. He felt so sick he really didn't feel like doing anything. But this was important. He'd made an arrangement with his radio contact in St. Thomas to stand by at nine every evening until further notice. Tuning in on 2638 kHz he made his call.

"Shorebase one, this is flagship one. Do you copy?" Henderson repeated this call three times before a reply came back over the air.

"Flagship one, this is shorebase one, I copy. Go ahead. Over," the voice came through the static.

"Shorebase, this is flagship one, Acknowledge ETA day after tomorrow, location T. And don't forget trolley. Do you copy?"

"Roger that, I copy. ETA Wednesday, location T, with full tanks. Over."

"Flagship out," Henderson said into the mike and then he shut down the transmitter.

There was no need for any further chit chat and that logistical problem was at least taken care of. All they had to do now was to get there without drowning. Rushing back on deck, he only just managed to reach the cockpit rail before another wave of nausea washed over him.

The schooner heeled over, taking the waves on her starboard beam. Henderson and Garcia watched terrified as each ghostly breaker rose to windward. Eerily illuminated by the green starboard sidelight their frothy crests loomed twenty feet above their heads, clearly visible against the dark sky.

"We will drown," Garcia said.

Henderson turned to Cobb.

"Is there anything you can do to make it better?" he shouted.

"No, you bumbo clot, we all gonna drown tonight," Cobb shouted over the wind.

"Cobby? For true you tink we gonna sink tonight," Benny sounded worried.

"For sure friend, for sure," Cobb replied.

If they were going to come to grief at the hijackers hands, then why make it easy for them.

Under different circumstances Garcia would have taken offence at the West Indian's rudeness, but not now. The odd big sea broke on the vessel washing her decks, and he was convinced each one would capsize the yacht, but for the most part they just hissed ominously before rolling away to leeward. Fear paralyzed Garcia, and as the schooner rolled, his guts knotted until they hurt. The trip had barely begun and already they were wet and miserable.

"If I am to die, then I will die inside the ship," he said finally.

"You're not going to die," Henderson said and followed him below, but the effects of the waves were even worse in the cabins.

They tried to prop themselves in their bunks with pillows to counter the motion of the schooner, but every time she rolled, they had to hold on to the bunk sides to stop from falling out. They had no idea that there were bunk boards under the mattresses that could be set up to hold themselves in bed, and no one aboard the *Fandango* was going to tell them. Both were violently seasick and spent a lot of time braced within the confines of the small bathroom, their heads hanging over the porcelain bowls.

Laura stayed in the small pilot berth in the companionway. It was close to the deck where she could keep an eye on the two West Indian crew. She noted each trip made to the engine room and the foredeck to check the sails. She occasionally heard them slam the cover of the deck box hatch or the teak cabin sole as they checked the bilges. At least Carlton had trained them well.

Later on Laura went down to the galley.

"I brought you guys some hot coffee and the rest of Garcia's sandwiches," she said.

"Thanks," Cobb said.

He thought there might be a small conscience lurking in the blond head. After a couple of sandwiches he turned to her.

"It ain't too late to call for help on de radio for de skipper, maybe make it easier for yourself later," Cobb told her.

"I didn't bring the food out of sympathy. Want to make sure you guys stay awake, keep this boat on course," she told him coldly.

"You one stupid woman," Cobb told her, "Dat Spanish man going to kill you too."

"Oh shut up," Laura told him.

She was too tired to get into an argument, but the thought stuck in her head. It bothered her.

The *Fandango* made slow time of it, but at least every mile to the north was another mile away from Beatrice. The tropical storm held its westerly course and would during the course of the night pass astern of the schooner and over Aves.

Laura was satisfied the oncoming storm would take care of Jack and Megan and wasn't the least bit remorseful. In fact she smiled a little at the thought of Megan drowning in huge waves or dying from exposure and lack of water. The redheaded bitch had prevented her from making it with Jack, she thought. He might even have come along with them had it not been for her, but as she thought about it she realized he never would have agreed. He was one of those stupid bastards who always did everything right. Pity, had a great bod.

Sometime during the night a particularly violent squall caught the *Fandango* full on her beam and even with just the two pieces of sail she heeled over dipping her lee rail below the water. The schooner took power from the gusts of wind and with the engine going as well she surged forward. Leaping wildly from the crests of the big rolling seas, she plunged sickeningly into the troughs, burying her bow in a white froth. Her bow picked up a load of water on the foredeck when she poked her nose into a really big one, and the white water came racing aft along the deck like the rapids of a wild river.

Hearing a heavy thump in the wardroom, Henderson got up and dragged Garcia from his bunk. Taking some small line from the flag locker, he turned the overhead light on. The heavy aluminum cases had slid from the starboard side of the wardroom to the lee side where they were lodged under the big teak table.

"Let's tie them to the base so they don't move," Henderson ordered.

"Si Eduardo let us tie the gold."

Passing the white strap around the heavy teak table base and through the stainless steel case handle, Ed Henderson pondered that what they had on the boat alone should be worth a couple of million at least. Yes, at least two, he thought, and he wanted every penny for himself.

CHAPTER THIRTEEN

Hurricane!

Jack and Megan stood on the shore looking out across the Caribbean. The *Fandango* had disappeared to the north what seemed like ages ago, and as evening waned a long, dark band slowly grew on the horizon to the east. It looked ominous.

"What is it?" Megan asked, squinting as she raised her hand to her brow.

"A line squall, probably the first of the depression they were talking about on the radio," he answered in an even voice.

"Gilligan's Island with a storm thrown in at no extra charge," she said flippantly, "as if we don't have enough to worry about."

Jack recalled old Captain Neddy King's advice.

"Man, if there's ever a storm, don't even think of staying on that place. Sometimes, dem big hurricane seas just wash Aves away."

It was a lousy time for recollections, he thought.

Although he hadn't heard the latest weather report he could guess what was going on. The depression east of the islands was here. It had sure traveled fast.

What he didn't know was that it had developed into a spinning tropical storm that was rapidly approaching the rated seventy-five knots for a hurricane.

The big low-pressure system had crossed the Atlantic with subtle stealth, gaining strength as it came. The malevolent mass of thunderstorms and squalls made amazingly quick progress across the vast empty reaches of the ocean, staying for the most part near the fourteenth parallel of latitude. Three hundred miles east of the Lesser Antilles, the system began its malignant metamorphoses.

For some unknown reason, the surface of the ocean was a few degrees warmer than usual, and the system took sustenance from this. An eye formed and the storm started spinning. Sluggish at first it slowly picked up speed. The vicious squalls and huge thunderheads strung out loosely throughout the system were pulled into the cyclonic spin, and orderly feeder-bands formed like long claws emanating from the eye. The storm grew in strength and continued on its course of almost due west.

The sixteen thousand-ton Greek freighter *Athena Maris*, bound from the Straits of Gibraltar to Cartagena, Columbia, laden with general cargo was having trouble. Earlier in the day she entered the storm system about a hundred miles east of Barbados. They immediately ran into very rough conditions and the ship took heavy seas over her decks.

Captain Nico Aristotalis reduced speed to five knots to ease the motion of his vessel and he called the North Post radio station in Barbados to report the situation.

"North Post radio, North Post Radio, this is *Athena Maris*. Do you copy?" his voice crackled over the speaker.

"*Athena Maris*, we read you 3 by 5. Go ahead with your traffic, over."

"North Post, this is *Athena Maris*. We are presently experiencing force ten conditions, and the barometer has fallen over the last hour. There is a hurricane condition, I think, over."

The Captain sounded a little nervous.

"*Athena Maris*, this is North Post radio. What is your position? Over."

"*Athena Maris* back to North Post radio, we are now 216 miles due east of St Lucia. Over."

"*Athena Maris*, this is North Post radio. What is the present wind strength and wave condition? Over."

"*Athena Maris* back to North post, right now we have sustained winds of sixty knots and I estimate wave height at twenty-five to thirty feet at this time. Poseidon is angry I think," the Captain said, trying a little humor.

"*Athena Maris*, this is North Post. Thank you for the report and please continue to stand by on channel 2182 in case we need to talk again."

"North Post, I will make another report in four hours. Clear and standing by on 2182."

The duty radio operator immediately turned to the powerful ham radio set and switched to the select channel for National Hurricane Center in Miami Florida.

"Miami? Yes, this is North Post Barbados, we just got confirmation from a Greek freighter just East of the islands, doesn't look too good, over."

"What's he saying about conditions now? Over."

"Steady sixty and twenty plus seas, didn't sound too happy, over."

"OK, we'll get the Connie off ASAP, over."

"We'll keep you posted. North Post standing by on 2182."

Within an hour, one of the special long range Lockheed Constellation aircraft took off. Her pilot throttled up to best speed to intercept the system.

The aircraft was a variation of the successful Lockheed Starliner, specially outfitted for hurricane tracking service, and run by a unit that the pilots fondly called "The Hurricane Hunters." Four 3400 hp radial engines flew the aircraft to a top speed of 380 mph, and right now the pilot was pushing her.

The big, four-engine aircraft reached the storm four hours and ten minutes after leaving Miami. They flew around the perimeter first, taking various readings and relaying them back to Miami for analysis and dissemination to the areas concerned.

"Hold on boys, gonna be a wild one this time," the pilot said over the intercom.

The Lockheed "Connie" was sturdy and although the crew had done this many times before they were apprehensive as they approached the towering thunderheads forming the center of the tropical storm. It was a big one.

Lightening flashed and the crash of thunder was louder than the roar of the engines. The pilot flew the "Connie" directly into the black cloud mass. Within the storm the plane was buffeted and thrown around like a toy, her long wings flexing to the point where they were sometimes two feet out of true at the tips.

Suddenly they passed from the violent turbulence into the eye. Clear and calm, the crew could see the well-formed spinning wall as they circled in the center. There was no doubt about it. This one was breeding fast.

"I christen you Beatrice second storm of the season," the pilot told his crew. "And one nasty looking lady too," he added.

After twenty minutes more the meteorological boys in the lab section of the aircraft informed the pilot they'd finished.

"Tally ho Beatrice," he said, giving the storm their traditional departure shout and he thankfully took her back out through the wall and headed home.

Beatrice made the graduation from a tropical depression to a tropical storm just east of Barbados, and at the speed she was travelling; she hit the island with little advance warning.

The low-lying hills of Barbados offered meager protection and she passed directly over the island, ravaging the land. After the first few hours of torrential rain, large areas of land were under a foot or more of water.

Sixty-mile-an-hour wind blasted the sugar cane plantations, flattening the tall stalks and ripping the sheet galvanized roofing off the small houses dotted along the landscape. Where the wind was strongest the sheets flew around like giant razor blades, threatening to slice in half anyone who got in the way.

The distance from Barbados to St. Lucia was only ninety miles but this was enough of a run for Beatrice to strengthen even more before she rolled in on the high, mountainous ridges of the island's volcanic backbone. Beatrice arrived with more torrential rains and the deep ravines and rivers swelled into silt laden torrents, staining the Caribbean a dirty brown for many miles out. Bits of tree trunks and all kinds of flotsam and jetsam littered the surface of the sea as the storm passed.

A brilliant display of pyrotechnics accompanied the storm, and the dark sky was lit up almost continually with the strikes of lightning. Beatrice vented her fury with blasts of thunder that shook the earth, and for those islanders lucky enough to have any galvanized roofing left, it shook and rattled like the devil himself was trying to rip it off.

Leaving the coast of St. Lucia, she made her way inexorably westwards towards Aves continuing her anti-clockwise spin. The northwest corner of the storm consisted of a line of vicious outlying squalls extending some seventy-five miles from the eye. The infamous "leading edge punch" of cyclonic systems and potentially the most dangerous quarter.

The dark line of squalls Megan and Jack saw to the east of them were the first of the outlying feeder bands some hundred miles in front of the eye. They were weak compared to what would come later. The sky grew overcast and as the evening wore on the squalls closed the distance to Aves. By dusk, the horizon to the east was totally and ominously black.

"Is there a place we can hide?" Megan asked.

"The caves," he reassured her, "it's the only safe place for us."

"When I get out of here, Jack, I never want to hear the name Aves again."

"Might as well go in now and wait this out," Jack said, taking her by the hand.

It was getting cooler. As they approached the rock formations at the north end of the island, Megan shivered involuntarily. The wind built to thirty knots, blowing gritty coral sand across the atoll into their faces. The first line squall moved in on Aves, closing up the cloud cover and the last remnants of sky disappeared. It was as if a huge dark blanket was drawn over them. The sun was blotted out altogether and it grew strangely dim.

The low, scudding clouds dropped lower and lower until it seemed that Megan and Jack could reach up and touch the fast moving masses.

In the fading light two lonely figures, bent to the waist against the wind, covered the last few yards to the first of the stone monoliths. Something was puzzling Jack and he stopped walking for a moment, looking around.

"What is it, Jack? What do you see?" Megan asked, looking at him in alarm.

It took him a moment to figure out what it was.

"The birds have gone," he said, scanning the atoll.

It was true. Looking around, she listened. The almost constant squawking and crying of the birds had gone. There wasn't one to be seen or heard. They'd all flown away to escape the storm. The only sounds were the rumbles of thunder and a low ominous drone emanating from behind the dark clouds. Jack stood looking eastwards for a moment, feeling strangely detached. It was as if he wasn't really there, but they were, alone on a remote atoll with Mother Nature about to vent her fury on them. Too scared to think straight, Megan held Jack's hand in a vise-like grip. It was her only connection to reality in a world otherwise gone awry.

The first raindrops pelted horizontally across Aves, stinging their exposed skin. Without wasting any more time, Jack led Megan into the rock maze and made their way to the cavern of lights. It was already dim inside. The effects of the ocean swell were evident in the grotto. The surge from the waves came in and swept right up to their feet.

"We're not going to get much shelter here, Jack," Megan said, looking around, "unless you're a crab."

"There's another cavern, the treasure chamber. We've got to find it quick before it gets dark."

It didn't take long. As Jack made a round of the seaward wall he found the crevice.

"Follow me," he said, taking her hand.

He led her through the rift and the tunnel and finally into the treasure chamber. There was no wind there and it was still and dry. Although there were gold coins and ingots lying around everywhere, Jack and Megan had no interest.

"All seems kind of worthless now doesn't it," she said.

"Yes. All these millions and they can't buy a bumboat ticket out of here."

"Don't remind me."

They found a spot near the wall where the sand had been caught in a little stone gully.

Gathering armfuls of the dry seaweed lying scattered in clumps around the floor, he scooped out a shallow trench and put the seaweed down. It looked comfortable.

"We'll stay here until the storm's gone," Jack said, patting down the makeshift bed.

As the last of the light faded fast Megan could only make out Jack as a shadowy outline. Walking over from where she had been standing, she looked down at his handiwork.

"And where are you sleeping?"

"Right here," he replied. "Don't worry, I'll keep my hands to myself," he added.

"You'd better," she warned, "How bad do you think it will be? I mean, will we survive in this hole?"

"We'll be fine here. This place is higher up than the other chamber, so the tides won't get to us."

"You don't sound too sure."

"We'll be fine."

Her temper flared for a second. She was about to tell him exactly what she thought about his last comment, but she allowed herself a moment to calm down. Neither of them voiced any thoughts on how they were going to get off the atoll. For now they would just concentrate on getting through the night.

Total darkness fell, and Jack lay down on the seaweed with his back to the wall. It was going to be a long night.

"Come and lie down. Stay with me here tonight. Don't want you falling in some hole and breaking your leg," he told her.

It was sound advice. The inside of the chamber was pitch black and there would be no more light until the sun rose in the morning.

"Don't worry, I'm not going anywhere," she replied into the darkness.

Stretching out next to him on the soft seaweed, she reached out, laying her hand on his shoulder. He squeezed her arm gently in response.

"Where do you think they're taking the *Fandango*?"

"I'm not sure, except it must be somewhere to the north. Otherwise they'd have left around the southern end of the reef."

"Think Cobb and Benny are alright?" Megan asked thoughtfully.

"Yes, I don't think Henderson has the guts to kill in cold blood."

"It's not him I worry about, it's the other two. Garcia and that super bitch Laura," Megan said vehemently.

"You've got that figured," Jack agreed.

"Why'd you sleep with her? " Megan asked, her voice suddenly angry.

"Didn't, I was sound asleep in my cabin and she just came in. Nothing happened. Cobb knocked on the door a minute later telling me the boat was dragging anchor. The only reason I let her climb into my bunk was that I thought it was you."

"What's that?"

"The rest of the morning, when I was alone on deck, I kept wishing it had been you."

"You mean that?"

"Yes."

"You're not just saying this because we're probably going to die out here, are you?" She wanted to believe him.

"You know when they left me on the beach here, and you were still aboard?"

"Yes," she said slowly.

"I kept thinking that I might not see you again," he said, reaching out to touch her in the dark.

"I thought you didn't like me very much."

"You've got one hell of a temper," he teased.

"I'm the sweetest person when you get to know me," she said with all the charm she could muster, "If we ever get out of here, Jack, I'll show you."

"Promise?" he asked smiling.

"Definitely," she said sighed.

Megan felt better after the exchange and shifted towards him until she was lying next to his warm body. She felt safe and at home with him. Sleep was impossible, but as the hours passed they dozed on and off. Later he put his arms around her. Her cool breath caressed his throat and he kissed her gently, savoring her taste. Her skin felt soft and vulnerable and their mutual desires soon took over. Eagerly returning his kisses, her sexual awareness mounted. She'd never felt like this before and the sensation of his powerful body over hers was intoxicating. Her senses awakened and she responded gratefully to his skillful touches. In the darkness of the cavern their gasps of pleasure were drowned by the sounds of the wind as it swept above them.

Sometime later, while Megan lay in his arms, she related to him the entire story of the *San Idelfonso* and how it came to be wrecked on Aves.

*****

One hundred and twenty miles to the north the *Fandango* plunged through the darkness. Although she avoided the worst of the storm they still experienced violent squalls and heavy seas. Cobb and Benny went about their duties like automatons. Benny wished he were ashore. He kept thinking about the warm, plump dark skinned ladies at the Frederick Street address back in Antigua. He never imagined things would turn out like this. But when he got home he'd have money and he'd really show the girls a good time.

Cobb was more pragmatic. He realized there was good chance that he and his shipmate would never see Antigua again. He caught snippets of conversation regarding the problem of witnesses to this piracy, and he realized Henderson wouldn't leave anybody around to tell the story. He was tormented by two thoughts. His wife and children depended on him and then there was his friend and skipper. He had a vision of Jack and Meg on Aves with storm seas breaking over the atoll. Cobb knew Jack was a resourceful, tough man and if there were a way for them to survive, he would make it happen.

Holding the *Fandango* to her course, he remained quiet, turning a few spokes now and again, but his mind conjured up interesting fantasies. He felt a pleasant sensation as he envisioned his big, razor sharp fish knife pulling up through Garcia's white belly. That was a good thought. He would just wait and watch, and if an opportunity arose, he'd take it. He thought about trying any one of a dozen different plans to derail Henderson and Laura, but they were all too risky. Garcia seemed too keen to use that gun of his and he didn't want to die just yet. So they sailed on.

Henderson stayed below for the first part of the night, but after midnight he came up with Garcia and they lay down to sleep on the cockpit floor with blankets. They were there for only a minute before a good-sized sea came aboard soaking them, and they went miserably below again. Laura found herself watching him more closely. She didn't trust Henderson and that phony smile of his.

*****

On the atoll the hours of darkness dragged on and the storm raged. Beatrice's eye came inexorably on, bringing the spinning wall of wind and rain ever closer to Aves.

Jack and Megan craved sleep, but they only managed to doze for short moments. Even when their lassitude overpowered them during momentary lulls, howling gusts rudely yanked them back to reality. Blowing over the rock formations, the wind made strange noises like air passing over the mouth of a giant bottle. The many openings and cracks in the cave acted like a giant organ and the stones of Aves vented their anguish in loud groans and shrieks.

"I'm scared," Megan said, trying to hide her head in his big shoulder.

"Nothing going to move these rocks," he said, pulling her closer, comforting her.

The long low swell that had appeared from the north so many hours before built steadily. A forty-foot surf hurled itself on the atoll's bulwarks, but as it had done over the centuries the coral fortress would once again protect Aves from destruction. Huge waves hurled themselves on the reef, their awesome power breaking into maelstroms of white, frothy surf. Jack and Megan felt the rocks tremble beneath them. With the increasing wind the surf climbed higher and higher up the shore. Soon the storm surge crossed the atoll in its center, washing tons of sand into the shallows.

In the early hours of the morning Jack woke with a start. The sounds that old Neddy King had spoken of. The cries of dead sailors. He hadn't understood what the old sea captain meant, but now he heard it.

"Give anybody the creeps," he said.

Megan didn't stir. His voice was drowned by the howl of the storm.

Somewhere beneath them, hollow passages ran inland from the sea. Cracks and tunnels in the coral formed a millennia ago channeled the sea inland below the rock maze. The raging surge came over the reef, forcing air through the vents like flutes, producing strange human-like cries. The ghostly sound echoed in the darkness. Jack felt very alone.

Brilliant forks of lightning rent the blackness above the atoll again and again and the smell of ozone pervaded the night. The flashes penetrated through the fissures in the roof of the stone caverns, playing eerily on the walls, and the blasts of thunder shook the stone ramparts of the atoll to their very foundation.

The eye of the storm passed right over Aves, and all of a sudden it was still and quiet. In the space of only a couple of minutes the wind dropped from seventy knots to zero.

"Is it over?" Megan sat up, listening intently to the silence.

"No. I think the eye is right over us. It'll probably start again in a while," Jack replied, giving her a little hug.

Laying there in the quiet waiting for something to happen, he wondered if he was right. The drone and howl of the wind had gone, leaving only the powerful sounds of the huge seas breaking on the reef and the air venting within the subterranean caverns. Sure enough, it began again with a vengeance. The night seemed to go on forever and through the early hours, the storm raged on and the huge seas threw themselves upon the atoll.

Huddling together in the safety of the cave, they were grateful to be away from the fury outside. Finally, they both managed some sleep, the kind one falls onto when exhaustion takes over. Jack awoke once and putting his hand out realized Megan was no longer next to him.

"Where are you?" he called out in the darkness.

"I'm still here," she said lightly.

She came back after a minute or two, lying down next to him again.

The last of Beatrice drifted away to the west at daybreak. An unnatural stillness hung over the atoll as if father death had passed over them. The wind disappeared for good this time and the sea condition dropped almost as fast as it had risen. The strange, fluting cries vanished and the only sound breaking the peace of the inner cavern was a faint hiss as the last of the surge came over the reef. Opening his eyes, Jack caught the first faint rays of sunlight dancing in through the hidden openings in the ceiling. Facing him, Megan snuggled up close to his chest and he looked down at her sleeping figure. For the first time he realized what a truly beautiful woman she was. In the diffused light, with her head cradled in the crook of her arm, he marveled at her long eyelashes and luxuriant red hair. Her tee shirt had risen high above her waist during the night, exposing her flat tummy. She really wasn't as skinny as he'd first thought. Her body was fuller in all the right places and her long shapely legs were perfect. She woke up that minute, as if sensing him watching her. She smiled slightly.

"What are you looking at, Jack Carlton?" she asked in a husky voice.

"I'm just making sure the beautiful woman I caught during the storm is still here."

"You haven't caught me yet, but last night was a promising start," she said, smiling mischievously.

"I'm glad."

She sat up and stretched.

"Tell me the storm's gone," she said, a tone of fear returning to her voice.

"Oh it's gone alright," he said, sounding frustrated. "Problem is, we're not."

"Any ideas about how we might get off here?" she asked.

"We just need to conserve our strength until somebody comes, that's all," he replied, not looking at her.

It wasn't an honest answer. The chances of anyone showing up at Aves right now were slim.

"I'm really thirsty. Do you think there's any water to drink outside?" she asked in a dry voice.

"I'm going to try and find some," he replied, running his dry tongue over his lips, "Maybe there's a dip in the sand with rain or something. Enough of it fell last night."

They wouldn't survive very long without water. He touched his head where Garcia had swiped him with the Uzi's butt. The one-inch gash was crusted over and sore to the touch. Looking at Megan's mouth, he felt a new admiration for her. The cracked lip looked painful, but she wasn't complaining.

"Let's go," Jack suggested, standing up.

"Alright, give me a minute," she said, walking slowly to the other side of the chamber. Afterwards, she dusted off the sand and picking up the green bikini bottom from the stone floor, she put it on again. She hung the little black purse she'd been carrying over her shoulder.

Crawling out through the opening to the tunnel, they passed through the rift into the chamber of lights. It was much brighter there, but as he looked towards the end of the cave where the passage to the outside had been, Jack gasped involuntarily.

"Oh man," Jack muttered.

"What, what's wrong?" she asked, worried.

Jack pointed to exit tunnel. The storm surge had packed tons of sand up against the opening. A good bulldozer would be a day clearing that lot. They wouldn't be going anywhere that way.

*****

For the *Fandango* daybreak came and passed almost without change. The sky remained dark and overcast and the dark clouds scudded so low over the pitching schooner, Cobb thought they would touch her mast cap. He and Benny were exhausted. They'd steered all night sharing two-hour stints. Now they were wet and tired. The sea condition had become confused as Beatrice swung around to the southwest of them. Short, steep seas broke in confusion around the *Fandango*, seeming to come from different directions all at the same time. The steel schooner was doing her best though and Cobb and Benny checked the running gear again and again to make sure that everything was as it should be. They took an inch or two on each of the running backstays as they stretched to protect the masts from the vessel's wild corkscrewing. Seas repeatedly came aboard, threatening to float the Whaler and the little lapstrake skiff away, but they had been well lashed down.

Beatrice continued to pull away to the west-northwest after passing astern of them and the dark squalls changed direction throughout the day. By evening, the wind dropped and hauled to the southeast, and Cobb tended the sails as they changed tack.

*****

Back on Aves Jack weighed up their options. He knew that they didn't have any choices, there was only one escape route.

"Please don't tell me we're going to die trapped in here?" Meg asked in alarm.

"There's another way out," he replied, looking towards the underwater grotto.

The pounding surf had kept it clear and bright sunlight beckoned at the far end.

"Oh no. No way. You're not even thinking of us swimming out through there?" Megan asked, her voice trembling.

"It'll be a walk in the park, Meg, and you're a good swimmer," he reassured her.

"Oh no. No way. You know I can't even put my head under water," she said angrily.

"Listen," he said, gently shaking her shoulders, "we're going to swim through the opening to the sea. That's the only way out of here. I'll be right there with you."

She looked grimly at the calm, clear water of the grotto before turning to him.

"What do I have to do?"

Jack had never actually swum through the opening; he'd just seen it from the inside and he had only a rough idea of where it exited on the outside. He suspected it would be just around the rocks where the reef started at the north point. He'd walked by there on the outside and seen the ledges jutting out into the sea.

"Here's what we're going to do," he said, trying to make it sound like they were planning a holiday outing. "We wade in here, and when we get to the end where the roof meets the water, we'll stop for a minute or two. With me so far?"

"Yes, I'm with you, but you're scaring the life out of me already, and I haven't even got my feet wet."

"OK, then we deep breathe for a minute. We want to really charge our lungs with oxygen so we can stay under for as long as possible."

"How far to the outside?" she asked, fidgeting nervously with her t-shirt.

He felt really bad for her. She was so upset about swimming under water her whole body was trembling, but it was the only way they would get out of the cavern. It probably wasn't more than forty feet, but he couldn't be sure. He decided to tell a little white lie, figuring it would help them get through this.

"It's only about thirty feet, Meg. I checked it out last year. It'll be a breeze, you'll see," he said, putting his arms around her and giving her a squeeze.

"If you're lying to me, I won't forget it," she said, pointing her finger at him.

Moving to him, she let her head rest on his chest for a moment. It felt good and she wished she could stay there just like that.

"Trust me, you'll wonder what all the fuss was about."

"If you say that one more time, I'll hit you," she snapped, pulling away.

She was really unhappy about his plan to dive through the grotto and stood there wrapping her arms around herself to try and stop shivering. She realized with an awful sinking feeling that this was their only way out. She had to believe deep down Jack would look after her.

He still had on the bathing suit he'd been wearing for the last dive. Megan knotted the bottom of her tee shirt at the waist so it wouldn't balloon out. She still had the little, five-inch black leather change purse that she'd been carrying since the day before and she stuck it in the waistband of her bikini.

"Why don't you ditch that? It'll just slow you down," Jack suggested.

"Good luck," she said, patting it, "it goes where I go."

"Suit yourself," Jack said in a slightly exasperated tone.

He took her hand and they waded in until they were both up to their chests in the warm water. The white sand was soft beneath their toes and the water was crystal clear.

"OK, now take some deep breaths," Jack said, holding both of her shaking hands in his own. They stood there for a minute breathing deeply.

"Ready?"

"No, but let's go quick before I change my mind," she replied shakily.

"On my count," he said.

She nodded.

"One, two," and on the third count they both took a huge breath and plunged into the mouth of the grotto.

Diving downwards about ten feet, they reached the mouth of the underwater tunnel. Kicking energetically, they swam horizontally along the underwater passage towards the sunlight at the seaward end. The well-lit tunnel was at least twenty feet wide and the white sand bottom lay some fifteen feet below the arched roof. The stone was smooth and clean, worn by the trillions of gallons of surging Caribbean Sea and sand that had passed there over the aeons of time.

As soon as Jack opened his eyes underwater he knew they were in trouble. He had estimated the sandy floored tunnel to be no more than forty feet, but as he looked, he could see it was much farther. It stretched out in front of them for at least seventy feet. It took Megan only a moment to make the same assessment. Opening her eyes, she looked forward into the tunnel. Although her vision was blurry she could see that it was a long way to the opening and her next breath of air. She stalled.

Grabbing her by the wrist, Jack pulled her on. The grey stone sides of the passage lightened as they struggled towards the opening. Twenty feet from the exit they both needed air. Megan was remarkably game, he thought. She was giving it her best shot, swimming as fast as possible, and she glanced at Jack for a split second before pressing on. Finally with the end only about ten feet ahead Megan got into trouble. With tiny bubbles escaping from her lips she began to exhale. Jack knew this urge was caused by the body's need to get rid of carbon dioxide. He also knew that the next sensation would be the undeniably strong urge to take in a breath of air. It was the moment when many people drowned. The urge to breathe overpowered all other senses and the victim took in a huge, struggling breath under water, filling the lungs.

Dragging a struggling Megan forward by the wrist he tried to control his own desperate urge to breathe. With only a few feet left to swim to the opening she began fighting like crazy. Megan's exertions used up the last molecules of oxygen in her lungs, and she tried to surface. Her head hit the hard stone roof and she passed out. In desperate need of air himself Jack swam on, pulling a limp Megan behind him. Suddenly they were out and above their heads the silvery surface shone brightly. Pushing her upward with all his strength, he followed.

His head broke surface in a rush of huge, choking gasps. Megan lay motionless and facedown on the surface in the brilliant sunlight. Grabbing her under the arms, he flipped her onto her back, holding her head out of the water. He'd guessed right. They were near the edge of the rocks and only fifteen feet away to the south a small sandy beach rose from the water. Luckily there was no coral, just the white sand bottom a few feet below them.

"Come on, Meg," he said to her, "Come on."

Holding her around the chest, he summoned the last of his strength and stroked towards the shore. A few seconds later his feet touched the sand and he carried a limp Megan up the tiny beach, laying her on the warm sand. Bending over her, he immediately began to give her CPR. Desperately carrying out the routine, he heard a pleading voice he almost didn't recognize as his own.

"Come on, breathe, breathe."

Fighting down the panic welling inside his chest, he tried to push aside any thoughts that she might not make it. He kept on breathing for her, unaware of the seconds ticking by.

"Come on Megan, come on."

It seemed like an eternity and Jack began to feel that she was gone, but he kept on going. And then miraculously she coughed, her body wracked by spasms as she came back from the brink. Dropping down in the sand, Jack felt a wave of relief sweep over him, and he gently took her head in his lap, stroking her forehead.

After a few minutes she settled down, and his heart went out to her as he wiped the tears away from her eyes.

"Am I dead?" she asked shakily.

"You made it just fine, Meg, you made it," Jack said, still stroking her forehead.

His hands shook as the realization of how close he had come to losing her set in.

CHAPTER FOURTEEN

The Ruby C

Megan was alright. She was breathing normally and Jack began to relax. Inevitably his thoughts returned to their immediate situation and he wondered just how they were going to weather the coming trials. Dying of sunstroke on a desert island was a hard way to go.

Helping her higher up the shore, they collapsed again at the base of a huge slab of rock.

"Let me have a look at you," he said running his hand over her head.

"I hurt all over," she said gingerly touching her lip.

"You hit yourself pretty hard in the tunnel he said.

Her struggle had started her lip bleeding again, but a new crust was already forming.

"Got to rest," she said, "tired."

Megan was mentally and physically wasted. The swim through the grotto had sapped her strength and she lay with her eyes closed against the slightly overhanging stone. It offered only a sliver of shade but she was grateful for even that.

They lay quietly for a while not saying much. After an hour, he felt stronger. As the tropical sun rose higher in the sky, so did the heat and the torture of their thirst.

"God I'm thirsty," Megan said, her voice raspy.

He stretched out his long bronzed arm and touched her shoulder gently. "I'm going to see if I can find us something to drink," He told her.

Nodding weakly, she raised her arm up over her eyes.

He had absolutely no idea where he'd find any. The atoll was flat and porous and the abundant rain that had fallen during the night seeped into the fine coral sand as quickly as it had come down.

Wandering around the rock maze he looked for any trace of fresh water. The storm had altered Aves's face, sweeping away a large section of the island to the east and the sand around the rocks had shifted as well exposing new faces of stone while covering others.

The blue Caribbean rose and fell in sparkling splendor around the atoll, and the sky once again held the fine puffy white clouds that had accompanied him on so many voyages. A good sailing breeze blew his blond hair back from his forehead and his dark brown eyes looked seaward but all he saw was an empty horizon, void of any promise.

"Right out of the damned tourist magazines," he said almost resentfully.

Walking away from the rocks he looked towards the south end of the atoll. A vast area of sand had been shifted. Suddenly he spotted a small pond of water separated from the sea. It was a hundred feet ahead. Running to the edge he fell to his knees, dipping a handful and putting it to his lips. He choked; it was foul and salty.

Disappointment overwhelmed him. Walking back to the rocky area, his thirst seemed even more oppressive. Further searching proved unproductive and he returned to Megan.

"Find any water?" she croaked.

"Not yet but I'll go look at the north end in a minute," he promised before lying down next to her.

The sun rose and passed its zenith. Jack decided that while he still had strength he'd climb the biggest of the rocks in order to look out towards the east. Maybe there was a ship passing.

Megan lay unmoving with her arm across her eyes. He touched her forehead gently before leaving; it was hot.

Walking once more through the rock maze he recognized a sound that had been absent. Great seabirds circled once more over the sandy atoll. A large albatross swooped low over his head and it's yellow eye seemed contemptuous of his inability to leave his sandy prison.

A few moments later he reached the biggest of the rocks. In a daze he climbed the gently sloping slab of grey steely stone. He reached the top and scanned the horizon. It was still empty, which didn't surprise him.

Standing there wondering what to do next, he felt another sensation; his toes were warm and wet. Looking down in disbelief he couldn't believe his eyes; he was standing at the edge of a large pool of water. Falling to his stomach he pressed his cracked dry lips to the liquid praying it wouldn't taste salty. This time it was fresh and wonderful. The rain puddle lay in a dip on the top of the rock about eight inches deep and ten feet across. There was probably more than fifty gallons there. Jack stood up, cupping his hands in Megan's direction and called as loudly as his hoarse voice would allow

"Megan, Megan, over here."

She was less than eighty feet away and he hoped she'd hear him. After a minute she appeared walking unsteadily towards him through a passage in the rock.

"What is it? A ship?" she asked looking up towards him and shielding her eyes from the sun.

"Better, there's water. Quick, come around this way," he shouted, indicating the way up.

Slowly climbing the gentle rock slope she took his hand to help her up to the level section. Kneeling down she pressed her face into the puddle. The water was hot from the sun.

"God it's good," she said.

Beatrice's high winds and driving rains had scoured the bird droppings from the rocks and they looked new and steely gray. Neither of them had ever tasted water so good.

"Better than good," Jack replied drinking greedily from the puddle.

Suddenly he noticed something else. The water was evaporating fast. Wide damp margins surrounded the puddle's edges where the stone sloped gently towards the center. It would not last another day.

Quenching their thirst they dunked their faces briefly, letting the water revive them. Leading Megan back to the shade of the rocks he left her to scout for another pan or dip filled with water. After a thorough search it was clear that it was the only one. When it was gone there would be no more. If the water could be preserved it might last for a number of days, but there was no way to protect it. The sun was evaporating it faster than they could drink it.

Jack walked around the island looking for some sort of container he might use, but there was no trace of any human presence, not even an empty tin can. Patrolling the edge of the shore near the lagoon he found a large empty conch shell. Rinsing the shell carefully in the sea he carried it back to the puddle and filled it with fresh water. He stowed it in the shade of the rocks. Over the next hour he managed to find more than a dozen empty conchs and laboriously filled every one. The fresh water was a magic potion for them both physically and mentally. Their spirits rose and they began to feel hungry.

Jack waded into the shallows picking up four huge live conchs. Where man had never harvested them they were plentiful. Holding the big shells in his arms he carried them to the rocks and broke them open with a stone. It was hard work but well worth it. Although tough and rubbery the flesh was fine and white. Beating the muscles with a piece of dried coral until it was tender, he carefully washed two pieces in the sea before serving them to Megan.

"You don't expect me to eat that thing?" she asked screwing up her face.

"It'll give you strength," he said, and as he handed it to her a mischievous smile crossed his face; all across the West Indies, the tasty mollusk was highly prized for it's aphrodisiac qualities.

"What?" she asked suspiciously catching the smile.

"Nothing," he replied innocently.

"I don't trust you, Jack Carlton," she looked at his grinning face and handed back the piece of white meat, "I want to see you eat it first."

Without hesitation he took the white meat and popped it into his mouth, chewing slowly.

"Mmm, a culinary delight," he joked smacking his lips together.

Hunger took over and she picked up a smaller morsel and gently chewed it.

"Not bad," she said surprised.

In fact conch was often served raw in salads and tasted not unlike raw clams. Jack ate three of the white muscled conchs, while Megan managed only one. They were at least a quarter-pound apiece.

The day wore on and they tried to hide from the sun but it was merciless. They drank again from the puddle on the rock, but it was disappearing fast. By five in afternoon, when they went for another drink, it had all but gone. All they had left was the meager supply in the conch shells.

There was no question about going back into the cave for the night. They would sleep outside.

In the last of the day's waning light Jack dug a shallow trench for them in the sand against one of the rock faces and once again filled it with dried seaweed. The heat from the day's sunlight would emanate slowly from the stone in the coming hours, keeping them warm.

As they lay down together in their sandy berth, Megan took Jack's face in both hands and gave him a gentle kiss on the mouth.

"Thanks for saving me in the grotto. I lost it I guess."

"Hey, you were pretty gutsy back there, I'm proud of you."

After that they said little, keeping their thoughts to themselves but both felt the same uncertainties. Their second night on the atoll began peacefully but Jack knew one way or the other it would probably be their last.

Later when the full moon rose they awoke to strange grunting noises. Curious they got up and walked carefully towards the shore where the sounds were emanating.

"Turtles, they've come to lay their eggs," Jack said quietly.

In the moonlight glow, they watched enthralled as dozens of the three hundred-pound creatures crawled laboriously up the gentle slope to the high water mark. There the female turtles struggled to dig holes with their hind flippers. Then they laid their soft round golf ball sized eggs in the sandy holes, sometimes as many as a hundred before covering them back over.

"There must be dozens, they're all over the place," Megan said.

"Maybe we could get them to rescue us and carry us away on their backs," she added wishfully.

"I've never seen so many. Must be something to do with the storm they're all coming at the same time," Jack remarked.

They sat there totally absorbed; witnessing one of nature's great mysteries as it unfolded before them. They marveled at the riddle of how these ocean roaming creatures found their way back to this tiny spit of land without fail, year after year, time after time. Jack experienced a sense of despair. When the turtles were finished they would leave as easily as they had come. He and Megan had no such option. They would remain marooned on their tiny sandy kingdom. Later they returned to their hole in the sand and after drinking from one of the conch shells slept again.

Jack dreamt of a tall schooner with white sails making it's way gracefully across a deep blue sea. He heard the sounds of the schooner lowering it's sails and the voices of the crew as they approached the lagoon at Aves.

In the moments before dawn Jack sat up and opened his eyes. After a moment he suddenly realized that he wasn't dreaming at all. There in the distance to the southwest the ethereal form of a tall sailing vessel was lowering away it's sails.

"Meg wake up," he shouted jumping to his feet.

He wasn't dreaming. The voices were louder. Rushing a ways down the still shadowy shoreline to get a better look, his heart took a leap. The ghostly sailing vessel was real enough. She was taking solid form. Emerging into the early dawn, she headed towards the lagoon.

Running back he shook Megan by the shoulder. She was still sleeping the sleep of the exhausted.

"Wake up, wake up," he shouted excitedly.

"Jack you great oaf," she said annoyed, wiping grains of sand from her face and mouth with both hands.

"Get up," he said breathlessly, "there's a boat coming."

Looking over the sandy rise, she shrieked with joy. The dim outline of masts and sails was coming slowly towards the lagoon. His excitement was contagious and she ran towards the shore. A second later, a terrible thought crossed her mind and she grabbed Jack by the arms.

"What if it's the *Fandango*? What if they've come back?"

"It's not. I could recognize her spars anywhere. Come on, let's go!"

"Hang on," she said bending down to pick up her black purse that had fallen from her bikini waistband.

It was a traditional sailor's dawn. Still grayish with golden rays of sunlight filtering up from a sun still below the horizon to the east. Hundreds of sea birds began to stir, squawking and wheeling overhead before taking off on their day's missions.

Making their way quickly down the shore towards the lagoon they shivered a little. The cool harbinger of daylight breezes came from the northeast and they wished for the simple joy of a sweater.

"Who it is?" Megan asked, still unable to believe she wasn't dreaming.

"Not sure, look, he's nearing the mouth of the lagoon," he replied pointing to the southwest.

In the distance the ghostlike image of a dark hull and tall masts crept ever closer and despite the screeching of the sea birds, they could hear the sounds of a deep-sea schooner lowering her sails. The faint sound of canvas slating back and forth, block and tackle snapping and creaking and the faint whisper of voices relaying orders along the deck was unmistakable.

She was under power, motoring slowly into the lagoon and as Jack and Megan listened they heard the muffled rumble of her auxiliary diesel engine. It was a sweet sound.

Walking quickly towards the anchorage Jack felt as though he was moving in slow motion, he couldn't move fast enough. He was terrified that whoever it was might turn around and leave before seeing them.

As they got closer Jack suddenly recognized the vessel and gave a quick laugh.

"It's the *Ruby C*, Neddy King's fishing schooner. He's come for the turtles," Jack said amazed.

"I knew they were good for something," she said smiling.

As the sun rose in brilliant splendor, two figures ran along the sands of Aves atoll, their feet raising little puffs as their feet hit the sand. Stumbling breathlessly the last few feet to the water's edge at the head of the lagoon they waved as the schooner dropped anchor a hundred yards in front of them.

Jack and Megan began shouting at the tops of their voices across the water. Looks of amazement appeared on the faces of the crew as they pointed towards the shore.

"Over here, over here," he screamed waving his hands high above their heads.

Megan shouted too, jumping up and down on the sand in excitement. They watched impatiently as the crew of the *Ruby C* rigged the gantlines from the tops of the masts and launched the long boat.

Jack recognized his old friend Neddy's snow-white beard. The old seafarer and two crew climbed in and the men took the oars, pulling quickly towards the sandy shore. A few minutes later the bow crunched on the crushed coral at the water's edge. As Jack took hold of the bow he knew they were saved.

Captain Neddy King stepped over the gunwale of the wooden boat to the sand.

"Jack mon, what de hell you doin here?" he asked incredulously as he extended a huge grizzled paw.

A powerfully built man of some sixty odd years, his leathery looking face was deeply creased by years of sea and sun. He wore the usual island fisherman's garb of faded blue denim shorts and khaki shirt. A straw hat perched on the back of his head, held on by a heavy knotted cord under his chin.

"It's a long story," Jack replied shaking hands and in a torrent of words he and Megan told him their tale.

Taking off the straw hat Neddy shook his head of white hair and his blue eyes sparkled.

"So, what you tellin me Jack, dey steal your schooner and leave you here to die?" Neddy asked in amazement.

He suspected there was more to the story, but he reckoned Jack would tell him when he wanted to.

"Hard to believe isn't it," Jack said hardly believing it himself.

"Dammit mon, you lucky like hell, you know?" Neddy said shaking his head. "But, what happened to you when de storm come?"

Jack and Megan looked at each other before replying.

"We hid in the caves, Neddy. You know the caves at the north end?"

Neddy King's eyes opened wide.

"I know about dem well enough, but I never go dere. Is a cursed place, you know," he replied making a sign of the cross over his barrel chest.

"Got more damn Duppies an Zombies inside dere dan in de Martinique graveyard on a dark night."

"How about you Neddy? What made you sail out here so soon after the storm?" Jack asked a little surprised.

"It was a hunch mon. I reckoned dat if I sail right after de storm, I would have de longest time before de next bad weather to catch me turtles," Neddy explained. "Ain't seen none roamin about have you mon?"

"You may have just hit it right, my old friend," Jack replied laughing, "there was a whole army of the things up the beach last night. I think there was a big run."

Neddy was really pleased to hear this. It was a bit of a hit or miss bet to sail to Aves and coincide exactly with a good turtle run, especially during the few days you could stay. It was a certainty that you'd have at the most a week or so before having to leave for bad weather, but the runs usually lasted more than one night, and if the previous night were a heavy one, then maybe he'd make a good haul.

"Anyway, that's what happened to us Neddy. I can't tell you how glad we are to see you. I reckon if you hadn't shown up today, we would have ended up trying to swim for it," Jack joked.

"Long swim, Jack mon," Neddy laughed, "Now, come aboard and we goin get you some clean clothes and a bite to eat. By de bye, who your friend is?" he asked, motioning to Megan.

Jack suddenly realized he hadn't yet introduced her. Neddy was quite a character and stood on tradition and ceremony.

"This is Megan. She's the Chef on the *Fandango*. She ended up getting left here with me."

"Megan, is a real pleasure to meet you, sweet lady," Neddy smiled while reaching out to shake her hand. He did it with a lot of charm and a little flourishing bow.

Even though Neddy King was well into his sixties he had a lot of charisma and continued to enjoy a reputation in Antigua as quite the ladies' man.

"Well Jack mon, I got to tell you, your cook certainly more pretty dan mine," he said with a laugh.

Esau, his cook on the *Ruby C* had been with him for many years. A roly-poly Antigan with only half a nose, his wife had bitten the other half off during a domestic battle.

Laughing they climbed into the longboat and the two heavily muscled islanders rowed back to the anchored schooner where they went up the rope ladder to the deck. Jack had never been happier to step aboard a vessel in his life. At the back of his mind he'd had serious doubts about ever seeing a deck again. Megan was exuberant too. She had despaired of ever getting off the island, despite Jack's promises.

As they stood there near the rail, Neddy took a close look at Megan's face and her swollen lip.

"Megan, you come with me now. We goin fix you up just fine, come," he said with great authority.

She glanced quickly at Jack, who could only smile as Captain Neddy took her by the hand and led her to the galley house on the foredeck, just abaft the foremast. The crew had rigged an awning under the boom, and in its shade the morning trade wind was cool and refreshing.

Sitting her down on an upside down wooden deck bucket captain Neddy waited as one of the crew brought the small canvas bag that held his medical kit. Esau came out of his galley bringing a well-polished aluminum pan with fresh water and a soft cloth. He also gave her a tin mug with some water to drink. Neddy let her have a sip and then he carefully dabbed the cut on her lip with a cotton pad from his bag.

"Now, dis goin hurt jus a little, eh," Neddy said, his voice as soft as silk. "Jus be still."

Pouring a little red liquid from the bottle onto a piece of cotton he applied it to her lip. She didn't flinch and after a few more seconds of closer scrutiny, Neddy was satisfied the cut was going to heal fine.

"Now, dis way," he said, and taking her by the hand again like a child, lead her to the aft companionway.

Jack watched as they passed him again but couldn't resist a comment.

"Hey Neddy, what about me? Don't I rate any attention aboard here?" he asked laughing.

"You too damned ugly Jack, I goin atten you after I finish wid de young lady," Neddy replied with a wink.

Leading a bemused Megan down the aft companionway he showed her where to have a wash in private and gave her some clean clothing. There was only one private cabin on the fishing schooner and that was the Captain's. He emerged a moment later with a satisfied look on his face bringing up an old but clean faded denim shirt for Jack.

"Here you go mon." he said tossing it to him, "put dis on."

"Thanks," Jack said appreciatively.

"You have a lil wash up far'ard here if you want, jus don't waste de water. Den, we goin have some food."

Jack listened on as his friend berated old Esau the cook, but he could tell the words were spoken on the basis of a long and true friendship.

"Esau, you ball-head jackass, we got guests on board so trow way dat stinkin gash you cookin and get some good food goin'." he ordered him in a familiar tone.

Old Esau replied with a few ripe expletives and slammed the galley door. Jack could hear him grumbling behind the wooden panels.

"Neddy tink dat jus cause he got gueses on de vessel he could 'buse me? Well dat ain de case at all, at all. How de man could 'buse me so?"

The *Ruby C* was a traditional West Indian fishing schooner with only rudimentary facilities aboard, but Jack was appreciative. Going to the forty-five-gallon water barrel on the port side he dipped a ladle of cool fresh water into the tin wash pan. Scrubbing the three-day stubble on his face with the bar of soap on the side of the bulwark he began to feel alive once again. It was refreshing.

Putting on the clean shirt he joined Neddy and the rest of his crew by the galley house for a cup of strong, sweet Jamaican coffee and one of the fish cakes Esau was frying up and passing out to the crew. They were a motley looking bunch, with straw hats and large fish knives at their waists, but Jack knew old Neddy was a tough one and wouldn't have any, but the best seamen and fishermen on his schooner.

Megan came up at that moment dressed in a pair of Neddy's blue shorts and a faded white tee shirt, with 'Mount Gay Rum' stenciled on the front. She had rinsed her hair out and put it in a ponytail and looked gorgeous. She had the loose fitting shorts cinched up with a piece of twine and under different circumstances, might have looked funny, but Jack thought she looked as wholesome and beautiful as ever.

"You have a seat here now Megan, and we jus' goin' get you some coffee and a bite," Neddy told her in his deep, gentle manner.

He got up himself and went to the small window of the galley house to get the mug.

"Put in extra sugar too," He growled at Esau.

Captain Neddy never asked anyone to do anything. He always told them what to do. He'd been at sea for more that fifty years, starting out on a trading schooner at aged twelve and figured he'd earned that right. But everyone noticed that with Megan, he was gentle as a kitten.

The storm swell had subsided as fast as it had come up and even the cloudy remnants of the day before were gone. The sky was powder blue and the friendly puffy white trade wind clouds sailed gently overhead, occasionally filtering the golden blaze of the sun as it shone down on them.

Where the giant waves had washed away a section of the southern part of the atoll, it left a wide shallow area less than two feet deep. A school of sardines had already taken up residence, hoping to escape the hungry jacks in the lagoon. But now the birds, which had returned hungry after the storm, swooped down like dive-bombers picking them off at will. Even as they watched, the gentle surge was washing sand back up the atoll's shore and after a few months it would probably look much as it did before the storm.

In the lagoon, the *Ruby C* swung to her anchor comfortably, rolling only a little.

"So Jack mon, what you want to do den eh? I can't take you back for at least three days. I got to catch some turtle to make my trip pay or I in trouble," Neddy said a little apologetically.

"How's your radio working?" Jack asked suddenly, an idea coming to mind.

"Good. You want to try callin somebody?" Neddy inquired.

"Yeah, I was thinking maybe I could get Billy Ramsey to fly out here and pick us up before they get too far with my schooner."

"Kanga Billy? Well yes, if he ain't drunk maybe."

Neddy didn't have a lot of time for Billy Ramsey. He felt the rum was a lot like the Bible, real good in small doses. But Billy? Well, like he was on mission to drink all the rum in the islands.

"English Harbour should be on de air now. Is after nine." Neddy said, "Les go give dem a try."

They left Megan regaling the crew with her tale of survival on Aves. The rough looking men of the *Ruby C* gathered round, captivated by the flaming redhead in the baggy blue shorts, and every man had his eyes riveted on her. Jack suspected they rarely had female guests aboard and certainly none as foxy looking as Meg. She was having a ball telling them about it, and he could tell she was happy again.

The two men went below to the aft cabin. It was small and functional, just what you'd expect on a fishing schooner. It was neat though and the bright white walls showed that Neddy had recently done a paint job. There was a comfortable bunk against the port side and a small skylight opened to the deck. Jack noticed Megan's bikini sitting on the edge of the sink where she'd rinsed it out. There was a small pine topped chart table to one side with a chair in front. Neddy's ancient chart of the Caribbean was laid out on the top. It was marked with coffee stains and a hundred faded pencil lines, reminders of voyages long past.

The ship's radio was on a shelf just over the chart table and Neddy sat down in the chair.

"Jack, I just goin' tune you in and den I goin' leave you, could be a while gettin anybody," Neddy told him over his shoulder.

Tuning transmitter in to 2182 he tested the squelch and volume.

"OK man, all yours," he said getting up from the chair.

"Thanks," Jack said. "I owe you."

"I know dat mon," Neddy said, smiling as he left.

Jack gave a small chuckle as he picked up the big Raytheon's telephone handset and began calling.

"English Harbour Radio, English Harbour Radio, this is *Ruby C, Ruby C*. Do you copy?"

There was no answer, but he kept on trying. Every three minutes or so he repeated the call trying to make contact. After fifteen minutes a broken female voice rasped over the speaker.

"*Ruby C*, this is English Harbour Radio. What's your traffic? Over." It was Jen from the charter office.

"English Harbour, this is *Ruby C*. Is that you Jen? Over."

"English Harbour back. Yes it's Jen. Is that you, Jack? Where are you? Are you all right? Over," she asked sounding concerned.

"*Ruby C* back. Yes we're all right, but I need to contact Billy right away. Is he around? Over."

"English Harbour back. You're in luck Jack, he's right here. Do you want to speak to him? Over," Jen's voice faded in and out.

"*Ruby C* back. Yes, let me have a word. Over."

A second later, the familiar deep Australian accent came over the radio. "You've caused a bit of strife here mate, what's up?" Billy Ramsey never bothered with any radio etiquette, he just got on with it.

"I'll tell you all about it when I see you. Right now we could sure use some help," Jack told him briefly about their predicament.

"What do you want me to do, sport," Billy came back.

"*Ruby C* back. Billy, I need your Catalina to look for the *Fandango*. Can you fly out to get us? Over."

Billy Ramsey was a man of action and it took only a split second to decide.

"No worries mate, I've already left. What's the sea condition out there?" he inquired.

"*Ruby C* back to English Harbour. It's good Billy. The Cat won't have a problem. Over."

Billy knew Jack Carlton was an experienced pilot. If he said that it was OK then he'd take the report as gospel.

"No worries then. Look out for me in a couple of hours."

At the charter office in English Harbour, Billy Ramsey stuck his cigar butt back into his mouth.

"Poor Jack and Meg. Sounds like they've been through hell," Jen commented.

"Ah don't worry your little head Jen. I'm going to fly down there and fetch them up. Then we're going to find that boat of his," Billy finished dramatically, "Now, where's me hat?"

"There it is Billy," Jen said pointing over to one of the chairs.

She didn't question him further. If big Billy said it was going to be alright, then it would be.

Twenty minutes later, the half dozen tourists sitting on the terrace at the Admiral's Inn had their breakfasts rudely interrupted by deafening blasts as Billy fired up the Catalina's big Pratt and Whitney engines. They watched enthralled as the big silver plane rolled down the sandy ramp at the inside end of English Harbour and splashed into the water. The roar of her engines reverberated around the surrounding hills as Billy edged the throttles forward, taxiing the big amphibian around the dockyard towards the sea.

Pulling the Mount Gay rum bottle from its residence beneath the seat he took a long swig before replacing it. One of the local yacht crew was rowing his punt out to a vessel anchored in the outer bay at that moment and Billy almost ran him over.

"Outa me way, ye bloody moron. Can't you see I'm in a rush?" he barked out the small cockpit side port.

His mate, Jack Carlton, was in a jam and there wasn't any time to waste. Ramming the throttles open, the big Catalina thundered past the terrified crewman in the dinghy, leaving old Fort Berkeley to his right. The big silver bird roared out into the open Caribbean Sea where she bounced once before lifting off.

*****

Back on the *Ruby C* Jack secured the radio and climbed the ladder to the deck. Megan was still preaching to the crew from her upside down bucket. She even had old Neddy captivated, and that was saying something.

"And when the storm was at it highest, when the waves were just crashing over the whole place... Oh, hi Jack," she noticed him walking forward.

"I was just telling the guys about what happened to us back on the atoll."

"I hope you're not giving them all the details," he joked winking at her.

"Jack!" she blushed.

"You get through?" Neddy asked.

"Yes, Billy said he'd be out here in a couple of hours with the Catalina to pick us up."

Captain Neddy cut the session short then. His crew had a lot of work to do and he set them about preparing the nets for setting in the shallows for the male turtles. The males would follow the females in to mate when they'd finished laying their eggs and they were easy to catch.

Esau prepared the kerosene lanterns the crew would use as they walked around the shores of Aves during the night, searching for turtles. They would flip them over so they couldn't escape, returning for them the following day.

Jack and Megan sat in the shade together discussing the many 'what ifs' whirling around in their heads. Finally, they both dozed off in the shade of the awning.

Jack woke to a familiar noise. The deep throated drone built and suddenly he realized what it was. The distant roar of big Pratt and Witney radial aircraft engines. He'd heard them often enough. Touching Megan on the shoulder he stood up on the deck looking towards the east. The crew of the schooner stopped what they were doing and looked on as well.

A tiny dot appeared low on the horizon, growing slowly in size until the Catalina appeared to the east of Aves. The huge silver bird came in low over the *Ruby C*. The one hundred and four-foot wings waging in greeting. The sound of the twelve hundred horsepower radial engines was deafening. Billy sure knew how to fly that thing, Jack thought to himself smiling. They watched as the big twin engine aircraft banked again low across the island. They could see the logo *"Digeree Do"* in bright red letters on the side of the fuselage.

The World War II vintage amphibian aircraft was certainly an unusual looking plane. The main wing and engines perched over the wide fuselage, attached buy a large single pylon. The plane's most distinguishing features were the two large Perspex blister hatches on each side of the main float hull between the main wing and the tail. A pair of smaller folding floats hung at the ends of the wing. The Catalina had a top speed of 179 mph and cruised at a more leisurely 117 mph, but her most endearing feature was her range of 2500 miles.

The birds scattered out over the lagoon trying to escape the deafening roar of the engines and the huge strangely shaped bird. On the third run the plane went further off to the south and came back in low. He was going to land.

Billy was good and flew the big aircraft like a graceful bird. He came in low and slow, headed right for the mouth of the lagoon. As soon as he was out of the rough water he throttled the engines right back and the stepped fuselage settled gently on the azure surface of the water. Billy then pulled stick and lifted the nose. She stopped planing quickly then, coming to a halt in the center of the lagoon.

There was no way to really secure the big amphibian short of anchoring it, and Billy certainly didn't want to hang around out here at Aves if he could help it. It was time to go.

"Well Neddy, like I said, I owe you," Jack said as they stood near the rail.

"Eh, eh, don't worry, I know you do man," Neddy replied smiling.

"Could you get a couple of your guys to row us over to the plane?" Jack asked him.

At that moment Billy opened the little Perspex side window in the cockpit canopy and waved them to come over. He wasn't going to hang around.

"I goin' take you myself," Neddy said, motioning them to the rail.

Megan joined them then and gave the old West Indian Captain a huge kiss on the cheek.

"Captain Neddy, thank you for saving us. You're the best," she said smiling.

As they climbed down the ladder Neddy turned to Jack.

"Bes you watch out man, she likes me. I might jus steal her from you and replace Esau," he said wistfully.

Despite his advanced age, Neddy was still a powerful man, and he put the long oars in the oarlocks, effortlessly rowing Jack and Megan towards the amphibian. Billy had inched up to windward into the shallows at the head of the lagoon and shut down the starboard engine letting the big plane drift. A moment later Jack saw the starboard bubble blister pop open and Billy appeared, waving them on.

"Come on you lot, I'm drifting fast here," he bellowed.

Neddy expertly slid the long boat alongside the gently drifting Catalina, and Billy grabbed the gunwale as it touched the side. Billy Ramsey looked like hell. He was suffering the consequences of a two-day drinking bout at the Ad's and his bulbous nose had burst a few more blood vessels, it was as red as a beet.

"Thanks for coming, Billy," Jack said, "You know Meg and Neddy?"

"Yup, know them both sport. Come on up," he said a little impatiently. It was amazing how Billy could talk through his cigar butt, without ever loosing it.

Jack shook hands quickly with Neddy one last time as Billy helped Megan through the hatch.

"Neddy, I'll see you back in Antigua man, and thanks again."

Neddy King just smiled, motioning for him to board the plane. Jack climbed through the blister hatch. Billy Ramsey waved quickly to the old Captain and after fidgeting with the faulty latch slammed it shut.

"Right Jack, let's get this box of aluminum and baling wire off the wet before we get into the rough water," Billy said urgently.

Jack knew he didn't want to let the amphibian drift into the rougher water outside the lagoon, where they could dip a wing float and get in to a whole peck of trouble.

Inside the Catalina was littered with cases of whisky and other liquor, probably the remnants of Billy's last booze-run down to Venezuela. There was an old Lee Enfield and a shotgun tied to the airframe of the aircraft with small twine. Somehow they looked right at home there.

The big Australian moved quickly forward to the cockpit and hit the starter switch for the starboard engine. It roared to life after only a touch. Billy smiled and gave his head an appreciative nod. He did all of his own maintenance on the plane and kept it in top shape mechanically, if not cosmetically.

Motioning for Megan to take the little jump seat behind Billy, Jack sat in the co-pilot's seat. Billy gunned the port engine and the big aircraft swung around facing the open sea. It was going to be a down wind run, but there wasn't much wind.

Billy opened the throttles and the big Pratts lifted clouds of white spray. The Catalina took a few moments to get up on the step and then she picked up speed rapidly. They roared by the anchored *Ruby C*, no more than a hundred feet away. Her crew stood at the rail waving them off. When the air speed reached eighty-five Billy pulled the yoke back hard. The big Catalina shuddered a little and just as they left the protection of the lagoon she lifted off. They were airborne.

Billy climbed her slowly up to three thousand feet and steadied the aircraft on a southeasterly course. They decided to search the islands from St. Lucia northwards. These were the most likely possibilities of where the *Fandango* might have made landfall.

The Catalina was a fine aircraft, durable and dependable. It could carry a good load and was roomy inside, but she was slow. Her cruising speed was less than a hundred and twenty knots and it would take at least two hours to close the Windward Islands.

Billy Ramsey leaned towards Jack and shouted over the noise of the engines.

"Got to work your passage, mate," and with that he motioned for Jack to take over the controls.

Billy reached down and took the half-empty bottle of Mount Gay from behind the seat, took a good swig, leaned back, and closed his eyes.

It had been a few years since Jack had last flown, but the big aircraft responded to his touch. Megan smiled at him from the jump seat. He felt right at home and soon began to enjoy flying the grand old lady slowly along between the white puffy clouds.

After a while, Megan stood up and came beside him. He motioned with his hands to see if she wanted to try flying and she nodded. Sitting down on Jacks lap she took the yoke in her hands. The blue Caribbean crept past below and for the first time in many days, Jack Carlton relaxed a little. It was going to be a pleasant flight.

*****

The *Fandango*'s second night at sea found the wind definitely less violent and the schooner began making better speed through the water. Laura took the wheel for a few hours, allowing the two West Indians to get a little sleep, but she called them again at one in the morning.

The weather continued to improve with each mile sailed and by early afternoon on the following day, while the big PBY amphibian flew eastwards with Meg and Jack aboard, the *Fandango* covered the last thirty miles across the Anegada passage. By three in the afternoon they were closing the southern range of the British Virgin Islands.

CHAPTER FIFTEEN

Trellis Bay

Cobb and Benny had steered for most of the voyage and were exhausted. The schooner's course brought her in on the Virgins and the rocky islands appeared as a line of low hills on the horizon. The afternoon waned and the *Fandango* gradually closed the distance until finally she was within a mile of Virgin Gorda.

Laura took over the wheel. The islands presented a maze of shoals to the south and she needed to know where to enter the island chain.

"Where does Jack usually sail in here," she asked Cobb.

"Through de Roun Rock Passage," he replied in a tired voice.

He thought about giving wrong directions, but skipper Jack wouldn't want him to do that, it would surely mean a sad end for the *Fandango*.

"Show me where to go," she snapped impatiently, "and don't even think about doing something stupid, Garcia would really like to try out that little gun of his."

Cobb got the message. The Puerto Rican sat looking miserable in the cockpit. The rough passage hadn't done anything to improve his demeanor and he nervously fingered the Uzi resting in his lap. Cobb pointed to the high round headland a mile and half off to port. The deep entrance channel lay to it's right. "Over dere, dat's where skipper Jack does pass," he told her.

Laura turned the helm bringing the schooner onto a course that would take them through the passage. It looked very small from a distance but as they approached, the gap began to look wider.

Laura nervously slowed the engine. Steering the yacht into Round Rock Passage channel, she kept to the center. Although it was deep and there was in fact lots of room it seemed like a tight squeeze. Keeping the schooner on her course they passed from the waters of the Anegada passage into Sir Francis Drake channel and the sea calmed right out.

"Should I tell the guys drop the sails?" Henderson asked Laura.

"Yeah, it's time," she replied almost disdainfully.

He picked up his pistol and with Garcia's help, they shepherded Cobb and Benny about the business of lowering sail.

Sir Francis Drake channel ran some eight miles from one end of the British Virgin Islands to the other, east to west. The calm sheltered expanse of water was protected to the north by Tortola and Jost van Dyke and the islands of Virgin Gorda, Cooper, Ginger, Salt, Peter and Norman to the south.

It was still a little overcast and a few squally looking dark clouds remained overhead. The effects of Beatrice's wrath spanned many miles. The waters of Sir Francis Drake channel were, for the most part deep, and there were no obstacles between Round Rock Passage and Beef Island. Henderson asked Cobb to point out the island because they were hard to define and looked the same. Their destination lay directly across from the pass they had just come through and Laura turned the wheel a little bringing the schooner on to her new course.

They closed the mile and a half to Beef Island rapidly. Trellis Bay opened up in front of them and soon they could see tiny Bellamy Cay in the center. The water was crystal clear and as the sandy bottom came into view Laura slowed the schooner to idle speed. Henderson noticed the shiny skin of an aircraft's tail parked behind the high grass on a dirt airstrip and a brief smile crossed his face.

"Where do you want to anchor," Laura asked Henderson.

"Over there, as near to the little dock as you can," he replied.

"When I get in the middle, I'm just going to stop and then you can tell them to drop the anchor," Laura instructed.

Garcia escorted the two West Indians forward to the anchor winch, while Henderson stayed beside Laura at the wheel. The schooner glided serenely into the center of the bay and she put the engine in neutral and then reverse, stopping her forward motion.

"I'm stopped," she shouted forward to Garcia and he motioned for Cobb to drop the anchor.

The Danforth slipped out the hawsepipe and sank to the sandy bottom. It was just after four thirty in the afternoon when they finally anchored in Trellis Bay.

Cobb slacked out seventy-five feet of chain and screwed down the winch brake. It was calm and that would be enough. Henderson was about to have them launch the Whaler when Laura stood up in the cockpit.

"I can't stop this thing," she shouted, sounding confused and fed up, "The engine doesn't seem to have a stop button."

Henderson turned to Cobb.

"How do you shut down the engine?"

Cobb thought for a moment, an idea rapidly forming in his mind.

"Well sir," he said sounding cooperative, "De shut dung is bruken and I have to go in de engine room to stop it."

He was lying. There was a small brass lever inside the teak wheel box that shut it down, but neither Henderson nor the woman would ever find it, Cobb thought.

"You'd better not be playing with me, because I don't have time," Henderson warned him, "You say you have to go into the engine room to shut it down?"

"Yes sir, dat where de engine is," Cobb repeated sarcastically.

"Garcia, you take him down," Henderson ordered.

The Puerto Rican smiled and motioned Cobb to move. Going below, the seaman led him to the engine room entrance at the aft end of the main salon. A small varnished wood paneled door and behind it the steel watertight bulkhead door led into the machinery space. Cobb bent and opened both doors and with a grunt Garcia motioned him to enter first.

He went in and quickly shut the main engine down using the governor shut down lever. The big diesel died immediately. Garcia crouched warily in the doorway of the engine room watching. Cobb knew now was the chance he had been waiting for. Standing behind the big diesel engine he hit the spring loaded emergency shut down flap on the air intake blower with his foot while making a motion with his hand on the governor. It swung shut with a loud snap.

"What are you doing," Garcia asked him suspiciously.

"Nuttin sir, just re-settin de gov-nuh," Cobb replied innocently.

Garcia seemed to accept this and they returned to the deck where Benny had unlashed the Whaler. Hooking up the gantlines they quickly launched the boat and a few minutes later it was bobbing alongside. Garcia took the two seamen below to the wardroom and utilized the sail ties again. The Dacron strips of sailcloth were most useful, he thought. He took care to bind them well, tying their feet to their hands behind their back in the kneeling position so that they couldn't move. It would be painful. Cobb struggled a bit to try and get comfortable and Garcia took this as a personal affront. Taking the Uzi from his shoulder he put it on the sofa and spreading his legs above Cobb he looked down at him.

"You no like how I tie you up, crew man?" he sneered.

Cobb was angry and stupidly answered back.

"Why you doan haul you ass, you Puerto Rican bumbo clot." The West Indian invective made Garcia's blood boil. He pulled back and began to slug Cobb in the face. His big bony fists hitting the crewman made a sickening crunching sound and it was only Henderson's appearance in the companion way door a few minutes later that stopped him.

"Quit that," he yelled.

Cobb's face was a bloody mess. Garcia calmly took the roll of duct tape Laura had brought to use with the camera equipment and taped both their mouths shut. They were expendable now and he knew his boss would have no further need of them. Eduardo would not be leaving any evidence behind, alive or otherwise.

The older twin engine Piper was parked over on the sandy airstrip about two hundred feet from the beach. The plane's pilot showed up on the little dock after twenty minutes and began waving. Henderson and Laura climbed in the Whaler and ran in to pick him up.

Joe-Bob Benson was a lifetime looser and boozer. In and out of jail on various drug smuggling and other charges, he'd never been able to stay away from the shady side of life. He was like a bee drawn to nectar. Whenever a seemingly easy money job came along he seemed to be right there waiting. He seemed to relish work that required him to keep a low profile, perhaps because of the half dozen or so outstanding warrants on him in various southern states. Bent character aside he was a good pilot and the shady inter-island flying business was just up his alley. Overweight and forty, he looked a lot older. Short and scruffy he sported a ratty baseball cap perched on the back of his head. He wore a pair of oil stained khaki trousers and a checked shirt. His pockmarked face was unshaven and his long brown hair hung in wisps from underneath his cap.

"Hey Henderson, I brought the plane in at daylight, where the hell you all been?" he asked in his southern drawl as the Whaler came alongside the low wooden dock.

"We've been rushing to get here, that's where," Henderson replied fed up, "Is the plane full?"

"Nope, but I got a place in Dominican Republic where we'll fill her up."

"I told you to make sure you had full tanks. It was important you had them full," Henderson said angered by Benson's casual attitude.

"Well, I was going to stop in St Thomas, but there's folks there who know me and they might have asked questions," the pilot whined spreading his hands.

This wasn't good news, Henderson thought to himself. He wanted to fly straight to the southern U.S., to a secluded strip in south Florida, where they could land in private. Now they'd have to stop in some sticksville dump in the Dominican Republic to refuel. He decided not to waste time worrying about it.

"Get in then," Henderson instructed.

The pilot climbed aboard the Whaler.

"Anybody see you?" He asked as they cruised back to the schooner.

"Nope, ain't nobody around this pee hole that I've seen," Benson replied flippantly his breath reeking of strong liquor.

They came alongside the schooner a few minutes later. It was quiet in Trellis Bay and there was every chance that no one else would show up which is just what Henderson was banking on. There were only a few boats in the British Virgin Island charter industry and Henderson figured he could count on being alone at this point of the island. There had been no development on this small island, except the small airstrip.

A narrow isthmus separated Beef Island from the main island of Tortola. The only way across from the mainland was by the little barge that ferried back and forth on a wire cable and nobody came out here, except to meet the weekly DC3 cargo and mail flight from San Juan, and that was still three days away.

Laura tied the whaler alongside before following the others below into the wardroom. Garcia was there with his feet up on the couch. He'd found a cold Carib beer in the fridge and was relaxing, the Uzi machine gun cradled in his lap.

"Who's the spic?" Benson asked, motioning towards Garcia, who tensed at the remark.

"Garcia works for me, so you should watch your mouth," Henderson warned him.

"No skin off my butt," the pilot said, "Got anything to drink on this rust bucket?"

Henderson found the man distasteful and obnoxious and he was beginning to wonder why he'd hired him, but he was a good pilot and flew the plane without any questions.

"I think there's beer in the fridge," he told him.

Joe Bob Benson had been eyeing Laura and he turned to her grinning widely.

"Well hey babe, what say you and me have a brewski together?" He asked suggestively grinning at her.

She gave him a thoroughly distasteful look.

"I don't drink with bums like you," she replied caustically.

Before the conversation went any further Henderson butted in.

"The galley is that way," he said pointing to the forward door. "Get yourself a beer and then let's get organized."

Benson gave her a thorough going over with his eyes, giving her his best Lothario's leer before going through to the galley.

A few moments later Henderson took charge laying out his plans for the coming hours.

"It's too late to fly out tonight so we'll stay put and then just before dawn we'll transfer the gold, take the schooner out a little ways and sink her. At daylight we'll be able to take off in the Piper and head north," he explained.

It would be too risky to take off on the unlighted sand airstrip in the dark, and anyway everyone was exhausted.

Henderson actually had two plans. The first he was sharing with the others and the second he was keeping to himself for the moment. He turned to Laura and Garcia.

"At say four am when it's still dark we'll take care of the schooner. I'll stay ashore with the pilot while you two take the boat out and sink it," he told them, "all you have to do is open the big sea cock in the engine room and come back in the Whaler. As soon as this boat gets her port holes under water she'll sink like a rock."

Laura raised her eyebrows and looked at him in disbelief.

"Henderson, what kind of fool do you think I am? As soon as we leave you'll be out of here," she snapped angrily.

Henderson looked taken aback. He leaned slightly forward and spread his hands.

"Do you honestly think I would risk that? I can't leave you here to go tell the world all about this. We'll wait right here till you come back."

"Why don't you go out and sink the damn thing yourself and I'll wait with fly boy here," Laura argued.

"Neither Garcia or I can handle this boat, Laura. You're the only one who can do it,"

She didn't like it, but Henderson had a point. He wouldn't risk alienating the two of them she could spoil everything. Laura reluctantly agreed and as always, Garcia just gave a sneer as a sign of his agreement.

Cobb smiled just slightly beneath the duct tape. His left eye was beginning to swell shut, but despite his pain and discomfort he felt a deep sense of satisfaction. They wouldn't be going anywhere with Skipper Jack's schooner. With the flap down on the scavenger blower, the main engine would never start and none of them would be able to figure it out. He closed his eyes with a sense of relief. He sure hadn't liked the idea of going to the bottom with the *Fandango*.

Henderson wandered into his cabin thinking about Laura. She'd turned out to be far too pushy for his liking and now the bitch wanted a cut of the take, as well as her exorbitant fee. The second part of his plan concerned her. He would tell Garcia to dispose of her on the schooner as she sunk. It would be best. With that thought in mind, he finally felt things were falling into place and nothing was going to stop him now. As night fell over Trellis Bay, those aboard the *Fandango* settled down for a few hours of much needed rest. They were going to need it.

CHAPTER SIXTEEN

The Search

M egan was astonished, but Jack had seen Billy perform before. Lying back in the pilot's seat with his jaws wide open, his nostrils, mouth and tongue vibrated violently as he snored. Jack wondered how the Australian could sleep with the rumbling roar of the big Pratt and Whitney engines so close.

Sitting in Jack's lap Megan held the large yoke with both hands and flew the Catalina. The big bird pretty much flew itself but he had to admit that she was doing a good job. He wasn't sure whether it was the flying or not and didn't care, but he enjoyed it too. The two had donned the old cockpit intercom headsets to communicate. Although bulky and heavy they worked well and drowned out most of the engine noise.

Weaving slowly along the aircraft occasionally drifted from side to side as she strayed a little off course. Every once in a while, when she strayed too far, Jack pointed his finger in the direction he wanted her to go and she pulled the yoke around, bringing the plane back on course. He kept his feet on the rudder pedals giving only a slight touch from time to time.

"Just keep the aluminum ridge on the front of the windshield level with the horizon," he told her and she did.

Occasionally she gained or lost a little altitude but always brought it back. Every so often she wiggled back a little to get comfortable and Jack smiled over her shoulder. Her nicely rounded bum felt soft and comfy where it was and even though he was beginning to feel a little cramped, he wasn't about to say anything,

An hour and a half after leaving Aves a high landmass appeared dead ahead on the horizon.

"Look Meg, St. Lucia," he said, "There's the famous twin Pitons."

The two volcanic spikes rose precipitously from the sea to a height of some two thousand feet. The sea around the majestic landmarks was very deep giving the water a rich dark blue hue.

Jack pointed down towards a pod of sperm whales on the surface below the aircraft. There were six of the great leviathans, two of them calves. He'd seen them in that location quite often, basking on the surface in the calm lee of the island.

Billy slept on as they closed the island and Jack took the yoke from Megan. She got up and sat on the inside arm of the copilot's seat next to him. Taking the Catalina down to one thousand feet he flew to the south and a little to the right of the Pitons.

Winging their way slowly past the twin peaks, they enjoyed the spectacular view before heading south along the coast towards Vieux Fort. The old abandoned US Naval Air Station was deserted. The heavily constructed concrete runway was superb however and from time to time private aircraft landed there to pick up or drop off passengers. The anchorage next to the concrete airstrip was passable too.

Jack was gambling on Henderson going to an anchorage with an airstrip nearby, but no officials. It was the only way he'd be able to fly the gold out quickly, without interference from the authorities, but as the Catalina droned it's way over the south end of the island, there was no sign of the *Fandango*.

"It's a good day to search," Jack said to Megan over the phones, "it's clear and the masts will be easy to spot if we get near her."

Bringing the Catalina around in a slow turn he flew up the western side of the island. The ruggedly carved coastline was indented with luscious green ravines and many small coves and bays. They kept a good eye to starboard looking for the yacht's tall spars. They'd be hard to miss.

As the day wore on the casual atmosphere in the cockpit of the Catalina, evaporated. There was an air of urgency now and Jack felt increasingly frustrated. His search was actually based on sound premises. There were only a certain number of anchorages able to cope with the *Fandango's* deep draft and Jack knew them all well. He eliminated those that the schooner could not enter and made a mental note of the rest.

Then there were some really out of the way anchorages Henderson would have absolutely no reason to go to. That nixed a healthy number of the tiny coves and little bays in the islands. Jack would concentrate his search on the more likely locations. He hoped his deductions would prove right.

Flying close by the idyllic lagoons of Marigot Bay, he dipped the right wing to have a better look. Suddenly Megan saw him take a sharp breath. Leaning over, she looked out the side window.

"Tall masts in there, going to have a look," he told her.

Throwing the Catalina over on her ear Jack flew up the center of the bay. There was a big schooner anchored there along with a half dozen other yachts, no doubt sheltering form Beatrice.

"Not the *Fandango*," He said, sounding disappointed.

It was his friend Joel Bonnet's hundred and thirty foot *Polynesia*. Jack knew him well, another charter skipper trying to eke out a living in this new industry.

Passing the north end of St. Lucia, the Catalina winged over Pigeon Island and Jack saw the thatched roof shack where Dame Ingrid Russet ran her bar. An old, white haired English lady who'd performed with the Gay Follies way back when. Jack had been drunk there more than once, but there were no yachts anchored there today.

The Catalina droned on, passing Diamond Rock, Martinique and Dominica, but by early afternoon there was still no sign of the *Fandango*.

"I'm thirsty and hungry," Megan said, "I'm going back to the cabin to see if I can find anything."

"Good idea," Jack replied.

Billy was still snoring. He must have had one hell of a bout, she thought. Making her way aft she began hunting around. The fuselage was wide and the two large bubbles on each side of the aircraft offered a neat place to look out. There were loose cases of Gilbys gin on the floor and an assortment of other boxes and bags scattered around. Billy kept a small inflatable rubber boat right at the back and there were some paddles next to it.

Finally, Megan found what she was looking for. Under some rather nasty looking bedding on the port side where the old radio operator's table had been. There was a wooden chest and a white igloo cooler to one side. She pulled it open, but it was filled to the brim with warm Carib beer.

Meg was disappointed. She was thirsty and all Billy had was warm beer and booze. Unloading the igloo to see if there was anything else there, she had just about given up hope when a lonely liter bottle of Coke appeared in the bottom. She picked it up chuckling to herself.

"Oh Billy, whatever would the boys say back in Antigua?"

It was warm, but she opened it with the bottle opener on the side of the box. She also found some canned corned beef and a loaf of bread in the wooden chest. She found a rather unhygienic looking spoon, and after rinsing it with a dash of Coke took it all back to the cockpit and shared the meager meal with Jack.

There was still no trace of the *Fandango*. As they winged their way further northwards, Jack watched the fuel gauge. He gave it the customary flick with his finger to see if it jumped, but it was telling the truth. They were just over half now and he wondered if they would have enough to finish the job.

The little archipelago of Les Saints slid by to their right, producing nothing. Neither did Guadeloupe. Jack skipped by the islands of Marie Gallant and Desirade to the east of Guadeloupe. There would be no reason for Henderson to go there.

As they left the sugar loaf bluff near Anse Des Hayes, Jack steadied on a new course and the big Catalina settled down for the half-hour run to the western most Leeward Islands. A dogleg over St. Kitts and Nevis turned up zip, and with a heavy heart Jack turned for Antigua.

Using the binoculars they continued scanning the horizon ahead of the aircraft, but there was only the wide empty expanse of the blue Caribbean Sea.

Billy Ramsey woke up as they banked over English Harbour. There were a number of sailing yachts there, but no *Fandango*. Jack doubted Henderson would have been stupid enough to take the schooner there anyway, but he had to check.

"Nothing yet mate?" Billy asked.

"No nothing,"

"Want keep heading north?"

"No other place else to look," Jack replied.

"Keep looking mate. They could be further on," Billy told him.

He handed control of the aircraft back his friend. He'd been flying for a number of hours now and was ready for a break. Billy's eyes looked like a pair of large scale road maps, but after checking out the window to get his bearings, he took the yoke and settled down to fly.

Jack was worried. Passing St. Martin and St. Barts, there was still no sign of the schooner and he began to feel a sense of loss. Like most of the owner-operated charter yachts he carried no insurance and if they'd wrecked or sunk his schooner, he'd be shit outa-luck as they say. Jack felt a deep anger as he thought about the whole situation and Megan noticed the cold steely expression cross his face.

There was no point in looking at Saba or Statia and so they stayed to the east. Billy took the aircraft north across the ninety miles of the

Anegada Passage. It was almost evening as the aircraft crossed over Round Rock into the British Virgin Islands. It would be dark soon and if they hadn't found the *Fandango* by then, well Jack didn't want to consider that possibility.

Aboard the Catalina they were all beginning to fade. Billy was holding on, but Jack could tell he was ready to quit and go back to sleep. Megan was putting up a good front. She'd spent a lot of hours with the heavy Zeiss binoculars glued to her eyes and she was tired as well. Jack, on the other hand, was on the stress buzz. He could go along for forty-eight hours or so hours without sleep and perform at optimum level, but then afterwards, he would fall into a comatose state for at least twelve hours.

There was a feeling of hopelessness as Billy banked the Catalina over the eastern end of Virgin Gorda, the first island of the British Virgin Island chain. The sun was close to the western horizon by then, and there was only going to be another half-hour of light left at the most.

North Sound was almost empty, just one small sloop anchored in the southern corner near the beach. There was nothing of interest along the north coast of Virgin Gorda, just a few small craft and a little freighter unloading cement for the Little Dix hotel project.

As they began the flight down Sir Francis Drake channel, the islands sat like a chain of emeralds set in a sparkling sea of twenty shades of blue. The azure shallows with areas of adjoining coral reef could be clearly seen while the deeper areas showed as darker blue. In some places the white sandy bottom reflected the waning light at depths of up to eighty feet.

Jack was beginning to give up hope. It was all going to be a loss. He could always go back and work for Air America; they'd give him a job. He was just thinking of how he might be flying guns into Central America in a few weeks when Megan suddenly spotted something in Trellis Bay, a small cove on the east side of Beef Island.

"Look, something there," she yelled onto the mike.

Turning to look where she was pointing, Jack saw them too. The *Fandango*'s tall masts were sticking up behind Bellamy Cay, a tiny islet within Trellis Bay, where a she was anchored.

"See her?"

"Yes, it's her alright," Jack said.

He felt a rush of euphoria. He had found his schooner.

"That's her Billy," he shouted.

Billy looked over and smiled giving him the thumbs up before putting the Catalina over on her port wing. Taking her well to the south of Beef Island and away from the anchored schooner.

"We've got to land somewhere nearby," Jack said to Billy.

"I'll put her down over the hill from Trellis Bay mate. There's a tiny bay with a sandy beach. Ten-minute walk from the schooner."

When they were out of sight he cranked the flaps down and made ready to put her down on the water. Jack felt good and he was ready to do what ever had to be done.

Passing south of Beef Island's high bluffs and rugged hills Billy kept her a couple miles away, staying at two thousand feet. He didn't want to alert anyone on the schooner.

Billy knew the area well. Banking slowly around, they lost altitude around the back side of Beef Island.

A hundred yards further north a narrow isthmus separated the island from Tortola proper. A little wooden barge on a wire took people back and forth when the mail plane landed once a week. Jack remembered the dirt airstrip on Beef Island; it was just a few yards from the anchorage in Trellis Bay.

If there was any man alive who could handle the lumbering Catalina with style, it was Billy Ramsey. He came in with flair, flying the aircraft like a graceful bird. Jack had to admire him, the man was good. Billy throttled the engines back and let the big amphibian kiss the water so gently they hardly felt a thing. He brought her to a halt in the little cove, a hundred yards from the isthmus and about three hundred yards from the anchored schooner.

There was a sizable hill between the Trellis Bay anchorage and the little cove where Billy had set them down, so with luck they would have remained unseen and unheard. As the last of the days light faded they threw the anchor over and Billy checked to make sure it was holding. They were less than a hundred feet from the sandy shore.

Billy shut the engines down. The silence after so many hours of being next to the roaring Pratt and Whitneys was overpowering. Standing in the cabin of the amphibian, both Jack and Megan experienced a shrill ringing in their ears, but they both smiled when Billy pulled out a huge pair of filthy wax plugs from his ears, rolled them together and popped them in his pocket.

"Bloody noisy this plane," he said shaking his bushy red head.

CHAPTER SEVENTEEN

Trellis Bay

Although the sun had set twenty minutes earlier the moon was already rising over Beef Island. Switching on the twelve-volt overhead light in the cabin Billy popped the blister hatch on the port side. Tiny wavelets lapped gently under the Catalina's aluminum hull and further out the warm waters of Sir Francis Drake channel stretched away towards Peter Island. Billy managed to excavate some of the mess in the back of the hold and magically produced a small propane camp stove and some instant coffee, sugar and a small green jerry can of water. Boiling the kettle, he made up a strong brew and they sat drinking it on cases of gin while munching on some slightly stale crackers he'd also found.

"Meg, you should probably stay here while Billy and I go ashore," Jack told her putting his hand on her arm.

"Why, because I'm a woman?" she asked bristling.

"No, because there's a lot of money at stake here," Jack explained, "these people don't mess around and I don't want you getting hurt."

"Or killed," Billy interjected.

She wasn't about to be put off.

"Sorry boys, but I've already been a victim of piracy, beaten up, marooned, sat through a hurricane and almost drowned in an underwater cave, so I think I've earned my place," she said in a tone that left no room for argument.

Jack smiled, she sure had spirit.

"Alright then, we better go ashore and see what we can find out," he said.

Going to the side of the cabin Billy untied the two weapons lashed to the airframe, handing the first to Jack. It was a heavy Lee Enfield .303 caliber bolt action rifle of World War I vintage with a full box clip of eight rounds. Taking the second firearm down Billy gave it a loving caress. The shotgun was one of the magnificent ivory inlaid double barreled twelve gauge Purdys made in Great Britain. It had belonged to his long dead grandfather, who'd been a wealthy landowner in England. He had actually been posing as a wealthy landowner while working as a burglar at night. He'd been deported to Australia under the prisoner immigrant program generations before. Billy picked up a handful of shells, showing them to Jack. They were the deadly .00 buck, which could cut a man clean in half at close range. He also produced a venerable Webley revolver and stuck it in his right trouser pocket. Opening a small box hidden at the back, his Aussie friend pulled out a World War II vintage German potato masher hand grenade. Holding it up he smiled broadly.

"Christ Billy, what the hell are you doing with those things?" Jack asked jokingly as he examined it.

"Use 'em for fishing normally, saves a lot of time, but maybe we could put 'em to better use now mate," the big Australian replied seriously.

Jack agreed. He wasn't under any illusion about the situation. The people who had stolen his schooner were killers. He hefted the big Lee Enfield rifle. It was heavy and would be awkward to carry, but at least it would even the field a bit. At a distance it might even put them at an advantage. He worked the bolt on the rifle chambering one of the long shells. The action made a satisfying snick. Billy cracked the Purdy at the breech. It was loaded and ready. The Webley was loaded with six rounds.

Megan went through to the cockpit where she'd seen a big thermos flask. Bringing it back she poured the rest of the hot coffee into it.

"It's going to be a long night, isn't it." she stated, screwing the top on the thermos.

'Yes, you're probably right," Jack replied.

"I'll carry this bomb if you want," she said holding up the grenade.

"Alright, just don't pull that big ring ok?" he warned her.

"What, this one here?" She said, putting her forefinger through it.

"Christ, don't do that," Jack roared.

"Don't get your knickers in a knot, I was only joking," she replied smiling.

"You don't joke around with that kind of stuff Meg."

Wrestling the small Zodiac rubber boat from the back of the cabin, they opened the side hatch, pushing it out. It plopped down into the calm water of the cove and Megan and Jack got in with the thermos and the "bomb". Billy passed down two wooden canoe paddles as they held it alongside before ducking inside the fuselage again. A moment later he emerged with the old Lee Enfield and the twelve gauge shotgun. Handing the rifle down to Jack he climbed into the rubber dinghy cradling the shotgun in his arm.

Laying the firearms against the side pontoons they paddled towards the shore. The little craft was tippy but there was no wind and they made good headway. The round bow touched gently on the sand a few minutes later and they climbed out, pulling the boat up the beach. Billy tied the bowline to one of the low hanging branches of the numerous sea grape trees bordering the beach.

It was a quiet, clear night and the moon was rising early. Jack was always impressed at how fast the change between night and day took place in the tropics, one minute it was evening; the next it was night. There was little twilight in between. Glancing at his Rolex it showed seven o'clock.

The occasional fisher-bat flew along the shallows just off the beach, dragging its claws through the water, and the crickets and tree frogs threw a cacophony of cheeps and clicks from the underbrush. Wandering flights of fire flies wandered from bush to bush on some unknown tropical mission, blinking their bright little coded messages as they went.

Standing on the beach near the trees, Jack thought it was as good to let Billy in on the events of the past few days.

"Billy, before you get more involved in this, we need to tell you what happened down at Aves."

"I reckoned you would mate, when you was ready."

"There's a king's ransom in gold sitting on the schooner," he told his friend.

He quickly ran Billy through the bizarre tale, with Megan interjecting from time to time. They told him everything, including the fact that there was a large amount still out there on Aves.

"Crikey mate, when you get into trouble you really dive in head first don't you?" Billy remarked incredulously.

"My life's story man," Jack replied with a chuckle.

Billy turned to Megan.

"You see little lady, nice Sheila's like you shouldn't get hitched with bums like Jack Carlton,"

I'm not hitched to him," she replied quickly, "at least not yet,"

"What about old Neddy? He's still out there wrestling bloody turtles. Do you reckon he'll yank the gold?" Billy questioned.

"Let me tell you about Neddy. There's no way he'll go near those caves, he figures there's an army of zombies and duppies in there."

"Yeah, well, I just might just take another flight down there one of these days and relieve them zombies of some of that coin. Could always use some extra."

"Well Billy, my man, there's enough treasure sitting just over this hill to make us all rich," Jack said.

"Partners?" Billy asked holding out his hand.

"Partners," Jack replied shaking the Australian's big paw.

And then a lilting English voice came from the shadows beside the two men.

"Excuse me chaps. I'd like to get included in this partners business, if you don't mind," Megan said a little haughtily.

"Sheila's don't carry rifles and that means you can't be a partner, right Jack?" Billy said playfully.

Jack waited for the inevitable tirade. He didn't have to wait long.

"Why you overgrown, chauvinistic Dingo. If you think for one minute I'm going to bow out after all I've been through, you'd bloody well better think again. Don't think you can come waltzing in here at the last minute and push me aside, just because I'm a Sheila, God, just where did you Aussie's get that name from anyway..."

Jack cut her off gently, grabbing her and putting his hand over her mouth.

"Hey we're all partners, the three of us," he said, taking his hands away slowly, "just quit shouting".

"Make sure when you talk about treasure from now on you include me," she finished telling them in no uncertain terms.

"I never thought otherwise," Jack said chuckling quietly.

Megan secured her position by shaking hands with the two men.

"Cor," Billy said chuckling, "never been partners in crime with a Sheila before."

"Oh, sod off Billy. Just because I'm a woman doesn't mean that I can't be effective. For your information, this here Sheila managed to fly your bloody great plane most of the way to Antigua."

"Alright you two, are we going or what?" Jack interjected.

"We're going," they replied in unison.

Walking along the beach the full moon rose in the sky. They made their way silently up the hill overlooking Trellis Bay. Following a well-defined sandy trail that the local fishermen used they had no trouble keeping to the path. Megan was barefoot, but the sand was soft beneath her feet. Wild goats made an occasional rustling sound in the bushes as they scurried away from the trio.

Suddenly Megan uttered a sharp cry.

"Ouch!" she yelped jumping to one side of the path, "Something just tried to bite me."

"For Christ's sake be quiet Meg. Do you want them to hear us?" Jack scolded her.

"Look, there it is, it's still moving," she continued pointing to the ground as she backed further away.

Stooping to get a better look, the two men looked down. There was a large dark spider like creature moving slowly across the path. It was one of the big West Indian land crabs so plentiful on the islands. Growing to a foot or more across, they inhabited large holes in the ground, emerging at night to scavenge the surface. Although equipped with huge powerful pinchers, they were secretive creatures and usually fled quickly at the first sound of footsteps.

"No worries, just a land crab," Billy said, "though judging by the speed it's going, looks like you scared the poor little bugger."

"Right, that's it, I'm going back, I don't fancy stepping on another one."

"Wouldn't," Billy warned her.

"Why not?"

"First, you'll forfeit your share if you go walkabout now little Sheila."

"And the second?"

"There'll be a whole lot more of them critters down near the beach."

Megan muttered something under her breath and they walked on. Staying close behind Jack, she held onto his shirttail with both hands wishing she had worn shoes. But then she remembered the last time she had even seen shoes was quite a few days ago.

Clearing the rise of the hill above Trellis Bay Jack' pointed down the hill.

"Look, there she is," he said.

The *Fandango* lay anchored just inside of tiny Bellamy Cay in the center of the bay. She was the only vessel there.

He was overjoyed but the bile rose in his throat as he ran his fingers over the crusted scab on his forehead where Garcia had hit him and there was still a dull ache in his gut where the he had kicked him. He kept on thinking about Garcia running his hands over Megan's breasts and the sound of her whimpering. Unseen in the darkness he smiled a hard smile. He thought briefly about what he would do to the bastard when he got his hands on him. The small rickety wooden dock jutted thirty feet into the bay on the Beef Island side of Bellamy Cay and a rough track led to the dirt airstrip a hundred yards away. The night was clear and as their eyes adjusted to the rising full moon it offered excellent visibility. Suddenly Jack stopped.

"Well, what do you know," he said looking towards the airstrip.

"What is it?" asked Billy, straining to see what was piquing Jack's interest.

"It looks like our friends have some wings waiting. See over there, just to the side of the air strip, there's a plane parked."

Putting his hand on his friend's shoulder he pointed towards the aircraft. The moonlight reflected off of its shiny aluminum skin.

"You're right mate. Reckon they're going to fly their little box of goodies right out of here," Billy said quietly.

"Not if I have anything to say about it," Jack replied evenly,

"Looks like an old twin engine Piper Aztec," he added after another second.

He was familiar with the aircraft; it was one of the types he'd flown in the Far East for Air America. The plane had two one hundred and fifty-horse power Lycomings and although the cruise speed was only two hundred miles per hour, it had good range.

Following the path over the hill down to Trellis Bay it took only ten minutes before they were standing on the shoreline opposite the anchored schooner. Less than a hundred feet away, the moonlight displayed every detail of her hull and rigging, and from what little Jack could see she at least looked intact.

The old wooden dock stood a few feet further down the beach, extending forty feet into the bay. The airstrip with the parked aircraft was a hundred yards off to their left.

Jack turned to Megan and Billy.

"You two wait here a moment while I go have a quick look at the plane," he told them.

"What are you going to do Jack?" Megan asked sounding a little worried.

"Don't worry, I'll be back in a few minutes, just wait for me here."

"Be careful," she whispered.

He liked the way she'd said that.

"Just remember what they call me."

"I know, 'lucky come back Jack'," Megan said as she watched him disappear in the direction of the parked aircraft.

"What's this 'lucky come back Jack' rubbish?" Billy asked her, "I never heard that one before."

"It's what they used to call him in the navy."

"Well you know what? I reckon he is one lucky bastard. Spent his whole life getting in and out of scrapes, our Jacko has, and always come out with no more than a scratch or two."

She didn't know whether that was complimentary or not, but she was cognizant of the respectful tone Billy used. It was the first time she'd heard him talk that way about his friend.

Crouching at the waist he cautiously approached the airstrip. Jack felt there was a good chance someone might be guarding the plane. Reaching the perimeter he looked carefully around, but there was no one in sight, just the silver aircraft glimmering in the moonlight. Making a quick circuit of the plane he took in the low surrounding bush and trees as well. No one.

Walking up to the aircraft he touched the cold skin. It was a lovely old twin engine Piper with a polished aluminum finish. They'd been around a long time and Jack had a lot of hours in them.

For a brief moment he was taken back to the Far Eastern skies where he had flown the rugged little aircraft. There were two footsteps recessed into the fuselage behind the wing on the starboard side and he pulled them out, climbing onto the wing. He tried the cabin door but it was locked. Even with the ample moonlight the tinted windows of the plane prevented him from seeing within. Climbing down he ran back to the trees where Billy and Megan were waiting. He'd only been gone a few minutes.

"See anything mate?" Billy asked him.

"Nope, nothing," Jack replied out of breath, "couldn't see in."

He turned his attention to the schooner. Standing in the shadow of the sea grape trees they looked out across the bay. There was only a hint of a breeze rippling the surface of the water, as she swung imperceptibly to her anchor. Although there was no one visible on the *Fandango*'s decks, they heard the muffled rumble of the Atlas generator set as the exhaust exited under the stern. Lights showed through the hull portholes, but Jack noticed that the usual deck lights were off. They were keeping a low profile. The starboard boarding ladder was in place and the Boston Whaler lay astern on a short line.

Near the dilapidated dock, a number of small wooden fishing skiffs lay pulled up on the sand.

"Why don't we just call the Tortola police?" Megan suggested in a whisper.

"Waste of time. By the time we get to Road Town and convince them we aren't lying, these bums will have split," Jack replied.

"I reckon you're right, sport," said Billy seriously. "I think we're going to have to cause a bit of strife around here by ourselves."

"Look, there's definitely someone aboard," Jack said pointing out to the schooner, "The Whaler's astern and I can hear the generator going."

"It's your call sport. What do you want to do?" Billy asked him.

Jack was silent for a moment considering the options. There just wasn't enough data to work out a decent plan, but it would help if they could find out what Henderson was up to, he thought.

"Come with me," he said.

Getting up they moved towards the wooden fishing skiffs drawn up on the beach.

"We'll just borrow one of these for a while," Jack said choosing an eighteen footer with a decent pair of oars.

Pulling the skiff down the beach into the water, Jack held it as Megan and Billy got in with the Purdy and the Lee Enfield. Wading out a little he pushed off before jumping in. Picking up the oars he fitted them into the oarlocks and rowed slowly towards the darkened schooner.

"Those oars are making one hell of a racket mate," Billy whispered.

Jack lifted them from the oarlocks and handed one to Billy.

"We'll paddle, it's quieter," he whispered.

Jack was certain the muffled rumble of the generator exhaust under the stern would make it difficult for anyone below decks to hear them. They approached from the starboard quarter and when they were less than a hundred feet away Billy suddenly put his hand on Jack's arm stopping him from paddling.

"Bloody hell," he whispered, "someone's coming on deck."

A shadowy figure emerged through the aft companionway hatch and went to the rail on the port side. Putting his paddle down Billy slowly lifted the Purdy, but Jack pushed the twin barrels gently down. The darkened figure moved to the aft deck and lit a cigarette. The flame of the lighter briefly cast an eerie glow upwards, illuminating the man's face. It was Garcia.

"Quiet," Jack whispered trying to hold his paddle still in the water.

If Garcia saw them now the jig would be up, but he didn't seem to be looking in their direction. He stood there smoking his cigarette and the little red glow burned brighter each time he inhaled. A minute later they saw the red dot arc into the water.

Billy dropped the shotgun. It made an unbelievably loud thump on the wooden seat as he tried to grab it.

"Bloody hell," he gasped, fumbling in the bottom of the skiff trying to retrieve it.

Garcia turned suddenly, looking in their general direction. He scanned the darkened bay, and for a brief moment seemed to look directly at them, but then he walked back to the companionway and went below.

Jack heaved a sigh of relief. Henderson and the others could have no idea whatsoever that they'd managed to escape from Aves. They at least had that advantage. Picking up the paddles they continued slowly towards the *Fandango*.

"We'll go alongside where the main salon porthole is," Jack suggested, "Maybe we can see what's going on inside."

"Okay, sport," Billy said picking up the Lee Enfield and laying it carefully against the thwart.

Jack paused for a moment turning to his friend.

"Billy, do me a favor and don't drop that damned thing," Jack whispered sharply to him. Billy grunted.

They paddled the final distance and lifted the oars out of the water as they touched the schooner's hull on the side facing the shore. The steel topsides were cool and white, and as Jack ran his hands lovingly along, they came away coated with dried salt crystals from her recent sea voyage. There was no one on deck, but they could hear the sound of muffled voices below.

"Move up to the portholes," Jack whispered holding on to the cap rail, "they're open. Maybe we can hear something."

Hand over hand they pulled the skiff along holding the heavy teak rail. Soon, Jack's face was near the first of the two portholes opening to the wardroom. They'd obviously opened them upon their arrival to cool down the interior of the vessel. He recognized the voices immediately and he felt his anger surge. Henderson was talking.

"Listen," he said, "I'm the one giving the orders around here, not you."

There was no civility in his tone, Jack noted.

"I just don't think we have to sink the boat. Who's going to figure it out anyway? We'll be long gone," Laura snapped back at him

"We're going to stick to the plan," Henderson replied jabbing his finger at her, "and at the crack of daylight we'll be on our way out of here."

"Why can't we just leave now? There's a huge moon up," she said angrily spreading her arms.

"Because, Laura, we've got to dispose of this yacht, otherwise someone will get suspicious, that's why," Henderson said in an exasperated voice.

"And I have to wait until daylight so I can see the airstrip to take off, otherwise they'll be serving up our remains over-easy with a plate of grits," Joe-Bob Benson added in his whinny voice.

Henderson turned to the pilot. "Benson, you've had the most rest, so you pull watch on the aircraft."

"That's cool," he said in a slightly slurred voice.

"And stay off the sauce dammit. I need you sober in the morning."

"Hey, I ain't drunk, just had a few brewskis is all. No need to get bent out of shape."

Henderson seemed angry and nervous. The guy was certainly stressed out. Jack risked a peek through the porthole and quickly evaluated the situation in the well-lit wardroom. Benny and Cobb were hog tied on the far side. They'd both been gagged with duct tape across their mouths. Cobb had a lot of dried blood on his head and face. Somebody had done a real job on him but at least they were alive. The sleazy bastard stood over them with the ever-present snub-nosed Uzi machine gun draped over his shoulder.

Laura sat on the couch alongside another man. Jack figured he must be the pilot of the Piper Twin. A short pot-bellied man with lanky, shoulder-length hair, Jack judged him to be about forty years old. He looked like just the kind of guy who'd get involved with Henderson.

The aluminum trunks containing the *San Idelfonso's* gold lay on the floor. Jack's mind was cold and clear as he strained to catch every word of the argument. He took his face away from the porthole and signaled for them to push off again.

As soon as they drifted far enough away, they picked up the oars again and paddled silently towards the shore. Megan noticed the stony look on Jack's face and felt her stomach knot. She sensed something terrible was going to happen and very soon.

The bow of the skiff grounded on the beach a few minutes later and they pulled it back up to where it had been before.

"So, what do you reckon?" Billy asked eagerly as he stood the two weapons in the sand against the skiff.

Megan put her arm through Jack's, but she remained quiet.

"The bastards are planning to sink the schooner tonight sometime and fly out with the gold in the morning," Jack said his voice shaking with fury.

"What about Benny and Cobb?" Meg asked anxiously. "Are they alright?"

"They're alive, but it looks like Cobb got beat up pretty bad," Jack told her.

"Oh no," Meg said sadly shaking her head.

"He's alright Meg, he's a tough guy," Jack assured her, "they'll be fine, just as long as we can stop them in time."

"What about the gold," Billy asked nonchalantly, trying not to appear too mercenary.

"It's still there, sitting on the floor of the wardroom in the same aluminum cases. There's another guy aboard now; some sad looking bum called Benson. Sounds like he's their pilot."

"So, that makes four of them," Billy stated slowly.

Jack looked pensive for a moment.

"Listen, they're going to have to come ashore with the gold before they take the *Fandango* out. So that will be our chance. When they come to the dock in the whaler, we'll be right there waiting for them. We can hide in the sea grape bushes, near the dock," he said.

"Definitely worth a try, mate," Billy concurred.

"Listen Jack, I'm scared. We're not going to shoot them?" Megan asked, concerned.

"Not if we can help it, Meg, but I'm not just going to stand by and let them kill Benny and Cobb," he replied evenly, "or sink my boat."

"What, you think they're planning to murder Cobb and Benny?" she asked in horror.

"Yes," Jack replied, "they can't afford to have any witnesses. Those guys will die if we don't stop Henderson, and if I have to shoot him to stop him, then I'll do it."

"I'm with you, mate. My feelings for them fellas aren't worth a pile of wallaby shit." Billy said.

He was at his most eloquent when he got riled up.

At that moment voices carried across from the deck of the *Fandango* and two dark figures climbed into the Whaler. A moment later the outboard roared to life and the boat came speeding away from the schooner headed towards the dock. Laura and the pilot were aboard.

Taking cover in the sea grape trees near the dock the trio watched silently. Coming alongside the dock, Benson got out and turned to Laura. Their brief conversation carried easily to where Jack and the others were crouching.

"Hey babe, why don't you come over with me, I got an air mattress in the back of the cabin big enough for two," he said in a slurred, syrupy voice.

Laura's reply was clear.

"Oh, piss off Benson," she snarled and a moment later she roared off towards the anchored schooner.

"Bitch," Joe Bob muttered to himself as he strode off towards the plane.

He moved surprisingly fast for a chubby fellow and Jack nudged Billy in the ribs.

"Let's be friendly and go introduce ourselves," he said.

Ordering Megan to wait in the cover of the trees, Jack leaned over and gave her a quick peck on the lips before moving off with the big Australian. They followed the pilot towards the plane. He was clearly inebriated and obviously not bothering to conceal his passage through the bush. He walked right up to the side of the aircraft and after unlocking the cabin door, climbed in shutting it behind him. A light came on in the cabin but few moments later he came out again with a pistol in his hands. Benson made a circuit of the aircraft before stopping at some bushes near the plane.

Jack and Billy followed him crouching from tree to tree. Joe Bob Benson was getting rid of the last three beers he'd consumed on the schooner. He was just zipping up his trousers when the two men took him.

Jack and Billy grabbed his arms from behind and pushed him into the bushes. Although Joe-Bob was marginally under the influence, he was surprisingly strong and struggled like hell.

"Let me go you sonovfabitch," he squealed, writhing in his efforts to get free.

He was making altogether too much noise and Billy quickly grabbed him around the chest putting his big hand over Benson's mouth to shut him up, but a second later Billy yelped, yanking his hand away.

"Streuth, the little bastard just bit me," he shouted unbelievingly.

"Bad mannered little shit," Jack growled, trying to hold the struggling man.

Joe Bob tried to retrieve the gun nestled in the front of his waistband and Jack reacted almost instinctively. Raising the steel shoed butt of the heavy Lee Enfield he brought it down on the side of Joe Bob's head. It made audible crack as it came into contact with the man's skull and he stopped struggling instantly, dropping like a stone.

"Little bugger bit me finger," Billy repeated again, shaking his hand up and down.

"He was just getting ready to do more than bite," Jack said removing the pistol from the pilot's belt. It was a heavy Colt .45 and there was one in the spout.

They dragged the unconscious man over to the trees where Megan was waiting.

"Is he dead?" she asked shocked.

"He will be if he tries to bite me again," Billy threatened.

"No, he's still alive, but we'll just tie him up before he comes around," Jack told her.

He looked over towards the wooden skiffs. Hopefully, there'd be some rope in them. Sprinting across the thirty feet of open ground to the beached boats he looked in the first one. Sure enough, there was a coil of quarter-inch manila anchor line in the bow.

Trussing the pilot like a turkey they dragged him fifty feet down the beach away from the dock, propping him up against a sea-grape tree trunk. Megan ripped off the bottom section of the 'Mount Gay' tee shirt Neddy King had given her and they gagged him as well.

Joe Bob Benson was going to have one hell of a headache when he came too, and this time it would have nothing to do with the booze. It was unlikely he'd cause them any further trouble that night.

'You must have hit him pretty hard, Jacko," Billy chuckled, "he's still sleeping like a baby."

As they settled down to wait for Henderson and the others to come ashore Jack counted to himself; one down, three to go.

CHAPTER EIGHTEEN

Jumbies In De Bush

Standing behind the sea grape bushes near the little wooden dock, Jack peered out across the bay. It seemed as though he been there forever waiting for some sign of action on the schooner. The mosquitoes found them and there was an almost continual slap, slap as they fought off the blood-sucking pests. The insects flew into their ears and Jack found the incessant buzzing almost as irritating as the bites.

The moon reached its zenith and began its downward arc. The occasional cloud crossed its face throwing the shoreline into dark shadow. Billy and Megan managed to nap on and off, but Jack remained alert keeping a close eye on both the parked aircraft and the anchored schooner.

At three in the morning Billy got up and checked Benson. He was still lying there like a corpse and he wondered if Jack had killed him. Bending over he put his face close to the pilot's to see if he was breathing but quickly pulled away. The man was breathing alright but he smelled like a bar urinal on a Friday night. Twenty minutes later Jack thought he saw something. Straining his eyes he tried to focus on the deck of the schooner, but there was nothing. It must have been a trick of the moonlight he thought.

"See anything?" Megan whispered appearing silently at his side.

"Not yet. No wait, something's happening," he replied pointing to the dark form of the anchored schooner.

Three dim figures emerged from the main companionway. Something was happening on the deck. Billy rubbed his eyes and looked across the bay.

"Looks like they're getting ready to come ashore," he said tiredly. "Can you make out who's on deck, mate?"

"Not from here."

The dark figures pulled the Whaler up on its bowline, bringing it alongside the schooner to the ladder. A moment later they manhandled a large oblong object over the rail. There were thuds and Megan caught the glint of polished metal in the moonlight.

"Look," she said pointing, "it's those aluminum camera trunks. They're probably going to bring them ashore now."

"You ready Billy? " Jack asked him.

"Ready? I'm set to blow their bloody arses away," he said with bravado, "let the bastards come."

"We can't just lay here in the bushes and pop them off in cold blood as they walk by," Megan complained emphatically.

"That's what they'd do to you little lady," Billy replied pointedly, "and without a second thought."

"Listen, here's what we'll do," Jack began and the other two bent their heads towards him as he quietly outlined his plan.

Picking up the old Lee Enfield. He looked at the big Australian.

"We're a little shy on shells. I've only got the one clip in the Enfield and your two slugs in the shotgun. That's not going to give a very convincing performance."

"Wrong," said Billy. Dipping his hands into the voluminous military style khaki trousers that he always wore, he pulled out a handful of .303 shells and a few more of the 00 twelve gauge slugs.

"Got a whole mess of these .303's," he said, "Old Chief Balfont of the Antigua Police gave me a few cases free. "

"That was mighty generous of him," Jack said looking at Billy suspiciously.

"Not exactly," he replied a little self-consciously, "the cheap pommey bastard was paying me for a load of duty free gin from St Barts. He came up short on cash and paid me the last fifty quid in old ammo."

"I thought you'd quit smuggling Gilbeys for the Antigua police."

"Well, I was short of coin," Billy replied defensively, "I just figured one more haul wouldn't hurt, and besides they asked me, I didn't offer."

Billy Ramsey was incorrigible.

"How many shells do you have?" Jack asked him.

"I got maybe twenty round of the .303 and, let's see," he paused for a second counting. "I have six more twelve gauge here," he said, handing Jack a dozen or so of the .303's.

He put them in the pocket of the denim shirt Neddy had given him. They were as ready as they were going to be.

In Trellis, Bay the shadowy figures on the deck of the schooner slid the second heavy silver case over the rail, lowering it into the Whaler. It was taking a long time and there seemed to be some sort of a discussion going on. Another figure came up on deck. A few moments later loud shouting came across the water from the yacht. The figures moved rapidly on the stern and then there was a flash of light.

Out on the *Fandango* a problem developed. After the heavy gold bearing cases were safely loaded in the launch, Laura picked up the flashlight from its holder in the companionway and went over to the cockpit console to start the schooner's main engine. After a lot of arguing with Henderson she finally agreed to go out with Garcia to sink the yacht. They wouldn't wait; she would just open the seacocks and leave her adrift. There was good deep water only a half-mile out and that would do. Her guarantee was the fact that Henderson couldn't risk having her and Garcia talking about their little caper. People had died and that was serious business. That was enough to convince her that Henderson wouldn't be stupid enough to fly off without them. Laura reminded herself that she had the snub nosed .38 and this gave her some sense of security.

Stooping down in the cockpit she shone the light on the console and hit the switch marked 'Main Engine Start'. The big diesel ground over and over, but refused to start. The flap on the scavenger blower that Cobb had let down prevented any air from getting into the cylinders and as a result she wouldn't fire.

"Shit, it won't start," she said frustrated.

"What's wrong with it?" he asked agitated. He didn't need any surprises at this late stage.

"I don't know, it just wont start." She thought for a moment before adding, "I bet Cobb did something to screw it up."

"Get him up here," Henderson instructed Garcia snapping his fingers and pointing to the companionway.

Garcia went below, coming up a moment later with Cobb at the end of his Uzi. Rubbing his wrists where the Dacron sail ties had bruised him, he took in the situation from one eye. The other was swollen shut. Garcia brought him round to the starboard side, stopping in front of Henderson.

"Alright smart ass, what did you do to the engine," Henderson asked him in a dangerous tone.

"I ain't do nutting. Maybe is de fuel shut dung lever in de wheel box," Cobb said, trying to sound convincing.

"Shut down lever?" Laura asked him suspiciously.

"Yeah miss, de same one ah tell you about before, you remember de one dat bruken."

"He did say something about that when we got here. Let him have a look," Laura said

"It have to reset by hand to start de engine," Cobb explained.

"You've got one minute to fix it, clear?" Henderson told him angrily.

"Yes sir, clear as could be."

Henderson motioned for him to move toward the helm box. Cobb took the flashlight from Laura and moved to the other side of the schooner's cockpit. At the aft end he lifted the varnished teak top of the wheel box. It was a fine piece of woodwork, about four foot by three and curved across the top. For a few seconds he was at least partially hidden from view. Wiping the sweat from his forehead Cobb made as if he was going to look in the box.

"Go and see what the hell's he's doing," Henderson ordered Garcia.

As he moved to walk around the cockpit, Cobb took a deep breath, brought the flashlight up to chest level and shone it directly into Garcia's eyes, blinding him momentarily. A split second later he threw the light at the Puerto Rican and sprang over the rail into the dark waters of Trellis Bay.

"Bastardo," Garcia shouted, jumping clumsily towards the stern.

As his eyes struggled to readjust to the moonlight, he tripped over the cockpit coaming and fell to his knees. Raising the Uzi, he blindly fired a burst of bullets over the rail into the water, hoping to find his mark. Rushing to the rail on the port side Henderson and Laura looked into the water, but all they saw were a few startled fish swimming near the stern.

"Shit," Henderson shouted. This was a development he hadn't planned on.

As soon as he hit the water, Cobb dove down a good ten feet, swimming for the shore. Opening his one good eye the salt water stung the cuts where Garcia's fists had broken the skin, but he didn't care. The moonlight reflected off the white sandy bottom of the bay and as he glanced over his shoulder he saw the huge blurry shadow of the *Fandango*'s keel suspended a few feet above the sand. He was an excellent free diver and could normally make an easy sixty feet horizontally under the surface. But on this occasion he was highly motivated and he breast stroked for more than eighty feet before surfacing. He gasped for breath.

Aboard the anchored schooner Henderson was furious.

"Did you hit him?" he growled at Garcia.

"I don't know, Eduardo"

"You let him get away."

"The light, it blinded me," Garcia replied nervously.

"That's just great. We're really screwed now," Laura shouted at them, "he'll go straight to the police."

"Shut up Laura the police are hours from here. Get the whaler ready and we'll go catch the bastard before he gets ashore," he snapped back at her.

"Forget it, have you checked the Whaler lately?" she pointed out snidely.

"No, why?" he asked impatiently.

"Look at it, it's loaded. The water's almost up to the rail. If we swamp it looking for that stupid crewman, our gold's going to the bottom of Trellis Bay."

It was true. Looking over the side he saw that the small boat's rail was close to the water. Two aluminum cases filled with treasure along with their duffel bags filled the bow. It would be too risky to go racing around the bay so heavily loaded and it would take too long to unload it again. Henderson was exasperated and he hadn't missed the fact that Laura said "our gold." It angered him.

At that moment he caught sight of a ripple and swirl in the water about eighty feet away.

"Quick, there he is," he yelled, pointing towards the shore.

As Cobb's head broke surface, he heard the Uzi's rip, and the menacing slaps as the bullets flew into the water only a few feet short of him. Without wasting any more time, he took another deep breath and dove again, heading for the beach.

By the time he surfaced again the sandy shoreline was only fifty feet ahead. He was far enough away from the schooner and stayed on the surface, swimming swiftly.

There'd been a very good reason for Cobb to chance making his risky move. He'd caught snippets of the conversations between Henderson and the others and he knew they planed to kill him and his shipmate. If he got free, maybe there would be a way to help Benny later.

Swimming parallel to the beach about thirty feet off he moved as far as possible from the dock and the yacht before gingerly letting his feet touch the sandy bottom. As he stood up in the three feet of water he noticed dozens of big black spiny sea urchins. He waded out carefully, making sure he didn't step on the long poisonous spines. Crouching, he made his way up the beach. His head and face ached and he was exhausted from lack of sleep, but he'd made sure the schooner wouldn't be going anywhere and he smiled as he thought about that and the fact that he'd finally escaped.

Disappearing into the line of trees he walked slowly towards the old dock. Suddenly he stopped. Somewhere ahead he heard whispering voices and without waiting to find out who or what it was he turned and took off at a sprint.

Further down the shore there was a fishermen's hut. He'd been there once before and knew exactly where it was. Making his way quickly and quietly he was soon there. In the darkness of the open sided shed the nets and bamboo fish traps lay packed neatly to one side. He found the familiar smell of old fish comforting. On the opposite side an old skiff sat perched on its supports with a sail draped over it. Crawling in he pulled the sail over his head and lay down. He would wait until daylight, when the Zombies had to return to the nether regions below the ground.

Back on the anchored schooner Henderson gave up on catching Cobb. He was probably dead anyway, he reasoned to himself. Garcia had spent three full clips spraying the water where they had seen the swirls. His thoughts turned back to the other problem they were trying to deal with. He needed to get the damn engine going right away. His plans were starting to go awry and they still needed to take the schooner out to sink her.

"Give me the damned flashlight so I can have a look in the box," He snapped.

Picking up the flashlight from the starboard scuppers where it had landed Laura fiddled with it for a moment before handing it to him. He shone it into the wheel box. There was a clutter of mechanisms, including the large worm gear controlling the rudder. The Morse control cables ran through the box as well as a bunch of electrical wires and switches for the various deck lights. Near the front corner on the left hand side was a small brass lever half hidden behind the Morse cables where they disappeared below. Henderson rubbed the grease from the side of the lever with his thumb revealing some stamped lettering. It was marked with two positions, 'Shut Down' and 'Reset'. He pointed it out to Laura.

"That's it," he said, "you didn't look very hard Laura."

"Yeah, but what position should it be in?" she asked impatiently.

He moved it back and forth a couple of times before leaving it in the reset position.

"Try it now," he said gruffly.

She hit the start switch on the cockpit console again, with the same result. The big diesel ground over and over but didn't fire. Unbeknownst to them, the blower flap would have to be reset from the engine room manually before the engine could start.

"Try it the other way," Laura suggested.

Henderson pulled it to the opposite position and Laura tried the starter again. Nothing.

They'd been fooling with the engine for while and Henderson gave a start as he looked at his watch.

"Shit, look at the time, it's after five already," he snapped, glaring at Laura.

"Don't look at me, I don't know anything about engines," Laura replied defensively, "Why don't you get that boozed up pilot of yours to come and have a look, if you can wake him up that is."

"Alright, you and Garcia take the cases ashore then get Benson and bring him back here. Garcia can wait by the plane," he told her, "and for Christ's sake hurry it up."

Climbing gently into the Whaler, Henderson leaned over the side.

"And remember, Benson parked the trolley at the end of the dock," he reminded them.

He wasn't overly worried about letting them go on alone with the gold; it was still too dark to take off.

Starting the outboard they left for the shore, moving dead slow so not to create any bow wave. The bow was only a few inches from the surface of the water as it was, and if it dipped the Whaler would swamp. Bringing it carefully alongside the dock they secured both the bow and stern. Luckily, the wooden planks of the dock's surface were almost level with the Whaler's rail and it wasn't too difficult to heave the aluminum cases ashore.

Garcia walked off to find the trolley. He found it right where it was supposed to be. The two-wheeled aluminum luggage cart was capable of holding a lot of weight. Wheeling it the forty feet back to the dock they loaded the large case first and then the smaller one on top. Leaving the Whaler at the dock they took off pushing the cart towards the plane. The first hint of dawn had already appeared to the east.

Jack, Megan and Billy watched from the cover of the sea grape trees, and as Garcia pushed the cart in the direction of the plane, Jack turned to the Australian.

"Billy, hand me your Webley, will you."

Billy pulled the revolver out of his pocket and handed it over to Jack, who then turned to Megan.

"I want you to stay here and keep an eye on fly-boy here," he told her. His voice had an authoritative, almost dangerous ring to it. Megan found it both unnerving and thrilling, and this time she didn't argue.

"You know how to use one of these?" he asked her.

"Yes, I've shot pistols a few times."

Jack gave her a quick kiss and handed her the gun.

"Watch him, and if he comes to just whack him on the head like this, OK?"

He motioned with the pistol like a hammer.

"I will, and Jack?"

"Yes?"

"When you find Garcia, remember what he did to us."

"Don't worry, I've been thinking about it all day. "

Jack and Billy followed Laura and Garcia carefully, using the cover of the trees and bushes whenever they could. The airstrip was close by and the cart's big wheels made it easy going. Approaching the plane Laura called out quietly.

"Benson, Benson you there?"

There was no answer.

"If that asshole is drunk, I'll be really pissed off," Laura said.

Jack and Billy followed silently, until they reached the low bushes nearest the airstrip.

"Benson, where the hell are you," Laura called out again as they stood next to the plane.

The cabin door was open, but still no answer from the pilot.

"Something's wrong," she said nervously.

Garcia climbed the wing and opened the hatch to the cabin.

"He ees no here."

"Shit. He's probably passed out somewhere, the fucking drunk. I'm going back to tell Henderson."

From behind the bushes, Jack heard the uncertainty in her voice. Turning to his friend, he whispered quietly into his ear.

"Looks like we'll have Garcia on his own. It's time to take him down."

"Couldn't agree more, mate," Billy whispered back.

"We'll wait till she's back on the *Fandango*, then we'll make our move." Turning they looked back towards the plane. Garcia spoke to Laura.

"We put the boxes in the plane first no?" he asked in his dull monotone.

"Yes, but be quick," she told him nervously.

Positioning the trolley close to the hatch he manhandled the heavy cases into the plane.

"I will wait 'ere," he said lighting a cigarette.

Laura took off running towards the dock leaving Garcia crouched under the Piper with the Uzi over his shoulder. The reddish glow of his cigarette cast an eerie light on the underside of the aircraft's wing.

She passed within forty feet of Megan, but had no idea she was there crouching in the trees. Laura quickly untied the Whaler's bowline before jumping in. Pulling the outboard to life she careened wildly away from the dock towards the schooner.

Jack watched the boat approach the *Fandango*. His pulse began to quicken and his muscles tensed. This was his chance.

Billy looked closely at his friend and saw the cold, determined look on his face. Streuth, I'm glad I'm not on the receiving end of that, he thought.

"You ready?" Jack asked

"You bet mate," Billy replied

"I'll circle around to the right and you take the left. When I get around the other side of the strip, say in three minutes, I'll need you to create a diversion to bring him out from under the wing. Then I'll take him with the Enfield."

It was sensible plan, because Billy's .00 shotgun load would be pretty inaccurate at anything over a hundred feet.

"What kind of diversion do you want?"

"How about I do one of me Tasmanian Devil imitations?" Billy asked seriously.

Jack smiled. If anything would attract Garcia it was on of Billy's Aussie animal sounds. They were unique in the world.

"OK, just make sure you make it loud enough," he warned his friend.

"No worries mate. Loud it'll be."

After checking their watches, they split up and circled. Crouching, Jack ran towards the seaward end of the airstrip closest to Trellis Bay, dodging through the sea grape trees. They provided good cover, and as long as he stayed within their low hanging branches he'd stay pretty well hidden.

Three minutes later he reached the other side of the airstrip. The low brush was closer to the plane on that side and he used the cover to creep a little closer. An open stretch of ground ran a hundred and fifty feet from where he crouched to the Piper. Garcia stood just to the left of it in the shadow of the wing.

It still wasn't quite light yet, and as Jack squinted over the rifle's sights, the Puerto Rican appeared only as a dim blur. The old Lee Enfield's bore had seen better days and Jack knew he was just too far away for a sure shot. The Puerto Rican was half hidden in the shadow of the wing and he needed to step out into the clear before he could fire.

He wished Billy would hurry up and make the diversion to draw the Puerto Rican away from the aircraft. He'd at least be able to see well enough to try a shot then. Billy obliged right then, but it wasn't exactly what they had planned. The Aussie's big left foot suddenly caught in a large crab hole and he tripped and fell sprawling out into the open, only a hundred and fifty feet or so from Garcia. The Purdy shotgun went flying.

"Shite," Billy gasped under his breath, trying to locate the shotgun.

Garcia heard him and moved like a cat from the shelter of the plane's wing towards the prostrate Australian.

"Ben-son ees you?" he called in Billy's direction.

There was no answer and he got suspicious, thinking next that it might be Cobb. Billy found the Purdy and picking it up, shook the sand from the barrels where it had dug into the ground. He came to his knees at the edge of the bushes lining the airstrip.

"Marinero, ees you no?" Garcia tried again, but still there was no answer. The silence was enough to trigger an aggressive reaction and he began firing quick, wild bursts while moving in Billy's direction.

Jack took off running. He was still too far away and the light too vague for a sure shot. He kept to the trees moving adjacent to the Puerto Rican.

"This'll have to do mate," Billy muttered to himself and a second later two loud blasts rent the morning as he fired the Purdy. He fired one barrel at a time but too quickly and from too far, and the 00 shot ripped the bush on the far side of the plane. There was no doubt where the shotgun fire had come from, the big twelve gauge made bright muzzle flashes in the dim light.

Garcia spotted Billy's shadowy figure kneeling at the edge of the bushes, struggling to reload the shotgun. He fired the Uzi again, this time from about fifty feet and Jack heard his friend cry out.

"Streuth," Billy Ramsey said falling on his side.

The shotgun fell to the sand again and he felt an intense spreading pain below the waist.

Slowing to a walk Garcia smiled as he neared the Australian, Uzi at the ready. He was going in to finish him.

Jack knew he had to draw him off and quick, or he would kill Billy with the next burst. Running out clear of the trees far enough so that Garcia would have no problem seeing him he stood up.

"Hey, Garcia, stupido," Jack yelled as loud as he could.

He was a hundred and twenty feet away with the Lee Enfield cradled in his arm. The startled man turned in Jack's direction. As it happened in the tropics dawn was breaking fast. The sun's red rim rose above the hills of Virgin Gorda some miles behind him and the Puerto Rican could see him clearly.

"Yes, you dago piece of shit. You remember me?" Jack yelled again, trying to goad him away from Billy.

Garcia smiled and taking aim at his new target he fired. The Uzi was less than accurate at that distance, and the bullets wildly kicked up little puffs of sand around Jack, none closer that twenty feet.

Jack quickly raised the Lee Enfield, aimed and fired. The recoil surprised him, even though he had used large caliber rifles before. The report reverberated around the surrounding hills but he missed. The weapon was old and the sights were way off.

Garcia realized he was too far away to be effective. Crouching he ran towards Jack, dodging and twisting. Jack's plan worked and he retreated into the tree line, running further down the boarder of the airstrip away from Billy. After a few moments, he glanced back over his shoulder. Garcia was still chasing him.

"I am coming for you, gringo. I will kill you soon. Then I will kill your whore." The crazed Puerto Rican yelled.

He was angry and when a man gets angry he makes mistakes.

Jack knew Billy had been hit, but he had no idea how bad. At least he was drawing Garcia away. The Puerto Rican was still running in the open, seemingly oblivious to his own vulnerability.

Back on the *Fandango* Laura found Henderson waiting impatiently at the rail.

"Where's Benson?" he'd asked realizing something was wrong.

"Don't know, drunk maybe. Or maybe something's happened to him," she replied her face showing signs of strain.

Henderson thought for a second before replying

"We're going to have to forget the schooner and get out of here. I've got a bad feeling about all this."

"How? The pilot's gone."

"The plane's mine, I can fly it " he revealed, "Is the gold aboard?"

"Yes Garcia put it aboard a few minutes ago. What about the other crewman?" she asked referring to Benny who was still bound and gagged in the salon.

Suddenly, the sounds of gunfire reverberated from the shore.

"What the hell," Henderson started.

Things were going wrong fast. There was another burst of gunfire and Henderson recognized the rapid zipper tearing sound of Garcia's Uzi.

"Quick, we've got to get to the plane," Henderson said.

"What about the other crewman?"

"Forget him, I'm not hanging around here any longer."

Climbing quickly into the Whaler, Laura started the outboard and drove in slowly, hoping to keep the outboard engine noise as quiet as possible. Arriving at the dock, they jumped out and began running towards the plane. A second later, another burst of gunfire exploded around the bay and they dove into the first group of sea grape trees.

Megan also heard the gunfire from where she was hiding but after a few minutes of waiting, she couldn't stand it anymore and took off running towards the sound of the shooting. She knew Jack wouldn't like it, but she had to find out what was happening.

She hadn't gone very far when she practically stumbled over Billy Ramsey. Lying there on his side, he had his hand on his bum. Kneeling beside him she tried to see what was wrong. Dark blood seeped slowly from between his fingers.

"Oh Billy, are you alright?" she asked, concerned.

"No, I ain't, I been shot," he replied gasping in pain.

"Where? Here, let me help you," she said trying to pull him up.

"No, don't," he grunted, "I can't sit up."

"Let me see," she said bending over him trying to help.

"I can't," Billy replied, sounding painfully embarrassed.

Jack continued drawing Garcia away from them and further up the airstrip. Letting him come closer he tried to think how he could take the advantage. The opportunity presented it self a moment later. The Puerto Rican systematically worked the bushes as he came firing a few rounds on single shot and then quick bursts. Dawn was breaking and it was only a matter of time before he spotted Jack.

"I know you are there little gringo, come out so I can kill you," he mocked.

Garcia was overconfident but as he fired another burst into the bushes Jack realized he was getting too close. He had to finish it now.

The Puerto Rican was seventy-five feet away when Jack suddenly stepped into the open. He was close enough. Raising the old Lee Enfield he drew a bead on the man's torso and pulled the trigger. The big rifle barked and recoiled heavily.

Garcia dropped the Uzi and fell to his knees clutching his left shoulder. Running over Jack stood above him as he knelt in the sand. He kicked the Uzi away out of reach.

"You've caused me a lot of misery you bastard," Jack told him coldly.

"And you gringo, you still live, and where is your red haired whore? I will let you live if you give her to me," he taunted in a half-crazed voice while looking up.

"She sent you a present asshole, and here it is," Jack snapped raising the rifle butt.

He brought the heavy steel shoed butt of the Enfield down hard on the side of Garcia's head. There was an audible crack and he dropped like a stone. Damn, Jack thought to himself, I'm getting good at this.

Dropping the old Enfield to the sand, he picked up the Uzi. Taking a full clip from the little black Addis bag Garcia was carrying he ran back towards his wounded friend.

The big Australian stood leaning heavily against Megan with one of his huge arms draped over her shoulder. She looked tiny next to him as she tried to help him stagger back into the cover of the trees a few feet away.

"Billy Ramsey, you weigh a ton," she scolded him.

She just about to heave on his shoulder again when a big black hand appeared from behind, taking Billy's other arm. It almost scared her to death.

"Cobb! God, you startled me," she said, laughing.

"Eh, eh, I heard all dis noise an' tought was Jumbies in de bush," He said amazed to see her.

Jack appeared at that moment, out of breath.

"What de hell you all doin here mon?" Cobb asked incredulously.

"Getting shot, that's what," Billy groaned.

"You okay?" Jack asked, wincing as he saw Cobb's battered face.

"Skip, I alright you know, but how you reach here?" he asked, totally bewildered.

"I'll tell you everything later."

"Are you're alright?" Megan asked turning to Jack.

"I'm fine."

"Did you get him, mate?" Billy managed to gasp as he gently knelt down and then lay on his side.

"Yes, he's got a bullet in his shoulder and a busted skull. No thanks to your lousy attempt at a diversion," Jack teased his friend.

"Hey, don't josh a fellah when he's down."

"How bad are you hit?"

"I'll live."

"I'd better take a look, Billy."

"Christ Jack, leave a man a little pride. You're not going to strip me naked in front of a Sheila?" he asked wincing.

"Don't worry I won't look." Megan promised.

Jack carefully eased his shorts down before he had a chance to complain any further. He was lucky, the bullet had passed clean through the outer fleshy part of his left buttock, and although he'd lost some blood, he'd recover. Jack took off the denim shirt he was wearing and wadding it up pressed it against the slowly weeping wound.

"You'll live. Wait till we tell the boys back in Antigua," Jack teased him, "The great Billy Ramsey, shot in the ass."

"You wouldn't tell, not on a mate?" Billy asked, concerned about his image.

"Depends, Billy," Jack said, winking at Cobb. "Now, hold this on tight."

Billy held the wadded shirt on his rear end as they gently pulled his shorts back up.

In the bushes on the other side of the airstrip, Laura and Ed watched.

"How the hell did they get here?" she asked stunned.

"Right now, I don't give a damn. Look, they seem to be busy. Now's our chance. Keep low, use the bushes for cover and approach the plane from this side. That way, they won't be able to see us. Ready?"

"Yes."

"Make sure you keep it quiet. They're armed now and we aren't. Let's go."

Laura and Ed took off as quietly as they could in the direction of the Piper.

After they'd sorted out Billy, Jack's thoughts turned to Laura and Ed. He needed to find them and stop them.

"I've got to find out what's happened to Henderson and Laura. Meg, you stay here and look after Billy, and Cobb, you come with me."

"Right Skip."

Reaching the dock Jack was surprised to find the Whaler tied up there. He thought they were still been aboard the schooner.

The grind and cough of one, and then the second of the Piper's engines suddenly interrupted his thoughts as they caught and fired. The aircraft's tail glinted over the short bushes as it turned and began taxiing down the runway.

"Who the hell?" he muttered to no one.

Unless, but no, Benson was still hog-tied in the trees. It meant that either Henderson or Laura could fly and they were going to take off with an airplane full of gold.

Jack was angry. He couldn't believe they were going to wing the gold right out of here after all. He turned to look at Cobb, standing in the

Whaler waiting. He was pulling the big Arbalette speargun from under the seat.

"We have to get back to the airstrip."

"Sure, Skip." Cobb said, and he bent to put the speargun down again.

"No, bring that thing with you." Jack said for no special reason.

Running the seventy-five feet back towards the strip, Cobb followed him a second later.

An idea was forming in Jack's mind as he held Garcia's Uzi. He remembered why he'd quit Air America way back then. The light aircraft's susceptibility to small arms fire at low altitude.

The Piper's engines revved as the aircraft rolled down the coral strip. The twin Lycomings steadied at a high pitched scream and the props raised a faint cloud of dust behind the aircraft. It was going to take off right over them.

Jack set the Uzi's selector on rapid fire and raised it. The silver skinned aircraft lifted off gracefully, passing directly over their heads. Aiming quickly he pulled the trigger, emptying the magazine into the underbelly of the plane. Fifty feet above them the bullets found their mark. As the aircraft lifted slowly into the air they looked upwards to see if the slugs had done any damage. Jack smiled. Silvery streams of fuel trailed away. The bullets had torn numerous holes through the tanks, and it was loosing fuel fast.

"Well, would you look at that," he said proudly. "They're dropping fuel like crazy."

"You is one good shot skip," Cobb said smiling lopsidedly. "Dat plane like it had need to pee real bad."

Even as Cobb spoke, Jack was thinking about the gold in the Piper's belly. They wouldn't get far with the amount of fuel they were losing. The Catalina still had at least another three hours of endurance left. Enough to follow the Piper.

Jack checked the load in the Uzi, but it was empty and he tossed it away and he and Cobb sprinted back the twenty yards to the others.

"I hit the fuel tanks. She won't last long up there, so I'm going to chase her and see where they end up," Jack told them.

"And just how do you plan to do that sport?" Billy interjected in mock anger.

"With your Catalina of course," Jack said matter of factly. "I need to borrow your plane again."

"How did I know that was coming? Listen sport, if you promise not to mention my little problem to the boys back in Antigua, I'll let you take her. Deal?"

"Don't worry, I'd never let the boys make you the butt of their jokes," he said with a slight chuckle, "and I'll treat the *Digeree* with kid gloves."

He turned to Meg and Cobb.

"Can you two get him back to the *Fandango*?"

"Oh no you don't, I'm coming with you," Megan told Jack looking him straight in the eye.

He was about to argue, but then he thought she might be able to help him search for the Piper.

"Cobb, think you can get him back aboard the schooner?"

"Yeah Skip. Ah tink I could manage de man," Cobb said, "An Benny can help me. We goin' hoist he aboard like one of dem big assed Aves turtles."

Billy Ramsey didn't look all that impressed, but for once remained quiet. Seeing his Arbalette in Cobb's hand he reached out.

"I may need that."

Cobb handed him the speargun and as Jack checked it over, Billy looked at him with a grin.

"I pity anybody who runs into you with that thing today."

"We'll catch you guys later," Jack said grabbing Megan by the hand.

"Good luck, sport," Billy yelled as they moved quickly off in the direction of the Catalina, "And for Christ's sakes don't prang me poor *Digeree*, I've still got to make a living with her," he added without humor.

CHAPTER NINETEEN

Digeree Doo

Reaching the crest of the hill overlooking Trellis Bay Jack and Megan paused for a moment to catch their breaths before jogging down the slope towards the cove where the anchored Catalina waited quietly. Making their way along the goat path she noted with satisfaction that with the coming of daylight, the wandering land crabs had disappeared into their holes for the day.

Crossing the grove of coconut trees near the head of the cove, they we shocked by the suddenly blast of a heavy caliber handgun.

"Shit," Jack swore, "who the hell?"

Reacting swiftly he tackled Megan around her waist bringing her to the sand behind a pile of dried coconut husks. As they rolled another shot rang out raising puffs of sand only a few feet away.

"Who's shooting at us...?" he asked again.

The shooting stopped for a few seconds and Jack took the opportunity to peek from behind the husks in the direction of the shooter. He was totally incredulous.

"Christ's sake, it's Garcia again," he said, his anger rising.

"How?" Megan said, "I thought he was dead."

"Me too. I thought I laid him out stone cold back there."

The heavy .303 bullet Jack had fired had hit the fleshy part of Garcia's left arm, leaving a serious, but non-life threatening wound. He'd come around a while after being knocked out by the rifle butt only just in time to see the Piper roll down the airstrip and take off. Incensed at being abandoned by Henderson and the American woman, he decided to take his frustrations out on those responsible for his dilemma. Watching Jack and Megan head off to the cove he followed.

It wasn't safe to stay where they were. The man was mad and dangerous. He would kill at the first chance. Hefting the Arbalette speargun he placed the pistol grip handle in the pit of his stomach and pulled back all four rubbers hooking the bridles into the long spear. It was useless at more than twenty feet, but closer than that, it could be deadly. Removing the tether line he left the six-foot stainless steel harpoon free to fly. Pausing another second he put it on safety.

Creeping along the line of coconut trees near the water's edge, they tried to remain hidden behind the sea grape bushes. Only a hundred feet out in the shallow cove the Catalina rocked gently tugging at her anchor rope. The small rubber zodiac was pulled up on the sand in front of the amphibian, just forty feet from where they now stood.

"What now Jack? He's going to kill us," Megan said frantically.

"Not if I can help it," he replied sternly, "before he gets any closer, we're going to make a run for the dinghy."

"You sure we can make it?" she asked sounding unsure, "I don't want to end up like Billy."

"We won't, run like hell, now!"

Sprinting towards the rubber boat they managed to cover half the distance before Garcia spotted them. Glancing over his shoulder Jack saw him staggering from the coconut grove with the pistol raised. He was two hundred yards up the beach but moving in their direction quite quickly. It was going to be a close call.

Covering the last few feet to the inflatable they frantically untied it from the bushes and pushed it into the water before jumping in. Garcia fired again, hitting the sand a few feet away. Preparing for more gunfire Jack tensed, but it miraculously fell silent. He glanced hastily over his shoulder. Garcia's gun was empty and was fiddling with the magazine, desperately trying to eject it so he could put in a full one. He was having difficulty because of his wounded arm.

What a break, Jack thought, and grabbing the paddles he handed one to Meg.

"Paddle!" he urged her.

"Right," she gasped, dipping the wooden paddle into the water.

The inflatable made infuriatingly slow progress towards the Catalina. It had lost air from a slow leak and it was like trying to paddle a soggy sponge. Megan was alarmed.

"Can you really fly this airplane, Jack? I mean, Billy was the one who really flew it last time, you just steered it for a while."

Jack pondered on that piece of logic for a second and then gave up. "Have I ever let you down? Of course I can fly it," he said as they came along side the Catalina.

Climbing in through the aft port blister hatch, they pushed the rubber boat adrift. It would float back to the shore where they'd pick it up later. Slamming the hatch shut they rushed forward into the cockpit. Motioning for Megan to take the right hand seat Jack fell into the pilot's. He set the Arbalette speargun on the floor beside the control column with the business end pointing aft. For a moment the complex array of switches and instruments in front of him seemed alien, but then in an instant it all came flooding back. Running his eyes over the dash he realized it was like riding a bike, you never forget how. His flying skills had saved him from death a dozen times during the war and the test business, and he was sure they wouldn't fail him now.

Hitting the starter switch for the starboard engine, it fired right away. Letting it rev for a second he hit the port engine. It coughed a couple of times but didn't catch.

"Come on you sonovfabitch, catch," he said urgently.

After what seemed like a long time the port engine caught and roared into life. Jack remembered that unlike the many other planes he'd flown, this one had an anchor line, and right now they were still attached to it.

"You'll have to cast us loose," he shouted to her above the roar of the engines.

"What do you want me to do?" she yelled back puzzled.

"You need to get into the forward compartment. There's a little hatch there and the anchor line is probably tied to a cleat," Jack shouted pointing to the line coming out of the front of the plane and leading down into the water.

Nodding, she descended the little alleyway into the nose of the aircraft. There was a hatch fitted with a special anchoring system, where the heavy forward machine gun had originally rested. The small three-foot square hatch lay open and the half-inch Dacron anchor line lead out. It was made fast to the twelve-inch stainless steel cleat on the airframe and Big Billy Ramsey had cinched the knot bar tight.

As Jack watched Megan, he caught a movement off to the right. It was Garcia. He had managed to push one of the small wooden skiffs into the water and was paddling erratically but quickly towards the amphibian with one arm and a determined look on his face.

"What the hell is it with this guy? He just keeps coming back," Jack exclaimed.

The large bloodstain on his shirt where he winged him with the .303 was obvious. He was slowly but steadily bleeding. Would the guy ever quit? Jack thought to himself.

"Have you got it untied yet?" he shouted the words through the windshield.

Megan's red head stuck up through the hatch. He was already revving the engines, and his feet went automatically to the rudder pedals, swinging the tail so the big amphibian would begin its turn to face the open sea.

Megan noticed the plane slowly turning and instinctively glanced out the hatch to see which direction they were going. She spotted Garcia coming towards them again and started to panic fumbling even more frantically with the knot, trying to undo it.

"Jack, it's stuck, I can't untie it," she screamed through the hatch.

"Is there a knife you can cut it with? He asked, making a cutting motion with his hands.

Scanning the small compartment she shook her head. Jack looked at the center console between the throttles. Billy had an open buck knife sitting there and Jack picked it up, throwing it through the passage to the aluminum floor at Megan's feet. A moment later he saw her hand with the knife cutting the half-inch Dacron rope.

"Come on, we can't wait much longer," he shouted, although he knew she couldn't hear him.

He didn't want her to look out again; Garcia was only twenty feet away from the side of the plane now.

He watched helplessly as Garcia lifted the pistol, aiming it unsteadily at the Catalina's cockpit. He fired three times hitting the *Digeree Doo* just aft of the Perspex canopy but the rounds passed harmlessly through the aluminum skin.

Finally, the frayed end of the anchor line fell into the clear water, and Megan's hand came up through the hatch with the thumbs up sign. A split second later she disappeared, whipping the small cover shut.

Gunning the starboard engine the big amphibian spun around to face the open water of Sir Francis Drake channel. It would be another down wind run, Jack thought, but there was plenty of room.

The port wing tip passed over Garcia, and the wooden skiff collided with a thump on the aft quarter of the rapidly turning aircraft near the blister hatch. Jack quickly rammed the throttles all the way forwards and the powerful engines threw up a maelstrom of spray. Megan reached the cockpit just in time to see the wooden skiff flip over behind the wing, and she leaned out over Jack's shoulders desperately trying to follow Garcia's movements, but she couldn't see him in the prop wash spray.

"He went overboard," she shouted, sinking into the co-pilot's seat opposite Jack.

The Catalina picked up speed and Jack smiled. It was just like old times. The sense of danger and urgency gave him a little buzz. He knew he could fly the plane without a problem. The airspeed indictor climbed and he took the amphibian up onto the plane. There was loads of power in the big Pratt and Whitney radials, but he hoped she would unstick before they got out into the rough water.

Fifty, sixty, seventy knots. It was almost time to rotate the aircraft when Megan thought she heard something come loose in the back of the cabin. Turning to see what it was, she shrieked in terror.

"Oh, my God, Jack!"

The loud engine noise muffled her voice but as he looked over at her quizzically, he noticed she was staring towards the back of the aircraft.

Glancing over his shoulder, he couldn't believe his eyes. Garcia glared malevolently forward. He was on his final legs but still deadly dangerous. The bastard had somehow managed to climb in through the aft hatch while he was turning the plane in the cove. From the aft end of the cabin he started walking unsteadily up the passageway of the plane. The big Colt in his left hand remained steady and level. Using his bad arm, he steadied himself against the even increasing bounce of the speeding amphibian. Blood oozed from his shoulder, and the wound on his head where Jack hand cracked him with the rifle butt still dripped. Although painfully injured, he was far from done.

Garcia screwed his face into a grimace as he leveled the gun. He was determined to kill them. It was hot in the closed fuselage and as Jack wiped the sweat from his eyes he saw the big Arbalette near his feet. It was still loaded and the wicked three-inch stainless steel barbed tip glittered only six feet from the doorway.

Jack thought desperately; he needed to do something fast. He could throttle back and stop the plane but the bastard would just shoot them anyway. He looked like he was hell bent on self-destruction. Time ran out as Garcia neared the cockpit bulkhead doorway. He moved forward in an unsteady fashion and Jack could see the pain in his face. Leaving a steady trail of blood on the cabin floor but he came through the bulkhead to the cockpit. He smiled again. It was one of those cruel smiles that meant I don't give a damn. He was only eight feet away when he very slowly aimed the Colt at Jack's head.

Megan froze in her seat. Pulling her eyes from the pain crazed Puerto Rican, she glanced at Jack. He wore a stony expression as he looked back at Garcia. Suddenly, he winked giving her a tiny smile, and before she could figure out why the hell he was smiling, he hit the right rudder pedal, while pulling the yoke hard right at the same time. The big amphibian dipped her starboard float in a tremendous shudder before lifting again. Garcia's mouth opened in astonishment as he stumbled onto one knee in the doorway and for a moment, the pistol barrel lowered.

It was all Jack needed. With a speed motivated by impending death, he whipped the Arbalette from the floor with his right hand, flicked off the safety and swiftly lifted the long speargun until it was pointed at Garcia's chest. He pulled the trigger without hesitation and the handle jerked as the heavy harpoon left the gun.

It seemed to happen in slow motion. Garcia looked down with a puzzled expression and dropped the Colt as the polished quarter inch spear shaft penetrated his chest. The razor sharp three-inch barb went straight through his heart and his face changed to an expression of bewildered horror. He was dead before he hit the floor. He lay there motionless, with three feet of stainless steel growing out of his chest. Megan gave a shriek and hid her head in her hands.

The Catalina bounced violently as she met the rougher, open waters of Sir Francis Drake Channel. Jack pulled the yoke back hard. As the big amphibian thumped dangerously over the first of the larger waves she came unstuck and took to the air.

Banking to the left he flew east around Guano Cay, slowly gaining height, before coming around to a northerly course. The Piper had gone that way and if they were headed for the U.S. mainland, it was the most likely course they would have flown. Jack took the amphibian up to fifteen hundred feet and steadied her out at a cruise of 110 knots.

It was difficult to speak because of the roar of the engines, and for the moment they remained silent. While Jack concentrated on flying the plane, the spearing of Garcia had left Megan a little subdued. She got up and stood by Jack's side, resting her hand on his right shoulder, while trying to stop herself from looking back to where the Puerto Rican lay dead.

Jack motioned for her to come closer and she bent her head towards him.

"I'm going to fly north," he shouted in her ear and she nodded.

They flew across the stretch of water between Tortola and Jost Van Dyke. The sky was clear and the sea had calmed following Beatrice's wrath. The surface of the ocean was as still as a millpond and it would be another day before the great Trade Winds returned.

Jack's thoughts returned to the Piper aircraft. At the rate it had been dropping fuel, it certainly couldn't have flown very far and if the pilot was experienced, they should have been able to ditch it. Jack knew if he was the one flying the Piper right now, he would be looking to ditch her in shallow water. At least then, the gold would be easy to retrieve.

Approaching the mountainous ridges of Jost Van Dyke at a thousand feet, Jack peered from the side of cockpit canopy he saw the thatched roof bar on Conch Shell beach. Smiling he remembered his friend Leroy and "Calabash", his faithful old donkey.

Passing over the rugged cliffs on the windward side of the island they scanned the rocky shoreline. Nothing. Then they were out over the Atlantic and the water turned an even richer shade of royal blue. It was deeper here but the hundred fathom curve still lay some miles ahead. There the famous 'Virgin Island Drop Off', held the giant record break-ing blue marlin which seemed to congregate for some unknown reason. Flying on they looked from side to side.

Jack held her at a thousand feet. The Virgin Islands receded until they were only a line of low lying hills to the south. They were nine miles northeast of Jost now and he began to wonder if the Piper had just gone down and sunk without a trace. Suddenly Megan shouted in his ear while tapping him on the shoulder.

"There, look," she shouted pointing to the right.

A tiny orange inflatable raft floated below them on the calm surface of the blue Atlantic. Banking hard Jack lost altitude quickly, taking the amphibian down to sea level where they made a circuit of the raft. A soli-tary figure lay prostrate in it and as they passed directly over, Megan rec-ognized the face.

"God, it would have to be Laura!" she shouted, her face screwing up in distaste.

There was no sign of the Piper. All that remained were a few pieces of foam and a seat cover floating near the raft to indicate the plane had gone down. Laura lay sprawled in the gently bobbing raft with her arm shield-ing her eyes against the glare of the sun. She didn't seem to take any notice of the large amphibian flying over her.

Jack brought the big Catalina in to land. It was a slow approach and he let her loose altitude quickly. She hit the surface of the Atlantic hard with a loud thump before lurching sickeningly into the air again. Megan glared at him. The next moment the Catalina hit again but she stayed down this time and Jack pulled back on the yoke to slow her down. Taxiing to the slowly drifting raft Jack cut the engines. Popping the starboard aft bubble hatch he threw a line across. Laura caught it and he began to pull her in.

"Well, well, look who we've caught," He said in a satisfied tone.

"I hate to say it, but I almost feel like leaving her out here to drift into oblivion," Megan told him in an angry voice.

"Now that would make us no better than them," Jack replied as he continued pulling on the line, "We'll take her aboard."

"I know, I'm not really a vindictive person," Megan said seriously, "Are we going to hand her over to the Tortola police?"

"No, They'd have us tied up here for years while they tried to unravel this mess. I think we'll take her back to Antigua, and let old Balfont take care of her and the pilot."

Jack pulled the last few feet of line in through the hatch and the orange colored life raft gently bumped against the side of the amphibian. Leaning over the edge they looked down at Laura.

"Looks like the tables have turned," Jack said smiling.

She lay on her side in the raft. Nothing she could possibly have said would have made her feel any better, so she kept her mouth shut.

Megan leaned out the hatch to take a look at her and maybe gloat just a little.

"I suggest you keep that bitchy mouth of yours zipped shut this time, otherwise we might decide to cut you up and feed you to the sharks," she told her venomously.

Jack looked at Megan in surprise. She'd said it with such conviction he believed she might just do it.

Reaching down they unceremoniously grabbed Laura's arm, hauling her aboard through the cabin hatch. As she fell on the floor, she let out a low wail of horror as she saw Garcia's bloody corpse laying a few feet away.

"What happened?" Jack asked her.

Laura just lay there for a moment, her chest heaving.

"We ran out of gas and then it crashed into the water. I was sitting in the back and I got out with the life raft. Henderson got knocked out when we hit and he sank with the plane," she stammered averting their gaze.

"After all that's happened, I'm not too worried about your sorry ass, but I want you to listen up," Jack replied tersely, "I'll be turning you in when we get back to Antigua. Until then, don't even think about causing me any trouble."

"I won't," she croaked staring up at him like a little child.

"I know you won't," Jack said coldly.

Jack turned to look at Garcia. As he started to move away, he caught a swift movement out of the corner of his eye and he glanced back just in time to see a flash of red hair as Megan hauled back and cracked Laura on the chin with a ripping right hook. Laura went sprawling backwards on the floor, and when she put her hand to her mouth, it came away bloody.

"I owed you that," Megan snapped at her.

"What are you doing?" Jack asked, stunned. "I thought you just said you weren't vindictive."

She glared at him briefly with those blazing green eyes of hers before replying.

"That wasn't vindictive, Jack. That was just me being a little angry."

Jack figured he better not say anything more on that subject. Megan was high spirited and he smiled to himself as he thought about the expression on her face as she'd decked Laura.

Taking some small line from the side of the cabin, she tied Laura's wrists behind her back, She wouldn't give them any more trouble; reduced from the arrogant, overconfident woman of a few hours before, she was a pathetic broken wreck.

Garcia had certainly made one hell of a mess of the cabin floor. Pulling the corpse to the entrance of the hatch he got ready to push it out. The sharks would take care of the rest. As he took one last look at the dead man's face, Jack noticed a peculiarity. In life, Garcia's expression had always been cold, even lifeless. Now in death, his face wore a softer, more humane look.

Without any more thought he pushed the corpse into the ocean. It tumbled slowly into the abyss the stainless spear glinting momentarily as the sun hit it. Eventually it faded into a vague, shapeless form and finally he could see it no more.

Afterwards he took a boat paddle from the cabin and a pile of rags lying near the old mattress on the starboard side. Mopping up the mess on the floor of the plane he threw them into the sea. He realized too late that he'd probably just trashed Billy's clothes.

CHAPTER TWENTY

The Green Flash

Jack and Megan took a miserable Billy Ramsey across the narrow isthmus from Beef Island to mainland Tortola in the Boston Whaler. They hailed a fisherman from the small village there to get a taxi. Securing the services of a beat up Ford station wagon they took him to the little hospital in Road Town. Perched in the back on all fours he swore all the way.

Melvina, the buxom hospital matron met them at the entrance. Billy would be under her direct care over the coming days.

"Sat on a speargun," Jack lied.

Melvina didn't doubt him. She hadn't seen very many bullet wounds in her day and anyway her patient looked just the kind of oaf who would sit on a spear. She lost no time putting him in his place. Helping him hobble to the only available bed, which happened to be in the maternity ward, she held his arm ever so gently as he climbed up to lay down on his stomach.

"Oh de poor likkle man, he look so weak ain't it?" she'd said smiling.

"Bloody hell," Billy exploded, "You aren't going to just leave me here with her, are you?"

"Doan get rude wid me, eh. Fust ting you need is a good powahful enema. In fact, you bum so big, ah tink is maybe a double enema you need," Melvina said mocking a scowl as she prepared the extra large gallon jug.

There was no doubt about who was in command at the Road Town maternity ward.

Leaving a surprisingly subdued Billy Ramsey with the very capable Melvina they returned to Beef Island.

Cobb and Benny had the *Fandango* ready to go and they hauled anchor immediately.

Jack was in a pensive mood. Although there was a generally good feeling aboard the *Fandango* as they left Trellis Bay, he couldn't help but wonder at all that gold on the bottom to the Northeast of the Virgin Islands. They had been so close, but it had vanished again for the second time. Still, he thought wistfully, you had to look at the bright side. They were all safe and no one was seriously injured, although Billy would probably argue that point. Jack knew he had a lot to be thankful for. His schooner was still in one piece, and he'd found the charter fee still neatly packed away inside the drawer. Plus he had Megan. He'd have to square Billy for the Catalina, but there would still be enough left for him to call the trip at least a financial draw.

They left Tortola without any trouble. There was no trace left of the Piper aircraft and Henderson and Garcia were fish food. Laura was locked in the cabin below along with a very sore Joe-Bob Benson, who had finally emerged from his deep slumber complaining bitterly about a headache. The stupid bugger had slept through it all. Patch appeared as if by magic. He had hidden himself somewhere on the yacht for the last couple of days but seemed no worse the wear for his stormy adventure. He stood guard on the two in the cabin giving a tiny growl from time to time. It almost seemed as though he knew they were both rotten. They weren't too happy when Jack told them that they were headed straight for a date with the Antigua police and probably a stay in their five star slammer.

Jack decided Antigua was the place to hand them over. There was probably going to be an investigation, requiring his presence, and he'd rather let old Balfont handle it back in English Harbour. At least if he needed to go on a charter, he could pass him a case of whiskey and leave unhindered. Laura's passport had been stamped in there anyway; she was on the crew list departing from English Harbor. As for Benson, he hadn't been stamped anywhere in the islands, but that was his problem.

Billy would be in the hospital for at least a week before he'd be able to fly the Catalina home. Until then, the big silver amphibian would rest on the side of the coral sand airstrip in Trellis Bay, none the worse for wear following her adventure. He would probably get totally legless at the waterfront Tavern once before leaving Tortola, and a new legend would be told of Spanish gold laying on the bottom, somewhere to the north of Jost van Dyke.

Cobb wasn't as badly hurt as Jack had first thought. In fact, he seemed totally unaffected psychologically by the beating Garcia had given him. Megan had bathed his face with antiseptic, and apart from a lot of swelling around the eyes and a few small cuts, he seemed fine.

"Me head jus real hard, Megan," he'd said grinning.

Both he and Benny quizzed Jack about the details of Garcia's sudden disappearance and his final demise.

"Well, let's just say I finally nailed him," Jack said, teasing them a bit.

"You shoot him Skip?" they both exclaimed.

The two rugged West Indian sailors listened in awe as Megan recounted the whole incident, telling them how Jack had speared him at the last minute to save the day. They weren't interested in Henderson; he was a non-entity as far as they were concerned. His destiny had been mapped out years before when he'd first chosen to walk the dangerous life.

They got underway and the schooner's bowsprit pointed south. As the two crewmen went about their duties Jack noticed that they seemed altogether too happy. Cobb kept on breaking into peals of laughter for no reason, and Benny would chuckle along with him.

Jack and Megan sat close together in the cockpit as he steered the schooner across the calm of Sir Francis Drake Channel towards Round Rock Passage, where they would set sail for Antigua. She'd found a tin of polish and a rag and was working on the brass binnacle which had become tarnished over the last week.

"Those two guys are way too happy," Jack said suspiciously looking across at Megan.

She was wearing her favorite green bikini and matching sarong. The swelling from the cut on her upper lip had gone down leaving a sexy curl to her mouth. At that moment Jack thought she was the most beautiful woman he'd ever seen.

"Well, they have a right to be happy," she replied. "Like we do, Jack."

"No, I know those guys like family, and they're acting real strange. Look at him," Jack said pointing to Cobb, "you'd think he just swallowed the proverbial canary."

When the two sailors finished securing the anchor, they came walking back to the helm their faces lit up with huge smiles.

"Skip we got a lil someting to show you," they said in unison.

Jack and Megan looked at them in puzzlement.

"What is it, Cobb?" Jack asked slightly bemused.

"I tink is bes' you stop de boat here for a minute, skip," Cobb told him.

"You want me to just stop here, way out in the middle of nowhere?

"Yes, skipper Jack. You and Megan bes' stop an come wid me," Cobb urged again.

Jack shook his head and pulled the throttle back, putting the Morse control into neutral. The schooner coasted slowly to a stop.

"Alright you guys, what's so important that I've to stop in the middle of Sir Francis Drake Channel."

"We got someting to show you," Cobb said light heartedly as he indicated for them to follow.

Megan and Jack were completely mystified now. Jack did a quick scan of the area to see if there were any other boats around before following the others down the main companionway. When Cobb had them assembled in the wardroom he bent over and opened the after most floorboard section over the shaft alley. This was the area where the propeller shaft led from the main engine aft to the stern of the vessel. It was a small varnished teak and holly hatch, two by three feet, and as he pulled it open they could see the thick stainless steel propeller shaft. The bilge of the vessel was another foot and a half below it. There were always a few gallons of water there and inevitably a sheen of oil floated on the surface.

"So what? The shaft alley has some water in it, just pump it out," Jack said getting slightly annoyed with Cobb's pantomime "You didn't have to make me stop to show me this, Cobb, you know as well as I do there's always a little water in there."

"We goin to pump it out now, skip. You jus watch."

"Well do it quick then, I've got to get back on deck."

Benny disappeared into the engine room where he hit the bilge pump switch. They heard a low hum as the pump cut in and the level of water began to drop quickly.

"Now skip, you got to look inside again," his first mate said pointing into the bilge. As the water level dropped an oil covered twelve-inch oblong block appeared and then more. Lying down on the floor, Cobb stretched one of his long arms into the bilge, picking up the closest one. It was obviously very heavy. Smiling broadly he raised it up for all to see.

"Now skip, I goin' to show you some real voodoo magic," he said, wiping the oily ingot on his tee shirt, it came away a brilliant gold.

"What the hell?" Jack exclaimed incredulously.

Taking the heavy bar from him, he almost dropped it. Wiping it across his hand, the gold shone through. Cobb told them his tale.

"You see skip, when we was sailin north, Henderson an' de Spanish man was sick, sick, an de Laura woman was sleepin' on and off in de companionway. So, whenever we saw de chance me an Benny steal a piece of gold from de boxes in de wardroom an when I made de bilge check, I trow it in de bilge."

Jack and Megan were dumbstruck. She laughed then until her sides hurt and gave Cobb and Benny each a good buss on the cheek.

"And how many bilge checks do you make during the trip?" Jack asked.

"Plenty skip, plenty," Benny replied smiling.

As they went back on deck to get underway, Jack turned to his two island seamen.

"You know guys I'll have to charge you freight for carrying that heavy gold back to Antigua," he joked.

Cobb looked serious for a minute.

"I talk wid Benny, skip. You save our lives back dere, so we want to split de gold wid everybody. Dat be you, Megan, me and Benny."

"Sounds like you have a deal man," Jack said, and they all stood in the cockpit of the *Fandango* and shook hands.

"What about, Billy?" Megan suddenly piped up, "Jack wouldn't have got to Beef Island to save you two, had it not been for him."

"Yeah, you're right," Jack said, turning to Cobb and Benny, "We've got to cut Billy in too. If it wasn't for him, I'd be out one schooner and you two probably wouldn't be here today."

They all agreed Billy would be up for a share as well.

"Partners?" Megan asked, and each person repeated the word as they shook hands.

Two hours later, the *Fandango* was close hauled with her rail down, racing across the Anegada Passage south bound for Antigua. There was a good stiff breeze and the schooner ate up the miles. Cobb and Benny busied themselves with a hacksaw on the leeward side cutting the gold ingots into smaller more manageable pieces.

By dawn of the following day, the fast moving yacht had closed the last few miles to the low lying island. By noon she was laying peacefully at her anchorage in English Harbour again.

Jack had radioed ahead and old Balfont was waiting on the dingy dock at the Admirals Inn with a trio of Constables. He took Laura and Joe Bob Benson into custody, and Jack passed him the two cases of Gilbeys gin he'd appropriated from the Catalina, indicating Billy would have a few more for him when he got himself out of hospital.

"Good show, old chap," Chief Balfont said happily, "Jolly good show. Do drop by sometime tomorrow and give us a statement, will you?"

He strolled off behind the two constables, sternly warning them to take good care of his gin.

Cobb and Benny went ashore wealthy men. Jack paid each of them off, adding an extra bonus. Their shoulder bags were heavy with their share of gold and as they stepped out of the Whaler onto the dock near the charter office, they turned to Jack.

"When you need us back skip?" Benny asked, frowning.

"Guys, after that little adventure, I think we all deserve a break. Lets take a couple days off, then we'll see. How does that sound?" Jack suggested.

"It sound real good skip. We'll see you den."

As they walked away, Cobb suddenly stopped and looked back at Jack.

"Skip, one ting. Next time we get a charter, check to make sure dem ain't criminals. Ah had enough of dem guys to last me a lifetime."

"You've got it," Jack said bursting into laughter. "And Cobb, I'll be buying a new speargun, so when you come back, we'll dive, just like before."

The two West Indians smiled at Jack and Megan and, giving them a quick wave, strolled towards the taxi stand. Cobb's wife and family would enjoy the benefits of his good fortune and the girls at the house behind Frederick Street would treat Benny like a king for a long while.

That evening Jack and Megan were alone at last on the schooner. The sun was setting on the western horizon. Jack was in his cabin drying himself off after his shower, when the door opened and Megan came in.

She looked gorgeous, wrapped in one of the ship's beach towels, her red hair hanging in wet tendrils around her face. They'd had a swim together in the bay and she'd just finished showering as well. Jack had promised to show her the fabled Green Flash.

"Ready to see the green flash?" Jack asked smoothing her hair away from her face and giving her a kiss, "We can sit on the stern and I'll make you one of my special rum punches."

"I've got a better idea," she said smiling mischievously.

"Oh, what's that?"

"I'm going to show you a real green flash," she said cryptically.

"On deck?" Jack asked looking into her lovely green eyes.

"No, I want you to climb up on the bunk and I'll show you right here," she said huskily.

Jack raised his eyebrows a little, then he climbed up onto the bunk, watching her.

"You've got to close you eyes and promise not to open them," she said smiling at him.

He was enjoying the charade and went along willingly, closing his eyes.

"You promise not to look, Jack."

"I promise," Jack assured her. He heard the swish of her towel sliding to the floor of the cabin, but he kept his eyes shut as Megan climbed up onto the edge of the bed and then he felt her warm, soft thighs straddle him.

"Alright, you can open them now," she said.

Jack opened his eyes. Megan was kneeling over him and the rays of a fading West Indian sun filtered through the skylight, silhouetting her perfect figure. She was holding up her little black purse.

"Meg, what is it with you and that purse of yours?"

She answered by flipping it upside down, and Jack watched opened mouthed as an impossibly brilliant stream of green fell through the rays of light, landing as huge emeralds on his chest.

"See Jack, now that's what I call a real green flash," she said laughing seductively.

"Meg, you little devil. Where the hell did you get these from?" he asked, stunned.

"Well, during the night of the storm, whenever the lightning flashed they made little green sparkles in the stone gullies and I picked up some of the bigger ones. I've already given the guys some so these are for you and me"

"Now I know why you were hanging on to that little purse of yours," Jack said shaking his head in wonder. "You're just one surprise after another, Megan."

"Think so? Well, just wait until you see what I do for my next trick." She leaned over and after looking longingly into those deep brown eyes of his, kissed him passionately on the mouth.

As the last of the day's sun shone through the skylight, it hit the scattered pile of emeralds laying on the bunk, and the bright green reflection danced playfully around the cabin walls as the *Fandango* tugged gently at her anchor. That night Jack Carlton dreamt of Aves. He and Megan walked the distant sandy shores and the grains were of gold.

The End

Born in May 1951 in Baddeck, N.S., Robert Louis (Lou) Boudreau, author of **The Man Who Loved Schooners**, first went to sea when he was six months old aboard the famous schooner *Yankee*. His father owned and sailed the schooner in the beautiful Bras D'or Lakes of Cape Breton, Nova Scotia, Canada.

When Lou was a year old the Boudreaus left Canada and voyaged south to warmer climes. Sailing out of Miami, Florida, they eventually ended up running their charter cruises in the West Indies. Lou spent his early childhood on the island of St. Lucia, where he became fluent in the local patois language. Lou grew up sailing the Caribbean aboard such vessels as the 100-ft schooner *Doubloon* and the 98-ft Howard Chapelle designed Baltimore clipper *Caribee*, both owned by his father.

In 1957, the Boudreau family embarked on a 10,000 mile deep sea voyage on the *Caribee*, visiting many interesting ports in the Mediterranean and North Africa. The adventure under sail made a deep and lasting impression on young Lou.

In 1968, at age 16, Lou joined the crew of the 135-ft Hereshoff schooner *Ramona* on a voyage to Nova Scotia, and following this, left school to follow the sea permanently. The young seafarer's apprenticeship saw him on some well known sailing vessels including the 143 ft schooner *Bluenose II* and the 137-ft Hereshoff schooner *Le Voyageur*.

After sitting for his master's papers, he ran the 90-ft ketch Atlanta, and the 138-ft Hereshoff schooner *Mariette*, noteworthy because she was the only schooner other than the mighty *Bluenose* to beat the Gloucester racer *Gertrude L. Thebaud*.

Over the years, Captain Lou Boudreau has experienced the exciting and the terrifying. He became an avid spear-fisherman, free diving for grouper on Bahamian reefs as well as an avid big game fisherman. Through hurricanes, an attempted drug hijacking in the Bahamas and a shipboard fire during a storm off the African coast, he has led the adventurer's life.

Swallowing the anchor in 1996 he returned to Canada where he devotes his time to writing. His first book, **The Man Who Loved Schooners,** was published in 2000. Lou has completed a number of other manuscripts, two of which are tentatively titled **Tales From the Captain's Table** and **Where the Trade Winds Blow**, which chronicle his own life.

Lou's Claim to Fame!: At the tender age of five, he ate coconut ice-cream with Ava Gardner while his father drank rum with Ernest Hemingway in Havana, Cuba.